About the

Lifelong romance addict **JC** ⋯ Zealand. Writing feeds her very ⋯ ⋯ ⋯ with happy endings and the endorphin rush they create. You can follow her at jcharroway.com and on Facebook, Instagram, and X @jcharroway

Award-winning author **Louisa George** has been an avid reader her whole life. In between chapters she managed to train as a nurse, marry her doctor hero and have two sons. Now she writes chapters of her own in the medical romance, contemporary romance and women's fiction genres. Louisa's books have variously been nominated for the coveted *RITA* Award, and the NZ Koru Award and have been translated into twelve languages. She lives in Auckland, New Zealand.

Helen Lacey grew up reading *Black Beauty, Anne of Green Gables* and *Little House on The Prairie*. These childhood classics inspired her to write her first book when she was seven years old, a story about a girl and her horse. She continued to write with the dream of one day being a published author and writing for Mills & Boon is the realisation of that dream. She loves creating stories about cowboys and horses and heroines who get their happily ever after.

Friends to Lovers

Friends to Lovers:

Something More

JC HARROWAY

LOUISA GEORGE

HELEN LACEY

MILLS & BOON

First Published in Great Britain 2024
by Mills & Boon, an imprint of HarperCollins*Publishers* Ltd
1 London Bridge Street, London, SE1 9GF

www.harpercollins.co.uk

HarperCollins*Publishers*
Macken House, 39/40 Mayor Street Upper,
Dublin 1, D01 C9W8, Ireland

Friends to Lovers: Something More © 2024 Harlequin Enterprises ULC.

Bad Reputation © 2020 JC Harroway
A Baby on Her Christmas List © 2014 Louisa George
Lucy & the Lieutenant © 2016 Helen Lacey

ISBN: 978-0-263-39774-1

This book contains FSC™ certified paper and other controlled sources to ensure responsible forest management.

For more information visit: www.harpercollins.co.uk/green

Printed and Bound in the UK using 100% Renewable Electricity at CPI Group (UK) Ltd, Croydon, CR0 4YY

BAD REPUTATION

JC HARROWAY

To love in all its forms.

CHAPTER ONE

Neve

THE RED BIKINI seemed to cover more in the shop but, as statements go, it screams *notice me*. But will it work on my best friend? Simply craving such a risky thing makes me want to abandon him here in the Maldives and catch the first flight back to London.

I slide my finger under the edge of the bikini bottoms and retrieve the shrinking triangle of fabric from between the cheeks of my backside. The elastic pings with a snap. I should never have taken my tall, athletic sister bikini-shopping. This would look way better on her svelte frame.

Panic squeezes my abdomen. Oliver might notice me all right, but for all the wrong reasons—like a catastrophic wardrobe malfunction when I dive into the pool…

'Careful what you wish for,' I mutter as I strike a sideways pose in the mirror, observing from a different angle how the teeny tiny scraps of fabric barely seem to cover my nipples. What the hell happened between my last-minute shopping spree—when despite my winter-white flesh, I'd convinced myself this bikini made me invincible—and now, when even an entire bottle of fake tan and twenty-four hours under the Maldivian sun couldn't stop me feeling almost as exposed as being naked?

My best friend Olly happened, that's what.

Oliver Coterill and his bedroom eyes, damn him.

Of course, those smouldering, come-hither looks aren't intended for me. Not today, not ever. I've witnessed them being flashed at countless women over the nine years we've been friends. But a girl can dream, and my imagination sparks with what-ifs every time he flashes his gorgeous, slightly lop-sided smile.

I sigh and tug the two triangles of the bikini top closer together to cover my cleavage. How would it feel, just once, to be visible to him in a sexual way? To be the recipient of that dazzling, bone-melting attention I've watched hordes of lucky women receive over the years? To step out of the friend zone and have him see me as a flesh-and-blood woman…?

'Pathetic,' I say to my reflection with an accusatory point of my index finger. Unrequited lust sucks.

I slap a smile on my sun-blushed face, stick out my chest to its best advantage and snap a selfie, firing it off to Olly on the message app we use to keep in daily contact.

I'll be out in a second…

He replies straight away.

Chop, chop, Never. I'm stuck with an investment banker wanker friend of my cousin. It's snorkel time.

So impatient. So easily bored. So fucking hot…

Ignoring his use of the nickname he'd christened me with the first day we met in a uni bar—he'd asked me to spell my name and I'd said, 'It's like never without the r'—I sidle up to the window and squint through the mosquito net for a clandestine glimpse of him semi-naked. I catch sight of his damp, dark-blond hair. He's chatting to some guy while draped over a sun lounger wearing only a pair of board shorts, which are wet and cling to his thick, muscular thighs as if they want intimate knowledge of what he's packing underneath.

Lucky board shorts. Of course they want intimate knowledge. The whole world wants intimate knowledge and, if I had my way, I'd be first in the queue.

Familiar longing fizzes in my pelvis.

Why are you doing this? Don't torture yourself. Whatever you do, do not look at his crotch.

Too late.

I press my thighs together and allow my mouth to hang open while my greedy, glutton-for-punishment stare traces the over-achieving bulge between his

legs. It meanders with blissful agony up the ladder
of his abs, touching on the scattered ink decorating his torso, then idles over his buff pecs, which
are sprinkled with manly dark chest hair. His single
nipple-piercing glints in the sun.

I swallow my drool. How will I survive the rest of
this holiday as his plus-one for his cousin's wedding
and ignore my constant state of lust? How will I get
through the toughest friend mission to date without
confessing the depth of my un-platonic feelings…?

The shrill cackle of feminine laughter drags me
from my perv-a-thon. Two women from the wedding party loiter near the edge of the pool, their
leggy, lithe and toned bodies presented for his in-
spection and their eyes flicking in his direction with
nauseating eagerness.

I step back but can't look away. The constant
female attention he attracts is the only downside
of our friendship. That and the fact I want to shag
him, of course…

Unlike me, these two are exactly his type—
exquisite, body-confident women who probably
achieve multiple orgasms during tantric sex… I
force myself to watch the impending train-wreck,
as if in slow motion, seconds before impact.

Thanks to Oliver's workplace stance on 'healthy
body, healthy mind', he's always at the gym he installed for his employees. But even with a flabby
dad-bod he'd turn heads. It's his arresting eyes—too

blue to look natural. Plus the cheeky, wonky smile and the God-given confidence he wears almost as well as his bespoke suits.

I massage my temple, breathing through the bout of testiness, which shunts my hormones into the danger zone. Why doesn't he put on some bloody clothes? It's only a matter of time before he gets bored of waiting for me to freak out over my shrinking bikini and approaches his admirers. Then I'll have to spend the rest of the holiday being the third wheel. Again.

At least his deluxe bungalow is at the opposite end of the resort from my single room. Despite his cajoling, I insisted on paying for it myself so I won't have to hear the sex noises coming from his bedroom.

Ignoring the women, Olly picks up his phone, reads the screen and frowns. He looks straight at my window from across the pool, as if he's staring right at me. I catch my breath and, even though I'm hidden behind the gauzy curtain, jump back for cover. Don't want to come across as pathetic and needy by being caught mooning at him and his female groupies.

I fire off a second message.

On my way.

My heart thumps my ribs with excitement and dread. How will I survive day two of his barely clothed company with nowhere to hide in this miniscule excuse for a bikini? I retie the bottom ties to give my nerves time to settle. But I can't go out there in this state—flustered, turned on, distracted. I dither in front of the mirror, my gaze flitting longingly to the contents of my partially unpacked suitcase.

I tap my teeth with a fingernail. Do I have time? The vicious throb of my nipples against my bikini top demands that I *make* time.

Oliver's already bored of waiting. He's probably flashing his bedroom eyes at the blondes as we speak. His reputation for stunning dates is renowned, although the chosen ones never last beyond a couple of weeks. In all the years I've known him he's never invited a woman to a family or work-related function. He says that's my role. We argued about it once, back in the beginning, when I accused him of wanting to have his cake and eat it. He'd stated reasonably that he preferred my company and didn't want to give his casual hook-ups the wrong impression. When he was ready to commit to a relationship, he'd introduce a woman to his family.

Prickles dance over my skin, the constant longing turning into a fire I have no hope of extinguishing if I'm spending the day with the man who presses all my sexual buttons. Unknowingly, of course.

Why not take the edge off?

Better to present myself for snorkelling somewhat satiated than in a sexually charged frenzy of frustration. That way I won't be tempted to take up the challenge issued in a margarita-fuelled pact by my girlfriends, Brooke and Grace, and hurl myself at him lips first.

No. I can't think about the promise I made to them to use this trip to finally confront my feelings for Oliver. Not in my current state.

Instead, I rummage in the bottom of my case for the bag buried under my clothes. I am going to need every single toy I possess to survive this beach holiday with my sex-on-a-stick friend. Why, oh, why couldn't his cousin's wedding have been held in Siberia or Alaska?

I select my favourite vibrator from my single woman's survival kit —the trusty Rabbit— then I toss the bag onto the bed and stamp off to the bathroom. If forced to watch Olly's semi-naked, wet body all day, I need to take care of myself first.

I slam the bathroom door closed, switching the vibrator on and off to test the batteries.

How would it feel to have him notice me, just once? To look at me with those ready-to-fuck eyes he usually bestows on other women? To see me as more than his reliable friend—a woman who would literally drop everything to be at his beck and call?

No. I know what happens to those women. They come, they go. Always temporary. Oliver isn't relationship material, and having him the way I want him could make me temporary too.

It's not worth the risk. I made my decision years ago—better to be his friend than to pass through his life in a brilliant flash of burning metal for a few heady seconds and then fizz out to nothing.

But, oh, how I'd love for once to feel that incandescent heat…

Brooke and Grace were right. I need to stop this unhealthy and long-standing obsession with Oliver. He didn't notice me at nineteen and he certainly never would now at twenty-nine. I've been single for eight months. Time to keep my vow, to open up that dating app and give some other guy a chance.

Right after I come…

Before the mood completely deserts me, I swish back the shower curtain and plonk my butt on the edge of the bath. I fire up the Rabbit once more, slide my bikini bottoms down my thighs and close my eyes, summoning my favourite fantasy.

The first shocking touch forces a gasp from my throat. I drop my head back and imagine Oliver striding across the tiles around the stunning infinity pool outside, making a beeline for my room, his handsome face taut with single-minded determination. I ease the vibrator inside as fool-proof, Oliver-themed images flash behind my scrunched-up eyelids. Imaginary Oliver throws back the curtains at the French windows, calls my name in his husky, nipple-tingling voice and slams open the bathroom door…

I want you, Neve. I've always wanted you...

I bite my lip, adjust the angle of the toy and spread my thighs wider, the fantasy fuelling my exhausted libido. He's here, his eyes on fire and glued to the action between my legs. But dream Oliver is no shrinking violet. He strides into the bathroom, takes my face in his hands and kisses me the way I fantasised the first night we met. Bold. Unapologetic. Frantic. As if he'd die without the connection of our lips...

Chasing the pleasure, I focus on his dreamy eyes, the sinfully thick black lashes and the mischief glinting in his penetrating blue irises. Mischief I love, even if it does put me squarely in the category of friend.

I press the Rabbit's head to my clit with a gasp, recalling how fantastic he smelled last night on the dance floor—clean, spicy top notes, exotic mid notes and uniquely Oliver base notes.

I'd tried to pay attention to his hilarious, implausible tales about his extended family, whom he'd flown here in his company jet—did I mention kind and generous?—but I'd momentarily lapsed into what it would be like to bury my face in the open neck of his shirt and suck on his skin until he growled my name with arousal... The sexy scruff on his chin scraped against my face as he'd pulled me in close for a slow dance. The smell of his shampoo from his slightly long, unruly, dirty-blond hair.

His broad, hard chest grazing my nipples awake as we'd swayed together on the dance floor…

My head falls back, one foot braced on the edge of the bath, as the Rabbit and I find the sublime rhythm I need.

I gasp. Make-believe Oliver grips my wrist, withdraws the vibrator and unbuckles his jeans. His mouth opens to speak. Perhaps a throaty, *'Let me help you with that,'* or a husky, *'Why not have the real thing?'* I can always rely on my Oliver fantasies to get me there.

So close… Just a few more seconds…

A harsh rap sounds on the bathroom door.

'Come the fuck on, Neve,' Oliver calls. 'You're taking for ever in there.'

I yank the Rabbit from between my thighs and slam my legs closed, as if he can see what I'm up to through the closed door. My face burns, my clumsy hands fumbling with the vibrator's off switch as it hums with the force of a million mosquitos. At last I silence the device and shove it into the back of the cupboard under the sink, behind the spare toilet rolls. Breath gusts out of me in a panic. Did he hear me? Does he know what I was up to? Did I say his name aloud?

I jerk my bikini bottoms up and run water to hide the thunderous sound of my erratic heartbeat.

'I'm coming.' I wince at the irony, splashing cold water onto my face to extinguish the scalding heat.

Perhaps I should blast the showerhead between my legs to douse my lady-boner.

Bloody Oliver…

I dry my face with a fluffy hotel towel and force my breathing to slow while I stare down my flushed reflection.

Keep it together. Act like nothing happened. Pretend, same as always.

When I emerge gingerly from the *en suite*, Oliver is collapsed on my bed, his arms spread-eagle and his stare trained on the fan spinning lazily overhead. His board shorts are dry and he swings his feet over the edge of the bed, because he's not very good at keeping still.

My clit throbs in retribution. I want to climb onto him and…

'How can it take you half an hour to clean your teeth?' he says without looking up. 'You'll have no enamel left at this rate.'

I shuffle over to a chair near the window, pretending to hunt for my prescription sunglasses while I boil inside—one, because I'm always simmering when Olly is around, and two, because my primed clit didn't get the memo that fun time is over.

'I should never have given you a key to my room,' I snap, venting frustration. 'Why can't you just be by yourself for five minutes?'

He looks up, props his elbows under him and stares, as if seeing me for the first time—his piercing eyes narrowed a fraction and his big, manly body still for once.

I freeze, unease dancing over my exposed skin. Why did I wish for that focus to be turned on me? Its intensity makes me want to run back to the bathroom and hide in the shower.

'I can be alone,' he says. 'The investment banker started asking me about work and, aside from the Japanese telecommunications deal, I don't want to think about business. I'm on holiday, and I thought we were going snorkelling.' His voice, as deep and magnetic as always, and tinged with a transatlantic twang from his dual nationality, carries that 'lost little boy' edge that keeps me enslaved. I can't help it. I have a terrible case of saviour complex where Oliver is concerned. I always have. I see something in him from which he needs rescuing. Although, clearly *I'm* the one in desperate need…

'Sorry,' I say, sighing. 'I didn't mean it.' I perch my sunglasses on top of my head and turn my back on him to push my feet into my flip-flops. 'I didn't sleep well last night. I'm testy.'

Oliver is quiet, so rare an occurrence I'm terrified to look down in case I still have my Rabbit in my hand or I forgot to re-don my bikini bottoms. I tense, my back aflame with the thought of his eyes on me, exactly the scenario I wanted when I purchased this teeny tiny excuse for a bikini.

I spin in a tentative arc to face him.

He's still laid out on my bed like a sacrificial lamb, still propped up on his elbows like some male pin-up, only now he's looking at me with a puzzled expression. Only Oliver could pull off that face and still look entirely fuckable.

'What?' I demand, in no mood for the usual teasing banter we share.

'Nothing,' he says, his jaw slack. 'It's just…'

His eyes stay on mine, but I look down anyway in case one nipple has made a bid for freedom. But no, I'm good.

'Why are you staring?' Perhaps the sexual frustration is pasted all over my hot face.

'I'm not. I mean…it's nothing. It's just that…you look good in red, that's all.'

That's all? I deflate. I want to cry and laugh in the same breath. I want him to scour every inch of my body with his sexy stare. I want him helpless to look away. Helpless against the transformation into my daydream Oliver, who would have stripped me naked and been rattling the headboard by now.

I snort. Move towards the mirror, where I pretend to tweak my messy hair that's caught up in a topknot, while my body tingles with awareness that I'm scantily clad, alone in a room with the object of my every adult desire.

'Thanks,' I say in my best unruffled tone, forcing my muscles to relax. My head spins and I talk my overactive imagination back from the ledge. Olly—

despite his infamous reputation with women—is a gentleman. He's always complimenting me when I dress up, or cheering me on when I crack a tricky case at work. Just as I listen to his work woes about his tech company, even though I don't understand a word. But that's what *friends* do. Support one another. He doesn't mean anything by his comment. Certainly not what I'd like him to mean.

'Are you wearing sunscreen?' I ask to cover my full-body meltdown because, where I turn lobster-pink before returning to pasty, Oliver tans to a deep bronze almost overnight. So not fair.

'Yes, Mum.' He grins.

I toss my tube of factor fifty at him, sighing when he sits up and catches it in one hand with lightning reflexes. See? Good at everything…

'Ha ha,' I quip. 'You can do my back.'

No! Fuck…why did I ask him to do that? His hands on me…touching…with my aroused state heightened and my orgasm interrupted. Not a good idea.

'I will.' He drops the tube onto the bed and leans back on his hands, arms straight. 'First tell me why you're testy. You're on holiday too. You're supposed to be relaxing.'

How can I relax when I'm on high alert for any sign he might've noticed me in a sexual way, or when I'm just waiting for him to hook up with one of the wedding guests right in front of me? It's happened before. He wasn't a dick about it, giving said woman enough breadcrumbs to keep her keen while also attending to me, the friend he brought along as his plus one. But the next morning the smug look on his face told me she'd miraculously found her way to his room once we'd said goodnight.

'I am relaxed,' I say, grimacing past my clenched jaw.

'You don't seem relaxed.' Amusement tinges his tone. 'You've put lip gloss on three times. Without wearing your glasses.'

Sometimes it sucks that friends know you so well… I cast him a glare, something so rare it seems to shock both of us.

'I'm fine,' I bite out, desperately trying to blank out the pact I made with Brooke and Grace—to orchestrate a holiday fling with Oliver. I should just embrace a bloody dating app. At least then I could vet prospective boyfriends from the comfort of my pyjamas. Instead I'm standing here dithering over the merits of actually confessing my feelings of lust to Oliver versus spending the rest of my life always wondering.

At my lame assurance, Oliver flops back down onto the bed in disgust. I ignore him. Continue with my rant, because it's *his* fault I'm in this state.

'I just…needed a few minutes to myself,' I say, huffing. 'I told you I'd meet you by the pool. Plus my bikini seems to have shrunk since I tried it on in the shop, and I wanted to make sure I didn't have any tan lines showing.' I pace to my suitcase and find my sarong, then knot it around my waist. Makeshift body armour.

'It's all right for you guys,' I continue. 'You can just throw on a pair of shorts and parade around in all your manly, hairy glory, attracting stares of appreciation from the opposite sex…'

He's fidgeting, another of his annoying habits I find attractive. Damn, everything he does appeals to my libido, but now I've started it's as if my sexual frustration has discovered an oral pressure valve.

'But us women, we have to wax shit and plump stuff and squeeze our bodies into ridiculous, minute fashion statements…' I grab my mascara and slick a layer over my stubby upper lashes. I locate my glasses, push them on and check my mascara. I'm happy with me. Mostly. I'm an attractive, smart, bordering on a proud nerd with my own forensic-accounting business.

But I'm not done venting.

'And you know how challenging it is running your own company,' I say, wiping a smudge of black from my cheek. 'I've had a very stressful week, with three new clients and meeting deadlines in order to have this week off. So forgive me if I can't simply switch on the party girl just to keep *you* entertained.'

I can sense without turning around for confirmation that he's stopped listening. But, instead of riling me further, his inattention deflates me. I'm being unfair. I'm not really angry with him. I'm frustrated with myself, at my continued inertia where he's concerned, because maybe Brooke and Grace are right. Maybe I should have told him I fancied him the night we met. Maybe it's time to tell him how I've felt about him all these years… At least then we could laugh about it, clear the air and move on.

My blood runs cold at the very idea. No. A swim in the ocean is what I need. Douse my hormones and reboot my mind-set to fun, holiday Neve.

'Neve…? What's this?' he asks, with the rustle of a plastic bag.

'Hmm?' I mumble as I tackle my lower lashes with the mascara wand, a feat that requires a bizarre facial contortion while my glasses are perched on the end of my nose.

'I said, what's this?' His voice has dropped several octaves to that smoky quality of all my filthiest fantasies.

But there's no time to enjoy the sound.

I freeze.

The mascara wand hovers near my eyeball, ready to blind me with one false move.

No, no, no… Please, no.

I turn, horror a tight ball cramping my stomach.

Dangling from Oliver's long, elegant and tanned index finger is my bag of sex toys.

CHAPTER TWO

Oliver

THE PLASTIC HANDLE digs into my fingertip, so monumentally weighted are the surprising contents. I swallow past my dry throat, my body heat rising as if I've sat too long in the sun. The minute I peeked inside the bag, Neve became a living, breathing sexual being in my mind. I've spent nine years avoiding thoughts of her that way. Thinking about sex and my best friend in the same head space…

Nope.

I'm not a masochist and that would have rendered our entire long relationship hellish. It's bad enough that she's amazing—kind, smart, funny. Plus, she just gets me. Hence, best friend.

The knock of my excited heart against my ribs mocks the boundaries I've used to keep our friendship intact. It's too late to un-see the sex toys. Too late to switch off the torrent of erotic images featuring my astounding Neve and her gorgeous body.

I grit my teeth and keep my eyes away from the tiny red bikini I want to rip off so I can complete the Neve jigsaw. The triangles of fabric concealing her best bits remind me I'm not supposed to wonder what she looks like naked. But my imagination is intent on torturing me.

I focus on her pretty, familiar face as the silence pulses around the room. She's panting, flushed, realisation dawning. I stare into her eyes, because that bikini fried my brain the minute she stepped from the bathroom and I can't think of a single nonsexual thing to say to my friend. At least this red offering is better—and by that I mean worse—than yesterday's white one, which was hard enough to ignore. Or maybe she's actually growing sexier day by day...

Of course, a gentleman would have ignored the bag on her bed. Even a degenerate would have discreetly closed it on discovering its contents. But I've been labelled worse—womaniser, lothario, playboy—my reputation is renowned. Just like my father's.

More seconds, more silence.

Part of me wants her to deny that this bag of dildos and vibrators belongs to her, to say that she found them in the wardrobe, anything that might stop me imagining her using them. The very idea sets me on fire, balls first.

At last, she lifts her cute, slightly upturned nose

in defiance. 'It's a bag.' She crosses her arms under her breasts, pushing them up and accentuating her cleavage, all seen with my highly evolved peripheral vision. Because I've perfected looking indirectly at Neve's forbidden zones.

I release a curse in my head for the thousandth time today and it's only ten in the morning. I've seen her in a bikini before. What's changed? Why am I struggling with the line, a heavily policed line I put in place nine years ago when I realised she was different and some smart corner of my primitive, immature brain decided to keep her as a friend? My first instinct was to shag her of course—she was striking, beautiful in that girl-next-door way, nerdy just like me and with a sense of humour dry and dark enough to make me forget all my troubles. Upon meeting her, my day went from shitty to 'it's going to be okay'. No mean feat, considering I'd just been through my one and only heartbreak and learned some valuable life and love lessons from my asshole father.

But despite fancying her I instantly knew she was too good for me—a messed up, commitment-phobic charmer with a bad reputation and an embarrassing family. I'd selfishly wanted her in my life, the act of keeping my hands off my proudest moment.

Of course, I'd tarnished my mature conduct by sleeping with Neve's then-roommate that night, but I *am* the son of a rock-and-roll has-been.

'Did you look inside?' she says at last, her cheeks darkening while she waits for my answer.

'I might have looked inside,' I say, fighting the urge to smile, because this is serious. How will I spend the rest of the week, with her in those barely-there bikinis, knowing the intriguing and highly informative contents of this bag? Knowing the girl I made asexual in my head, to keep me sane, is all grown up and likes to play?

Damn, could she be any hotter?

I shift my hips, trying to get comfortable while my shorts garrotte my dick.

'Okay, I lied,' I say, giving free rein to my smile. 'I definitely looked inside.' I don't know what I'm doing, but I know the lid to Pandora's box has flown off with this discovery.

The idea of my beautiful, funny, sweet Neve using sex toys does strange and wonderful things to me. Dangerous things, because now I just want to get my hands, mouth and dick on her.

Will I ever be able to contain my desire for her again?

This is the first time I've seen her this naked while she's been single. Since she dumped her latest serious, hoity-fucking-toity boyfriend who wasn't good enough for her. What was his name… Liam? Yes, that's it. I christened him Limp Liam.

Not that I'm good enough for her either. The opposite, in fact. Otherwise I wouldn't be snooping in her bag of dildos more turned on than I've ever been in my life. For a woman who's always been there for me, always believed in me, even when I didn't value myself.

Finally snapping into action, Neve stamps closer. 'Don't mess around—you have no personal boundaries.' She snatches the bag from my hand.

I grab the bottom of the bag in an immature game of tug-of-war, my fist curling around a phallic object inside.

'You've always known I'm an arsehole—it's genetics,' I say, waggling my eyebrows. 'Tell me, do you always travel with such an extensive toy collection?' I don't want to tease her, but it comes out dripping with playful challenge. Because that's the way I've always skirted my attraction to her. But something inside me, the part seeing Neve in a whole new and sexy light, doesn't want to play games. I want to know more about her sexual side.

And I always get what I want.

My blood thrills, hot and laced with adrenaline. She's so close I can see the delicious flush of her neck and the tiny teardrop-shaped imperfection of her right pupil with which she was born with and that makes her uniquely Neve.

'I'm not ashamed of my needs,' she says, lifting her chin. It's an adorable display of grit that's at odds with her petite stature and freckled nose... and the fact that I know her so well I'm certain she'll forgive me for this indiscretion. Damn, she's so sweet. I fight a smile at the fact she's wearing two pairs of glasses—her regular pair and her sunglasses perched on her head.

'Quite bloody right.' But now I'm incandescent with curiosity. Does she use them all? Every day? In the shower?

Bile hits the back of my throat—did she use them with Liam? Or with the dick-wad boyfriend before Liam—Tristan? Or, as I liked to call him, Tris Tosser? The one who disliked her girlfriends, Brooke and Grace, and suggested she try a carb-free diet… He'd been heading for a rendezvous with my fist, right before Neve dumped him.

Then it hits me, my lusty sluggish brain fitting the pieces together. The noise coming from the bathroom when I came in. It wasn't an electric toothbrush.

My cock surges against the fabric of my shorts. If she happened to look down she'd see how inappropriately perverted I am. Lusting after my only true friend. The only person who knows the real me and all my fucked-up family bullshit. The only person to unconditionally, unselfishly care about me—not for my famous father or because I can get free tickets for his reunion tour.

My precious Neve.

But I can't resist. I have to know.

'Were you just using one of these? When I

knocked on the door?' I tilt my head towards the bathroom, my eyes burning with the effort of steering clear of her delicious body.

She flushes a deeper shade of puce. 'I might have been—your timing sucks, by the way.' She snatches the bag free of my grasp and tosses it into her open suitcase. 'I've been single for way too long.' She braces one hand on the curve of her hip. 'In fact, I've finally downloaded that dating app Brooke recommends. After eight months, it's time to get back out there.'

She over-talks when she's nervous. But this little nugget of information is like a slap in the head. Neve's past boyfriends have all graduated from the school of Serious Boring Fuckers—or the SBF Club, as I like to call it—but at least she met them in person, got to know them, dated them for a while before making it official. Not that any of them had particularly taken to me, of course, even though I was no threat—I've never laid one finger on her in a sexual way. A few of her exes even tried to break up our friendship or insinuate themselves into it by throwing a sister or cousin at me in the hopes the four of us could double date.

'What…?' I drop my voice from the squeaky pleading that tries to escape. 'Dating apps aren't the way to go. I know. I've used them.' As far as I'm aware, she's not into one-night stands. She'll be eaten alive in the shark tank of the dating app scene. She's way too kind and sweet.

'Why not?' She holds eye contact, waiting for my explanation, but my brain is still mush from the knowledge that I interrupted my sexy goddess friend taking care of business with a battery-operated phallus.

My flesh-and-blood phallus throbs.

'Because…' Comprehension kicks in. She's back on the market. Actively seeking the next wanker who'll probably wind up hurting or disappointing her. I was certain the last one would have the balls to pop the question, but I'd known almost instantly he wasn't man enough for Neve…

But the next one might be. And then what? A husband won't have the tolerance that a boyfriend might for me in her life. We're close and I don't want that to change. But, as this current little pantomime proves, I'm selfish, inappropriate and lack boundaries. She'd choose, and I'd lose. Lose my Neve.

I swallow hard, the razor blades slashing through the lust gripping my throat.

'Do you have a better suggestion?' She offers a nervous laugh and looks down at her pretty painted toes in that way that tells me she's feeling vulnerable. 'Any dishy single friends who want to date a woman who works ten hours a day running her own business and prefers a night in with her cat watching baking shows to an evening out on the town?'

My thoughts turn murderous at the idea of any of my single friends with Neve. I want to rush to the bathroom, scoop up as many towels as I can find and cover all her gorgeousness from view in case any other single wedding guest gets any ideas.

'Don't put yourself down,' I say. 'Any guy would be lucky to have you—you're intimidatingly intelligent and have a wicked sense of humour.' The Neve I first met used to compare herself unfavourably to her younger sister, who's a professional swimmer, although I've never understood why; Amber bores me to tears.

Neve sighs, shoving a beach towel into her bag. 'Look, I know it's not the best way to meet someone, but beggars can't be choosers, and I'm heading towards my thirties—'

'In a year,' I scoff.

She shrugs and flashes her playful smile at me, the one that kicks me in the gut every time. 'Yes, but my toy habit is pretty expensive—time to find a real live substitute with enough staying power that I don't need a truckload of double As.'

Of course my accountant friend would balk at the cost of her sex-toy addiction. She has a spreadsheet for every occasion, including her grocery list. 'Wait, are you saying Limp Liam…?'

'Don't call him that.' Her eyes flash with censure.

I ignore her outrage. 'Are you saying he was lacking in the bedroom?' I bite down on my glee that the patronising, toffee-nosed Liam with his old Etonian judge father was somehow flawed, even while my chest clenches with sympathy for my wonderful Neve, who deserves all the good things, including well-hung, attentive boyfriends with extreme stamina.

I think I'm going to puke.

She shrugs. 'Not so much lacking... I guess it was largely down to me. Why are we talking about this? Let's go snorkelling.' Neve develops a sudden fascination with her outfit: a shift of a bikini strap here and retightening of her sarong knot there.

What the hell...?

'Nuh-uh, no way.' I shake my head and lean back on my hands to show her I mean business. At least these latest revelations—that she's joined a dating app and that her relationship with Limp Liam wasn't all roses and screaming orgasms—douses the heat in my shorts, shrinking my hard-on quicker than a cattle prod to the arse.

'What was down to you?' I can't let this go, torn between arousal and jealousy of the exes who saw a side of her I can only dream of.

She looks down, thinks better of it and slams her eyes back to mine. She's ballsy and brave even if we've never skated this close to deeply personal— read sexual—details before. At least, not *her* sexual details. Mine tend to make it into the celebrity gossip headlines thanks to my reckless teens and the example set by my ageing-rocker father. Stories which feature me apparently out-debauching him with beautiful women seem to sell twice as many newspapers and magazines.

'I'm saying that amazing sex, mutual, perfectly timed orgasms—angels singing, stars bursting and unicorns prancing—don't happen for everyone.' She sighs. 'Not that you'd know anything about that with the amount of practice you've had.' Her eyes roll with derision.

My shoulders hunch with tension. I knew it. Those *are* the sex toys she used with Limp Liam… I'm going to have to bleach my brain once this conversation ends.

'Hey,' I say, holding up my hands in supplication. 'I have no beef with however your ex got the job done.' I just don't want those images in my head. Images of Neve pleasuring herself, on the other hand, I can surely keep for later personal use.

'In fact,' I add, 'I'm quite impressed he was man enough to buy you sex toys.' I nod in the direction of the bag, which might as well be filled with snakes. Green snakes. Their venom fuelling my envy. 'He didn't seem the type.'

Neve huffs. Collapses into a chair and narrows her eyes behind her glasses. 'I bought them myself. And I didn't use them with him.' She nibbles her lip and examines a fingernail. 'He was a bit insecure in that department, to be honest.' She flushes, as if she can't quite believe she's telling me all of this.

I'm a little gobsmacked myself, truth be told, my body veering wildly between excitement and sick, twisted fascination.

'So what do you mean it was down to you?' Creepy-crawly legs skitter up my spine. Part of me dreads her answer in case it fundamentally changes something between us, although haven't things already changed? Like me allowing myself to look at her in a way I've spent years shying away from? My inexplicable jealousy over the dating app? The idea that she might have been short-changed by the men in her past…?

'Well…you know. I…' She covers her mouth with her hand, as if holding in some terrible secret, and then blurts it out. 'I never had an orgasm with him.'

'What the hell?' I clench my jaw when I realise I've actually said this aloud. But I'm livid enough to crack my own teeth. I hold up my hand. 'I'm not judging you. It's his fault, not yours. If he didn't know his way around a woman's body, and he was insecure about using toys, that's on him.'

I fume inside; I knew he was a dick-wad.

Instead of nodding in agreement or telling me to shut up, like she usually would, she turns pale, her vulnerable stare cutting me to ribbons. 'Thanks for being so loyal, but it can't be him, because it's happened before.'

I curl my fingers into fists to stop myself pulling her into a hug and holding her until that look fades from her eyes. We've hugged a thousand times— brief, platonic hugs, preferably where her breasts don't come into contact with my chest and my boner doesn't show—but this time I wouldn't stop. I'd kiss her. Taste those soft lips she habitually nibbles when she's pretending she's not upset. Kiss that ticklish spot on her neck. Stare into her mismatched eyes until we both feel better.

'So you've had a couple of dud boyfriends.' I shrug, torn between utter horror for my friend and a gleeful delight that the intimidating, serious number-nerd arseholes she's dated in the past were lacking in the most crucial department. The urge to kiss her builds, a furnace in my chest. There's no way I'm introducing her to any of my single friends now.

She's special. She needs a special guy, one who'll worship her the way she deserves, treat her right and rock her world.

No. Don't think about your friend orgasming. That's shit you'll never erase from your brain…

Then again, none of those exes of Neve's dragged her into the gutter by splashing her picture all over the tabloids in some salacious story like *Latest Squeeze of Layabout Son of Rock Royalty!* or *On Again, Off Again Girlfriend of Serial Philanderer Oliver Coterill!* The consequence of our friendship.

Guilt makes my skin crawl.

'It happened with *all* of them, Oliver. All.' She stares, her green eyes huge and mesmerising. 'I've never once had an orgasm with another person.' She stands now, as if she can't contain the tension her confession has produced and needs to move. I, on the other hand, am shocked to stillness, gaping like a stunned mullet.

She pulls on a T-shirt as if she wants to hide. My horny and flabbergasted brain recalls how we're supposed to be going snorkelling. She's supposed to be taking clothes off, not putting them on.

My entire body is aflame now, my eager dick twitching in my shorts. Neurones fire. One single coherent thought emerges: I could give her what others failed to do, now I'm a man. I'm not a teenager with no control over his poor decisions or his dick, like I was the day we met.

What the hell? No, no, no, no...

'So it must be me,' she says with a sad little laugh. 'Perhaps there's something wrong with me...' She looks away, her lip taking a thrashing from her teeth as she fiddles self-consciously with the hem of the T-shirt.

'There's nothing fucking wrong with you—I can assure you.' Her back is to me so I indulge in a quick perv of her arse, a cute heart-shape that does things to my pulse. Even though it's covered by a sarong, I can picture the way the bikini bottoms disappear between her cheeks, exposing her glorious globes in an adorable, lopsided way. I want to lick and suck…

'How do you know?' she hurls over her shoulder.

My ire rises, drowning out testosterone and propelling me from my slouch on the bed so we're standing face to face. 'Tell me, do they work?' I point at the open suitcase and the bag of toys, praying my hands aren't shaking with the adrenaline pouring through my blood. I want to touch her so bad. Just once.

She splutters, her mouth opening and closing, making me notice her perfect little kissable Cupid's bow. 'What?'

'Do they work? Can you make yourself come with your bag of tricks?'

Stop talking. Walk away.

'Yes, but—'

'Well, then,' I say, my hands on my hips. 'There's nothing wrong with you.' My fists clench, my heart jackhammers in my throat and lust boils in my belly at the very idea of Neve making herself come with a dildo.

For the first time in the nine years I've known her, I free myself to look at her the way I want, my stare travelling her body.

From her green eyes, gawping at me as if I've lost the plot, to her lush lips, parted so her breath can gust in outrage. Down the slope of her neck to her freckled shoulder, which has escaped from the wide opening of her T-shirt. The swell of her generous breasts straining against the fabric, with her laboured breathing and curvaceous hips screaming 'woman', right down to her pretty toes painted with purple nail polish.

The release, the euphoria, the freedom fills me in a rush so deep-seated I want to groan aloud and fall to my knees.

I feel the vacuum created by her indrawn breath. Force myself to look up.

Our eyes meet.

This is hallowed ground. Forbidden territory. A no-going-back moment. I watch her lips, which seem to tremble, waiting to hear her thoughts.

But now I know her secret, know the rough deal she's had with the SBF Club, there's no way I'm allowing her to meet some jerk from some app who wants nothing more than to get his rocks off.

I stare at her lips. If she asked me to kiss her now, I would.

But, oh, the price of that kiss. Just one foot over that line could ruin everything...

But didn't I already ruin her long ago—her reputation, at least—by simple association? Hasn't she already paid the price for being my friend? Not that she ever complains, so steadfast is her loyalty—which I don't deserve.

'This conversation is getting weird,' she says in a breathy voice, ignoring the fact I've just ogled her, with lust, from head to toe. Her gaze flicks to the door, to escape, but it's back before I can draw breath.

'I think we bypassed weird a long time ago,' I manage to say past my constricted throat. 'I'd say we're well and truly in outlandish territory. I'm not happy, Neve.'

Her eyes widen, her plump lips pressed together in a line. 'Why not? It's my situation. I don't see how it's your problem.'

Her point is valid on every level except for one rather crucial and burning logic.

I take a calming breath, fully decided on my course of action. Exhale. Stare deep into that unique pupil so she senses the import of this moment.

'What if I want it to be my problem?' I say.

CHAPTER THREE

Neve

COULD HE MEAN what my addled brain thinks he means?

As far as my libido is concerned, there's only one interpretation…

But no… Of course not. The excited fluttering in my belly peters out. I'm nothing like his usual women—glamorous, immaculate, sexual beings only looking for a brief, casual fling. There's no way I want to become one of those temporary women. Never once in all these years I've known him has he had a relationship that lasts longer than a week. Emboldened by alcohol after a few too many drinks, I once asked him about his relationship avoidance, and he said that he only had to look at his father— who's been married six times—to know that he hadn't inherited the commitment gene.

'What? Do you want to have a crack at it?' I

snort, trying to make light of a situation that makes me feel like I've waded into the sea up to my neck.

'I could. Why not?' he says, regarding me intently, as if with new-found fascination, until I burn with exquisite temptation.

I finally look away from his handsome, deadly serious face. 'Very funny, Olly.' *Oh...yes, please.* 'No, thanks—I'll stick to the dating app.'

He rolls his shoulders back, a move that pushes his buff chest closer to my peaked nipples. 'Why? So you can have a string of depressing dates with a string of selfish guys who can't keep a girlfriend— because otherwise they wouldn't be on the dating app in the first place? No way am I watching you put yourself through that, not after what you've just told me.'

'Then close your eyes,' I snap. He's crossing the line here, and part of me is enthralled and part of me equally appalled.

He carries on as if I didn't speak. 'You deserve so much better than that after your experiences with your exes, who I assumed were at least satisfying *your* needs, despite acting like superior wankers towards me. All of your needs.'

My eyes burn with incredulity just looking at him; he's seriously not joking...

'Most men our age use dating apps for hook-ups,' he ploughs on. 'Do you think those types are going to be any more attentive to your needs than Limp Liam or Tris Tosser?'

I fist my hands on my hips, ignoring his nicknames for guys who'd disliked him in return, their animosity a source of many an argument during our respective relationships.

'You've had your fair share of hook-ups,' I say, 'So I bow to your superior knowledge. But it's not your place to determine what I deserve.' I aim my index finger at the centre of his sternum. 'And don't you dare feel sorry for me.' If I'd wanted to feel second rate again, I'd simply have watched him crack on with the blondes outside. There's always a queue for Oliver's attention.

He leans closer, eyes sparking with gravity, until my finger brushes his chest. He tenses his pectoral muscles, the tip of my finger almost swallowed in the deep valley formed.

I drop my hand, retreating from the physical stand-off.

'You're my best friend,' he says, his seductive voice almost unrecognisably un-friend-like. 'I care about you being hurt or disappointed again.'

His words wash over me, wonderful and irritating at the same time. Because I want to be more than his friend. A part of me always has. 'You're hardly qualified to speak about relationships—you've never had one in your life.' Something that, for me, helped maintain the boundaries of our friendship. I might not have been the chosen one in his bed, but for sheer staying power in his life I had all those other women beat.

He grits his teeth. 'I may not want a relationship, but I'm damned well good at fucking, which is all that's on offer here. I could make you come until you screamed your throat raw. I promise you that.' He steps closer, so close his tall frame and broad chest eclipse my vision, so he's all I see.

I sway on my feet, weak with lust just from the ecstasy of his words. But I'm used to ignoring my libido where Oliver is concerned. Used to lecturing myself on protecting a good thing—our friendship—from something as underwhelming as sex, which has been my experience.

Although, I know with him it would be far from underwhelming. In fact the English dictionary boffins would need to come up with a new adjective—perhaps ultra-whelming. Still, can't tell that to Mr Cocky.

'Oh, I believe you.' I say. 'I've seen and heard enough of your conquests over the years to know that's no idle threat.' I close my eyes and drop my head back in mock ecstasy. *'Fuck me harder, Olly. OMG, Olly. Olly, I'm coming!'* I mimic the sex cries of Oliver's past lovers, who hadn't been able to contain their delight during that brief and hellish-for-me month when he'd lived with me in our early twenties.

When I open my eyes there's amusement in his intense stare, his lips twitching with barely concealed mirth. I want to kiss the smirk right off the self-satisfied prick's face.

He leans in, his manly scent washing over me until I'm weak from the head rush.

'Jealous…?' he says, his voice low and enticing enough to vibrate the air around my nipples through two layers of clothing. But no amount of armour can protect me from the effect he has on my needy body. Because I've always been jealous, part of me desperate to be on the receiving end of some Oliver loving just one time…

And isn't this that chance? A once-in-a-lifetime offer?

I huff, brace my hands on my hips and stick out my chest. 'I am perfectly capable of taking care of myself, as you can see.' I wave my hand towards my bag of delights. 'I don't need you or anyone else.'

But how would it feel to cast off the exhausting battle of denial just for a few minutes? To throw myself into his bulging arms and say, *Yes, I am jealous, show me what I've been missing!* To surrender to every desire I've kept at bay all these years and allow my rampant libido loose on Oliver Coterill?

Would I survive? Would he?

The day I met him in a student pub, he was so charming, but with a sadness in his eyes that seemed to fuel his behaviour and a cynicism too profound for someone of our age. We'd clicked immediately. My attraction was instant, and for a few heady hours—laughing over stupid jokes and being competitive over game after game of pool—the insecure younger woman I was back then had hoped that maybe, just once, I might score the sexy, funny, charming and best-looking guy in the bar.

Then, green with longing and furious with myself for daring to dream I'd be his type, I watched him slope off with my room-mate of the time. Back in our tiny student flat with paper-thin walls, the sounds of Oliver's sexual prowess kept me awake most of the night. Fortunately for my ears and my sanity, their relationship ended after a couple of days—she didn't get his dry sense of humour and she hated pool. When he spent more time talking to me than he did fucking her, she turned on both of us. I tried not to take sides, but as soon as she realised that nothing would put her back in Oliver's bed she called me his pathetic puppy dog and moved out, leaving us to our budding friendship and me to cover all of the rent.

'I know you don't need me, or anyone else,' he says, his beautiful eyes temptation enough. 'But I'm not talking about disappointing dates or relationships or second-rate, battery-operated orgasms.'

Simply hearing him say the word 'orgasms' aloud in his sexy baritone sends shockwaves of delirium down my thighs, almost triggering a mini-climax.

'I'm talking about sex,' he says. 'Full-blown multiple orgasms that will make your extensive, and I might add impressive, toy collection redundant.'

I can barely stand, my lower limbs like rubber, even though I know he's teasing. But he's sown seeds of 'if only' in my brain, and it's like a greenhouse in there, shoots sprouting all over the place, each possibility more graphic than the last until I'm a turned-on mess. I want to beg him—*please stop for the sake of my hearing...*

But he's still talking, his sinful mouth crafting wonderful, dangerous words. 'You should at least experience that once, so when you do date the next serious, condescending arsehole you'll have expectations beyond discovering his career aspirations, whether he's allergic to your cat and if he's prepared to watch those baking shows you love.'

A gasp slips out through my slack mouth at his expression. 'You're *actually* serious?' It's finally computing in my head that this isn't some elaborate, bored Oliver practical joke at my expense, although he's not usually cruel.

I grow lightheaded with need, my imagination running at warp speed. Oliver and me. Sex. Orgasms.

'Deadly,' he says, no hint of amusement now. 'Why not? Apart from today's shocking revelation, we know everything there is to know about each other.'

I have to bite the inside of my cheek to stop myself wincing. Oh, Oliver, if only you knew how long I've lusted… How many fantasies, how many orgasms, you've already aided unbeknown…

'I'd never hurt you,' he continues. 'And, as you said, I'm an expert at casual and I deliver. Blokes on dating apps lie—they'll claim to be the best lover in the world and send you some Photoshopped picture of their enormous dick…which begs the question why they can't find dates in the first place.'

The room starts to spin, so oxygen-deprived is my brain.

'So how will that go?' I lash out, because he's made me hornier than ever before with the way he's looking at me and with all his talk of orgasms. But I'm not a toy. He can't take me out of the friend box, play with me and then put me back. Red rage boils behind my eyes. 'Would I be some sort of altruistic pity-fuck?'

My question falls into the tense silence.

I've only seen Oliver truly angry once—with some pap who stuck a camera in my face outside a swanky restaurant he'd taken me to for my birthday a few years ago. It's not a thing I ever wish to revisit, especially if said anger is directed my way, but there's no escaping his furious stare and the strain radiating from his rigid body.

I hold my breath, my heart leaping through my T-shirt like that of a cartoon character.

'Don't.' His single-word reprimand is little more than a throaty whisper with the effect of a blow, given the sincerity in his eyes and the harsh set of his jaw. 'Don't you dare demean my respect for you. You're more precious to me than the sum of everyone else in my life.'

I shudder, confused by his words, but ready to swoon at his feet. Like this, all sexy, commanding and self-assured, he's ten times as hot as when he's just laughing, friend Olly.

We're so close, I feel his heat. When my head starts to swim because I've forgotten to breathe, I inhale his air.

'I want you. And I'm a selfish bastard. An orgasm for you means an orgasm for me.' He clicks his tongue, a hint of that roguish smile of his. 'Come on, Neve. You're a feminist—you know the way equality works.'

He wants me the way I want him? I open my mouth to speak, to tell him to stop teasing because it's not funny, to argue that there are willing blondes more his type out by the pool, but he silences me, a finger resting on my lips with infinitesimal pressure.

I try not to pant my excitement onto that solitary fingertip, because then he'll know all the longing and conflict bubbling inside me.

'If I have to watch you parade around in these sexy bikinis for the rest of the week, fighting my hard-on for you, we might as well both get our money's worth, don't you agree?' He lets the last question hang for a beat or two, his mouth kicking up once more, although his eyes stay banked with heat. 'You know how much you enjoy being frugal.'

Two compliments in a row from Oliver scrambles my disbelieving brain, especially when one of them contains the words *sexy* and *hard-on*. He thinks I'm sexy. Has a hard-on for *me*.

Go red bikini!

But, no, I can't. There may as well be a neon line painted on the timber flooring between his toes and mine. Even the tip of a toe over that boundary changes everything. If only we could somehow forget that line for a while.

His finger slides down my chin and falls away. I groan in my head because his touch, flirtatious bordering on seductive, may as well have delved into my soul to massage my wildly beating heart. I want him to touch every part of me in that way until I'm so full of sensation, there's no room for reason, doubt or fear.

And it seems I can have what I want.

'But…' Why am I stalling? This is what I secretly craved when I agreed to Brooke's silly pact, back in London. That he'd suddenly wake up and notice me. Why am I not laving my tongue over his pierced nipple, over every inch of him as if he's a giant lollipop, and then ripping off those shorts with my teeth?

'It's a stupid idea,' I say, 'because it will change things between us.'

I'm not naive. Oliver is Oliver. He's not going to miraculously morph into boyfriend material overnight. He doesn't do relationships, just sex-fests. We'll sleep together, and it will be great, but then what? Will we be friends with benefits every time we're both single and feeling horny? Will our friendship end as soon as the shagging ends, Oliver reverting back to type, growing bored and moving on? The roll of butterflies reminds me of his value in my life. And to risk it all… For sex. Probably one-sided sex, like all my other experiences. No—it's not worth the price.

But, couldn't I have a little taste of what I've always craved? Just one time?

'It'll only change things between us if we let it,' he says with a shrug. 'It's just fucking. You'll tell me what feels good,' he says, his stare tracing my mouth. 'And we'll get you over this hurdle, no big deal.' He's still the voice of reason, and if I didn't know better I'd think he'd waited all these years just for this chance. And he makes it sound so easy. So neat and compartmentalised.

'Don't you want to know what your body is capable of?' His voice brims full of delicious promise. 'I want to be the one to show you.'

At my continued hesitation he holds up his hands, palms out, and moves back a fraction. 'I don't want to pressure you. It's your decision. And if I'm being inappropriate here I'll apologise and we'll never mention this conversation again.'

Panic flares in me. I grip his forearm, stalling. 'Hold on a second. I'm thinking.' Could I keep my distance emotionally and just enjoy the sex? Take the orgasm on offer, learn from the master and keep feelings and expectations out of it? Would I be any worse off? And at least I'd know one way or another if there's truly something wrong with me. If I can't come with Oliver, no other man stands a chance. And he's right. I shouldn't dive back into dating with such depressingly low expectations.

As long as he keeps his word that it won't change our friendship, this is my best shot at a safe space of sexual exploration...

He stands stock-still, his stare glued to mine while my pulse flies.

I narrow my eyes to what he calls my 'mum look'. 'Let's say for argument's sake we're the first couple in the history of the world to make friends with benefits work... We'd need to have a defined set of ground rules.'

His lips twitch. 'Of course. A person with an analytical, spreadsheet-wielding mind like yours could rattle those off in seconds.' He crosses his arms and lifts his chin, playfulness deepening the creases around his eyes. 'Hit me with it.'

My voice is too breathy, because the longer we talk about this the hornier I grow. And the more of an actual possibility it seems, not just talk. But there's a riot going on inside my stomach as I ponder the practicalities, nerves beading perspiration on my top lip. Still, he's right. Rules and numbers don't lie.

'You've already stated rule number one,' I say. 'That it won't affect our friendship.'

He nods. 'Done.'

'Rule number two,' I say, ignoring the way he finds this amusing, warming to my theme. 'What happens on the island, stays on the island.' As long as I keep the rules coming, I can delay the moment when I have to make an actual, life-changing decision. But is there really any question? Am I really going to turn him down when a part of me has never had platonic thoughts where he's concerned?

'Yes, of course…' He's growing impatient. Bored.

I roll back my shoulders. If we're doing this, I'm putting in the safeguards. I won't let him railroad me. 'Rule number three—we *never* speak about this with each other after today. Ever.' Perhaps that way we'll both forget it happened and therefore protect our friendship.

He gestures a mock salute. 'Roger that.'

'And four—no kissing and telling.' Heat boils up my neck at the hypocrisy of this last point, because if Oliver lays one finger on me in lust there's no way in hell I'll be able to keep it from Brooke and Grace. I'll be spilling my guts in our group chat before he can say 'take off your clothes'.

My heart thuds.

'As if I'd do that. And I've already agreed that we keep it a secret. You're repeating yourself now,' he says with an indulgent smile. Oliver slowly reaches for the sunglasses I'd forgotten were still perched on my head, folds them and tosses them onto the chair.

Of course I'm babbling—I'm a bundle of nerves.

'Let's shake on it,' he says, his deep voice more dark and dangerous than I've ever heard before. With eyes locked on mine, he holds out his hand palm-up. His big, sexy Oliver shaped hand is so familiar. But the gesture, us shaking on a deal to step over the friend boundary together, is so alien that the scant inches between us may as well be miles. My own arm feels leaden, hanging at my side with paralysing inertia.

My fingers twitch. Burn for his touch.

My eyes burn with longing, trapped by his vivid blue stare.

My throat burns, all the reasons and arguments and conditions dried up.

I lift my hand so it's hovering over his.

Before I can vacillate further, Oliver closes the gap and slides his palm against mine in a strong grip. I suck in a gasp and then flush, because there's no way he missed the sound. We're not hand holders, Olly and I. Despite the hundreds of sexless touches that have passed between us, this touch is breath-stealing, scorching.

But, if I'm gasping at hand-to-hand contact, what happens when there's some breast action going on? I'll probably self-combust.

My thighs quiver at the very idea.

This is the longest handshake in history. I try to pull my hand free, but Oliver holds firm, using the momentum of my recoil to propel me closer, my breasts now only millimetres from his hard chest. I look up from his mouth, the breath panting from my lungs.

'Olly,' I plead, my body almost touching his in all the places that matter.

'Rule number five…' he says, his stare blatantly tracing my parted lips with the hunger I've longed to see a million times—the bedroom eyes.

'No more Olly.' His deep voice is full of unfamiliar command. 'Only Oliver.'

I nod my agreement, my knees too weak to keep the tremble from my legs.

Olly is my friend. Oliver will be my lover.

Temporarily.

'Say yes,' he says, tempting me.

I feel my pulse to the tips of my toes.

'Yes,' I say, on a heavenly wave of surrender.

CHAPTER FOUR

Neve

HIS NOSTRILS FLARE, as if he's sucking in a silent gasp, but he's outwardly calm and so controlled. My friend has a sexy alpha side… My entire body feels stiff enough to snap. Not that I want to escape but, now this moment is here, the actual realisation of all my hopes and dreams, I'm a physical and mental wreck. So high on longing and the thick thud of desire, I can almost imagine the orgasm he claims to be able to deliver.

'Fact one about orgasms,' Oliver says huskily, his full, sensual lips only inches from mine. 'They start in your mind.'

I look up from his mouth and the expectation of his kiss, my stare clinging to his for fear I'll pass out before we even get to the good stuff. Because bedroom Oliver is even more confident than when he's running his multi-billion-pound company. I went to a tech conference with him once in Silicon Valley, where he'd been invited as a speaker. His intelligence and authority was so hot, I'd had to leave before the end of his talk to rub one out on the bathroom.

'Close your eyes,' he says, voice low and seductive as he woos my body to his will. 'Let me paint you a picture.'

I obey his hypnotic words, although I don't want to miss one second of the look of lust on his face. I'd walk over hot coals for him on any given day, so on *this* day, where I'm so close to the fulfilment of my deepest fantasy, I'm his to command. One hundred per cent.

When he speaks again, I'm so attuned to every nuance of his voice—as if I'm hearing it for the first time, so heightened are my senses—that every word is audible over the sound of my own ragged breathing.

'It's hell watching you walk around in these sexy bikinis,' he says, his breath warm on my cheek. 'I don't know what's happened, because I've seen you in a bikini too many times to count, but I haven't been able to keep my eyes off you, off your gorgeous body, since we arrived.'

My neck collapses, my head falling back, a gasp of ecstasy floating past my parted lips at his arousing confession. I'm petite, curvaceous. Why have I never known that he thinks my body is gorgeous? His poker face must be a good as mine.

He lifts my glasses from my face and I fight the urge to open my eyes. 'I want to see what's underneath these tiny triangles,' he says, his dark voice vibrating the air between us.

Moisture gushes between my legs. I want to show him. How can he do this to me with his voice alone? With his ordinary words? But to me, they're not ordinary.

'I want to taste the sweet little nipples I see poking through the fabric,' he says, his warm breath now feathering over my neck, my collarbone, as if he's about to take off my T-shirt and bikini top to do exactly that.

'I want to know if you're wet while I stand here speaking my dirty thoughts aloud.'

I am, oh God, I really am.

I grip his fingers more tightly because I feel faint with desire.

He hums a sexy noise in his throat. 'I want to drop to my knees right now and suck on all that heat and sweetness. And I will. Soon.'

My pants grow frantic, as if I'm a vixen in heat. I want to open my eyes, to see the lust I hear in his smoky voice. I've never been this turned on before, and he hasn't really touched me yet, but I don't want to break the spell. I'm high on the promise in his voice, which I've waited so long to hear.

Wave after wave of delicious spasms clutch at my core muscles. I might actually come standing here. With him touching nothing more than my hand and my mind with his aphrodisiac words. How can he do this to me? And why did I wait all these years to be this brave?

'But more than any of that,' he whispers, worming his way deeper into my mind, 'I want this.' The heat of his breath registers on my lips a split second before his firm kiss lands, and I go into meltdown. With an impatient grunt, he drops my hand to grip both sides of my face and holds me still, captive, enraptured, while his firm, thrilling kiss directs my pliant lips apart. His tongue delves inside my mouth at the same time his leg slides between my legs, my sarong parting so the only thing between my very wet crotch and fizzing clit and his muscular thigh is two thin layers of fabric.

My pulse whooshes in my head; I'm kissing Oliver.

As if my brain is jolted with electricity, I snap out of the seductive trance he put me in the minute he touched my hand. My eyes snap open to see his swimming before me, out of focus but bold with triumph and challenge. I could die happy right now, because I've taken that giant leap, I've made something happen.

His strong arm scoops around my waist, hauling my body up and mashing my tingling breasts to his hard chest, so I feel the bar through his nipple. I'm desperate to discover if it's sensitive for him. My tongue pushes against his, a mewl forcing its way from the back of my throat as I claim the kiss I've only dreamed of for nine years. It's everything I imagined and more. A first, but somehow familiar, because he's no stranger. I know him inside out. And I want him with terrifying ferocity.

My hands tangle in his hair, fighting to bring me closer to the source of such wrecking pleasure as Oliver Coterill's kiss.

I want it never to end. I want to rush it along. I want so many things, I'm practically levitating, only the tips of my toes grounding me to the timber floor.

Then my analytical mind starts a placard-waving demonstration. I scrunch my eyes closed in the hope of silencing the protests. I don't want to see sense. I don't want to think of all the reasons that this shagging my best friend dooms me to a lifetime of heartache. I just want him. Just one time before I abandon my futile crush for good and give up my fantasy.

Because there's been a secret, shameful part of me convinced I've held something back from past boyfriends, as if waiting for this moment. For my shot with Oliver. Perhaps I even sabotaged my own past relationships, holding out for this long-coveted eventuality. Perhaps that's the reason my exes were jealous of our friendship; they saw what I tried to conceal.

And Oliver's right. I want to experience the amazing sex everyone talks about. That it might be with him, is too perfect to contemplate.

Without breaking the kiss, Oliver releases my face to work on the knot of my sarong. My lips cling to his like limpets, my arms so tight around his neck, I might inadvertently strangle him. But if I let go he might change his mind. I might change mine. That he wants me, that he's actually fumbling to get me naked and it's not just a figment of my rampant libido and overactive imagination, already makes this the best sexual encounter of my experience.

His mouth tears from mine, his head bent closer while he struggles with the knotted fabric.

'Let me,' I say, swatting at his fingers. 'Take off your shorts.' I'm almost too afraid to see him naked—the experience will likely be life-threatening. And he'll see me—uncharted territory.

He abandons the knot in the sarong and steps back. 'Oh, no. There's no way we're rushing this.' He lifts the hem of my T-shirt at the same moment I free the knot around my waist. With a whoosh of falling fabric, and a tantalising glide of his knuckles over my waist and ribs as he divests me of the T-shirt, I'm back to just my tiny red bikini—my lucky charm. For all the heat in his stare as he eyes me up and down, I might as well be naked.

My knees knock. *I'm going to let Oliver see me naked.*

'We'll get to the good stuff,' he says with a hint of his teasing smile. He grips my face once more and slides his mouth over mine. 'But first you need warming up.'

I thought men couldn't multi-task, but Oliver is a pro. His lips never leave mine as he manoeuvres me, inching me back to the bed. My thighs hit the mattress and I collapse backward, clinging to his waist to pull him down on top of me.

It's a 'sprawl of limbs, clash of teeth and grunt of laughter' moment, but then his arm scoops my waist and he rolls me on top of him, my body in contact with his hardness from breasts to thighs.

I drag my mouth from his, every inch of me on fire. 'I'm warm, trust me.'

'Good,' he says, his hands gripping my buttocks.

Laid under me, his hair desecrated by my hands and his eyes dark with desire, he doesn't look like my Oliver. But he's never looked hotter. And, considering he rocks business suits like a Hollywood heartthrob, wears jeans and a T-shirt well enough to make designers weep and struts his board shorts like he's modelling surf wear, that's no mean feat.

I push up onto my haunches, kneeling astride his thighs for a better view of his sculpted chest and abdomen. That's when I see the thick rod of his erection for the first time I actually whimper behind the hand pressed to my mouth.

'Oh…' My words dry up as I salivate, blatantly staring at the object of so many of my fantasies. A taboo object, which until now has been as shrouded in mystery as the Bermuda Triangle.

His sensual mouth, slightly swollen from our kisses, stretches. 'It's showing off—ignore it.'

That he talks about his penis in the third person makes me want to laugh, make jokes, start some of our usual banter, but I want him too much for levity. The fact that he's here with me with that snake in his shorts, and that he's mine to touch and kiss as I please, starts a series of body-racking trembles.

Desperation makes me a little fractious. 'I thought the whole point of this was that, for once, I didn't have to ignore it. In fact, I thought I could lavish all my attention on it.' I deliberately lick and then bite my bottom lip.

His pupils dilate, his breath coming faster. 'You've had to ignore it in the past?' The look of mild incredulity on his face confirms my excellent acting skills.

I shrug. 'I'm a woman, you're a guy… Not that I've ever seen it showing off before, of course.'

He smiles, a hint of his friend smile hidden behind the lust transforming his features into those of a man I don't recognise. 'Well, you can lavish all the attention you like on it,' he says. 'Just not yet.'

My sulk evaporates when he reaches up and unties the bikini strap at the nape of my neck. 'The first thirty minutes are all about you.' He peels down the triangles and my breasts spill free, just like that, my nipples peeking out, as if they don't know we're supposed to be just friends.

'Thirty minutes…?' I croak. Won't it all be over after ten? We'll probably be snorkelling in thirty minutes…him satiated and me still wondering if there's something wrong with me…

No. I trust that he's good at this. He's had enough practice. All I have to do is surrender to his plan.

'Mmm-hmm. Lean forward,' he says.

I brace my arms on either side of his head on the bed, my freed breasts dangling. I have a fleeting thought that it's not the most flattering angle, but then Oliver does two things that blank my mind. One, he cups my aching breasts in his warm hands and, two, he jerks his hips up from the bed, as if he can't keep still, the thick ridge of his erection bumping my clit and making my eyes roll back.

'Argh…' I love this plan. Best plan ever.

'Tell me.' His thumbs rub my nipples in small circles, his big hands cupping and caressing. 'Are you feeling turned on?' Another tilt of his pelvis. Another nudge of my clit.

Turned on? I'm molten. He'll feel my heat, my soaking bikini crotch. He'll know it's for him… But we crossed the line where I hide my raging attraction to him long ago.

'Yes.' I open my eyes to see him studying me with fascination. 'I was turned on before you walked in here.'

His nod is lazy, his eyes hooded as if he expected that answer and is picturing what he interrupted in the bathroom.

'What do you think about when you use those toys you love?' he asks. 'And don't you dare say nothing, because I won't believe you.'

I flush—I feel the heat spreading across my skin like a tidal wave. This is Oliver... He rolls each nipple between his thumbs and forefingers, the bite of pressure enough to make me forget everything but how good he's making me feel. I'm so aroused by what he's doing and the way he's looking at me, as if he can't wait to put that magnificent penis inside me, that my mind forges ahead with blatant honesty.

'You.' I realise my mistake immediately and bite down on my lip to engage some filters. 'I imagine you making all your women come hard enough to release those screams I've heard through the walls.'

'And?' he says, his fingers stroking and pinching at my nipples in perfect synchronicity so that I'm gasping.

I want to hide from being this vulnerable with him, but I don't want him to stop what he's doing. I look deep into his eyes. 'And I imagine it's me you make scream. Me you make come.'

Fire rages through me, scalding, scorching. But there's no room for shame or awkwardness because his pupils flare, his stare burning hot. 'I will. More than once.'

I close my eyes. I love this confident side of Oliver. That his commanding conviction extends beyond business to the bedroom fills me with trickles of hope and excitement that, this time, I might just make it over the finish line.

My hand makes a dive for his erection, but he intercepts, gripping my wrist. 'Twenty-seven minutes until you get anywhere near the contents of my shorts,' he says, his voice gruff, body strung taut beneath me. He abandons my breast and grips my hips in his hands, grinding me over his hard length, meeting the helpless undulations of my hips with small thrusts. Teasing. Tempting.

I release a frustrated yelp and slide my lips down his neck to his nipple piercing, which I flick with my tongue until his fingers dig into my skin.

Oliver tugs the side ties on my bikini bottoms and peels fabric away from my backside, his hands grasping and massaging the bare cheeks of my arse. Then he pulls the front of the bikini until I push up onto my knees a fraction, the whole garment sliding between my legs with a scrape of fabric over my most sensitive parts.

He tosses the bottoms and releases the final tie on the top at my back, throwing it after its partner, so I'm now completely naked astride him. At the mercy of his fierce stare and exploring hands.

'This isn't fair,' I choke out as he roams my nakedness freely with eyes and hands. I want to see all of him too.

'Who said it had to be fair?' Giving my hips one final grind onto his erection, he jack-knifes up into a sitting position with a crunch of his sexy abs so that we're nose to nose. 'Kiss me,' he says in his husky voice.

No second time of asking required. I forget I'm stark-naked astride my friend's lap, drape my arms over his broad shoulders, tangle my fingers in his hair and go to town on his mouth, my heart thumping that I'm allowed to kiss him, touch him. Will I ever be able to stop? To go back just to watching his mouth move when he talks and recall how it tastes?

No. No time travelling. Enjoy the moment.

We kiss for what feels like an hour, me naked and writhing in his lap and him displaying a degree of restraint and patience I hadn't believed possible from my highly sexed friend.

If he wasn't intermittently grunting and moaning, his cock rock-hard between my legs, I might have thought he was bored. I've never known a guy to turn down dick action. For thirty minutes!

'Oliver…' I moan, need building in me like steam.

'Tell me how it feels.' His familiar face is almost unrecognisable, slack with desire, his lips swollen and eyes hooded but penetrating.

I can't keep still, my hips jerking on his lap. 'I'm burning up. I need you.' My mind clears from the lust fog and I realise I'm actually close. Amazingly, unbelievable close. As if a stroke or two of my clit could carry me over the edge. But surely not? It can't be that easy.

But I've been here before, the high elusive, my orgasm building only to fade away again.

But he hasn't even touched me there yet, only my breasts. And his kisses.

He must hear my thoughts, because he slides one hand between my legs, his other a vice around my back, as if he doesn't want me to get away.

But why would I go anywhere? I'm exactly where I want to be. He's still wearing his shorts—there's been zero penetration—but already it's the best sex I've ever had.

He stares at my face while his fingertips slide over my mons, my skin sensitive thanks to the full Brazilian wax I had for the holiday. I grip his shoulders, fingernails digging into his skin, anticipation coiling in my belly. And I can't look away from his eye contact, even though I'm burning alive at the unchartered intimacy.

He grazes my clit with his fingertip, bolts of electrical current zapping along my thighs. 'Tell me what you like.'

I nod, so desperate now to know if his skills, his boasts, are justified. 'Touch me again. Like that,' I say, beyond caring that my voice is a breathy pant and I'm barking sexual orders at my best friend.

Another glide of his fingertips, and then another. Delicate circles growing in pressure until it's too much to bear and I throw my head back on a desperate cry.

He pushes a finger inside me, then a second, his thumb still circling my clit, and then his facial scruff scrapes the skin of my breast, his mouth devours my nipple and I clench in a violent spasm around his fingers.

'Yes… Oliver…'

This is happening. It's really happening… I'm so close, and not a battery in sight.

He sucks down hard, pressing my nipple flat between his tongue and the roof of his mouth before releasing it to the rapid lap of the tip of his tongue. I look down, watch his mouth on my breast, feel his hand doing incredible things between my legs, and the tension builds.

'Harder,' I say. 'Suck me harder.' And he nips at my nipple with the barest scrape of his teeth.

Fire races along my nerves, thick, languid heat pooling in my pelvis, a desperate empty feeling deep inside.

'I want you inside me,' I manage huskily.

'Not yet.' His tone is final.

'Suck harder, then!' I gasp, my hips joining the rhythm of his pumping fingers. He obeys, his mouth clamped down on my nipple, pushing a third finger inside me and pressing his thumb down on my clit.

And then he looks up, his eyes searing into mine while his mouth is at work, the contact bold and intimate, and the final catalyst igniting my pleasure.

'Oliver…' His name is all I can utter before I fall. The waves of sensation batter my weak body, spasm after miraculous spasm wracking my internal muscles.

I buck and jerk in his lap, both seeking and avoiding the heavenly pleasure, but his grip around my waist shackles me, so I'm his puppet until the last wave smacks my spent body and I slump forward with a strangled plea.

'Enough…enough!' I'm limp in his arms, collapsed against his broad chest, his scruff scraping my shoulder and neck as he nuzzles his mouth over my skin.

'I'd say that's one orgasm down, one point to us, wouldn't you?' I feel his heart thudding against mine, feel his smile against my neck. I can see it in my mind's eye—smug, playful, those grooves bracketing his beautiful mouth.

I want to call his bluff, to pretend I faked it, to wipe away the arrogance I'm certain is on his face.

But, even if I hadn't all but snapped off his fingers with the force of my orgasmic spasms, I'm too wrecked to do more than offer a lame huff of protest.

I have nothing to say. My mind's blessedly blank. I can't believe what just happened. With Oliver, of all people.

But then another thought occurs to me, sending my heart leaping into my throat. Because before this one time is over I have a few more demands. I straighten and look him straight in the eyes—although he's a little blurry because I'm not wearing my glasses—and test out my croaky voice.

'Now I get to touch your penis.'

CHAPTER FIVE

Oliver

'OH, NO, NO…NO.' I check my watch behind her back. 'You still have sixteen minutes of your time left.' I hold her to my chest and turn my face into her mussed hair to inhale the scent of her shampoo. My brain battles the frantic rage of testosterone in my blood to make some coherent thoughts. What the hell has happened to my Neve? Was she always this hot, this sensual, provocative and demanding? I've been walking around with my eyes closed. For self-preservation. But how can I have missed so much for so long? Been so idiotically stupid?

Because she's my friend and I was terrified I'd fuck it up. Because, unlike Neve, I've only had one relationship. As a teenager. Jane was a lot like Neve, except that she broke my heart. Then my father's cynical take on women and love—and my own reckless behaviour—taught me to shut myself down to that kind of risk.

But I can do this—keep my friendship with Neve separate, sacrosanct, and enjoy the sex. Fuck, I gave her her first shared orgasm… And I still have sixteen minutes to touch and lick every gorgeous inch of her until she's imprinted on my mind. I want to get up close and personal. I want to taste her and force her back into orgasm number two, now I know she's had a rough deal from her exes. If I can reset the sexual imbalance she's tolerated for way too long, the risk is worth taking.

I slide her languorous body from my lap and she collapses onto the bed, her face buried as she gifts me a vision of her sexy backside. My dick throbs, pushing at the front of my shorts in revenge for having to wait. But I'd walk around with blue balls for a week in order to show Neve the good time she's missed out on.

I can't resist touching her, though. My fingers trace her ribs and the tattoo of an infinity symbol she got for her twenty-first birthday. I'd held her hand, jealous as fuck of the dude inking her skin just to the side of one full, beautiful breast. Not that I'd fully seen them then. But, now I have, the delicious images will be scored on my memory for evermore. Although, somehow, I'll have to try and forget the details once we return to being just friends…

Neve stirs, rolling onto her side and propping herself up on one elbow.

'How did you do that?' she asks, her flushed face full of genuine awe.

Pride builds in my chest. I may be related to a man-whore who sucks at commitment, but I've given her something those other supercilious dick boyfriends of hers couldn't. I shrug, stroking her hip with my thumb. 'Sex is easy. You just have to be honest about what works.'

I lie on the bed facing her, my head on my bent arm, and caress her buttock, filling my hand with her pale rounded cheek. 'Tell me. What was the best part of what just happened?'

She huffs, rolling onto her stomach again to hide from my question. 'You don't need your head to grow any bigger.'

'Come on, I'm serious. Tell me. There's a reward for the best answer.' We've always been playful with each other, shared a similar sense of humour. That I get to combine one of my favourite parts of our relationship with one of my favourite activities— sex—makes me feel more alive than ever, and I haven't even come yet.

Then an idea occurs. 'You think about your answer.' I rise from the bed and march to her suitcase, retrieving a toy from the bag—a bright-pink dildo—while she buries her face in the pillow and grumbles about being so candid. But I need to know. I have plans.

I place the toy on the bed, out of her line of vision,

kneel astride one of her legs and brace myself over her back. While she mumbles excuses into the pillow, I push her hair out of the way and kiss her freckled shoulders and the valley between her shoulder blades.

'If you want to replicate an outcome,' I say, my voice thick with lust, 'you must analyse how you arrived there. Consider it an audit, if you like.' All the while my mouth is occupied with her satiny skin and my questions, my throbbing dick is distracted.

'Mmm,' she moans, her breath catching. 'It was all good.'

I can see she's going to need a little encouragement. If she's allowed herself to be short-changed by her exes, talking dirty probably doesn't come naturally. 'Was I too rough with your nipples?' I slide my mouth down the bumps of her spine, learning new things about her, like her sensitive, ticklish spots.

'God, no.' She groans. 'That was good. Perfect. I liked the nibbling and tweaking.'

'See, that wasn't so hard—this is what I want to hear.'

I press kisses in the small of her back and then kiss each cheek before pressing my teeth there with the barest hint of pressure. 'And the biting? Too much?' Oh, how I'd love to mark her, give her a hickey so she remembers this in the days to come every time she looks in the mirror.

'Um…no!' she squeaks, bucking her pelvis. 'That was good too.'

I grip her hips and encourage her to roll over onto her back.

I look down at the woman I know so well, pride building in me that she trusts me enough to gift me this incredible privilege. Flushed and panting, looking at me as if I'm the only man on earth.

Not a womaniser with bad genes.

Need roars through my head. Why have I denied myself this possibility for so long, and how can I take full advantage of my luck before Neve wakes up to my true nature? Because not all my decisions have been as awesome as this one.

When I met her I was a monumental fuck-up, more like my father than I care to admit, and she was amazing, someone I knew I wanted in my life despite being out of her league. But I'm older now. More mature. I have no intention of losing her or allowing her to regret this.

But the clock is ticking.

'So the nipple play was good.' I scoot down the bed and lift one leg, bend her knee and press her ankle up to my lips. 'What about the kissing?'

Her mouth hangs open, her breasts rising on every laboured breath. 'That was fine. Oliver, do we have to talk?'

I swirl my tongue around her anklebone. 'Oh, yes, I'd say the talking is essential for orgasm number two. I'm not sure I'm happy with just fine.' My tongue laves up the curve of her calf to a sensitive spot behind her knee. 'Mmm… I'll have to try harder with the kissing.'

She's panting now. 'Okay. Good. The kissing was good. It definitely helped. But I don't think I'll be able to come again…'

I slide onto my stomach, shouldering her thighs open until I'm positioned exactly where I want to be. I press a kiss beneath her belly button, smiling up at her outraged but aroused expression. 'Don't make this even more exciting by issuing a challenge.'

Slowly, deliberately, I look down between her legs. Lust robs my breath. She's completely bare, all that gorgeous pink pussy on display for me.

Neve whimpers and covers her face with her hand. 'Oh…'

'Don't you hide from me,' I say, tracing kisses and licks up her smooth inner thighs, while my stare jumps from her face to my new favourite view.

She lifts her head and glares. 'Oliver…' But the reprimand lacks conviction, her voice so strangled and needy.

'Tell me,' I say, sucking in the scent of her arousal until my dick starts to weep, 'was two fingers enough? Is three too ambitious?' I trace her opening with one feather-light fingertip.

She shakes her head, her bottom lip trapped under her teeth, her eyes wide, pleading. Her lips actually tremble.

Damn, she's incredible.

'No?' I press a kiss to her mons, swirl my tongue there, avoiding her most sensitive areas until I'm certain she's ready to beg…or demand.

'I loved everything you did to me.' She's panting with need now, desperation hovering in her eyes. 'Couldn't you feel how hard I came?' she whispers.

I grin; my Neve is warming up. 'I could. Let's see if you're ready for another.'

Panic flares in her beautiful eyes, but there's desire too. 'I…I can't.'

I grin, blow a stream of air over her exposed lips. 'I think you can,' I say and lower my mouth to her, sucking and tonguing her sweet flesh like I'm French-kissing her pussy.

She cries out, her thighs jerking and her head falling back between her shoulders. I part her with my thumbs and find her swollen clit, plump and ready.

'Oliver…' She says my name on a gasp that makes my blood pump harder because there's reverence in her voice that makes me feel invincible somehow. Right now, I'm so much more than the sum of my parts. More than her commitment-phobic friend. More than a casual fuck. More than a man.

I'm everything she deserves in this single moment.

'Why don't you watch what I'm doing and direct proceedings?' I suggest, my pulse hammering hard enough to deafen me. 'That way, I'll know what you like.'

Her huge eyes are round as she stares at me between her legs and then watches my mouth lave kiss after kiss to her pouty clit.

She's addictive. Her scent is so arousing I'm worried I might come in my shorts. I ease my hips back to dampen the friction and flatten my tongue over the taut bundle of nerves that all my verbal preparation has swollen to a tight bud.

'Yes...' Neve hisses, grasping my head with both hands so she can rock her pelvis against my mouth.

I keep up the suction, searching the bed for the dildo with one hand. I see the moment she notices the toy, excitement flaring in her eyes. I look down, lining it up at her slick entrance, and then search her face for permission. Her nod and whimper is the green light I need. I ease the thick toy inside her, my dick throbbing as we both watch the shocking-pink shaft disappear between her lips.

'Oliver,' she pants, her thighs trembling at the invasion. 'Suck me.'

I want to beat my chest in triumph at how perfect she is. Sweet, shy Neve has left the building. This Neve is greedy for orgasm number two. And I'll give her anything. Do anything to make her happy. To watch her come again.

I obey, my mouth finding her once more, alternating sucks and flicks of my tongue with plunges of the dildo inside her, knowing all the while she's watching.

This time her orgasm builds slowly. Her cries, her chanting my name over and over, and the jerks of her thighs, are all clues of the impending climax. Number two looks and sounds as good as the first. Neve's pleasure is one of the best sights I've ever seen, as she shatters and collapses back onto the bed, spent.

Testosterone roars through me, my abstinence equally depleted. 'Do you have any condoms?' I toss away the toy and race out of my clinging shorts, which feel two sizes too small. Have I ever been this turned on? This hot for a woman? Is it just because I know it's a one-time deal? A novelty? Forbidden? Or is it wonderful Neve and her addictive abandon?

Neve waves her hand in the direction of her wash bag on the nightstand and I rummage, my shaking fingers quickly locating my prize. I sheath myself and climb on top of her still spent body. She welcomes me, her kisses fast and frantic and her hands grabby, tugging on my shoulders and buttocks as I line myself up.

Part of me can't believe I'm actually doing this— about to penetrate my beautiful Neve, a woman I've forced myself to ignore sexually for so long. But, just as her pleasure is precious to me, so is she. I'll pay the price, make everything all right between us, if I can just have this one time.

With teeth gritted against the impending ecstasy, I sink forward into her tight warmth, my mind blank from all the reasons this is a terrible idea and I plunge home, thrust after thrust. Her cries and kisses urge me on. Sweat breaks out, stinging my eyes. But I don't want it to be over so soon, even as animalistic instincts take hold of my hips. I brace my arms either side of her head, my thrusts rocking the bed into the wall. She feels amazing. She is amazing. Perfection.

'Touch yourself. Your nipples. Your clit,' I bite out, and she nods, whimpers and obeys, one hand delving between our hips and the other plucking at one red, swollen nub.

Her pale skin is marked from my mouth and my facial hair, the sign of possession I craved.

My climax builds at the base of my spine, fire boiling in my belly. But still I want her with me, coming around my cock the way she milked the toy and my fingers. I want everything she has now I've stepped across the line. I want her corrupted. Ruined for mediocre sex for ever. Not my sweet friend, but this sexy woman who's ripped apart everything I thought I knew about her.

'Are you close?' I grit out, hips slamming into hers.

Miraculously she nods, her head thrown back as she wails, and we come together, angels singing, stars bursting and unicorns prancing.

CHAPTER SIX

Neve

I GRIP OLIVER'S waist and rest my cheek against his sun-warmed back, hiding from the worst of the sea spray as he spins the jet-ski in a tight arc. Adrenaline forces a squeal from me. I grip the seat with my thighs and cling to him for dear life. My heart thumps so hard, I'm sure he must feel it against his back.

After the astounding and miraculous orgasm medley this morning, we took the jet-ski and snorkel gear and headed out for the afternoon, exploring the pristine lagoon and teeming reefs of the Maldives. A good thing, because if we'd been anywhere near our rooms at the resort I'd be dragging Oliver back to bed.

I close my eyes and rest my forehead between his shoulder blades. How can I know him so well but still feel like I don't know him at all? The sex was everything I imagined and more, no fantasy able to compare with Oliver's sexual talents and my body's wondrous release. I'm still unsure how he managed to drag not just one but three orgasms from me in quick succession. Perhaps it was his bedroom eyes, or the bossiness, or the dirty talk… Or a winning combination.

But, while I'm still celebrating the miracle, a part of me hasn't been able to shake the doubts since.

Because we can never take back what happened.

I was blind to the shoal of tropical fish decorating the reef while we snorkelled, my mind occupied with how I'd had the most incredible sex of my life, but that it couldn't happen again, because it was with my best friend. A man with no interest in forming anything long term. And that's good, right? Because one time is recoverable, but more than that could become habit and therefore dangerous.

Over the years I've watched Oliver perfect the several-nights stand, which never turns into a relationship. And while right now, with my body still singing hallelujahs, several nights of Oliver's brand of sex sounds like the best plan ever, I cannot get carried away. There's a real risk if we did it again and again and again…

I suck in the scent of his skin, my body aching. How will I survive the next few days if it doesn't happen again? How can I go back to pretending that I don't crave his touch, his kisses, his body? I'll need to learn to lie all over again.

And is he still my best friend? Is it possible to return to what we were after such an incredible but disastrous side-step over the line?

Oliver swings the jet-ski in a figure-of-eight through the warm Indian ocean, as if it's business as usual. True to his word and the strict rules we'd set out, we haven't discussed it since, even though the memories are fresh enough. If I close my eyes while I suck in the scent of his warm skin, I can recreate a thrilling, involuntary clench of my internal muscles.

I sit up straight, mentally shaking myself. Olly and I are good enough friends, mature enough adults, to make a one-time holiday hook-up work. Our relationship is too important to spoil because we had sex… Even the kind of sex that surely sets off seismic activity on the ocean bed…at least for me. Perhaps it's always that way for him.

And there it is, the core at the centre of my doubts—that I'm an anomaly for him. Not his usual type. He's had a lot of partners, but he always manages to find women who want the same things—a casual good time.

One of the major reasons my last few relationships ended was because I'd grown a little more committed than my exes. I seem to have a knack for choosing men who aren't quite as invested in the relationship, and no one wants to feel like a stop-gap until someone better comes along. And then, of course, there was the bad sex...

But I can learn from my experience with Oliver. Now that we've proved there's nothing wrong with me, that I've just been sleeping with the wrong partners—selfish partners uninterested in my pleasure—we can go on as if it never happened.

Right?

But, oh...it *did* happen, and I'd do it again in a heartbeat. My heart thuds against his back, excitement building at the idea that, if I'm disciplined with myself, I can have more of him...perhaps until we have to go home...?

No—if Oliver can stick to the rules we laid out at the start, I sure as hell can. And there's no way I want to be the friend he hooks up with every now and then. A sexual placeholder in between his other women.

'Let's get a drink,' he yells over the sound of the engine. I give him a thumbs-up and he slows the jet-ski and heads for shore. In the shallows we dismount and tug the craft up onto the sand, handing our life jackets back to the waiting resort staff.

There's a bar on the beach, tables and chairs spilling from the deck onto the sand. We head for the sun-loungers underneath palm-thatched umbrellas that face the endless blue sea and give our order to a nearby waiter.

'That was so much fun,' I say, flopping down onto a lounger and relaxing back against the pillows as if I'm not sneaking looks at Oliver's wet, ripped body from behind my dark glasses.

'Mmm...' he mumbles, settling beside me.

We sit in silence, punctuated only by the arrival of our drinks, a cocktail for me and a beer for him. The warm breeze raises goose bumps over my skin, each excruciating second stretched indefinitely.

What now? This was exactly the kind of awkwardness I feared.

Both of us take a generous swallow, as if we're avoiding the moment when we'll be forced to have a normal friendly conversation. A conversation that has nothing to do with nipples, erections or orgasms.

Why is this so hard? He's still Olly. Still my friend.

I take a second gulp of the delicious drink and then place it on the table between Oliver's lounger and mine, presenting a calm, unaffected exterior while my heart thumps against my ribs and my stomach sinks.

I can't think of a single thing to say to a man with whom conversation has always flowed easily. My mind snags on the image of Oliver's face as he'd come inside me this morning. You should never know what your best friend's sex face looks like. I can't un-see that. I can't go back to thinking of him *just* as my friend, because he's more now. Can I even pretend he's a friend when the lust incapacitating me makes the previous nine years of lusting seem inconsequential?

Do I even want to go back to being friends now that I know how devastating sex with him is? But I've already written off being his lover, the potential heartache too risky.

Ugh—I'm going around in circles. I grab my drink once more, an occupation for my fidgety hands. We've ruined what we had and there's no future outside friendship in which we can both be happy.

'Okay,' he says, shaking me from my brain freak-out so that I literally jump, spilling a splash of sticky cocktail on my belly. 'I know we promised we wouldn't talk about it, but let's talk about it.'

I wipe at the spill with a napkin, delaying the moment when I have to look at him. 'Is that a good idea?' I mumble, settling my eyes on the view while the renegade neurones in my brain fire silent question after silent question.

Is our friendship irreparably damaged?

How was it for you?

And, most pressing, can we do it again?

'We said we wouldn't talk about it. Ever,' I remind him. I just need to prepare for the return of abstinence.

'I know.' He shoots me that look, the one he issued earlier when he said those magical words *I could make you come until you scream your throat raw.* 'But that was before you started to freak out.' His voice is way too calm for my liking, as if for him what we shared this morning is no big deal. It's a big deal for me. Gargantuan. It was spectacular and my body wants a repeat I know I can't have. I'd say that's worthy of a decent freak-out.

'I'm not freaking out,' I say, chasing full-blown denial. 'We agreed the subject was closed. You're breaking the rules.'

Thank goodness he raised it—I was close to cracking myself.

I'm still avoiding looking his way, but I feel the smile in his voice. 'Ah, come on, Never, you've always known I'm a bad influence,' he says. I've previously secretly adored my nickname, because it was just between us, like a secret handshake. Only now its use douses me with chills.

Neve was his lover. Never is definitely his friend.

'Can't a guy gloat when he's having the best day of his life?' he says, and my head whips around. He's having the best day of his life? I narrow my eyes. Is he teasing?

As if he's perfectly content with his revealing statement and my shell-shocked reaction, he stretches out his long body on the lounger.

Then he looks at me, playful once more, his voice

low. 'Oliver and Neve, three,' he says about my orgasm tally. 'SBF Club, zero.'

He grins, and I want to kiss him so badly, to sit astride him out here on the beach and take his magnificent penis into my mouth until it's all he can do to lie helpless and turned on under me—the way I behaved earlier. He's far too smug for my state of mind, which veers from wildly aroused to cranky and confused.

Bloody Oliver...

'SBF Club?' I ask, fully aware I'm skirting a forbidden conversation and indulging Oliver's ego. Part of me dreads knowing what he means by the initials.

'It stands for Serious Boring Fuckers,' he says, looking faintly annoyed. 'Your lazy exes.'

I gasp, casting a frown in his direction. 'You had a club name for them?' I knew there was little love lost between Oliver and the men of my past, especially after I split with them, but this is the first time he's ever admitted it aloud. But why, unless he was... No, he couldn't be... Jealous?

Trickles of sick delight run through my veins, knowing that misery loves company and that he might too have suffered frustration over the years. Until today, he's never given one indication that he sees me in a sexual light—probably the reason I'm reeling about what this morning's deviation means. And his jealousy could just be possessiveness over our friendship, nothing more.

He nods, resting his head back on his hands so all his delicious bronzed chest is on display and his arm muscles flex, distracting me from mounting sufficient outrage. 'To think I used to feel intimidated by them. If only I'd known they weren't taking care of you properly.'

'What are you talking about?' I vent my frustration. He's making me all kinds of hot and bothered. Turned on, then annoyed and then overjoyed… We're not supposed to be discussing this morning. It's hard enough to forget when he's stretched out semi-naked, calling to me like a feast catered to my specific needs. When I can still smell his scent on my skin, can still recall the taste of those lips and the commanding scrape of his sexy voice.

I scoff. 'You design outrageously clever software for a living that I don't even try to understand. Your tech company is worth billions, and no doubt the current negotiations with one of the world's largest telecommunications giants will make you insufferably wealthy. Why would you be intimidated by anyone?'

I stare into his beautiful eyes, see the doubt that lurks there whenever Oliver talks about his father, whom he's christened the world's crappiest role model. Kids, even teenagers, shouldn't have to drive their parent to rehab or attend their string of celebrity weddings. It's a miracle—one Oliver often incorrectly attributes to me—that he isn't an alcoholic junkie himself, although he's often wondered if he's something of a sex addict.

But I can guess the answer. His success is due to how hard he pushes himself, almost as if he's outrunning both the reputation of the Oliver I first met and the reputation of his outlandish, rock-and-roll father as well as the frequent comparisons made by those who don't know the real him, especially the media.

One of the hardest things to do during the early days of our friendship, while our competitive natures bonded over pool tournaments and university maths club, was to watch him sabotage himself time after time with bad decisions—partying, skipping lectures and frequent one-night stands—which only seemed to increase the hollow look in his eyes.

'The Kimoto deal has reached a delicate stage,' he says about the Japanese telecommunications corporation, displaying an uncharacteristic flash of vulnerability that I haven't seen in a long time. This business deal means a lot to him.

I soften my tone, probing. 'This is the artificial intelligence software you launched?' I ask, in no way pretending to know what he does for a living. His company has so many irons in the fire, it's hard to keep up. If it's cutting edge, Oliver and the geniuses he recruits to his company are all over it.

'Yes. Kimoto is passionate about robotics. They want my AI software, but they're haggling over the small print.' He takes a swig of beer. 'Anyway, I'm not intimidated by your exes anymore. Although a couple of them did their best to remind me how my family skeletons and past reputation made me unworthy of your friendship.' He looks away, focussed on the horizon. 'And, while they may not have taken care of you between the sheets, at least they didn't taint you, expose you to their embarrassing, media whore of a father and all the baggage he attracts.'

My heart clenches for him. He's referring to articles written about his misspent youth, painting him as the philandering, layabout son of rock royalty, a chip off the old block, which I know he despises. Try as he might, despite his self-made billionaire status or his business success, he feels he can't shake his past. Or comparisons with his father.

'I've never met your father,' I say, my voice tentative, because I know this is his weak spot, the only part of his life where he seems to doubt himself and his intuitive instincts.

As a teenager, growing up on two continents, shipped back and forth between his acrimoniously divorced parents—his father in LA and his mother in London—he struggled with his identity, which was defined by celebrity gossip mongers before he had a chance to develop his own sense of worth. In the shadow of an extroverted, outrageous and perpetually adolescent father, and an embittered mother who'd been passed on for numerous younger models over the years, it's no wonder the Oliver I first met had hang-ups of massive proportions.

'Too right, and you're the better for it, trust me. He'd probably try to marry you or something. No wonder Kimoto Corp are cautious about doing business with me.' He snorts, but there's no humour in the sound. There's a tension in his body, one that regularly accompanies any mention of his father.

'He's already married,' I say about his famous father, a larger-than-life character who grew up in South London before hitting the big time as part of an eighties rock band. 'And I'm sure the business community sees what you've achieved, not who you're related to.'

Of course, he could simply have embraced the role of LA layabout, living off his trust fund, but he had too much pride and integrity for that, determination he'd channelled into a global success. Just as numbers and balancing accounting records keeps me grounded, nerdy tech-wizardry fuels Oliver's sense of worth. Despite him looking like the archetypal beach bum layabout the press would have the world believe.

'Anyway, I thought we were discussing this morning,' I say as a distraction.

'We are, but being friends with me isn't easy,' he says. 'You were accosted by some journo sniffing out a story at that Christmas gala last year. And I've lost track of how many times you've had your picture splashed over the gossip rags in some speculative bullshit story about us every time you're single. It's as if they can't believe I could attract a friend of your calibre.'

He's agitated. I want to comfort him, as I normally would on this subject, but touching him more than absolutely necessary could overwhelm my already strung out body.

'I can't imagine what it was like for you to grow up in the public eye. To have everything you do scrutinised and gossiped over.' No wonder his sense of privacy is fierce—he's the exact opposite of his father, who seems to court the attention, good and bad.

'I'm grateful to your exes, actually,' he says, his mouth a grim line. 'At least they protected you from the stories that tried to paint you as pitiful and in love with me, something I failed to do.'

My heart stops beating. Because, while I too hate the mocking tone of those stories, I fear the world will see that they carry a grain of truth; part of me was, is, a little bit in love with him.

As his plus-one, I'm the woman most often and consistently photographed with him, often dubbed the desperate off-again, on-again girlfriend. Exactly the thing I'm anxious to avoid, now we've crossed the line of physical intimacy.

'I don't care about the gossip sites. We know what we are to each other—just friends.'

Or at least we were, before today. Have I become what the world sees? A woman clearly besotted, content to wait in the wings for my chance with him while he takes his time deciding if he's ready to commit?

Have I subconsciously followed him around for the nine years it took him to notice me? Yes, I chose friendship over a relationship, but was part of me too scared back then to force his hand and make him choose, knowing he wasn't ready for a relationship?

'Have we ruined it? Us?' I ask, my voice barely a terrified whisper. I don't want him to choose any more than I want to make that decision. I want us to have both, just a while longer. Because I crossed the line with my eyes wide open, knowing that, one way or another, things would be different.

But I need to know.

Oliver jack-knifes into a sitting position, swinging his legs over the edge of the lounger to face me. 'No. Don't say that. We're fine.' The same panic gripping me seems to flash in his eyes. 'You know your friendship is the only good thing in my life beside my work—I'd never jeopardise that. Ever. I know I broke the "talking about it" rule, but I'd never break the first rule.'

I warm at his words of reassurance then break out in shivers. 'But—'

'No. There is no but.' He scoots to the edge of the lounger so he can reach across and grab my hand. 'I need you. You know all my family bullshit. You understand me like no one else—see things in me no one else sees. You've never once made me feel like I have to be something I'm not or prove myself. You've got my back and I've got yours.'

I shiver at the vulnerability of his pleading expression, struck dumb by my outpouring of feelings for this man.

'Perhaps I was just jealous of your exes,' he says. 'Jealous that they could give you something I can't. Anonymity, normality and protection.'

His fingers squeeze mine so hard I press my lips together to hide a wince.

'Well, there's no need to envy them.' I point out. 'I dumped them for a reason.'

He shrugs. 'It just didn't work out. Now I know about the sex, I'm not surprised.'

I hedge, reluctant to continue down the heavy turn this conversation has taken. 'But the predominant reason for me was the disparity in our investment in the relationship. A woman likes to feel adored. To never have to doubt that she's the number one priority, not just convenient.'

He stares, silent, his eyes burning my skin. Why am I telling him this? He's not interested in relationships. He doesn't need the pointers. He has as much success with the ladies as he wants.

'Promise me again,' he says, throwing me off my guard. 'Promise me that you won't let what happened this morning change anything.' He punctuates his words with tiny tugs on my hand. 'Because I'm not sorry it happened, but I'll always need you in my life. You'll always be my best friend.'

The words stick in my narrowed throat, because our relationship has already changed. Almost beyond recognition. Yesterday morning I wanted him in an abstract, imaginative way. Today I want him with a fire hot enough to turn the sand under us to glass, even though I should be sated, satisfied and heeding the warning signs flashing before my face.

'I promise,' I whisper.

What else can I do? We crossed the line. I had my orgasms. It's time to be mature and remember everything else we've meant to each other all this time. Support, laughter, someone who just gets us.

As a friend, I know I hold the number one spot in Oliver's life, which is why he always wants me around when he has a social event like his cousin's wedding. He's loyal and thoughtful, always on hand when I need advice or a shoulder on which to cry, even if it's in the middle of the night. Despite his busy schedule, I know he'd drop everything for me if I asked. And he's my biggest fan, as I'm his, championing my endeavours, celebrating my successes and reining in my insecurities when they surface.

'Besides, no one else would put up with you, so I'm kind of trapped,' I say to lighten the mood, grateful for his familiar grin, which tells me we'll be okay.

Just then the engine of one of the many sea planes that ferries tourists around the atolls snatches our attention. The small sixteen-seater aircraft comes in low, landing in the sea at the far end of the island.

'New holiday makers arriving,' I say, because I want to return some semblance of normality to our conversation, one that seems to have left us both exposed and raw.

Oliver's hand tenses around mine. He looks past me, squinting, as if trying to spy the passengers disembarking the plane onto the small wooden jetty down the beach. Then he stands abruptly, dropping my hand.

'Fucking fantastic. I'll see you at dinner,' he mutters, sliding his sunglasses onto his face and heading in the direction of the plane.

'Wait, Oliver,' I call after him, but he's already striding away, his back rigid.

I look past his stiff frame, trying to focus on the people some distance away cluttering up the tiny jetty, spying a group of four or five bodies. One's taller than the rest, his body language more exuberant.

When combined with Oliver's emotional shutdown and abrupt departure, it can mean only one thing.

His father has come to paradise.

CHAPTER SEVEN

Oliver

WHEN I STAMP into the restaurant thirty minutes late, thanks to some emails from my legal team that required urgent attention, Neve is already seated between two of my cousins. Two of my male cousins.

A bonfire builds in my chest. I'm jealous? Comparing myself to her exes wasn't such a brilliant idea on my part. Yes, I'd given her the orgasms they'd failed to, but that's where the benefits for her end. Because I also crossed the line, selfishly putting her and our friendship at risk. And no amount of damage limitation, now that Slay is in town for his niece's wedding, will make me feel any better. Because now I'll be obliged to introduce them. Fucking disaster waiting to happen. Disaster follows Slay wherever he goes.

I breathe through the red fog clouding my vision. In some ways, the jealousy is a welcome distraction from the usual shit show that accompanies my father. A shit show I'd spent the rest of the afternoon trying to minimise, because it would be just like Slay to rock up with the media and outshine the bride, probably dragging me in too and jeopardising my deal with Kimoto.

Nausea threatens. What if Neve sees how similar we really are? What if she learns about my past indiscretion and despises me for my immature weakness? What if she finally sees through me and decides I'm not good enough?

I can't lose her. She saved me nine years ago. Her sense of humour and her take-no-bullshit attitude were exactly what I needed to pull my head out of my arse and take myself seriously. If it wasn't for her, I'd probably have dropped out of uni and become more like my old man than I already am.

I shudder.

And now, when I'm on the cusp of a deal that will cement my company's position as a serious player in the international tech world, I need her grounding influence and belief in me more than ever.

Enter Slay and his impeccable timing.

Fuck!

Neve looks up and catches my eye. She's glowing, beautiful, despite her concerned expression. Her hair's piled on her head in some sort of casual up-do, her red dress making her fair skin radiant. She's always looked great in dresses and red is definitely her colour.

I want to whisk her out of here, hide her away from Slay—I messaged her the news of his arrival—because having my father here so close to Neve, when I've managed to keep him well away for years, makes me feel as powerless and gullible as I did at nineteen.

Because Neve is part of my real life. Nothing to do with my life growing up in LA. A life of excess and parties. A life of fake, superficial popularity with my peers. A life devoid of the male role model and the consistency a teenage boy needs in order to find his place in the world. At least I'd been smart enough to use school as an outlet. My scholarship to a London university enabled me to break free of any financial dependence on Slay.

I should never have invited Neve to this family wedding when there was a risk Slay might attend. Perhaps I should have stayed away myself, given the current delicateness of the Kimoto deal. The last thing I need is negative press.

I sigh and cast my gaze down the length of the table, looking for my seat, which is at the opposite end from Neve and my cousins.

Mike, the cousin to her left, is newly divorced. His round lawyer's face flushes with excitement as he laughs at something Neve has just said.

Bastard.

Rob, the cousin to her right and five years her junior, waits impatiently for his turn for her attention, his fingers tapping the table.

Why didn't I organise a private dinner for two? And how long will I have to tolerate this evening before I can get her alone? Then again, if the old man does plan to make a grand entrance, I want her as far away from me as possible. Perhaps she'll slip under his radar—not that he's ever overlooked a beautiful woman, regardless of whether he's married or single.

I take my seat between the bride, my cousin Shelley, and her maid of honour, who I met for the first time this morning. I smile, desperately trying to recall her name, and then sag with gratitude for my cousin, who had the foresight to arrange place settings. Of course, that means she deliberately sandwiched Neve in between the only two other single men here...

Shit, I'm a mess. A mess I created the minute I lifted the shutters from my eyes and allowed myself to truly look at Neve. To admit long-buried desires. I should never have touched her, but can I stop now I've indulged? Because, despite the rules she needed and the risks involved, I want more. I swallow hard. I don't think I'll ever get enough.

After my brief interaction earlier with my father and stepmum number five, and the threat that they could turn up any second, my appetite is nonexistent. I grab a waiter, order a bottle of beer and make trivial conversation with Shelley, an attempt to distract me from my fury.

Why is Slay here? It won't just be to celebrate his niece's nuptials. My father rarely does anything that doesn't also further his career somehow. But I'm out of the loop. Despite never quite achieving the former heights of his glory days, he's always tried to stay relevant. Perhaps he's promoting a tour, or a new album. God forbid it's a tacky reality TV show… It would be just like him to rock up partway through the meal and buy everyone at the bar a drink—maximum impact set to ensure he, and only he, is the centre of attention. I wouldn't put it past him or a member of his entourage to have invited the press here so he can upstage the bride and groom and feature on every celebrity gossip site by midnight.

I glance at Neve, trying to catch her eye again, inadvertently landing myself in conversation with Amelia, the maid of honour, who punctuates nearly every sentence she speaks by touching my arm. Unlike Neve, who'd never heard of my famous father when I first met her all those years ago, Amelia clearly thinks she already knows everything about me and my rock star parent. She fires question after question about what it was like to grow up in the LA scene, which famous people have I met and do I know if my father is coming to the wedding?

Before sleeping with Neve, I'd have tried to shag Amelia, if for no other reason than to shut her up. Sometimes it's just easier to go along with a stranger's assumptions and play my designated part than to be real and open.

Women like Amelia don't want the real me—the nerdy, tech businessman who works a hundred hours a week and designs software in his spare time. The me I've worked hard over the years to reinvent, to separate from everything Slay represents. They want the caricature from my past that, acting out as a younger man, I once embraced. One my father's team of publicists still churns out because it fits his rock and roll lifestyle. They want the image of me the media continues to spawn, the one who is never spotted with the same woman twice, with the exception of Neve, even though the women I date are equally into casual sex and avoiding commitment. They want to be able to say, 'I slept with Sid "Slay" Coterill's son'…

I spin some crap about wild parties chez Coterill to appease Amelia and feast my eyes on Neve once more, knowing if I could get her alone, bury myself inside her again, I'd feel like myself.

I'm so selfish. Just like him.

Because the crap which accompanies my father, and by unfortunate association me, is exactly the reason I should never touch her again. She's too precious. She's the only woman I've ever told about my famous father who didn't simper and giggle at the idea of meeting him some day, like a star-struck groupie. And now I've fucked things up by fucking her because, no matter what I said on the beach earlier, it's changed things.

How could it not?

Instead of quenching a long-standing fantasy, I want her even more now I've experienced her passionate enthusiasm and heavenly body. And my jealousy…? Did that burn as fiercely with Limp Liam or Tris Tosser as the current hellish fire scorching me alive? I could easily climb over the table and gouge out the eyes of my cousins with a dessert spoon just for looking at *my* beautiful, sexy, funny Neve.

Where has this possessiveness come from?

I neck a swallow of beer, trying to ease my parched-with-panic throat. Now Slay is here, I can almost feel her slipping through my fingers. I am so fucked.

She pauses in her conversation with Mike and looks my way with a small frown. Heat flares from every pore as our eyes collide.

I try to smile but my face feels frozen.

Slay's arrival hot on the heels of the massive shift in our relationship seems to have awoken all my insecurities, reminding me that, no matter what I do, people will always compare us, and maybe they're right to.

It's glaringly obvious I'll never be good enough for Neve. Never be able to protect her from him, from the pervasive side effect of his fame. From the circus that surrounds him. The only way to do that is to turn back time nine years and ignore her in that student bar.

Would I have acted out the way I did at nineteen if I had a normal dad? One content to take pride in his son's achievements and not try to compete for all the attention all the time, even when it meant hurting his only son. I've never told Neve my worst secrets about Jane, and what I did the night we split, and she doesn't understand life under a public lens. At times, it's made me feel like I'm going crazy, and I don't want that for her.

But I can't lay the blame solely at Slay's door. The speculation around my private life is due to my media reputation, fuelled by my notorious commitment avoidance. I'm responsible for the media interest in my relationship with Neve. I've denied my feelings for her and, through my past immature actions, I've offered her up for comparison to the other women I see when there is no comparison. But does she know that? Maybe before this morning, but now…?

My fists curl with impotence. Why jeopardise what she means to me with something as common as sex? Not that sex with Neve was remotely humdrum—I haven't stopped craving her since the moment our lips touched. But if my father's lifestyle proves anything it's that real, long-lasting relationships take work, commitment and compromise, things I'm certain I can't possibly have inherited from him, unlike my borderline addictive traits…

If Neve couldn't make it with those serious, upright men of her past, how the hell can I—a man with Slay's genes—have anything to offer?

I catch Neve's eye once more, desperate to know the thoughts behind her unreadable expression.

As if sensing my distraction, Amelia touches my arm once more, saying something about catching the reunion tour of my father's band last year.

Neve's stare drops away from that hand on my arm before she turns away from me and engages with Rob on her right.

I grit my teeth, furious with myself. She probably thinks I'm interested in Amelia, when all I want to do is drag her out of here and... What? Shag her again? Remind her just how much like my father I am—a philanderer with the emotional depth of a rock pool? Only the fact that her own appetite for the mouth-watering menu seems healthy enough stops me—I'm *that* selfish.

The rest of the meal is torture. I ache head to toe to get her alone. By the time dessert is served, I'm crawling out of my skin, desperate to talk to her and dreading the surprise arrival of the star of the show. I slide my phone from my pocket and message Neve.

Do you want some of my dessert?

I deliberately chose the coconut-free chocolate creation from the menu—Neve despises coconut—

and I noticed that she chose something else. She's a self-confessed foodie who struggles with menus because she wants to taste everything. So we've developed a routine. I order something different from hers, and she steals a taste of my food.

She reads my message but simply shakes her head in response.

I grow restless, shoving away the plate while I try to listen to enough of Amelia's droning voice to seem polite.

After five more agonising minutes, as soon as Neve's spoon hits her empty plate, I try again.

Want to go for a walk on the beach?

Her answer comes blessedly quickly.

Okay.

I excuse myself from the table and head out into the night to wait for her at the short path that leads from our resort down to the beach.

She doesn't keep me waiting long, padding up on bare feet, her shoes swinging in her hand.

I sling my hands in my pockets because, in my current mood, I'm likely to do something I'll regret. Like kiss her again. Or fall at her feet and beg her to...

What? She deserves the moon, not some hypocrite friend who doesn't know the first thing about relationships, something I've avoided for years, because I never again wanted to feel as vulnerable as Jane and Slay made me feel.

Yes, in theory Neve and I have the best foundation blocks—friendship and astounding sexual chemistry. But I'll fuck it up, just like Slay did, because we're father and son. His blood runs in my veins. We're more alike than I can ever admit.

Nausea rushes to the back of my throat. Whatever happens during the rest of our time here, I have to keep Neve away from Slay.

She keeps her distance as we head to the beach, her wary eyes almost crushing me. 'So you met Mike?' I say after we've walked a few minutes in silence, my jealousy getting the better of me. 'I'm surprised he let you escape—I haven't seen him that animated since he met his wife.'

It's not her fault she's kind and funny and gorgeous and I don't deserve her. Mike is a way safer bet—I should step aside or foster the relationship once we're back in London. What little dinner I managed to eat threatens to make a reappearance.

She looks at me as if we're strangers. 'Yes, he's a nice guy. He was kind enough to introduce me around.'

I wince. I deserve that for being so late. I brought her here as my guest. But I allowed Slay to worm his way into my head, the way he always does.

'How's Amelia?' she asks. 'Waiting for you in your room, no doubt?'

'I'm not interested in Amelia.' It wasn't until I kissed Neve this morning that my life, full of shallow, pointless hook-ups, snapped into focus. Depressing focus.

'I don't care either way. I've spent the past nine years watching women throw themselves at you.' She strides ahead towards the water's edge, irritation visible in her rigid shoulders and raised chin.

I catch up, sickened by how much I'm messing this up. 'Well, I care if you're interested in Mike. Are you? He's a great guy.' The last sentence takes effort.

Neve shoots me a murderous look. We retreat to angry silence, following the line of lit torches pushed into the sand, away from the resort. My pulse ratchets up with every step. Not just from the jealousy. Out here in the dark, alone, I'd hoped that we could just be us. The usual us, where I can be myself.

But perhaps *us* no longer exists.

I want to tell her all the things bottled up inside me—how crazy Slay makes me, how fearful I am that I'll never be able to be my own man, no matter what I do or how successful I become, and how sorry I am for putting that disappointed look on her face. But now we've slept together the dynamic has changed. Will she still forgive my thoughtless cock-ups? Can I still confide in my best friend, the only person who knows the real me—good, bad and ugly? Would she admit she liked Mike and wanted to date him? Or do I no longer deserve her confidences?

My hands curl into fists and, not for the first time in my life, I curse my father. I still recall his sage wisdom when I had my heart shredded by Jane. I'd genuinely fallen in love for the first time and I believed she felt the same way. But when I told her I'd be spending the summer with my mother in London, because I'd needed to get away from Slay, she dumped me out of the blue.

A year and many casual sex-ploits later, I met Neve, a miraculous woman who'd never even heard of Slay. She's been a breath of fresh air in my life ever since. But have I robbed myself of that life-giving air?

'Why are we fighting?' I ask, my vision now adapted to the dark, so I see her still-wounded expression in profile.

'Because sometimes you're an arsehole,' she replies.

'This is true, but you knew that the day we met.' I'm joking; I hope I've matured a little in the subsequent nine years, but she's in no mood for humour. 'Tell me what's really bothering you.' I want to take her hand. Instead, I shove my hands back into the pockets of my chinos.

'You invited me here,' she says, 'suggested we have sex, of all the stupid things, and then as soon as it's over you shut down. Shut me out.'

Bugger…it does look that way. 'I'm sorry for deserting you this afternoon,' I say. 'But I've had to run damage limitation since Slay arrived to ensure he doesn't upstage Shelley tomorrow with some audacious publicity stunt. It wouldn't be the first time, believe me.'

Rather than placate me with suitably soothing condolences as she normally would on this topic, she spins on me and says, 'I know you think he's a diva, but he *is* Shelley's uncle. She invited him and she must know what he's like. You flew her entire wedding party here on your company jet, and goodness knows how much it's cost you to run interference. You've protected her wedding day as best you can.'

I'm struck still, my mouth hanging open. But Neve hasn't finished the home truths.

'I know you struggle with your relationship with him, but you don't need him. You're independently wealthy, you've built your own life, a life you should be proud of, and yet the minute he arrives you go running as if for a dose of punishment or something. As if you somehow take responsibility for his actions.'

I rub my forehead, bitterness burning my throat, because I know I'm responsible for my own actions, and in the past I've allowed Slay to mess with my head until I've acted shamefully. My biggest regret.

'My main motivation was to keep any media he might attract the hell away from you. I brought you here.'

Some of her anger seems to dissipate as she comes to a halt and turns to face me. 'This has nothing to do with Slay. We were in the middle of a conversation earlier today and you rushed off… without explanation…as if I deserved less than common consideration. You said it wouldn't change our friendship, and then you fail at the first test.'

'I'm sorry. I should have explained. That was rude.' I try to take her hand, but she snatches her arm away.

'Nine years I've known you and you've never once introduced me to your father,' she says.

'Because he's an embarrassment. A cliché. It has nothing to do with you.' I curse the mess I've made by indulging my need for her. None of this would have happened if I'd just maintained the distance I've always kept where she's concerned. Of course, none of it would matter if I stopped allowing Slay to get to me. Or if I'd been open from the start— but then she probably wouldn't have stuck around if she'd known.

She continues as if I haven't spoken. 'You couldn't even be bothered to be on time to escort me to a meal with *your* family, introduce me properly to people I barely know and who looked at me with…pity or something.'

'What do you mean?' I ask, every muscle strung taut. If someone has upset Neve, they'll be walking back to London. 'What the hell is there to pity? You're amazing—'

'You, Oliver. You. Everyone knows what you're like—I saw it when they looked at me tonight. Oh, here's Olly's sad little friend, always following him around in between his women. Well, you can't just slot me in and out of your bed whenever there's a vacancy just because we had sex.'

The vulnerability slashed across her face cuts me deep.

'I'd never do that,' I say, aching to hold her until I feel better and she looks at me the way she did this morning, when it seemed like I could do no wrong in her eyes. The same disbelieving eyes that I'm looking into now.

Her lips move, as if in slow motion, every heartbeat a tick of impending dread.

'I told you it was a bad idea,' she says. 'We should never have touched each other.'

CHAPTER EIGHT

Oliver

SHE STAMPS OFF, muttering something about sorting out her love life once and for all.

My blood runs cold with panic. I race after her. 'No one pities you. And I'm sorry I made you feel that way.' I'm messing up this apology because I feel her slipping through my fingers. I'm terrified Slay will meet her, see what she means to me and deliberately screw me over.

'Just forget it. It's my own fault. I should never have agreed to such a stupid plan.' She's still simmering.

I clutch at straws, so out of my depth. Neve and I have never argued before. 'Look, I'm sorry I was late for dinner. Kimoto Corp is getting cold feet. I had a to make a few calls to the UK. But you're right, okay?'

She stops. Spins. Stares.

I take a deep breath, broken glass in my chest.

'It was rude of me to rush off, but I don't want Slay anywhere near you. He's…' I grip a fistful of my hair and tug, searching for the words to make her understand, words that rip me open. Words I've never spoken aloud to anyone. Ever since the age of nineteen, since I've forgone feelings and relationships, I haven't needed to worry. But Neve is more than my friend.

Now I have everything to lose.

'He's a narcissist. He makes people like him, but it's not for their sake, it's for how they fuel his ego.'

'I don't care about your father. I'm not impressed by his fame,' she says, her eyes wide, as if she senses how close to the bone this subject cuts me.

'I know, and I've always completely adored you for that, believe me. But that doesn't mean he wouldn't try to flirt with you, even in front of his wife. He comes onto anything with a vagina, and I can't bear to see him look at you that way, okay? Not you. You're my person.'

My Neve…

I'm panting, wound so tight by foreboding. I've inadvertently hurt her and she regrets what we did.

'I'm sorry to hear about the Japanese.' She deflates. 'I know how important this deal is to you. Why didn't you tell me?'

I step close. I can't stand the distance any longer. I reach for her chilled upper arms. 'I got distracted with fears of paparazzi following Slay here—it feels like every time I think I'm breaking free I'm tugged back down to reality. I wanted to blow off the family dinner and just eat with you—just the two of us. Then I saw you with Mike, and stupid jealousy took hold. I'm sorry.'

Her eyes are round, as if she's shocked by my jealousy. 'I don't fancy Mike. I know you have this notion that I'm sweet, but as far as your father is concerned I can handle myself.'

'I know, but you don't know what he's like.' I press my lips together. She doesn't know the full extent of his depravity, or mine. I've never told her how Slay claimed Jane made a pass at him. How, stupid and heartbroken, I'd rushed to her that night for confirmation and the truth had flashed in her defiant eyes. She'd never loved me. She'd used me because of who I am. Who my father is.

And I've never told Neve how I exacted my drunken revenge…

'I know what you've told me, so consider me warned off Slay,' she says. 'But you shut me out earlier. Just because we had sex doesn't mean I'm going to let you walk all over me.'

'I won't.'

'You do it every time,' she says.

'What do you mean?' Unease raises the hairs at the back of my neck.

She looks at the sand and shakes her head. 'You sleep with someone and, before they have a chance to get to know the real you, you withdraw. I've spent nine years watching you do it. It's your modus operandi. And why have you never come close to a relationship?'

'I never lie to women—they know what they're getting into with me, and they say they want the same thing. Casual.'

'Yes, I'm sure you're honest about it, but people develop feelings. Every time a woman gets too close, you shut her out and move on without a backward glance. But that's not going to work for me. We agreed we wouldn't let this morning come between us.'

Rage clenches every muscle in my body. 'I'd never shut you out of my life. I've never come close to a relationship because I choose to avoid them. With my father on his sixth marriage as a role model, can you blame me?'

'I guess not.' She shrugs. 'Olly, I know that you had a pretty shitty time growing up with Slay, but please don't let him come between us.'

'I'd never allow anything to come between us. I need you.' I tug her closer, squeeze her fingers with one hand and cup her face with the other so she can't escape. 'I'm sorry that I allowed my father to distract me. It's just that…you're my weakness and he can't know that. I want to keep him the hell away from you. For your sake. To protect you.' I can't stop looking at her tempting mouth. I want to kiss her so badly, to demand her forgiveness. Because I need her now more than ever.

But she's right—if I don't open up, I might lose her anyway.

I sigh, let go of her face and tug her down to sit on the sand, close enough for me to feel comforted by her body heat.

'I've spent years trying to carve something for myself completely unrelated to him or my past,' I say, spilling the words that will make her understand what she means to me. 'My relationship with you, my work—there's no hint of him there, and I love that, take pride in those areas of my life.' I can't be all bad, if she's believed in me all these years, but she deserves to understand the way I feel about Slay.

'Remember when I told you about Jane?' I say, gripping her hand.

'Your teenage girlfriend?' She nods, her eyes wary.

'Yeah. Well, when she dumped me, I was pretty cut up. When Slay noticed me moping, after a rare bout of parental observation, he insisted that the best way to get over her was to take me on a bender.' I let lose a hollow laugh at my own naivety. 'I fooled myself we were finally bonding in a meaningful father-son way rather than the superficial crap of most of my life up to that point.'

'Wasn't he ever a normal dad?' she asks, scooting closer, her shoulder pressing against mine in comfort and solidarity.

'If he was, I don't remember. Sid Coterill is always Slay, always on show. I'm not really sure why he even had a kid, but at least he didn't knock up all my stepmothers, so that's something.'

'So did the bender help with the heartbreak?' she asks.

I snort, continuing the sordid little tale I wish she didn't have to know. 'He took me to an LA strip club, the last place I needed. I was nineteen. Confused, because I was desperate to relate to him somehow, but also reeling from the loss of first love.'

Neve's hand squeezes mine.

'I realised he didn't know me at all. He didn't care enough to see how I felt. Instead of compassion and genuine connection, he bought me a table full of shots, a lap dance and then passed on one of his most valuable fatherly insights: "Plenty more willing pussy in the world, son".'

He'd then proceeded to tell me how my ex wasn't worth my regret, because she'd made a pass at him on more than one occasion and he'd nobly turned her down, as though he'd done me a favour or something.

I'd rushed to the bathroom and hurled an evening's worth of drinks into the toilet, along with any belief that I could trust a woman to want me for me, or that Slay actually cared for anyone but himself.

Eaten alive by the crippling humiliation, I can't look at Neve. I don't want to see horror or pity. But the memories stiffen my resolve. I won't allow Slay to ruin the one good relationship in my life.

I face her. 'I don't want a man who talks about women that way anywhere near you, the woman I respect most in the world.'

She's silent for a few painful beats of my heart. Then she whispers, 'I'm sorry you had such a crappy role model who didn't know what an amazing son he has. You're nothing like him.'

My gut twists. If only she knew how alike we truly are.

'What did you do after that?' she asks, and I stiffen. I can't confess how later that night I executed my revenge on Slay, with his third wife, although my shameful act hurt me more than it seemed to hurt him and still haunts me to this day.

'I moved out of his LA mansion and never went back.' I tug her into my arms then, squeezing the life from her and burying my nose in her hair so I can suck her comforting scent into my lungs. I can't fuck up again. I can't risk losing her, as I surely would if she knew the full story.

I feel her relax against me, relief shuddering through my frame.

'I'm sorry you had your heart broken,' she whispers.

'And I'm sorry about dinner.' I press a kiss to her temple. 'You never got to try my dessert.'

For the first time since we crossed the line, she laughs her familiar laugh. 'You can buy me another one tomorrow,' she mumbles against my chest and then pushes at my hips to break my hold on her. 'But we need to follow the rules if we're going to survive the rest of this holiday and go home still friends. No more discussing the sex.'

Relief pours through my veins. 'Okay...' I say, because I'll do anything for her. 'But it's hard not to discuss such awesome sex.' My dick twitches in my trousers. I shift my hips so she doesn't see how turned on I am and think I'm not taking her seriously. That she's giving me a second chance fuels my blood with adrenaline.

She wriggles, but I tighten my arm on her waist. I've held her before, of course—chaste, brief encounters when she's been upset or needed solace. But she feels different in my arms. More real. I don't want to let go, possession adding to her arousing closeness.

'Yes, it *was* awesome, but now it's over. And we both need to navigate this new territory.'

My fingers tense on her back. Everything inside me slows, apart from my uncontrollable galloping pulse. 'I don't want to it to be over.' Because now we're more than friends.

I've always wanted more. And now, when it's

hard to think of anything but how good we are together and how much I ache for her… There's no going back to a version of us without this intimacy. Not for me.

'Oliver, let's be realistic.' Her eyes cling to mine. 'We'll go home and go back to normal. You avoiding relationships and me looking for one.'

I stare so intently, I feel like my eyes are diamond-cutting lasers. 'Don't talk about dating other men when I can still taste you on my tongue. Still hear your cries in my head. Still feel you clamped around my dick.' The thought that she can easily forget what happened between us and move on to some dating-app jerk leaves me trembling with agitation.

Her tiny gasp, the excited flare of her eyes, contradicts her next words. 'We can't do it again…'

Despite her caution, I feel the moment excitement grips her, the increased breathing and the softening of her muscles from rigid to slack. She still wants me, and I want to lose myself in her. To relive how good it was this morning, even though every detail is etched into my brain.

I slowly nod my head, lowering my mouth closer to hers while I keep eye contact. I want her in no doubt of my feelings, and I want to witness her reactions. 'We definitely can. We were good together. Astounding, in fact. Fuck the rules.'

She closes her eyes, as if seeking strength. Then she opens them again. 'Olly—'

'Oliver,' I interrupt, because I'm not going backward. Not when her eyes dance over my face as if she's debating where to kiss me first. Not when her lips are right there, soft and inviting. Not when I know how one kiss will turn her passionate and demanding.

'I want you more than I did this morning,' I murmur, my voice low, my mouth so close to hers, one lunge is all it would take to put us out of our misery. 'I've wanted you ever since.'

My declaration is dangerous because this isn't an impulse driven by lust. I've had all day and the previous nine years to open my eyes and admit this fierce attraction, and I finally feel that if I work hard at it I could be man enough for Neve. Because she's my priority. There's no future I envisage or want without her.

I hold my breath while she says nothing, tension juddering through her small frame with each laboured breath.

Then, with a sexy little feminine groan, she lurches against me and presses her mouth to mine. Her arms encircle my shoulders and she straddles my lap as we kiss—lips devouring, tongues surging, breath mingling.

Unlike this morning, when I'd taken control, Neve's frantic kisses and grabbing hands are more demanding. More desperate.

Thank fuck, because I'm wild for her, and I was beginning to think I was in this state alone.

I collapse back onto the sand, my arm around her waist so she's sprawled over my chest. I slide my hands over her hips then cup her buttocks, pressing her closer to assuage the demands of my aching cock.

Neve breaks free of the kiss, braces her hands on my biceps and gives me a small shove as she sits up. I like the view of her over me, but I need to hear that she's with me before I vacate the driving seat.

'Tell me you want more awesome sex too,' I say. 'I want to hear it.'

'Yes, I want more. Of course I do,' she pants out, dropping kiss after kiss to my mouth and then nuzzling my neck in a way that has my hips bucking up between her legs.

I cup her face while my pulse pounds in the tips of my fingers, scared she'll feel it on her skin. I need to show her how important she is. How much I value her beyond this physical compulsion, which seems to have gripped us both.

'I'd never do anything to risk losing you. You're too important. Understand?' I hate the doubt I saw in her angry eyes earlier. Hate that I was the source. She's the most important person in my life. And if this was just sex, perhaps I'd find the strength to resist this chemistry, but it's more than that, more than I ever dreamed or knew was possible.

Her eyes droop, half-closed, and I feel her tiny nod between my palms.

She shuffles back and shoves my shirt up, trailing burning hot kisses over my chest. Staring up at me, she flicks her tongue over my pierced nipple. My abs crunch involuntarily and her hips grind on my erection, which is steel against the fly of my trousers. Damn, I want her, and I definitely don't have a condom.

'Now it's my turn to explore,' she says, attacking my fly with determined hands. My cock surges free between the open zip, the relief overwhelming, but reality dawns.

'I don't have a condom.' I doubt she does either, given her disappointment with me and her skimpy, pocket-less dress.

'I don't care.' She palms my erection, rubbing me through my boxers until I fist the fabric of her dress, which is ruched up over her pale thighs.

'You were so bossy this morning, I never got to put my mouth on you,' she says, licking her lips as she scoots back onto my thighs so she can tug my trousers and boxers over my hips.

'That's just the way I am, baby.' My voice is hoarse with longing, but laced with warning, because if that mouth, those plump lips and perfect Cupid's bow, gets anywhere near my dick… Game over.

'Mmm?' She bends close to trail her lips down my rigid stomach as she grips my aching length.

'I'll come…' I warn, my brain turning foggy with lust. God, she feels so good and looks even better, her beautiful familiar face slack with desire, her stunning breasts spilling over the top of the low neck of her dress, her hand and stare intent on my favourite appendage.

'Well, that's the idea.' She smiles up at me.

Any further argument evaporates as her hot mouth swallows the head of my cock and I'm there—helpless, craving, on the edge.

Neve sucks like she's enjoying a lollipop, her cheeks hollow, and then she releases me to trace the laving tip of her tongue down my shaft.

The cool night air hits my damp flesh. Dizzy with need, I prop myself up on my elbows, not wanting to miss one single second of this fantasy come true. How many times have I jerked off imagining her mouth on me, the daydream in no way preparing me for the fantastic reality? A reality which only gets better when she grips the base of my cock and takes me back inside the hot haven of her mouth while she moans out her pleasure at the power she wields.

'Touch yourself,' I bark, because there's no way I'm coming without her. My hips are already jerking of their own accord, my balls on fire and eyes gritty with the pressure of witnessing every incredible second of her mouth on me.

She looks up and slips her free hand under her

dress between her thighs. I fist her hair; she's killing me. Could she be any more perfect? Any more addictive? Why did I wait so long to discover this side of her? A side I guessed was there all along but refused to see to keep myself sane.

But now I can open my eyes. Focus on the way her beautiful lips stretch around me, delivering pleasure so intense, I'm seconds away from decimating my stamina record.

She smiles around me, actually smiles, looking up at me with such feminine power glowing in her eyes, I release a sort of feral growl. A noise I've never made before, like some kind of tortured animal.

What is she doing to me? Have I ever been this hot for a woman? This incapacitated by need?

I'm passing the point of no return. The sight of her sucking me while she touches herself, the pressure building in my balls and the heat boiling at the base of my spine watching her own me, glorying in her possession… It's all too much.

'Neve…' I cup her face, my thumb swiping her bottom lip stretched around me, my other hand tunnelling into her hair. 'I'm going to come. I'm warning you.'

I have no idea if my sweet friend will swallow me or watch me spill over my own stomach. And I don't care either way; I'm lost to her in this moment. Whatever she wants, fine by me.

She sinks deeper, sucks harder. Her hand gripping my shaft is her answer. She rubs herself more vigorously, her whimpers telling me she's close too.

I'm helpless to stop the cascade of unparalleled pleasure beginning deep in my pelvis, streaks of lava streaming along my length as I empty myself into her mouth with a broken cry.

She sucks me dry, swallowing every drop, her hand still working furiously between her legs, her hips undulating to her own blissful rhythm. I'm spent, still coming down from the incredible high, but I want to reward her for the best blow job I've ever had. When she releases me, I sit up, dragging her close with one arm around her waist so I can kiss her. I slip my hand between her legs, my fingers joining hers to rub over her slick, heated and swollen flesh. I push my tongue into her mouth just as she whimpers out the first crest of her orgasm, kissing her through spasm after spasm of her bucking body.

Sudden jealousy rages through me, smacking me like a rogue wave. I want to lay claim to all her orgasms. I want to be on hand to deliver all her pleasure now we've shared this, and there's only one way to achieve that goal.

'You're not sweet at all, are you?' I press my forehead to hers and scrunch my eyes closed, holding her while she catches her breath.

'No,' she pants. 'I'm definitely not.'

I squeeze her tighter, the beach spinning a little. 'I love that about you, you bad woman,' I say, pressing my lips to her temple.

Yeah, I'd say our friendship as was is pretty much over.

CHAPTER NINE

Neve

I WAVER BETWEEN sleep and wakefulness, emerging from the best dream, desperate to prolong the delirious pleasure. Dream Oliver is back, and he's kissing my naked body, each nipple, my stomach and then between my legs. Hot, sexy open-mouthed kisses…

I open my eyes, this dream so vivid. I look down, still groggy but rapidly waking with every zap of fire that knifes through me.

It's not a dream.

Oliver is licking me awake. I groan, gasp, my head falling back on the pillow and my thighs parting to accommodate his broad shoulders. Then I look back down, expecting some wisecrack or teasing glint in his breathtaking eyes. But he's serious, his stare intense, raking over my every reaction to the lashing of his clever tongue.

I can't look away from the sight of his mouth

on me. The heat in his eyes. The sounds of early-morning paradise beyond the window. My impending orgasm peters out—I'm in deep trouble, addicted to him, to his touch, now that of a lover. The best lover I've ever had. No surprises there.

How will I ever be able to stop craving this, him, when our every kiss, every caress, every intimacy answers a deep longing inside. A deeper connection with a man I already know so well. A complex man with demons and struggles, just like the rest of us. A man with a massive heart he's too scared to trust.

Last night at dinner, I thought this was over. Being shut out reminded me of all the reasons I've fiercely fought my feelings for him for so long. His past with Slay as a role model, his rejection of serious relationships—he's not ready to allow someone close yet. Perhaps he never will be.

My heart spasms, pain pulsing. I don't want to be his fledgling foray into something beyond sex. I can't afford to be the test case. I'm ahead of him where relationships are concerned and, after a few hard-learned lessons of my own, I know what I want.

But he's still content with casual.

I need to be careful, oh, so careful to protect my heart. Focussing on the chemistry, the pleasure, helps. Because right now that's all I can trust. All I can expect.

I cradle his face, my fingers tangling in his

messy hair, my stare locked with his, and whisper his name.

Wordlessly, and despite my cry of protest, he takes his mouth from me and crawls up the bed, settling his hips in the cradle of mine and pushing into me in one smooth glide. My sensitive peaked nipples chafe on his chest hair, his piercing adding an extra layer of friction. I tug his mouth down to mine, our tongues connecting, surging, duelling as sure as the deep and sublime ecstasy of his penetration.

We don't speak, but we don't need to. His fingers tangle in my hair, cradle my face in his hands, his arm gripping my shoulders as over and over again he thrusts into me in watchful silence. But there's nothing to say that we didn't cover last night. We both want this. We're both willing to endanger our friendship, both confident we can manage the fall out of this risky indulgence.

Oliver scoops one of my thighs over his arm and then the other, his hips sinking lower, closer, so that every thrust batters my clit until it's all I can do to hold on to him and trust that he won't leave me behind.

His mouth finds my nipple, licking, flicking, nibbling, and the flames start in the pit of my pelvis.

'Oliver!' I cry out with a desperate voice. That of a woman I no longer recognise, changed perhaps forever by allowing him this close.

Then he speaks at last, his voice gruff, perhaps

with the first words of the day or just with the emotion I see in his eyes. 'Say you're mine right now.' He clenches his jaw on the order, thrusting harder, deeper.

His eyes are almost turquoise with desire, more intense and serious than I've ever seen him, his ownership euphoric.

'Tell me,' he barks, his angular face taut with his own mounting desire. 'Before I give you your next orgasm.'

He's controlling this, us, and it's the hottest thing I've ever heard him say. Because I *am* his. He's taking me on a journey of discovery and I can't deny him, or my own needs, even as I try to hold something back for self-preservation.

My breath catches. I want to give him what he needs more than I want the pleasure he's holding to ransom. But I know it's a reaction to what he confided about Slay. I know it's not a lasting promise he wants from me.

'I'm yours!' I yell as he delivers thrust after thrust. Each blow devastates as I'm tossed over the edge into a rapturous climax, where my only awareness is how loud I scream his name and how tight I clutch him inside my body. He groans out his own release, collapsing his weight on top of me and burying his face against my neck.

I want to laugh or cry, but I do neither, because love, this fear of his power to hurt me, is no laughing matter, and I'm sliding, falling, being dragged under with every kiss, every touch, every orgasm.

No, that could all be lust, right? The inevitable side-effect of such amazing sex. Because I can't love Oliver more than I already do. I'll be torn apart.

My body grows restless under his crushing weight, fear snaking along my nerve endings, but I don't want to move. I want to lie here and pretend everything is as it was a few days ago.

He stirs, kissing my neck and then rising to take care of the condom in the bathroom. When he returns, he's donned his tight black boxers and hands me one of his white T-shirts. And everything seems normal. The new normal, anyway. No need to panic.

'It's a stunning day for a wedding,' he says. 'Come and have breakfast. I arranged it out on the balcony while you were asleep.' His face is relaxed, open, but goose bumps rise on my arms. I'm reading way too much into that possessive demand spoken in the heat of the moment.

I shrug into his over-sized shirt, take his hand and follow him out to his bungalow's private deck. We're faced with endless ocean views hazy with the fierce morning sun. I take a seat, my stomach flipping at the fact that he's been up early organising the delicious spread I see laid out.

'I asked the staff to prepare a coconut-free breakfast, so you can eat anything you like,' he says, removing covers from the food. My aversion to the tropical staple is well-known, but I'm still humbled that he went to such trouble. I tuck into some fruit and yoghurt while Oliver helps himself to toast.

'So what will you wear today?' he asks, scooting his chair a few inches closer to mine so that when we eat our arms graze. I force the mouthful past my tight throat, trying to pretend I haven't noticed.

'Um… I thought I'd wear a sundress.' This new attentive side of him, one I've never experienced on such an intimate level, blurs the boundaries I'm trying to reconstruct around our new but temporary relationship.

'Is it red?' he asks, his stare full of renewed heat. 'You looked beautiful last night in red. You should wear it more often.'

I almost choke on a piece of melon. It's hard enough to resist flirty, playful friend Oliver, but charming, sexy lover Oliver is almost too much for my frazzled ovaries. My mouth opens, no answer emerging, because this Oliver—sex-rumpled, attentive and romantic—may as well be a virtual stranger. If I'd known this side of him, would I have acted on my attraction sooner, confessing that my feelings for him had transcended platonic from day one? Would I have demanded the number one spot in his life and not settled for what at times over the years felt like second place?

Precarious breath shudders out of me as I shrug.

History's proved this privileged position of lover in his life is short-lived. As he admitted last night, he considers himself incapable of commitment because he's Slay's son, so there's no future for us.

I cannot get carried away by his romantic gestures. We said we wouldn't allow this to damage us. I have to have faith in my own abilities to stay grounded, and Oliver's word that he won't allow anything to break us. His over-protectiveness around his father is his way of doing just that.

'There's a swimming with dolphins experience tomorrow, if you'd like to go?' he says, pushing a lock of my hair back behind my ear. Then he slides the plate bearing his last half-slice of toast in my direction.

I nod, close to inexplicable tears. 'That sounds perfect. I'd love to.' Perhaps it's the emotion of the wedding brewing—I always cry at weddings. Or his gesture—saving me some of his food reminds me that my Oliver, the one I know beyond these wonderful new revelations, is still here.

I take the toast with a small smile. 'Thanks.'

His easy grin is infectious, settling some of my doubts. If I'm not careful, I run the risk of spoiling the best week of my life by over-thinking. I should just enjoy as much time as we have and deal with the fallout back home in London, where I'll be able to escape the daily addiction of him while we both live our separate lives.

'So tell me about the Kimoto deal,' I say, pouring some tea and taking a bite of his toast. 'Any news?' He's worked long and hard on the artificial intelligence software this past year.

He runs his fingers through his hair and puts down his mug. 'It's with the lawyers, so I'm hoping for good news today. I should really be back in the office, but I couldn't let Shelley down after promising to fly the wedding guests here. My team have everything under control. I just…'

I reach for his hand and he grips my fingers. 'This deal is important to me. I take my work very seriously and I want Kimoto to see that. The last thing I need is Slay causing a scene. It almost feels like he'd deliberately sabotage this for me.' His leg jiggles under the table.

'Why would he do that?' I ask, horrified that any parent could act vengefully.

He shrugs. 'There's no love lost between us. And if he can tag some mention of himself onto my company news…' He smiles a humourless smile. 'Part of me was naive enough to think I could have this one success all to myself.'

'It's a big deal for you outside of the financial gain, isn't it?'

He nods, tension radiating from his body. 'My team have been working on this software for years—they deserve to have their work valued. This will make international headlines for all the right reasons. And I hate the fact that my past… Slay's reputation…might ruin that for everyone involved.'

'You deserve the recognition, too.' My heart clenches. 'I don't think I realised how much you've struggled with the two sides of your life.' The self-made professional businessman and the privileged celebrity son growing up in the shadow of his father's fame. After what he confessed last night, it's no wonder the Oliver I first met was a little wild.

'Perhaps this deal will put an end to those comparison stories,' I say. 'It's not like you ever trade on Slay's fame.'

His grin is wry. 'I might have used that once or twice to impress women or get laid before I met you. And I fully admit I've done my fair share of acting out in the past, earned my own reputation…'

'Or perhaps you were simply out-running Slay's. From what you've told me, it's doesn't sound like he made any attempt to protect you from his fame or the excesses of his world, as some celebrity parents do.'

He stares, his eyes burning into mine, as if it's never occurred to him to show himself compassion for being young and rudderless and making a bad choice.

'We all make mistakes, experiment with who we want to be,' I go on. 'You've built a successful, innovative company from nothing. You look after your staff, attracting and retaining the best brains in the industry.' I offer him the last bite of toast, even though there's more on the table. Shared food somehow tastes better.

He eats it from my fingers, setting off delicious tingles of pleasure in my pelvis. 'Yeah, well, the tech world evolves so rapidly, experience only counts for so much.' He runs a hand over his face and I notice new creases at the corners of his eyes. 'It's a young person's field—even I'm getting a little long in the tooth to keep up.'

I can't resist a confirmatory ogle of his ripped torso, decorated with tattoos. 'Oh, yes, ancient. You're only thirty. And it may be a young person's game, but you're the one with the leadership skills and the vision to recruit those young geniuses. You're the one who built on the success of Never Scan.' I mention the software he developed at uni that launched him onto the path to his first million.

'Well, that was down to you,' he says, growing serious, his stare intent.

I laugh. 'Just because I did your company accounts for a few years doesn't mean I'm in any way responsible for the things you've achieved.'

His hand shifts to my arm, the slow swipe of his thumb back and forth sensual and distracting. 'You're totally responsible,' he disagrees. 'That's why I named the software after you.'

This revelation is news to me. 'But…' I gape in shock. 'I thought…' I had no idea the name of the first software he developed had been named after his nickname for me. I'd assumed it was the other, more common, usage of the word because, aside from the accounting software he designed especially for my business, I have no understanding of what he does. Teasing me for my technophobia is one of his favourite pastimes.

'You didn't know?' he asks, his eyes alight with mischief as he relaxes back in his chair, still gripping my fingers.

I shake my head, dumbfounded.

'It's true. You believed in me at a time when I needed someone. You listened when I spent hours talking about stuff I knew you didn't understand, and you convinced me I was onto something worth developing. Encouraged me to not give up. I wouldn't be here, wouldn't be making billion-pound deals, without you.' He leans close, lifts my hand to his mouth and kisses my knuckles one by one, his eyes on mine. 'That's why I gave you shares.'

Pressure builds in my chest, and the hot aching in my throat and the sting in my eyes returns. 'I thought the shares were a really nerdy birthday present.'

He laughs, tugging me into his kiss. 'Well, they were that too. But you see how I know this, us, is going to work out? Because you know me. You see *me*, when most other people see my reputation and family notoriety, the fickle bits of celebrity that have rubbed off on me over the years from living in Slay's world. But you understand that's not who I am, and you still like me.'

'I do like you,' I say, my breath trapped in my chest, because the other 'L' word wants to break free.

'The feeling is entirely mutual.' He kisses me again, long and lingering and ending on a sigh. 'We should get ready.' He looks at his watch. 'The bride will kill me if I keep her waiting because I'm buried inside you.'

The heat in his stare tells me he's serious.

I rouse myself, needing a few minutes away from his all-consuming presence to gather my wits. Oliver in flat-out charming mode is dangerous for my judgement, because I'm becoming more and more ensnared in him and the way he makes me feel... special.

Oh, how bright and brilliant it is here in the beam of Oliver's focus.

But special isn't enough. I want to be everything to him, and he's shy of commitment, something he's never wanted or even considered, thanks to Slay. While I will always support him, can I invest time and energy into guiding him through his relationship phobia when I'm already so emotionally attached? That seems like the road to certain heartbreak. And given the depth of his commitment issues, maybe he'll simply be content to slip back into his casual routine once we're back in London and he's surrounded by willing women.

I retire to my own room to shower and change for the wedding ceremony. I wish I could don a protective shell like the hermit crabs we see on the beach. Because my mind is foggy with Oliver's shock revelations and the flares of hope they've sparked. Do I really know him at all? Yes, I know the playful, generous friend he's been for nine years. But the man trying to outgrow his reputation and break away from any association with Slay—is this the part of him that's always called to me on a deeper level? The part I've been waiting for?

I'm putting the finishing touches to my make-up when there's a knock at the door.

My heart races with anticipation, because I've been away from him for thirty minutes and already I miss his company. Miss the way he takes my hand and does that swiping thing on my skin with his thumb. Miss his frequent passionate kisses, as if he can no more stop himself than I can. Miss those seriously hot looks that pass between us fifty times a day.

How did we look at each other before we began this intimacy? Will I always crave him this way, now that I know exactly how much more there is to lose? And can I risk exposing my heart to pain on the off chance he'll one day decide he's ready for more?

I yank open the door. Oliver stands on the other side, his hair still damp from the shower and his white linen shirt open at the neck to reveal a delicious triangle of tanned chest and a smattering of manly dark hair. In his outstretched hand is a single flower that matches the one he wears as a buttonhole.

The world tilts a fraction at the gorgeous sight he makes. I'm playing with fire, the flames already licking along my fingers. 'Have you lost your key?'

He shakes his head, his stare raking mine in that way that reminds me of how he looks at me when he's deep inside me, before swooping the length of my body to take in my outfit—a strappy, slinky sheath dress in teal, chosen for how sexy it makes me feel. For him.

Appreciation and something darker, more seductive, shines in his eyes. 'Can I accompany you to the wedding, Miss Grayson?' He tucks the single bloom into my hair, behind one ear and my core clenches with longing. I want to launch myself back into his arms, drag him into my room and keep him prisoner until it's time to go home and put an end to this dangerous fantasy.

His fingertips graze my cheek before he drops his arm and he holds out his hand for mine.

Oh, no, no, no...

I'm in deep trouble. Every second I grow more invested is a threat to my very being.

But I take his hand without hesitation, trying to put all of these burgeoning feelings into perspective. We pad on bare feet down to the beach where his family is assembled on the sand at the rustic altar, casting each other wider and wider smiles, as if we have a secret. I'm caught up in the romance, only vaguely aware of Slay Coterill and his sixth wife near the front; it's as if Oliver and I are sealed inside an invisible bubble, with eyes only for each other, the rest of the world shut out. I can't stop looking at him—so handsome, every inch familiar but in sharper focus—and every time I do his eyes are on me, ablaze with hunger that helps to remind me why we started this physical exploration. There's no place for my romantic imaginings.

The ceremony is short and beautiful. My hand rests in Oliver's throughout, exotic but so addictive, because it feels like it belongs. And of course he produces a crisp white handkerchief from his pocket when inevitable tears dampen my lashes. I stop fighting myself, uncaring who sees our togetherness. People can think what they like about me, his friend-lover.

I dab my eyes, careful of my mascara, while Oliver tugs me under his arm and presses a kiss to my temple. 'You are so adorable.' His smile is indulgent but still laced with that fervent hunger I burn for. Because now he knows I'm no longer just his 'sweet' friend. I'm badly desperate for him.

I laugh, drying the last of my tears and handing him back his handkerchief.

'I'm bad, remember? I want things,' I whisper. 'You, every way possible,' I go on, the scrape of my dress over my distended swollen nipples excruciating. 'How soon before we can sneak away?'

His stare darkens. 'I want you too, but we have to make an appearance at the wedding lunch.'

I sigh but smile. We have time. Days.

'An appearance' turns into hours—photographs, a delicious wedding feast, toasts and dancing. It's after a turn on the dance floor—a patch of the white sand beach under a gazebo decorated with fairy lights—that our escape is interrupted by Slay. We've managed to dodge him all day by avoiding the bar, where he's entertained his audience.

'Son! Come and have a drink with me and your stepmum,' he calls, making a grand gesture with his outstretched arms and booming voice, so Oliver is forced to stop to avoid a scene.

'I'm sorry,' Oliver whispers to me under his breath.

'Bring your lady-friend,' says Slay, winking my way, then laying twin kisses on my cheeks before either of us can utter one word of protest or make our excuses. Oliver's stepmother number five, who looks a couple of years younger than us, barely looks up from her phone.

'Sid,' says Oliver in a clipped tone. 'We were

just leaving, actually. And this is Neve.' The term 'lady-friend' clearly upset him more than it did me.

Slay's stare hardens at the use of his real name, presumably the reason Oliver used it. He slouches back in his seat, spreads his tight leather-trouser-clad thighs. His shirt hangs open to the waist to reveal a waxed, tanned torso decorated with ink.

'Leaving this early?' he asks, raising a near-empty bottle of champagne, waggling it at a waiter to indicate he wants a replacement. 'That's not very rock and roll.'

I rest my hand on Oliver's rigid back, stilling him from reacting to the puerile jibe.

'Fabulous resort, isn't it?' Slay lights a cigarette and squints at me through the smoke.

He's not exactly leering, but I grow conscious of the strappy nature of my dress and the fact I'm not wearing a bra. My body grows stiff, all the lovely feel-good hormones of the romantic day draining away.

'So, did you guys meet here?' asks Slay, with an oily smile.

I step closer to Oliver's side, my hand gripping his shirt at the small of his back—non-verbal communication that I don't need rescuing.

'Neve is a very old friend.' Oliver's voice is aloof, tension pouring from his body.

My insides jolt at Oliver's descriptor. I don't really mind that he introduces me that way, but Slay's clearly never heard of me. Not once in the past nine years has my name come up. To him I'm just another of his son's temporary women. And, like Oliver's current stepmother, one of a long list…

I know Oliver said he's trying to protect me, but I can't help the tiny stabs of insecurity that rain down on me. Perhaps he doesn't trust that I can handle Slay's celebrity. Perhaps he thinks I'd become starstruck after all. Hardly…

But it reminds me of my place in Oliver's life these past nine years, and it's not the place I want. The place I began to dream for.

Slay seems to relish the discomfort he's causing. 'Well, don't keep her all to yourself,' he says before taking a deep drag from his cigarette. 'It's rude not to share.' Something like menace or challenge sneaks into Slay's eyes as he toes out a spare stool in invitation. 'Why don't you both sit down?'

It sounds like a dare. The air around our small group seems to freeze. The smell of testosterone emanates from father and son, each locked into a stand-off that zaps the atmosphere with animosity.

What the hell…? I've had enough.

'That's really kind of you, Mr Coterill,' I say, coming to my senses. 'But I have a bit of a headache. Some other time, perhaps.' I tug Oliver's arm, trying to drag him away from the situation, which seems to have made him furious.

'Of course. I look forward to it,' Slay says, ignoring Oliver, his eyes on me in some sort of act of defiance.

We're almost back to Oliver's bungalow, my footsteps rapid to keep up with his longer strides and my hand crushed in his, before I risk conversation.

'What the hell was that all about?' I ask as he unlocks the door and strides inside.

He tosses the key card onto a nearby chair, flicks on the lamp and pours himself a whisky from the mini-bar. 'Want one?' he asks, ignoring my question.

'Yes please,' I reply, accepting the drink and watching him knock his back in a determined swallow. Why the hell is he so angry? I'm the one who was passive-aggressively insulted and ogled by Slay and reinstated to the friend zone by Oliver.

'I told you he's an asshole. I warned you he'd flirt with you—with his wife right there…. And he's an addict—he's not supposed to be drinking. Now do you see why I tried to keep you two apart? He's hardly the most flattering of fathers.' He yanks his shirt off, slings it onto the chair and strides to the bathroom.

I follow, sipping my whisky to calm my nerves at the vision of his naked torso, tanned and tattooed, his jeans riding low on his narrow hips.

'I told you I could look after myself. No need to go head-to-head with him. Don't you trust me?' I challenge, directing my disappointment away from the reminder that I'll soon be back to my former role—an old friend. And it shouldn't bother me, because I can't allow myself to harbour my growing feelings. Oliver turns on the tap and splashes his face with cold water, one hand braced on the side of the sink.

I understand that Slay and Oliver aren't close, but it seemed as if things would come to blows down there on the beach. If ever there was a way to land yourself in the news, it would be publicly decking a world-famous rock star. And why is he letting Slay get to him so badly?

'Of course I trust you, although I don't understand why you're not running away from me and my fucked-up family as fast as you can,' he says, drying his face with a towel. 'But, if you're staying…' His voice ominously grows quiet. 'I'll defend and protect you any damn way I like.'

My pussy clenches at his commanding tone even as I say, 'Don't be ridiculous. How Slay behaves has no bearing on my feelings for you.' I don't want to add to his mood by addressing the fact that the father he seems embarrassed of looked at me as if he might be lining me up to be wife number seven. 'And I'm tougher than I look.'

Am I tough enough? I *should* run, but only to protect my heart from a man who's a commitment-phobe.

The real issue here is us—our unfinished business. The reminder I'm just one of a long list of women makes my skin crawl. I feel the need to mark him somehow. To be memorable. To stand out so he'll never forget the madness of our holiday fling.

'Fuck Slay,' I say, venting my frustration that Oliver seems to be allowing his father issues to hold him back. I step closer, commanding his eye contact as I press my lips to the rim of my glass and take a slow swallow of whisky. 'I won't let whatever that was out there ruin today. Ruin us and the time we have left here. I want you. I've wanted you all day. I don't give a shit about your father. This is between us and I'm exactly where I want to be.' If I can't have more of him than great sex, I'll take it again and again as compensation. 'So, if you're so intent on looking after me, why don't you do something about my current state?'

His face is tight with a frown. I hold out my glass to him and he takes it, knocking back the dregs then placing it on the vanity. His arm scoops around my waist, hauling me close so I'm pressed against all that yummy, pretty, naked chest.

'Is that right?' His eyes glitter, the romantic lover absent while his heart thunders against my sensitive breasts.

I trace the piercing in his left nipple with one index finger, rubbing over the barbell, making his abs contract and his hard cock jerk against my belly. Feminine power ignites in me, my limbs languid and my body temperature spiking.

'Yes.' I slide the finger down the ridge of his abdominal muscles, dipping inside his navel before unbuttoning the top button of his fly. My teeth trap my bottom lip as I look up from the trail of hair dipping into his waistband. I slide my fingertip to the head of his cock, feeling the tiny wet patch where he's leaked on the fabric of his fly.

I lift his free hand from his hip and wedge it between my legs so he can feel the heat and moisture I'm generating. 'I need what only you can give me.' Can't he see we're all that matters? Can't he feel how easy it would be to lose ourselves and block out the rest of the world, just as we have all day at the wedding? Can't he trust that there's so much more to him than being his father's son and the limitations he's placed around his heart?

'Neve,' he warns, his tone still brittle. 'Don't goad me—I'm in no mood to go easy on you.'

I tilt my chin, pressing my open mouth to his collarbone, his neck and his stubble-covered jaw. 'I want you as you are. You know me as well as I know you. You know what I need, what my body likes, and I trust you. You'd never hurt me.' I slide my tongue over his parted lips, my hand stroking him through his jeans so I feel the jerks of his cock that let me know my words, my demands, excite him.

I gasp, laugh, groan as he snatches his hand from between my legs, cups my face and pushes me back against the tiles, kissing me and then dropping his mouth to my breast so he can tongue my nipple through my dress. I yank open the remaining buttons of his fly but, before I can get my hand on his erection, he bunches my dress around my waist and drops to his knees.

'Fuck, I can't get enough of you,' he says, his forehead pressed to my stomach, breath panting between my legs. 'I should never have touched you, but it's too late. You're addictive.' His audible, prolonged inhale ends on a groan as he buries his face against my mound and laves my clit through the lace of my panties. 'I wanted to kill him for looking at you that way,' he says about Slay.

My heart surges at the return of that possessiveness that weakens my knees. I spread my thighs to accommodate his broad shoulders and grip his hair in my hands, twisting the strands with enough force to tilt his eyes—which are impassioned and stormy—up to mine.

'I wanted you to touch me. So badly. Only you can give me what I need, what my body craves. I'm yours.' For now.

He seems to need my admission, his stare burning through me. 'Fuck yes, you are.' He groans, sliding the crotch of my underwear aside so he can put his mouth on me in that way I've come to expect— hot, greedy, carnal. I throw one leg over his shoulder, digging my heel into his back as his tongue spears me, his big hands filled with the cheeks of my arse, and I cry out, my head thumping the wall behind.

His tongue lashes my clit, alternating with deep plunges inside. I grip his hair and ride his face, desperate now for the orgasms he can deliver. Desperate to come for him and desperate for more. For it all. Because this isn't going away. This need isn't diminishing. And if I glut myself now, take all I can have of him, perhaps I'll be able to live off the memories when it ends.

I'm skirting the cusp of my climax when he slides his fingers inside me, two, three, stretching me. Plunging. I cry out in despair when his fingers leave me and I glare down at him, about to demand he put them back when I feel him probe my rear with his moisture-slicked fingers.

I stare into his fierce eyes, and a gasp rips from my throat at the foreign, thrilling contact. He watches my reaction, his mouth quirking a fraction, his groan of praise weakening my knees. Because I'm his, whether I like it or not. Whether he thinks he deserves me or not. And I trust him with my body, my pleasure, my life.

He's shown me what I'm capable of, shown me how well he knows me. And I want this, want him all the ways I can have him until my time is up.

But I also want to undo him. To take him on this roller coaster of need right alongside me. 'Oliver,'

I say, gripping his face while he eats at me. 'That feels so good, but I want your cock in me.'

He pulls his mouth from me, his fingers still working in my crease, massaging, gliding over my sensitive rear, waking up nerve endings I didn't know I possessed.

'Say it again,' he grinds out, his voice breaking. 'Say you're mine and I'll give you my cock. I'll make you come.'

'I'm yours,' I say, the words heavier every time I speak them. But I can't focus on the future, not when I want to burn in every present moment with him.

He rises to his feet, shucking his jeans and boxers and kicking them away, then he stands naked before me, his fist wrapped around his glorious penis, sliding and tugging his long length. Taunting me. I whimper at the sight. Slide my dress from my shoulders where it pools at my feet.

'Leave the thong on,' he commands, and I'm past caring that I'm half-in half-out of my underwear. I grip his hips and pull him close. 'I'm yours,' I whisper against his lips, which smell of my own arousal. 'What are you going to do with me?' I ask, before sliding my mouth to his nipple and gently tugging on the piercing with my teeth.

He grunts, his fingers digging into my hips as he spins me around so I'm in front of him, facing the sink, and his cock glides between my arse cheeks, the wet tip nudging the small of my back.

Our reflections stare back at us. Him a tall, bronzed god and me flushed pink with lust and longing. And something else. Something too terrifying to name, because it mustn't be true. I mustn't let it be.

'Bend over,' he says.

I obey, bracing my hands on the edge of the vanity, my focus on breathing, an act which should be automatic but feels precarious. He leans over my back, his scruff scraping at my neck and the juncture of my shoulder as his hands cup my breasts.

His thumbs rub my nipples and I cry his name. 'There's a condom in my wash bag there,' he says, sucking on my skin and sliding one hand back to my slick clit. 'Get it.'

I fumble in my haste, and when I locate the foil square I feel the nip of his teeth against my skin, as if he's reached his limit.

He sheathes himself quickly and then his stare meets mine in the mirror. We're both panting hard with anticipation and, just like our first time together, I marvel at his stamina, because I'm achy, needy, empty and ready to beg, to end this torture of wanting.

'Oliver…' I spread my legs in invitation, tilting my hips back. 'I want to be yours, to be bad for you.'

His eyes are so dark, so hooded, I can't make out the blue any longer.

'Even if I ruin you?' he asks, his fingers still strumming between my legs.

'Yes.' I don't hesitate. But he could never ruin me.

His nostrils flare and his jaw bunches as he seems to wrestle with my declaration. He looks down, strokes my back as if with reverence, and then slides my thong from between the cheeks of my arse. He positions himself at my slick entrance and then grips my shoulder in one hand, surging forward on a single, delicious thrust that has me rising up onto tiptoes to accommodate him.

His thrusts knock me forward. I lock my arms and push back, each slap of his thighs against mine thrilling and, oh, so debauched. He releases my hip, his fingers coming between my legs from the front to collect some of the moisture coating me, and then he returns those wicked fingers to my rear.

'Do you like this? Is this what you want?' he asks.

'Oliver, yes…' I mewl, my back arching as he strokes with increased pressure over my pucker.

'Rub your clit,' he barks, his face almost unrecognisable with the violence of his arousal.

I do his bidding with a helpless yelp, my fingers sliding around the base of his thrusting cock and then rubbing over my engorged, needy clit.

We lock eyes in the mirror, so many unspoken words passing between us in silent communication. I rub hard, so close to climaxing now I'm full of him.

'I trust you,' I say, because I want to give him all of me, but I can't trust myself that I won't fall so hard, so deep, that I'll never be the same.

At my words his fingers dig into my shoulder, his thrusts deeper, and he presses a fingertip into my rear.

I'm tossed into an orgasm so profound, I'm vaguely aware of screaming his name and of his own shout of unrestrained pleasure before the world seems to go black, my five fingers clinging to the edge of the vanity being my only grip on sanity.

Oliver leaves my body, tugging me into his arms and sliding us to the bathroom tiles. His kisses pepper my face, my closed eyelids, his gusting breath telling me he too is still reeling. He holds me tight, his arms possessive around my waist.

'You're mine,' he whispers against my temple. 'Mine.'

CHAPTER TEN

Oliver

I SWIM TOWARDS the back of the boat behind Neve after a day spent snorkelling and sailing, just the two of us. But I'm still distracted by what happened with Slay. I'd wanted to gouge out his eyes when he looked at Neve as if she was just another potential notch on his guitar. And when he disrespected her with that snide dig at me about sharing... I saw red, and for the first time in my life I'd wanted to hit my own father. To punch his million-dollar veneered teeth down his throat. And I might have, if Neve hadn't defused the situation.

But that would have shown her exactly what I'm trying to conceal. Proved how much alike Slay and I really are in some areas. And I'm not ready to have her despise me the way I despised myself for many years. How could I have allowed Slay to burrow so deep under my skin last night?

It's Neve. I've fallen for her so easily, and it's

as if Slay has deliberately come here to remind me of my every failing. I'm so buggered. I knew it the minute I opened my eyes after our first night together, and the fact was again cemented last night when Slay uttered the word *share* and I realised how much I had to lose.

Neve clambers aboard and then leans over to take my snorkel mask and flippers. We haven't discussed it since the conversation in the bathroom last night. We showered and lay naked and entwined beneath the cool sheets all night. I couldn't sleep, which meant I watched her sleep, marvelling at how perfect she is and how blind I've been all this time. But Slay's presence, his little pissing contest last night in front of Neve, brought all my fears screaming to the forefront of my mind.

I don't deserve her. All these years I've avoided relationships in order to protect myself from the pain and humiliation I felt at nineteen. I messed up following my split with Jane, crossing a line with Slay's then-wife number three, proving how much like him I am. And I'll likely mess up again if I try to have something real and committed with Neve.

But the selfishness that boils inside me won't allow me to give her up…

Silently, we rinse off the sea water under the deck shower and then stretch out on a couple of loungers to enjoy the rest of the cruise around the atolls. Meanwhile, I debate how much of my secret she needs to know. Probably all of it, before she hears it from Slay.

'I can't believe we actually got to see dolphins,' Neve says, excitement still gleaming in her eyes. 'And that turtle was so beautiful.'

'Pretty cool, eh? I thought the manta ray was the most impressive. Drink?' I ask, selecting two ice-cold beers from the mini-fridge on the aft deck.

She nods, accepting my offering with a smile I now claim as mine. Just for me. Because it lights her eyes so I see things there that give me hope. The sensual heat is an incredible privilege, yes, but there's also wonder and longing...as if she almost believes I'm the only man who can give her what she needs.

If only I was worthy of such belief. Statistically, I'm likely to disappoint and hurt her just as much if not more than the SBF Club...

'Thanks for organising this—it's a perfect way to have some space away from the others,' she says about our private cruise with an experienced local captain. I arranged it so we could be assured of the best snorkelling spots and for his insider knowledge of the spinner dolphins, which frequent these waters.

Her reminder of my possessive leanings and the way our day almost derailed after a two-minute conversation with Slay pricks my skin with guilt. I need to be more open. Her push-back last night shocked me. It never occurred to me that she'd assume I didn't trust her. It's Slay I don't trust. And myself.

But the last thing I want is him, or anything else, to come between us. I start with the easy news.

'I agree. I don't think we'll be seeing Slay again. I heard this morning that my latest stepmother is history and he's gone back to LA.' I try to keep the relief from my tone.

'Oh dear,' she replies not bothering with commiserations. Now that she's met Slay, she can see for herself that he'd stand a much better chance if he married a woman he shares something in common with.

'Yeah,' I snort. 'Don't feel too sorry for him. It's only a matter of time before the next twentysomething catches his eye.'

'How do you feel about that? Are you calm enough to talk about it?' she probes, her hand on my thigh caressing away my agitation.

I shrug, pretending I can't recall the sinking feeling every time a fresh wedding invitation from Slay lands on the mat. 'You saw them together last night. Hardly a love match. Next time, he should at least try to find someone who isn't after him for their fifteen minutes of fame. But perhaps that's the attraction for him—the adoration. Until they get to know him.' Resentment bubbles up anew inside me. I hate that I almost allowed Slay to ruin what I have with Neve.

Until I touched her, until he met her and showed me how much is at stake, I thought his hold over me was long past. In one way or another, he's influenced every relationship I've ever had, whether disabusing me of my faith in first love, or through the early days after I came to London when I slept around as if to prove something—maybe that I could switch off the emotions that made me vulnerable. Or simply that Slay didn't have the monopoly on bad-boy behaviour. And now I'm allowing him to cast doubt over what I have with Neve, this overwhelming need to protect her. I fear that I can't commit and be what she deserves.

Because, for the first time in over ten years, I want to commit.

But could she ever take me seriously, knowing me as she does? And now also knowing Slay...

'I have spoken about you to him before,' I say, needing to reassure her. 'He's just too self-absorbed to notice what other people say most of the time.' However Slay tried to paint her as some hook-up I'd just met, my feelings for her are deeper than ever. For the first time in a decade—not that the first time counted—I was barely a man. I think I might be in love. Terrifying, all-consuming love.

Panic beads sweat on the back of my neck. How can I confess that when there are more pressing things I need her to know? I feel like I'm about to split open, all my ugly secrets spilling free. Am I ready to expose my true self, the me I see every time I think about Slay? Will she still want me when she knows about my sordid past? At all, even as a friend?

I must have zoned out, because when she speaks I startle.

'What did he mean about the sharing? Is he into threesomes or something?' she asks outright, her mouth forming an 'O' over the neck of the beer bottle. She takes a long swallow, giving me precious seconds to formulate some words that don't sound like a script for some hideous reality TV show.

My skin crawls. If only I could say yes. Better than the truth, which still has the power to make me shudder with shame, both for how Slay acted and how I acted out in return.

'I wouldn't put it past him,' I say. I want to confess all my shameful truths to this woman who believes in my redemption. Who sees something that eludes me when I look in the mirror. But I also want more time. Because I'm learning new things about her every day.

'He's a drama queen who likes to stir up trouble,' I continue, scrubbing my hand over my unshaven face. 'He likes to get a rise out of me for sport.' Perhaps Slay sensed what Neve means to me, so delivered a low blow.

I want to erase last night's meeting with him from her memory, because standing in front of him beside the woman I love made me feel small and completely unworthy.

We'll ruin her. Drag her down to our level. I can't do that, but can I give her up?

Neve is watchful, silent. Waiting for more.

Unease creeps down my spine. I want to be honest. Every hour we spend together feels like we're moving closer, but some things are too devastating to confess. Perhaps half the story…the less damning half.

'Remember the night he took me to the strip joint?' My stare falls on the endless blue of the Indian ocean because it's hard to think about that night without feeling white-hot licks of regret and shame. 'Well, in addition to his unique advice on getting over a woman by moving swiftly on to the next, he also informed me that Jane, the girl I was crying into my beer over, had allegedly come on to him while we were together.'

Neve sits bolt upright. 'What? Seriously?'

I nod, my neck so stiff it spasms. 'Seriously. "No use crying over pussy you never really had in the first place",' I say, imitating Slay's words of wisdom.

She scoots to the edge of her lounger and reaches for my hand. 'Did she?'

I shrug. 'She half-heartedly denied it, but it doesn't really matter who was telling the truth. I was a teenager, full of emotions, and that felt like my lowest ebb. And Slay kicked me while I was down, whether intentionally or through tactlessness doesn't matter.'

I squeeze her fingers, needing to pull her into my arms but also hating that I'm the source of the appalled disbelief in her wide eyes. I know she feels empathy for my younger self, but she must also feel horror to a degree. No normal father behaves that way.

'That's horrible,' she says, gripping my hand more tightly. I shake my head, cutting her off. I don't deserve her pity, because I behaved as badly as him later that night. Worse, in fact. Because, whereas Slay claims never to have laid a finger on Jane, I went home alone to his mansion, furious and drunk after visiting her for confirmation.

Slay's third wife, Aubrey, was in the kitchen. She saw I was upset. Poured me another drink. Made me spill the whole story. And then, somehow, I'd kissed her, or she'd kissed me, and with pain and humiliation driving me I'd allowed emotions to rule my head. I didn't stop it. I slept with her. And afterwards she told me she was leaving Slay anyway so I shouldn't feel bad. But I felt worse than bad. Confused and ashamed, because I wasn't certain who had used who. But I was certain my actions were something Slay would have done.

And I was right. I'll never forget the look of anger tinged with pride on Slay's face during the inevitable confrontation the next morning. In trying to break free of him, I'd become something he could finally relate to and respect. My self-worth reached rock-bottom. Even now, years later, the shame defines everything I do. Why would my wonderful, beautiful Neve want anything to do with such a... weak degenerate?

'"Don't date with your head, boy. Use your dick".' I quote Slay, the sickening memories choking. 'That's the last time I turned to him for advice.' I swallow, my throat aching because I'm back there, feeling helpless, vulnerable and inadequate for a woman like Neve.

She slides onto my lounger, her arms around my shoulders and her head tucked into my chest. 'I'm so sorry you went through that.'

I press my lips to her forehead, selfishly sucking in the comforting scent of her skin. 'I was lucky enough to have dual nationality. I caught the first flight to the UK, applied to university, spent the summer working in London and then I met you—a brilliant ray of sunshine,' I say, trying to forget.

I acted out for months after that incident, some twisted part of me taking to heart Slay's unwanted advice about women as I tried to make sense of my teenage angst and confusion over what I'd done with my father's wife. But, aside from the attempt to protect myself from further heartache, it wasn't me. Not the real me.

I shelved that version of myself when I woke up to the fact that my behaviour made me more like Slay, not less—terrified of his celebrity world in which I'd become caught up, where outrageous things seemed commonplace. Although by then my reputation was set with the British media and exaggerated by Slay's publicists, who come from the school of 'no publicity is bad publicity'.

I'd plastered on a mask and tried to banish my disillusion for a while, living out my early twenties avoiding getting too close to anyone. With the exception of one person.

The person now in my arms, making my heart clench with every beat.

I can't lose her.

Not without losing part of myself.

CHAPTER ELEVEN

Oliver

I HOLD HER tighter to stop myself shattering apart.

'Let's forget about Slay. I have another surprise for you.'

She looks up at me with a small smile but concern in her eyes. 'Okay.' She sighs, dropping her head back to my chest and snuggling closer. 'But, for what it's worth, I hope you know that I would never betray you in any way.'

I love her for her reassurance, although I deserve neither her loyalty nor her caring.

'I never took a girl home after that. Never introduced him to anyone, especially not you. You're too precious. I couldn't survive losing you.'

Panic rumbles through me, a wave growing in momentum. Will she leave me when she learns just how similar Slay and I are?

'Why especially me?' she asks, stilling.

I exhale the tightness in my throat that tastes

like fear. 'Because you're different. You didn't care about who my father is. In fact, you'd never even heard of him. Right from the moment we met you've never taken any crap from me, even on that first night when I was immature enough to be full of crap. You made me earn your friendship, and that made it all the more valuable, because most things in my life came easy to me back then, just as they had for Slay. Why would I risk all of that, risk you, by exposing you to a man I wish I could disown, wish I didn't share DNA with?'

Her eyes soften and I want to kiss her so badly. To lose myself in her and our passion until I forget where I come from, what I did and start afresh with Neve.

'I admit the leather pants in this heat are a bit tragic,' she says, and then rolls her eyes, injecting the moment with humour.

A rumble of laughter resonates in my chest. That she can make me smile when I'm full of regret and frustration is a testament to how she enriches my life just by being herself. I fall a little bit more in love with her in that moment.

The boat's gently humming engine changes in tone. I look up.

'We're here,' I tell her. 'I hope you're hungry.'

I sling on a T-shirt and Neve covers up with a sarong, her excited eyes restoring my balance as she catches sight of the small thatched shelter on the island where we've moored.

'I arranged a treat for lunch,' I say as we walk down the gangplank and pad through the pristine clear shallows.

'Sounds intriguing, but you didn't have to go to all this trouble.' She smiles her smile; the one I'm head over heels for.

'Yes, I did,' I say, lifting her hand to my mouth and pressing a kiss to her knuckles. 'I was going to arrange a picnic. But you love cooking shows, so I thought we could have some fun and I could learn some skills—you know how culinarily challenged I am.'

'*Kihineh?*' Ali, our local chef, asks us how we are in Dhivehi, the official language of the Maldives.

Neve's excitement is infectious as she takes a seat in the open-air kitchen, which already smells of heavenly spices.

Ali explains the menu—*bis keemiya*, a type of samosa stuffed with gently sautéed cabbage, hard-boiled eggs and spiced onions, *garudhiya*, a fragrant fish soup, and a coconut-free version of *huni roshi*, a chapati-style bread.

Under Ali's instructions, Neve sets about grinding spices with a pestle and mortar and I'm tasked with rolling out the balls of chapati dough into circles.

Neve is in her element, her eyes bright as she

watches Ali with rapt attention and teases me for my oval-shaped bread.

'You're really good at this!' I watch her deep-frying rectangular samosas. 'Will you teach me some basics when we get home?' It's the first time either of us has mentioned reality, and my heart stops while I wait for her answer.

'Of course,' she says, laughing as I burn my first chapati to a cinder on one side. 'Don't worry. We'll make a cook out of you.'

When we're done, Ali carries everything to a solitary sheltered table for two near the shore. Despite my having a hand in it, the food is delicious.

'Try this,' tempts Neve, feeding me from her fingers, which are greasy and spicy.

Despite being ravenous, my tight throat makes swallowing a challenge. I love seeing her this way—excited, relaxed and happy. After all these years, I feel like I'm learning something new about her every day. An addiction I want to feed until she's woven through me.

'Thanks for this,' she says when, sated, we finally admit defeat.

'It's my pleasure,' I say, humbled and awed that I put the happiness on her face.

'Let's walk along the beach,' she suggests, standing and taking my hand. After we've walked in silence for a few minutes, she says, 'Can I ask you a question?'

'Of course. Anything.' I kiss the back of her hand.

'Is what happened with Jane the reason you avoided relationships—to protect yourself?'

I shrug and then sling my arm around her shoulders so we can be as close as possible while we wade through the warm, shallow water. 'Could you blame me?'

'No.' She looks gutted. 'But not all women are the same.'

'Of course not. But back then I felt like I'd tried to have something real and it backfired. Jane wasn't interested in a long-distance relationship with me, or travelling or studying abroad with me, as I naively dreamed. She wanted me for the LA celebrity lifestyle. She wanted me for Slay.

'As a kid, I used to wonder what it would be like to have a normal father who went to soccer games and taught me to surf. Instead I got the dad who offered me joints, took me to strip clubs and hit on my girlfriends...'

'Why didn't you tell me all of this before?' she whispers.

'I'm not proud of my behaviour when I first met you. I couldn't believe my luck that you didn't know Slay Coterill. I told him that you'd never heard of him once—best moment of my life. You should have seen his face...' My amusement quickly dries up. 'But my experience was of women who either assumed I'm just the like him or hoped that shagging me might earn them an introduction. The comparisons in the media didn't help, of course.'

Neve's arm tightens around my waist.

'After a while, I just played that role, because it helped me to lock down my emotions and armour myself against a repeat of the humiliation and betrayal.' But could I risk reaching for more? With Neve? Maybe the best way to have her in my life and protect her from Slay and my biggest fear—that she'll become embroiled in my family drama one time too many and decide I'm not worth the hassle—is to hold on tight and show her and the world her importance in my life.

She's everything.

'You know, I understand how you feel being compared. I used to feel like I grew up in Amber's shadow. She was taller, prettier, successful, even while we were still at school.'

I grow restless, a strong urge to kiss her senseless and confess how she makes me feel with just one of her beautiful smiles taking over. 'Amber is talented in one area, Neve. I doubt she could do what you do with all that auditing, number-crunching, investigative stuff you do. Height is part of the genetic lottery. And I one thousand per cent dispute the other claim.'

I bring us to a halt and turn, tugging her warm body into my arms. I press a kiss to her lips, gripping her waist with what feels like terrifying force.

During this trip, it's become crystal-clear that I'm one mistake away from sabotaging this. Unless I tell her how I feel about her…how I've always felt.

Or, better still, show her.

We pull apart, reluctantly on my side. Relief washes through me when I see her glazed eyes and parted lips, and feel the thud of her heart against mine, which tell me I'm not alone in this.

I press my lips to hers once more. 'You're beautiful and smart and funny and you fill my life with fucking sunshine.' I stare hard so she sees that I'm serious. 'You always have, Neve.'

'Not just regular sunshine…?' She smiles. I haul her up to my kiss as if she's my source of oxygen, breathing her in.

'I'm not insecure about it any more,' she says, dropping her face to my chest so I can no longer see her expression. 'And I love Amber, but sometimes it was hard feeling second best. First boy I ever fancied turned me down—not so unusual, I know—but then he asked me if my sister was single. That set the tone for my late teens and early twenties when we went out together—she'd attract all the attention, get the hottest guy, and I'd be left with the friend.'

I hold her tighter, my gut twisted with longing, wishing I could erase her past doubts. Because isn't what she just confided exactly what I did to her the night we met? 'You never told me that.'

Tension infects her body. 'Well, it seems silly

now. Besides, history repeated itself with you—I thought we were flirting that first night we met and before I know it you went home with my flatmate.'

I stiffen. 'Well, it was my loss. My immaturity and stupidity.' I hear her intake of breath, regret for the wasted time crushing me. I hold her and allow myself to admit I want to wake up with her every morning, not just the mornings we have left in the Maldives. My love for her is way beyond platonic. Perhaps it always has been. Perhaps that's why I freaked out when I met her so soon after having my heart broken, with my father's cynical advice ringing in my ears and the demons of that one terrible night haunting me...

'I fancied you back then, that first night. You knew that, right?' I should have told her this long ago. I had no idea I'd made her feel second best.

She freezes, almost as if she's stopped breathing. I've shoved us into uncharted territory. Discussing the night we met in any way beyond the sanitised version that spawned our friendship was previously taboo.

Then her chest slowly deflates, as if in a controlled exhale. 'You fancied anything with boobs back then,' she says, trying to downplay the seriousness of my confession. But it is fucking serious, the momentousness not lost on me if the band tightening across my chest is any indication.

'Not true. That university maths lecturer had a

very nice pair but I didn't fancy him.' I turn serious, grip her face and maintain eye contact, because I ache for her past disappointments. Knowing I might inadvertently have added to them by overlooking her that night through some sense of twisted, selfish self-preservation slices me open.

'I fancied you the minute I saw you,' I admit, recalling that night like it was yesterday. 'You were the prettiest girl in the place—why else would I make a beeline for you?'

I hear the breath catch in her throat, as if this is genuinely shocking news. As if she never, for one second, suspected I found her attractive before our fateful conversation about orgasms.

'But you didn't choose me.' Her voice is a whisper.

Shame streaks through my veins like lightning. 'That was because of my issues, nothing to do with you.' I lower my voice and force out the words I've bottled inside all these years. 'You were perfect that night. So perfect I'd never known anyone like you. But what I did know was that I wasn't in your league—that if I played my usual stunts, laid a single finger on you, I'd fuck it up. Ruin it for ever. Be just like my father. And I didn't want that with you. I wanted to keep you.' I brush my lips across her shoulder, feather-light.

She gapes, her eyes desperately flicking over my face, as if seeking the truth of my words.

'I was an arsehole,' I say. 'You knew it and, fortunately, so did I. I'm not proud of this, but I can't even remember your flatmate's name. And yet here you are, still the most important person in my life. I did choose you, Neve. It's just taken me this long to grow deserving enough to say that aloud.'

Wordlessly she wraps her arms around my neck and tugs me into her kiss. When we break apart for air, our foreheads resting together, weighty silence follows. I'm trapped, immobile, by my longing, and fear I'll ruin the best thing that's ever happened to me. But I know one thing for certain. I want more than this week. I want more than friends, even with the awesome benefits. I want Neve to truly be mine.

'I booked us a private island stay for tonight,' I tell her, my heart climbing into my throat. 'Will you stay there with me? Just the two of us?'

'Yes,' she says, with zero hesitation.

Hope soars in my chest. Maybe this time I've got this.

Maybe it's taken a trip to the world's most isolated group of islands to see what I've had in front of me all this time.

CHAPTER TWELVE

Neve

OUR LAVISH BUNGALOW on the private atoll is paradise. I emerge from the master suite, freshly showered and wearing the red dress Oliver liked from two nights ago. The silk glides over my tingling skin, which is sensitive from the sun and sea and the knowledge that I'm dressing sexily for a man with whom I'm falling desperately in love.

No. *Love* is too tame a word for the feelings crushing me. I loved my friend Olly. What I feel now is searing, out-of-control rapture. Bliss and dread rolled into one confusing tangle. Because I want Oliver, the Oliver I've come to know deeper than ever before, beyond this week. I want him for ever. And I want him to feel the same way about me. His confession about fancying me when we first met was achingly bittersweet and scary. Because it's given me hope. Hope to dream that maybe, this time, I could get the guy.

I step into the living room, catching sight of him staring out at the exquisite, uninterrupted ocean views. The setting sun halos him, pink and orange light streaming around his tall frame. My heart lurches against my ribs, pining for him.

I can't breathe.

I could go to him now. Tell him how I feel, how I've always felt about him. But to what end? I know my Oliver, and the odds are stacked against us. Yes, he had a crappy, erratic role model growing up, and had his teenage heart broken and trampled on by Slay's callousness. Only now do I fully understand the impact of that on his younger self-esteem, but there's no escaping the fact he's never once had a serious girlfriend since Jane. And, as much as I can't stop seeing a future for us romantically, I also don't want to be the guinea pig, the test case, even if he wanted more than our in-between relationship.

I've been there before with my exes, been the more committed person in the couple. I know where that leads—resentment, insecurity, heartache. And that's what I'd be with Oliver. While he bumbles along in his first relationship in nearly a decade, deciding if it's working for him.

What then? What if he decided it wasn't for him after all? How would I survive that?

If I can just get through the rest of the holiday unscathed… But it's growing harder to ignore how perfect he is for me, if only he believed himself capable of a committed relationship. If only he stopped comparing himself to a man he's nothing like.

If only he saw what I see.

My sigh expels a tiny part of my soul.

He turns, catching sight of me, and my heart stutters out of rhythm. He whistles, his eyes alight, as if with everything I wish to be true. Wish he'd say aloud. But I'm fooling myself. I feel as if I'm hurtling towards a brick wall with every hour that passes. The deadline to this fantasy looms.

'I love that dress.' He strides my way and my lungs try to escape my chest with every soft step of his bare feet in my direction. He presses his mouth to mine in a soft whisper of a kiss and takes both my hands. His eyes bore into mine, and I almost glimpse a flash of longing there, but then it's gone, replaced by his familiar grin. 'I've planned something special for tonight now I have you all to myself.'

My entire body shivers. Can't he tell I'd do anything for him? I've given myself over to him since we started this crazy sex-periment, and I have no regrets. Although I should have taken more care to armour my heart.

Nervous laughter bubbles from me. 'I'm not going naked scuba-diving, if that's what you have in mind.'

He shakes his head, a hint of mischief twitching his mouth. 'It's a little more personal than that—will you dance with me before dinner?'

'Of course.' Anticipation slithers down my spine. Why do I feel seduced, cherished? And ready to fling myself into the unknown, the way I dived from the back of the boat earlier?

He's arranged food, and the table on the veranda is beautifully set for a romantic dinner for two, but my throat is so tight with desire and love there's no way I could eat. Or even speak.

Soft music fills our bungalow, spilling out onto the beach from concealed outdoor speakers. He leads me onto the sand and then turns me into his arms. I settle against his chest with a soft sigh as he sways to the music. I breathe in the familiar scent of him, my face pressed to his shirt and the strip of his chest exposed at the open neck. I tell myself I don't need words or assurances, or for ever because this moment, this day, where we've laughed, shared and learned new things about each other, is perfect. He made each moment perfect, and that's enough for now.

His hands roam my back, holding me close, possessive but also restless, the same turbulence rolling through me because close isn't enough. It's never enough when we're together.

I look up and my breath catches. Playful, self-satisfied Oliver is nowhere to be seen. His eyes blaze with heat and vulnerability I've only seen in him once before, long ago, when he'd broken down after a few too many drinks and confessed sordid details about growing up with his father—finding

Slay passed out in the mornings after endless parties, driving him to rehab and standing by his side
at the altar for his many marriages, confused by his
own place in his father's cluttered and chaotic life.

But this has nothing to do with anyone else, only
us. How we've managed to carve out a utopian corner of paradise for ourselves to play out roles for
which neither of us has a script.

'Neve, I didn't know you could mean any more
to me.' He lowers his lips to mine, seemingly in no
hurry as he kisses and kisses and kisses me while
my toes sink deeper into the soft sand and I fall
apart in his arms. Because I love him so much, I
can't bear to think about the past we've wasted or
the uncertain future. Only this moment.

'Let's go to bed,' I say.

'If you insist,' he agrees.

Then I'm airborne, swung up into his arms, a
squeal breaking free. He strides towards the bungalow, carrying me. I want to make a joke about
my weight, or a quip about him working out, but
the look on his face, as if he wants to devour me,
stops such frivolity.

'Want to sleep out under the stars? I want us to
do more new things together. All of the things.'

My stomach flitters, but I nod my assent, because
I want the same. This unknown Oliver is as addictive as familiar Oliver.

At the day bed, a romantic outdoor canopied affair surrounded by gauzy curtains, he lowers me to my feet. He stands before me and without a word unbuttons his shirt, revealing the toned, tanned and tattooed torso I've learned by heart. I slide the straps of my dress from my shoulders, allowing the fabric to pool at my feet before kicking it away. I slide my hands around Oliver's waist, his warm skin over taut muscles the best aphrodisiac, if I needed one. But I don't. That I'm allowed to touch him after years of enforced hands-off makes for a dizzying reality.

He shoves down his shorts and boxers, adding them to the pile of discarded clothing. My strapless bra goes next—Oliver unhooks it with one hand. He drops to his knees, removes my thong and then he presses a kiss to my stomach, his hands on my hips, fingers gripping with passion that feels like ownership.

I cradle his head, slide my fingers through his flop of hair, which is less tamed and more beach-tousled than he normally wears it back in London—another thing that makes him seem old and new all at once. He climbs to his feet, his mouth sliding up the centre of my body, between my breasts, until he reaches my mouth. He kisses me, cupping my breasts, his thumbs working my nipples into sensitive, aching peaks. My core clenches, empty of him.

'Oliver,' I plead, wrapping my hand around his thick, erect length.

'Shh… Let me worship your body.' His mouth

closes around one nipple, stealing any argument I have with longing and sensation.

All he's done is worship me since that very first kiss. He's shown me what my body is capable of when I trust the person I'm with, when I surrender to his touch, safe in the knowledge he cares and won't let me down.

Or perhaps all I needed was love. To admit the depth of my love for him, and everything else would slot perfectly into place.

Somehow we make it to the bed, the cool slide of satin sheets a balm to my fevered skin. Oliver's mouth is all over me, kissing, licking, nibbling every inch of my skin from my neck to my thighs until I want to scream with frustration and I'm pink from the scrape of his facial hair.

'Please,' I beg again, my hand slipping between my thighs to give my clit some relief.

He pulls my fingers away and replaces them with his own, watching my reaction to his touch and his kisses.

'I'll never tire of making you come, of watching you come—it's addictive. Mine. You're mine, Neve.' He swaps his fingers for his mouth, sucking and laving my clit until I'm a writhing, shaking mess of need and yearning.

'I need you. Now. Oh, please, now!' I cry out as his mouth leaves me.

I grab his shoulders and tug, and he sits up between my spread thighs. His hand grips the base of his cock and he slides the tip over my engorged clit and through my moisture.

'Yes. Forget the condom,' I say, my voice breaking with urgency. 'I'm good if you are. Do it.' I'm aware I've reached the demanding stage of my arousal, but I'm helpless. He makes me helpless.

He scrunches his eyes closed and drops his head back. 'Neve, are you sure?' I've never heard his voice so dark with desire, not even last night, when our frantic coupling in the bathroom seemed to be about anger, challenge and claim.

'Yes.' I push up onto my elbows and grasp his steely buttocks, shunting his hips forward until the bare tip of him pushes inside me.

We both gasp. Oliver opens his eyes, takes my hands in his and slides the rest of the way into me until he's buried to the hilt and his face is transformed by his own desperate need.

'Fuck, you feel fantastic. I'll never want to leave,' he grits out, his eyes blazing into mine.

I'm so high on him, on us, the first flutters of an orgasm start. His slow, thorough thrusts shove me over the edge so I cry out, my stare locked on his beautiful face. But I'm greedy. I want more. I want everything he has to give me. I let go of his hands to squeeze my sensitive nipples as I lift my pelvis, meeting him thrust for thrust. Sweat breaks out at his hairline.

He's holding back. But I want him wild, teetering on the edge, a place I'm clawing at with my fingernails. I shove at his hips and roll over onto to my stomach. Before I can press up onto all fours, his body covers mine and he re-enters me from behind.

'Yes,' I hiss, because this way, me flat on my stomach and him deep inside, it's tighter, the friction almost unbearably good.

His hand burrows under my hip to stroke my clit as he pumps into me. 'Come again. Show me what I want to see,' he orders, and like his puppet I nod, because I'm almost there, my walls clamping around his shaft as a second orgasm strikes.

My cry is muffled into the pillow. And then I'm pressed into the mattress by Oliver's weight, flat out, his front plastered to my back and his face buried on my shoulder and the side of my neck.

'Neve!' He bellows my name seconds before he goes rigid and comes. And even then he won't stop. He flips me over and collapses on top of me where his hips buck, wringing the last of the pleasure from his heavy, spent body as he laves kiss after kiss over my chest, my neck and my face.

'I can't get enough of you,' he whispers, pressing his mouth to mine, and he's right. We're spent and sweaty, but already I want him back inside me. I feel his cock thicken and twitch against my stomach.

My final thought as we lose ourselves in each other's touch once more… How the hell will we ever stop this?

CHAPTER THIRTEEN

Oliver

THE PICTURE'S BLURRY, obviously taken using a tele-photo lens, but Neve and I are still recognisable, kissing on the deck of the boat after swimming with the wildlife. I make a fist and press it to the bridge of my nose, as if wishing it away will change the string of events. While Neve and I slept like two spoons in a drawer, blissfully unaware, the story of Slay Coterill's split from wife number six created a path of cyclonic destruction.

> *Bad rock and roll icon ditches wife number six...but will sometime on-again, off-again girlfriend of Coterill Junior ever make it across the finish line?*

My stomach roils with fury. I glance at the open windows. I left Neve in the shower five minutes ago while I ordered breakfast. I wanted everything about this day to be perfect. And now it's ruined. Because of me.

The story, which represents everything that's wrong about my life, everything I've tried to distance myself from, pulls me apart. It paints her not as the amazing, strong, independent woman she is— the most important woman in my life—but as the pathetic sidepiece of a man who can't commit. A man who doesn't deserve her. A man who is just like his father.

And perhaps the media is right. I've denied my feelings for Neve for nine years because of my issues. I've pretended and hidden away the vulnerable places in me that prevented me from considering a serious relationship. I've brought all of this down on her through my fears. It's a mess, exactly the kind I've dreaded, and I've dragged Neve into the circus.

I swear under my breath and slide my phone onto the table with jarring force. Her association with me—I can't bring myself to call it a friendship any longer—does nothing for her reputation. All I do is bring her down to my level. Slay's level. I can't protect her, and I've been fooling myself all these years that I could.

Further chills rack me—my romantic gesture of sleeping under the stars could have given the paps even more fodder, a more intimate photo…

With a stomach full of dread, I creep back into the room through the open French doors. She's towelling her hair dry, wearing one of my T-shirts, the wondrous sight of her making panic surge inside me.

'Breakfast is ready on the deck. It's another perfect day in paradise.' A perfect day for my perfect woman, only I have to spoil the mood with my news. I don't want to, don't want to remind her of the reality off this island, my reality, not when things between us are equally magical and fragile. Because I feel her emotional distance like a force field. She's holding back, and I don't blame her.

I need to tell her everything—secrets, declarations of my feelings, and of course the crap online. Perhaps then I can make all of this right. Because when I woke this morning, like every morning since we started our physical relationship, I watched her sleep, aching for her to open her eyes so I could be in her company. And I knew that, without her, I'm incomplete. I'm desperately in love with her, and I want to be her everything, as she is mine.

That means being open and vulnerable, and laying it all on the line.

I lift her hand to my mouth, brush my lips over her knuckles. My pulse leaps with trepidation. She's like hand-blown glass—one wrong move and I'll shatter the illusion of us with my bare hands—but a trickle of possibility meanders its way through the chaos in my head.

'I have ideas about how we can spend today horizontal, if you're interested,' she says, scooping both of her arms around my neck to draw me down to her kiss.

I lose myself for a few seconds, eager to blot out the world with her, naked and sated. But I'll have to tell her about the photo sooner or later. And I should have told her the other stuff long ago.

I pull back and hold her hand, my heartbeat seeming to resonate through my fingertips. The happy smile slides from her face.

'There's a photo on the gossip sites this morning,' I say, spewing out the words to get them over with. 'The two of us kissing yesterday on board the boat—there must have been left-over paps lurking, looking for Slay.'

She shrugs. 'So? I don't care. Forget about it.'

She's right—if it doesn't bother her, I shouldn't allow it to get to me. But it reminds me of the exposure I experienced as a child, growing up with Slay, and then later as a teen. Every move I made meant something to people I'd never met until I felt as if I didn't know who I was, just who I was supposed to be.

Slay's son.

And I'm more than that. I'm a man fit for this woman.

Neve, my safe haven—what I should be for her. I don't want her to read some garbage and doubt herself, doubt her place in my life, because she's a part of me, a vital part, and without her I can't exist.

'I know, I just…' I rub a hand over my face. 'I feel like I've let you down somehow, failed to protect you.'

'You haven't let me down.' She slides her thumb over my bottom lip. 'I don't care what they say about me.'

I want that to be true, but we all have our insecurities. Slay is mine.

I nod, although my head feels wooden, clumsy. 'I just… I don't want you to read it because I don't want you to believe what they say. I don't want you to feel inferior, pitied or second rate. You're not. The opposite, in fact.'

She stares, a million emotions flitting across her eyes, each of them leaving me more unnerved. 'Okay,' she says in an unconvinced tone.

But I can convince her. I can make this right. I can protect her and show her what she means to me in one move. Breath shudders out of me as the idea I've been ruminating on takes form.

Why not? We've known each other nine years. I'm in love with her. I want this. I can end the gossip and show the world exactly where my priorities lie.

I take her hands, gripping them tightly before slowly sinking to one knee.

She freezes, confusion slashed across her face, and then tries to tug me back to my feet. 'Oliver, what are you doing?'

I resist, looking up at her with a lump in my

throat. 'Neve,' I begin, ignoring her frown, 'you mean more to me than any other person on the planet. When I think of letting you go as soon as we touch down in London, I feel sick.'

Her breathing speeds up, her eyes swimming with emotions, not all of them good.

'I know you're pissed at me right now,' I add, 'because this is sudden—some would say crazy.' Yet, the more I think about it, the more sense it makes.

Please let her want the same.

'The caretaker here is a celebrant,' I continue as full understanding comes to her wary expression.

'So, Neve Sara Grayson, will you marry me?

CHAPTER FOURTEEN

Neve

I'M LIGHT-HEADED, AND the room is shifting alarmingly at the thought of what he's just asked me and what it means. He smiles, his beautiful Oliver smile that's playful and sexy and could be specifically designed to make me fall harder, although there's nowhere left for me to fall. I love him completely, bone-deeply, irrevocably.

But…

I grasp his fingers for fear of my legs giving way. This is off. Wrong. Perhaps some sort of sick joke, for which I'll seriously never forgive him.

My stomach rolls over with adrenaline. A few days ago I could only dream of this scenario. For a moment it makes me feel that, just maybe—the insanity of his timing and the motivation behind his proposal aside—this, us as a couple, could actually work. Haven't I always dreamed of being more to him than a friend, more than a friend he has sex with? Of being everything to him, the way he is everything to me?

But not like this—rushed, a rebound because of some negative press. I don't want to be a sticking plaster over the wound left by Slay. I want Oliver, but I don't want to be a relationship experiment. Whatever impulse or panic has him in its grip, he's clearly not ready for commitment. This is not the way I envisaged this fairy-tale moment.

I squeeze his fingers. 'Oliver, this is—'

'Don't say crazy,' he interrupts. 'Because it makes sense. *We* make sense.' He stands and grips both of my hands. 'You want to settle down, to find someone, but you won't find what you're looking for on a dating app.' His words are urgent, impassioned. 'I know. I used to be one of those guys using apps to hook up with women. But now we've broken down this barrier we used to keep our friendship intact. We're amazing together and we're still best friends.'

His words, wonderful words, would have thrilled me a week ago. But it feels like this proposal has more to do with Slay than us. If he'd simply asked for a relationship I would have said yes. Because we can't go back after everything we've shared. I'll never be content to meet him for coffee or go to a movie and say goodbye as if this week hasn't happened.

But neither can we rush this. We can't jump several dating steps just because we know all there is to know about each other. I have to make him understand, to salvage this.

'Why don't we try dating when we get home?' I say, my voice almost desperate. 'There's no need to rush.' Despite the temptation to say yes, to have the fairy-tale moment just this once. To be the first choice of the man of my dreams, a man I thought I'd have to give up soon. But I don't want to be temporary. I haven't waited nine years to be his commitment guinea pig, only to be cast aside when he discovers he's not ready to abandon his single life after all.

He's never had a fling that lasts longer than a week. Women come and go. Beautiful women, some he has lots in common with, some clearly keen for more than what's on offer. And the end has nothing to do with his father, as he'd claim, and everything to do with him. To do with his belief that somehow he's no good at relationships because of his role model, or that he doesn't deserve one because of his wild youth, or that he'll only get hurt again the way Jane hurt him.

But what if I surrendered to my weak inner voice, the one telling me that this is what I've craved all along?

No. It's a guarantee of the heartbreak I fear. He'll soon grow bored of trying to outrun those demons which, if his turmoil over Slay's latest antics is any proof, are still very much alive and kicking. He'll decide he was premature and still wants to play the field, something that helps him keep at bay feeling too deeply.

He's nothing like his father, but nor is he ready to commit or to be a husband.

And what then for me? I already know I want all of him, to be all to him.

No, I have to be strong.

I suck in a shuddering breath. I can't risk saying yes just to know how that feels before I'm flung back to reality. A reality without my lover *or* my best friend. Worse off than when I came to these islands. Because losing one means losing both. If I loved him less fiercely, maybe I could go along for the ride with this impromptu proposal.

Oliver steps closer and grips my face, his animated eyes holding mine. 'We've known each other a long time. Now that we've made the leap into lovers, this is just one more leap. I know I don't deserve you, but I can try.'

'Of course you deserve me. That's part of the issue.'

He's not hearing me and his touch, his palms on my skin, so familiar, so good, now feels too cloying.

'If you're worried about the ceremony here being legally binding, we can make it official as soon as we get back to London,' he says. 'Then I'll issue a press release. Announce our marriage.'

'What? Why would you do that?' I ask, dumbfounded. He's thought this all the way through, while I've been blissfully ignorant, simply celebrating our deepening connection and imagining that perhaps we could have something real. That perhaps he really has changed and is ready to settle down. But this feels like a circus act, exactly the kind of scene he says he hates and usually attributes to Slay.

'Because, if we make us official,' he says, taking both my hands and squeezing, 'they'll have nothing more to print about you the next time they print a story about Slay. Because that will stop my father coming between us.'

And there it is, his motivation for this rash proposal. Nothing to do with love or feelings for me. Not a reflection of the growing closeness I've experienced this week. Just another show of one-upmanship with his father, a way to ensure history doesn't repeat itself and a ruthless guarding of his emotions, just like the Oliver I first met.

My heart clenches so violently, I feel my pulse to the tips of my toes. And I know, with a certainty that leaves me hollow, that my fairy-tale romance with Oliver is over.

CHAPTER FIFTEEN

Oliver

'OLIVER,' SHE SAYS, her eyes full of pain. 'I know you've been let down in the past, hurt, but you can't control what other people think or say. Not the press, and not Slay. All you can do is control how *you* react,' she says, making all kinds of sense. But I'm crazy in love with her—sense left the building days ago. This isn't going the way I'd planned. We should be kissing through happy tears by now, back in bed or flying to Male, the capital, to go engagement-ring shopping…

I know on an intellectual level that what she says is rational, but I've spent my entire adult life trying to keep a lid on this kind of exposure, to distance myself from Slay and the type of publicity he invites. Only now it feels worse, because I love her. I'm vulnerable because she's under attack. What hurts her kills me, especially when I'm the one responsible for that pain. This is why I've always avoided this feeling—fear, loss of control, failing Neve.

My mouth feels dry. She doesn't love me back. Or she doesn't think me capable of the emotion. I've finally worked up the courage to be open about my feelings for her and she doesn't share them.

She tugs the neck of the T-shirt, covering her exposed, sun-bronzed shoulder from my view. That drives a stake through my heart and the romantic morning I had planned, ripe with fresh starts and possibilities. Now only the usual shit-storm Slay Coterill leaves in his wake remains.

No, this mess is of my creation. If I'd been honest from the start, if I'd done what Neve said and put to rest Slay and how I've allowed fear to hog-tie me, none of this would matter.

'So, you're saying no…is that it?' I ask, waves of dread rolling through me.

'It's not that.' She looks away. 'It's just… I don't think we should rush into anything foolhardy,' she explains, immune to my stillness. 'Isn't it better to let Slay's latest marital implosion blow over and focus on your deal with the Japanese?' Her expression grows decidedly shady, something that raises every hair on my strung-taut body.

My anger is self-directed, my secret past proving that I've inherited Slay's weakness of character.

Neve must sense my brittle tension. She looks up, her eyes pleading. 'You've avoided commitment all these years. I just want you to be sure you're ready. This…this was just a holiday fantasy.' Her words are a whisper, cautious and edgy. Pain lances me as if I've been speared through.

'So you only want the fantasy?' I knew this was too good to be true, that I wasn't good enough. I knew I couldn't truly have her. 'You don't want me?' Betrayal sours my tongue, even as my blood runs cold with the knowledge I've done this by keeping secrets and keeping a distance.

'Oliver, I'm not saying that… But you've never had a relationship that's lasted longer than a week.'

I can't look away from her eyes, which seem to communicate something different from the words she's using to destroy me.

'I'm just protecting myself from the inevitable.' She presses her hand to her chest, as if she too feels pain. 'Because of course this will end, and I'll just be good old friend-Neve again.'

'I understand that you want to protect yourself.' I've been trying to protect her from me for our entire friendship. I'm not a safe bet. My track record, my genes, the skeletons littering my closet… She'd be mad to make me the person responsible for her happiness. 'I want to protect you too—from gossip and from Slay.'

'But a rushed proposal doesn't do that, don't you see? You're just reacting to what's going on around you—this latest Slay scandal. Our physical connection is amazing, but shouldn't we see if we work in the real world first?'

Pressure builds in my head. She believes me incapable of more than sex, more than a superficial, hollow relationship. Just like the kind in which Slay specialises.

'So, you don't think I can do more than fuck?' I turn away, pace to the window and stare blindly through the mosquito nets while impotence and rejection crush me.

'I don't mean that. I just...' She growls in frustration, and in my peripheral vision I see her bury her face in her hands.

Icy calm settles over me, extinguishing the flames, razing us as a couple to the ground. 'No, it's okay. You're right. I'm no good at commitment, but I am good at fucking.' I spin to face her, my breath sawing through my lungs. 'You had your orgasms, but anything more... Hell, who are we kidding? I'm my father's son after all.'

She pales, her eyes huge. 'I'm not saying that. You're putting words into my mouth.' She deflates on a defeated sigh. 'Perhaps we were better off as friends.' The last is a hushed murmur, as if she fears the power of those words. With good cause, because they can end this, and what then? Is there anything left to return to?

'Olly,' she pleads, returning to the shortened version of my name I associate with her friendship and nothing more. 'I've seen new things about you this week, things I didn't know before. Wonderful things. But I've also witnessed how you feel about yourself when Slay is around. How this proposal seems to have arisen out of your fear that you're like him and can't commit. But I don't want to be just a quick fix.'

Uncontrollable need blasts through me. Need to destroy this once and for all to make this feeling of splintering apart stop. Because she's right. We've destroyed what we had and for what? So we could get our rocks off? So I could confirm what I already knew? That love is a mug's game, designed to weaken. And that I'll never be able to shake the association with Slay.

'It's okay, Neve. You're right. I would have screwed this up eventually. You know it. I know it. Hell, even Slay knows it. He tried to warn me the other night.'

She sits on the bed as if this conversation is taking a toll on her ability to stand. 'What do you mean?'

I scrub a hand over my face, wishing I could walk out of the doors and keep on walking. But every coffin needs a final nail and, if I hammer it in good and strong, I can retreat to lick my wounds safe in the knowledge I won't see Neve's disappointment ever again. 'His comment about sharing wasn't about threesomes. It was a warning. A reminder to me that we're more alike than I care to admit.'

'Stop saying that. It's only true if you let it become true.'

I nod, my grin sickening. 'It's already true. The night I learned the lessons of love from Slay, the night of the strip club, I went home alone while he stayed on to party.' My mind sounds an alarm. Once I tell her this, she'll look at me the way Slay did that night, with a slimy smile—part fury, part triumph—as if I'd played right into his hands and I was finally a son he could relate to and be proud of.

'I was drunk, furious with myself for being foolish enough to go to him for advice, humiliated and belittled. My heart was shredded, confused, uncertain what to believe but sick that what Slay told me might be true. When I slammed into the kitchen, in search of more beer to numb the pain and stupidity I felt, Slay's third wife, Aubrey, was there.'

The growing horror in her eyes should warn me off. But I'm too far gone, and ruining this for good is the only way to protect me from the pain of knowing I've lost her faith.

'She came on to me, right there in the kitchen of my father's house,' I continue. 'She was only a few years older than me, perhaps twenty-three. When she kissed me, I felt appalled, disgusted and euphoric all at once. It was as if I could exact revenge on Slay for a lifetime of being a shitty role model. For subjecting my teenage years to a string of stepmothers barely older than me. For caring more about fame and his rock-and-roll lifestyle than his only son. And most of all for kicking me when I was down, as if my feelings meant nothing.'

My fists clench at my sides and I stare deep into Neve's eyes.

'I kissed her back. Angry.' My words fall into the distasteful silence of the room. 'I knew it was wrong, we both did, but she didn't stop, and neither did I. I hated my life so much in that moment that hating myself for my actions seemed inconsequential.'

Neve shifts, her hands jerking in my direction as if to touch me, but I still her with a single quelling look. I need to finish the whole tale, because if she didn't want me before she'll definitely reject me after. At least then I'll know where I stand.

'After we'd finished, when I came to my senses, my head spinning drunk, I ran to the bathroom and threw up my disgust into the toilet until I could barely move. But the damage was already done. She'd wanted out of the marriage anyway, so she told Slay we'd slept together as a parting gesture.' A humourless snort blasts free. 'He wasn't even angry. He simply shrugged, as if I'd finally become what he expected.'

My stomach roils. 'I left that night, sickened by the fact that I'd become just like him, and burning from the humiliation that I might have been used in some sort of sick marital game.'

The filthy feeling returns now, coating me in its oily grasp. I stare hard at Neve, hating the unspoken judgment blaring from her hurt stare.

'That's what Slay meant by "sharing". His reminder to me that the apple never falls far from the tree, and that sex is just another form of currency.' But for a while, with her, I'd believed it could be different…

'So, don't worry,' I finish. 'You've made your feelings perfectly clear and, as you now know, you're right about me. I'm not good enough for you. I never was.'

I turn my back on her, swish the curtains aside and leave.

CHAPTER SIXTEEN

Neve

THE SPREADSHEET SWIMS before my eyes, the columns of numbers spinning like dials. I press my glasses to the bridge of my nose and close my eyes, hoping that when I reopen them the world will make sense once more.

It's my first day back at work since returning alone from the Maldives. Oliver's plane flew the entire wedding party back to London, minus our host, who, Shelley informed me, flew to Japan the day of our confrontation to run damage limitation on the Kimoto deal.

They had been long days since Oliver and I parted ways. Angry. Resentful. And, for my part, shattered into a million grains like sand.

How can we have gone so wrong? And why did I risk it all, risk what I had? Risk losing him.

It aches. My entire body. My mind. My soul.

I abandon my computer screen and open my

phone. I've composed and deleted hundreds of texts without sending a single message.

I've communicated with Oliver one way or another every day for the past nine years, and now, when I feel like I'm splitting in two, I need him more than ever. He's always been there to mop tears, hug me or tell me a stupid joke to cheer me up. But now there's radio silence. *Mutual* silence. Because I don't know how to reach out to him. I don't know what to say that he'll believe. All I know is that I fell in love with him all over again. Stronger, deeper, without hope of redemption. Because, where before my love for him was a puddle, this is the deepest fathom of the ocean.

And then I let him down. I didn't see what he tried to show me. I hurt him—an unforgivable act from a woman who's supposed to be his best friend, and in love with him to boot.

My phone pings, and my heart bangs against my ribs until I see it's from my friend Grace. She's replied to my SOS: I'm working a late shift today so can meet you for a cuppa in fifteen. Usual place?

I type out a reply and save my work, although there's not much point in being at the office today, I'm that ineffective. I tell my assistant I'll be back in an hour and then I wrap up in my coat and scarf and head out into a frigid London day.

The fresh, brisk walk should clear my head. But all I can see is Oliver's face swimming in front of my eyes, streaked with pain and betrayal. He opened himself to me and I ran from him, scared I'd never truly get what I want. Terrified that I'd never stack up, because Oliver's proposal, his solution to the photograph, had resounded with panic. And I couldn't trust it. I couldn't trust myself to be objective—something I've never been with my feelings for Oliver.

But of course he'd try to distance himself from his father, distance me from association. He's been doing it most of his adult life. Could it be that protecting me all these years might also have held him back from exploring us…?

And the rest… Slay, his stepmother… I only care that Oliver's punishing himself.

Grace sits at our usual table in the little tea shop not far from my office. Her tan from her holiday in Fiji last month has mostly faded, but there's joy shining in her eyes that not even my plea for help and my current expression can diminish.

She's in love.

The wind is knocked from me and it's hard to breathe.

'I've ordered our usual,' she says, although I doubt I'll be able to swallow anything past my constricted throat.

'Thanks,' I mutter, unwinding my scarf and draping my coat over the back of the chair. 'I wouldn't have texted on your afternoon off, except—'

'Except you needed a friend. And here I am.' Her sympathetic stare floods my stinging eyes with moisture. I blink it away and slump into a chair in defeat.

'Tell me,' she orders.

I drag in a shuddering breath. 'I messed up.'

'You told Oliver how you feel.' It's not a question and it makes me wince, because that's what I should have done. Right from the start. Instead I slept with him, ruined our friendship and then I still didn't tell him. I just turned him down and stamped on his feelings.

'Not exactly…' I hedge, dread rolling through me, because Grace will need all the details, which means reliving every wonderful and then disastrous moment.

She waits patiently. Grace is good at patience, and I need the breathing space, because I'm light-headed with regret.

'We slept together and it was great,' I say, holding up a hand to ward off any wise interruption. 'I know what you're going to say, and I didn't let it go to my head. But…somehow I ended up hurting him. Because I got scared…and I didn't trust in us… and now I don't know how to make it right. I don't know where he is or if he ever wants to talk to me again. I think I've killed our friendship. Lost him for ever.' I sag back in my seat, drained.

Sympathy hovers in her compassionate stare.

'Tell me everything,' she says, pouring tea into delicate floral cups.

So I do.

When I finish my rambling tale, my tea is cold, my scone is untouched and Grace's brows are pinched in a frown.

'So he actually proposed?' Her eyes flick to my bare left hand.

I nod. 'Yes, but you know what Oliver is like. It was an impulse, almost a joke... No.' I throw myself back in the seat, because I'm all over the place, my words as jumbled as my thoughts. 'Not a joke.'

'And you said no?'

I nod, my eyes stinging. 'It wasn't real. Tourist marriages in the Maldives are ceremonial only.'

'Did it feel real?' Grace asks tentatively. 'Because why would he ask if he doesn't love you and want to make a serious commitment?'

Good question. I open my mouth to answer. No words. My jaw hangs while my mind kick-starts and races for the first time in three days.

Could it be that simple...?

'Sounds to me like he's in love with you, sweetie,' says Grace when I remain stunned silent.

'No...' But...could Oliver really be in love with me? Could he want a real relationship? Have I been so desperate to protect myself from heartache, so convinced he wasn't ready for more, that I ignored the signs?

'And you're definitely in love with him.'

I nod, tears building in my aching throat.

Grace signals the waitress, who miraculously brings a fresh pot of tea for me along with a clean cup and saucer. 'Of course Oliver would doubt that he had anything to offer you after what you've just told me about his relationship with his father.' She covers my numb hand with hers. 'But you need to tell him how you feel. That you love him, more than a friend.' She pours me a fresh cup of tea, and this time I take a grateful sip, because tea makes everything better, so maybe it will infuse my mind with logic and clarity.

'What are you afraid of?' she asks, cutting right to the core of the issue.

I drag in a deep breath, steeling myself. 'That I'm not enough for him, or that I'm too much because he's avoided relationships all of his adult life. I'll be his experimental case. What if he decides it's too hard? Relationships take work. He'll tire of us and move on and I'll risk everything but still lose him.'

Grace nods, her face serious, so I feel marginally appeased for my rambling thoughts. 'Well, there are certainly no guarantees in any relationship, but you and Oliver have a better chance than most. You know each other better than anyone else. You have a long and solid friendship on which to build a relationship. And, if you don't tell him how you feel now, it might be too late.'

I nod, almost unconsciously. She's right. I do know him. I know everything about him, because he's always shown me that he values me. That he cares. He's capable of the kind of commitment I'm looking for, because he's given me that from day one. With his friendship. I have to trust that he can move past his insecurities over Slay and extend that commitment to our romantic relationship.

Perhaps I'm the one holding back.

I wince, because where he's confessed his deepest shame, making himself vulnerable like never before, I didn't fight for him. I allowed him to assume that I'd judged him. I didn't chase after him and explain myself. I've been the worst friend, too scared to put myself out there like he did, lay myself open and say the words.

Because he doesn't know me. He doesn't know everything. In order to guard my heart, I've fooled myself that all I want is the pretence of him, when really, I want it all. I don't need to cling to my fears, not when there's so much at stake. The ultimate prize. Oliver.

I stand so suddenly, my chair scrapes and several pairs of eyes look our way.

'Where are you going?' Grace asks, as with trembling hands I tug the end of my scarf from under the leg of the chair.

'I have to go and tell him that I love him. Because I don't think he knows.'

I flick her a wobbly grin, too panicked to say anything further, but she's a good friend. She understands.

Grace smiles widely. 'Of course he doesn't, otherwise he'd never have let you go.'

CHAPTER SEVENTEEN

Oliver

MY VIEW OF London from my Canary Wharf office holds none of its usual charm. I disconnect the call to a member of my legal team. The good news that Kimoto Corp finally purchased my artificial intelligence software for a nine-figure sum falls hollow. I stare blindly out of my window, frozen with inertia.

I'll probably make the business news tomorrow, for all the right reasons. But the victory means less—nothing, in fact—when I can't celebrate with Neve.

I scrub a hand over my face, closing my eyes for a brief moment. I see her face, her look of horror when I told her how much like Slay I'd behaved in the past. I wrench my eyes open. I don't need to see that expression to recall it, because that's the moment I knew I'd lost her for good. Both any feelings she had for me and her friendship.

So how the hell do I move on now?

My indiscretion is in the past. Teenage years are the time to make mistakes and grow up. The point is to outgrow that propensity. Some of us do, and some of us don't—like Slay. But I made another mistake back then. A worse one, with longer reaching consequences.

I hid my feelings for Neve. I told myself I didn't deserve her, and denied my attraction, and that's the thing I'd change if I had one time-travelling wish.

Because I love her and there's nothing more real, more deserving.

I don't want to move on. I don't have to. I just need to convince her that no one will ever love her more.

I jolt to my feet, energised into action. At that moment a message arrives from my assistant.

'I have Neve Grayson here. She says it's urgent.'

I fumble to fasten my jacket buttons as I stride to the door. I swing it open, my heart in my throat. And there she is.

Her cheeks are ruddy, perhaps from the cold outside, and she's huffing, as if she took the stairs all the way to the fortieth floor.

'Hi,' I say, stunned by the wonderful, beautiful sight of her, an automatic smile tugging my mouth. 'I was just on my way to find you. Come in.' I step aside, gesture her into the office and close the door.

I don't think my heart could beat any faster.

She turns to face me and for several endless seconds we stand and stare.

I snap to my senses. 'Would you like a drink?' I ask, not sure what to do with my hands short of touching her, so I stuff them in my pockets.

'No, thanks.' She fidgets with the scarf in her hand.

'Can I take your coat?' Why is this so awkward? And how can I make it right? Because I need to make it right. I refuse to lose her. I'll do whatever it takes, be whatever she wants. But her absence from my life is not an option I can tolerate.

She shrugs out of the coat and tosses it on the leather sofa nearby. 'I'm sorry to interrupt. I'm sure you're busy.'

'I'm not too busy for you,' I say, my mouth full to bursting with all the other things I want to say. 'You look great, by the way.' Her tan still glows, bringing out the flecks of moss-green in her eyes. 'I missed you.'

Fuck it. I don't care if she hates me now. I don't care that I might be repulsive in her eyes. I need to tell her all the things crushing me, because I should have said them nine years ago and I have nothing else to lose.

'Oliver…' Her hesitation sickens me, but I'm past caring, because I'm less without her, and I want to be whole. To be worthy of her, even if I can't be with her.

'I need to tell you something,' I say. 'I should have told you this nine years ago. I love you, Neve. I should have said it sooner.'

My voice catches and I make a fist inside my pocket. 'Perhaps you can't think of me that way, after...everything...but I still want you to know how I feel. Because you were never second best. I chose you the day we met. You were a breath of fresh air in my life. You rescued me from the destructive, self-loathing path I'd gone down. I wanted you in my life but I wasn't ready, wasn't mature enough to handle you back then, to deserve you. You mattered to me more than anyone else. You still do. And you always will.'

She swallows hard, her big eyes round.

'And you were right about me.' I rush on, saying it all before she decides to leave. 'Everything you said was true. I'm not Slay. Nothing like him. I don't care what other people say or think. Because all I really care about is you. Your happiness. And, if you're happier without me in your life, or if you want to just go back to being friends, then I'll do whatever it takes to fix this, because you make me a better man. You always have. And I absolutely cannot lose you.' I take a half-step closer. 'I can't.'

Her hands flinch at her sides, the only move she makes. I swallow down the crushing trepidation that feels like acid and force my features into some sort of neutral smile, while every emotion roars in my head, warp-factor ten.

'I don't want to be your friend,' she says.

I exhale a part of me I know I'll never get back.

'I understand.' I hate the flatness of my voice, because I'm a liar. I just told her whatever she wanted would be okay with me. But it's *not* okay. It will never be okay that she's not mine.

'No.' She shakes her head. 'I don't think you do, because I've always hidden how I feel about you.' She steps closer too, so we're only a couple of feet apart. One move and I could touch her, but instead I force myself to focus on her words.

'I lied and pretended and denied my feelings so I could be your friend. I told myself I stood no chance with you, so what was the point of risking your friendship?' she says. 'Because that was the only way I could handle my feelings for you and keep them a secret. I took any part of you I could get rather than being nothing to you.'

'You were never nothing,' I bite out, pressure building in my head. 'You're everything.'

She wrings her hands. 'But I deceived you. Because a part of me has always loved you from the start, and now I'm so desperately in love with you that I messed everything up.'

I shake my head. Her words make no sense. I'm the one who messed up.

'I hurt you when you opened yourself up to me,

because I was too scared to be as vulnerable as you were.' Her eyes plead. 'But friendship won't satisfy me any longer. I want more. I want all of you—every bad, sexy, playful, caring inch.'

I can hardly compute what she's saying. 'You should have told me.' It comes out sounding like an recrimination but the only person I blame is myself. 'Back then. And I should have told you.'

She nods. 'Maybe neither of us was ready nine years ago, but I should have told you how I feel in the Maldives rather than let you leave thinking I care about something you did as an angry, confused teenager. I don't care about anything but you. Us. I don't care about Slay, or the past or the press. I just want you. I love you.'

I stride to her, then scoop her up in my arms and kiss her. 'I love you too. God, do I love you.' I kiss her smiling lips. 'So much. So much it hurts.'

Her arms come around my waist, under my suit jacket, and she holds me tight. She laughs, tears in her eyes as she accepts my crazed kisses peppering her face and returns them with a few of her own. But it's not enough. It will never be enough. I'll always want more of my wondrous Neve.

'We're such idiots.' She sniffs and buries her head against my chest, over my pounding heart.

'I agree. There are elements of the ridiculous about us, but that's why we're meant for each other.'

'You really love me?' she asks, a soft murmur.

I nod, my chest full to bursting. 'I love you so much that I can't breathe or think or function without you. I love you so much that I binge-watched that baking show you love last night. I've binned any trace of coconut in my pantry, just in case, and I found four videos of cute puppies I want to send you—the ones that make you cry.'

Her smile tears my heart in two. 'That *is* a lot.'

I stride to the sofa, sitting down with her in my lap so we can resume the kissing in comfort.

She straddles my thighs, her skirt riding up as our kisses grow heated. Then she pulls back, the look of love and lust on her face making her more exquisite than ever. 'Do you have meetings this afternoon?' She wriggles on my lap and I forget what day it is, let alone what's on my schedule.

'Yes,' I say with a sinking feeling in my gut. 'You?'

'Yes.' She sighs, leaning forward to kiss my neck.

'I'll cancel them,' I tell her without hesitation. There's nothing more important to me than Neve.

She looks up with that naughty glint in her eye, her bottom lip trapped under her teeth. 'I will too. Let's be bad and play hooky together.'

'Deal.' I kiss her once more. 'But first I need to do something.' I retrieve the ring box from my pocket. Even consumed with business during my brief trip to Japan, she was at the forefront of my mind. Purchasing an engagement ring I know she'll love was my first priority when the plane touched down.

I take the ring from the box, feeling her held breath and her eyes on me, and hold it up between us. 'I should have done it properly the first time, because I meant every word. So I'll ask you again. A fresh start.

'Neve Sara Grayson, I'll love you for ever. I'm less without you. So, will you marry me?'

'Yes,' she says, laughing and crying at the same time. Kissing me, holding out her trembling hand for my ring.

I press a kiss to her ring finger, my lips lingering for a few heartbeats, and then slide the diamond in place. 'There—now you're finally mine.'

'Yes, and you're mine—so take me home, so we can do dirty things to each other.'

'Whatever you say, my darling. It will be my pleasure.'

EPILOGUE

Two months later, Christmas Eve

Neve

OLIVER AND I have spent Christmas together before, at my parents' or his mother's, but never just the two of us. And this year, as the song goes, he's all I want for Christmas. For ever.

I've lit the fire in his huge living room for that festive feel, but I've also deliberately cranked the heating up so high that he's wandering around in just his jeans and a Christmas apron I gave him as an early present. It says, *Screw nice, let's be naughty.* It's all part of my cunning plan to get him naked… And to think that he lived under the mistaken impression that I'm somehow sweet for nine years.

We've spent the afternoon baking mince pies together and drinking mulled wine. He suggested a Christmas movie, but his penthouse apartment is so pretty—both inside, with a huge tree, and outside, with views of a glittering London from the wall of windows—that together with the arresting sight of his sexiness there's enough visual distraction.

He comes up behind me and traps me where I'm leaning against the wiped-clean kitchen counter with one arm each side. He nuzzles my neck, sending delicious shivers down my spine.

'I'm so glad you're here,' he says, kissing my temple.

'Me too.' I lift my mouth up to his kiss and turn to face him, wrapping my arms around his waist. 'So, what's your Christmas wish?' I slide my hand up his naked back and walk my fingers over his shoulder and down his chest.

'Well, that's easy. You. For ever. You're also going to be my New Year's resolution, by the way.' His lips trail my jaw and down my neck and I loll my head to the side, giving him access as desire grips me. After all, it has been all of four hours since we were last naked together...

'Well, we'd better start planning our wedding, then,' I say, smiling when he jerks upright, his handsome face alive with wonder and hope.

'Really?' He grips my waist, lifting me up, and I cling to his hips with my thighs.

'Really,' I say, kissing him as he walks us to the enormous white leather sofa facing the fire.

We shed our clothes, laughing, kissing and loving each other, exactly the way we were meant to be. When he's laid out on top of me, love and passion in his expression, I'm momentarily distracted.

'Oliver, can you smell burning?' I ask.

He stops kissing my chest and sniffs the air. 'Fuck, I think it's the mince pies.'

I hold in a laugh. 'Oh, dear,' I say, wrapping my legs around his hips to stop his escape. 'So there is something you're no good at. Don't worry. Keep practising. We'll make a cook of you yet.'

'Sod it.' He grins, his mouth finding my nipple in a pinch of revenge that only encourages me to tease him more. 'I have smoke alarms.'

And then we lose ourselves in one of the things he excels at.

Friends. Lovers. In love.

* * * * *

A BABY ON HER CHRISTMAS LIST

LOUISA GEORGE

To Iona Jones, Sue MacKay, Barbara DeLeo,
Kate David and Nadine Taylor, my gorgeous Blenheim
girls – thank you for the great weekend at the cottage
and your amazing help to brainstorm this book.

You guys definitely know how to rock a
writing retreat. xx

CHAPTER ONE

Nine months ago...

'I'VE FOUND A baby daddy!' Georgie's wide grin shone brighter than the Southern Cross, her dark brown eyes sparkling even in the bar's dim light.

Liam watched, dumbfounded, as excitement rolled off her, so intense it was almost tangible.

'Well, not a daddy as such. I should really stop saying that. But I have found someone who would be perfect to donate his sperm...which I know makes you shudder, so I'm sorry for saying The Word.' She gave Liam a wicked wink that was absolutely at odds with this whole one-sided conversation.

Whoa.

Too gobsmacked to speak, Liam indicated to her to sit. She tossed her silk wrap and bag on the back of a chair, put her drink down on the table and plonked in the seat opposite him at the only free table in Indigo's crowded lounge.

A baby?

He felt the frown forming and couldn't control it—even if he'd wanted to—and finally found his voice. 'Hey, back right up, missy. Am I dreaming here? I thought you just said something about a baby...'

It had been too long since he'd seen her looking so happy so he was wary about bursting her bubble—but, hell, he was going to burst it anyway. Because that's what real friends did—they talked sense. Just like she'd done the first time they'd met, in the sluice room of the ER; he a lowly med student, losing his cool at the sight of a lifeless newborn, she a student nurse with more calm and control and outright guts than anyone he'd ever met. She'd let him shake, allowed him five minutes to stress out, then had forced him back into the ER to help save the kid's life. And they'd been pretty much glued at the hip ever since.

So he needed to be honest. He raised his voice over the thump-thump-thump of the bar's background bass that usually fuelled their regular Friday night drinking session, but tonight the noise was irritating and obnoxious. 'I go away for three months and come back to sheer madness. What happened to the *Nothing's going to get in the way of those renovations this time*? *I'm on the real estate ladder now and going up.* What the hell, Geo? A baby? Since when was that on your to-do list?'

Stabbing the ice in her long glass with a straw, she looked up at him, eyes darker now, and he caught a yearning he'd seen glimpses of over the last ten years. She thought she hid it well, but sometimes, when she was distracted or excited, she let her tough guard slip. 'You, of all people, know I've always wanted a family, Liam. It may not have been at the top of my list because I always believed it would just happen at some point. But I can't keep putting it off and leaving it to chance, because chance isn't going my way. And I refuse to prioritise decorating over having a baby. That would be stupid.'

In his opinion, having a baby was right up at the top of stupid but he kept that to himself. And, for the record, it wasn't just decorating—her house needed knock-down-and-start-again renovations. 'But what's the hurry? You're only twenty-eight. It will happen, you've got plenty of time. You just need to find the right guy.' And why that made him shudder more than the *sperm* word, he didn't know.

She let the straw go, then pulled a hair tie from her wrist and curled her long wavy hair into a low ponytail. Her hair was the same colour as caramel, with little streaks of honey and gold. He didn't need to get any closer to know that it smelt like apples or fruit or something vaguely edible. And clearly he'd been away too long if he was starting to notice stuff like that.

Luckily she was oblivious to him staring at her hair and thinking about its colour and smell. 'Oh, yes, and the candidates for husband are queuing up at the door, aren't they? You may have noticed that the pickings for Mr Perfect are slim and slimming further by the day in Auckland. There's a man drought. It's official apparently, New Zealand has a lot fewer men than women my age. Why do you think I've needed you to…*expedite* a few dates for me?' Her shoulders slumped. 'I know we've had fun setting each other up with potentials over the years, but I'm starting to think that—'

'That maybe you're too…picky?' He raised his glass to her. 'Hey, I don't know, but perhaps you could consider only having a one-page check-box list that potentials need to tick, instead of fifteen?'

Her eyes widened as she smiled. 'Get out of here. It is nowhere near fifteen.'

'Not on paper, no. But in your head it is. I've seen you in action, remember. *He's not funny enough. Too intense. Just a joker. Doesn't take me seriously. Just wanted a one-nighter.*' Truth was, Liam had been secretly pretty damned proud she'd spurned most of his mates' advances and that she'd ended most flings before they'd got serious. There was something special about Georgie and she deserved a special kind of bloke. He hadn't met one yet that would be worthy of her.

'So I have standards. I'd settle for Mr *Almost* Perfect if he existed—which he doesn't. I'm getting too short on time.' Her red, loose-fitting summer dress moved softly as she shrugged delicate shoulders. 'I don't know about you, but I get the feeling that asking a man to father your children on a first date might just scare him off.'

'Well, hell, if I asked a man to father my children on any date it'd either be in a nightmare or because I was hallucinating.'

She rolled her eyes. 'You know very well what I mean. And, yes, you are the straightest guy I've ever met.' Her eyes ran over his chest, lingering a little over his pecs, throat, mouth. Why he noticed he didn't know. And, even stranger, he felt a little hot. When her gaze met his she gave him her usual friendly smile. 'You're looking mighty fit these days, Dr MacAllister. How was Pakistan?'

'Hot, wet and desperate.' As with all his aid missions, he didn't want to relive what he had seen. Enough that he had those images in his own head, without sharing details with others.

'But at least you know you were doing good out there. What were the conditions like? Are you okay? How are you feeling? When do you leave again? Please be happy for me.'

This was always how it was with Georgie: random conversation detours and finishing each other's sentences. But things generally flowed and they knew each other so well that often they didn't have to speak to communicate. So with the sudden baby daddy bombshell he'd never felt so excluded from her life. 'I'm fine. Knackered, but fine, looking forward to a few weeks' locuming at the General's ER. At least there's running water and reliable electricity. And I have a decent bed to sleep in. The next planned rollout for me is in South Sudan in a couple of months.'

'But if they need you earlier…'

He nodded. 'Sure. It's the way it is.'

'I still don't know how you manage all that to-ing and fro-ing. Here a couple of months, then gone again. I like staying in one place.'

And he didn't. The longest he ever stayed anywhere was when he came back here because he needed a semi-permanent job to help fund his aid work. 'But I'm never going away again if it means I come back to crazyville baby talk.'

'It's not crazyville.' Again with the eye roll. He didn't even have to look. This time it was accompanied by an irritated shake of her head. 'I've made a decision to do this now. On my own. I know it'll be tough and it's not the perfect image I've always had in my head about a mum and dad and two point four kids, but that's too far out of reach right now. I've had to curtail my dreaming and get real. Being a solo mum is just fine.'

She stopped talking to take a long drink of what looked a lot like lemonade. On a Friday night? Could be that she was actually serious about this. 'I want to conceive and carry to term, and have a baby…*my* baby… and, if things work out, have another one too. But that's probably greedy and selfish.'

'You deserve to be, Geo, after what you've been through.' *But now? Why now?*

'So, I'm looking forward, and taking an opportunity.

Endo is a lot less active during pregnancy so if I could manage two pregnancies in quick succession…if the IUI works, that is… IVF would be a whole different ball game.'

Trying to keep up he lifted his palms towards her. 'IUI? IVF? Slow down a bit. So you're not thinking turkey baster? Or just plain old-fashioned sex? That is a relief.'

'Believe me, I'll do whatever's necessary.'

He didn't doubt it. And finally the reality was sinking in. She was going to do the one thing he'd sworn never to do—and because he was her friend she'd expect him to be supportive. 'So what tipped you over to the dark side?'

And, yes, his reaction would not be what she wanted, but: a) he couldn't help it and; b) he wasn't prepared to lie just to make her feel better. It was precisely because of their friendship that he knew he could be straight up with her.

'You are such a grump. For me there is no dark side. Being abandoned at two days old and having literally no one from then on in has made me want to feel part of something…a family. You know that. I just want what everyone else has, Liam—to feel loved, to be loved. To love. And I have no doubt that there will be some hard times, but I will never leave my baby on a doorstep for someone else to find, and condemn them to a life of foster-homes and social services, like my mum did to me. I will cherish any child I have. I've had my share of dark sides and being pregnant and a mother isn't one of them.'

Her nose wrinkled as she reached across and lightly punched him on the arm. 'So, I was worried things were getting worse endo-wise, so I asked Malcolm to run some more tests at work a few weeks ago.' Her hands palmed across her abdomen—subconsciously? Possibly. Protective? Definitely.

'You've been having more pain? Oh, God, I'm sorry, Georgie. That sucks. Really, I thought you were managing okay.' Liam hated that. Hated that even though he fixed people up every day he didn't have the answers to Georgie's problems and that they were running out of solutions as time ticked on. His heart thumped in sync with the music, hard and loud in his chest. 'What did he say?'

'That the endometriosis is indeed getting worse. That everything in there's getting blocked up and scarred and it won't be long before I'll need pretty major surgery. That it's only a matter of time before pregnancy is going to be nigh on impossible. At least, without a whole lot of effort and money and no promises at the end.'

Her eyes filled with tears. Which, for Georgie, was such a rarity Liam sat there like a useless lump and watched in horror, unable to move. She was the strongest woman he knew. She'd faced tough battles her whole life and she never tired of fighting. No matter how ridiculous her plan sounded, his heart twisted to see her hurting. 'You know how much I need this, Liam. I thought you'd understand. I thought you'd support me. You know, like good friends do? I've been there for you regardless and I kind of hoped you'd feel the same.' Her hand reached for her gut again. 'This idea? This is a good thing.'

It was the worst thing he'd ever heard. 'And so who is going to provide the…?' He couldn't bring himself to say the word. For an accomplished medic he had trouble imagining what went on behind closed doors at the IVF clinic.

'Sperm? I've decided I'm going to ask Malcolm.'

'What?' Liam almost choked on his beer. 'Your boss?'

'And that's wrong, why? He's smart. Not unattractive. Owns a successful IVF clinic and has helped thousands of women achieve their dreams, so he's compassionate too. Those are all the right kind of genes I'd look for in a father for my child.'

'He's still also your boss.'

She hip-planted both hands. 'And I'm pretty sure he'd want to help. He sees this kind of thing every day, so to him it's not an unusual request. I'll ask him to sign a contract to keep things simple. I have enough money put by to keep me going for a while and the clinic has agreed to reduce my hours after maternity leave.'

Maternity leave. Contracts. That sounded far from simple. And the money she had put by was supposed to be for renovations to help her become more financially independent. 'Seems like you have it all figured out.'

'He knows how much I want this. How much I need to know DNA and family history. It's been my life's dream. Just a little...*expedited*.' She gave him a smile at their shared joke.

Liam didn't feel much like laughing. Sure, she'd talked about this on and off over the years but now the reality hit him in the gut like a two-ton truck. She wanted a baby. A family. Kids. 'Surely asking your boss is downright unprofessional. Unethical.'

'A friend helping a friend? Since when did that cross any kind of line?'

'Where would you like me to start?' It crossed more lines than Liam cared to think of. It would be like...like if he offered to father her child. Ridiculous. Ludicrous.

Wouldn't it?

The thought flitted across a corner of his mind. He pushed it away. Ludicrous indeed.

'Malcolm saw how upset I was at the results.' As she

spoke she seemed to loosen up a little. Determined, but calm. 'I've asked to have a meeting with him next week. If he says no then I'll have a rethink.'

'It sounds messy to me. How about using one of the anonymous donors at the clinic? You get to know about their family history, too. You can choose anyone that ticks your fifteen pages of boxes.' He didn't know why someone anonymous fathering her child seemed like a better option. It just *felt* better. A long way from right, but better. 'And why didn't you ask me?'

What the hell?

He didn't even know where that question had come from. As she stared at him his chest tightened.

'Is that what this is all about? You're upset because I didn't ask you? Honestly? The man who comes out in hives when he even sees a baby?' As soon as the words left her mouth she closed her eyes and pressed her lips together. Too late. After a beat or two she slowly opened her eyes again and winced. 'Oh, my God, I'm sorry. Really. I'm sorry, Liam. I am. I didn't mean… I'm so sorry. But I just know how you feel about families.'

'Do you?'

She looked surprised at his question. Probably because he'd kept his past to himself and never spoke about what he wanted for the future. But families and babies were something he definitely had an aversion to. No, not an aversion, just a deep desire not to go there. Ever.

Her voice softened. 'Since you always refuse to talk about anything deeper than what you had for lunch, I have to surmise. You have a track record of emotional avoidance. So I've always assumed that big loving, meddling, messy, happy families aren't something on your wish list. In all honesty, you'd be the last person I'd ask. And, judging by your current reaction, I think I'm right.'

* * *

Liam's face was all shadows and hollows. His blue eyes had darkened to navy. Only once before had Georgie seen him look so utterly haunted, and that had been the day they'd met and she'd forced him to work on that newborn.

Later that night, when they'd gone for the first of many subsequent beers, the alcohol had made his tongue loose and he'd mentioned a family tragedy involving his sister, Lauren. But then had clammed up so tight Georgie had never been able to open him up to that particular hotspot conversation again. And since then he'd absorbed whatever it was that had thrown him off balance that day. Until now.

His voice was low when he eventually spoke. 'I just think you could have talked to me about it all first. Put more thought into it.'

'I don't think that's possible, it's all I've been thinking about for weeks, turning scenarios over and over in my head.' She watched as anger and hurt twitched through him until he wrestled it under control. Why couldn't he just smile and pat her hand and say what a brilliant idea it was? Her words had obviously been a low blow. She'd always respected that he had his reasons for not wanting a family, even if he'd never really fronted up and explained why.

Some support would have been nice, but hadn't she heard this kind of story so many times at work? Babies, IVF and the sometimes desperate journey towards parenthood made strong couples stronger and weak ones fall apart.

Then thank God she and Liam weren't a couple because, judging by this conversation, they'd fall at the first hurdle.

He was her friend, her closest friend in lots of ways;

she always took his advice, always went to him with problems. And now she was all kinds of confused, needing time to think and reaffirm.

She stood to leave. 'Look, this was clearly a mistake. I'm going to go home so we can both take some time out. I'm sorry if I've ruined our Friday night. But, you know, I don't know where we'd go from here. Trying to play your wingman and find a date for you with some poor unsuspecting woman just isn't my idea of fun right now.'

He tipped his glass towards her again, but he didn't get up. Didn't try to make her feel better. And he always tried to make her feel better.

Which was why his opposition was spooking her more than she'd anticipated. Still, she'd made this decision and she was sticking with it.

She had no choice. This was her life. Her chance.

And to hell with him if he wasn't going to be there right when she needed it most. She threw her wrap round her shoulders. 'I'll…I don't know…see you later?'

He watched her stand. He still didn't move but his voice was more controlled as he gave her a small smile. 'Heaven help us all when you start taking the hormone injections.'

'Oh? Why?'

'Aren't they supposed to make you all antsy and volatile?'

'What?' She couldn't bring herself to tell him she'd been taking them already. And, yes, she was being antsy. But it was his reaction that had made her like that, not the medications. 'Maybe, just maybe you have royally pissed me off. And to add insult to injury, you're now being condescending. Patronising.'

'Just honest. As always.' Yes, she supposed he was.

One of things she relied on him for was his frank honesty. 'So when is it all happening? The impregnating thing?'

'So very clinical, Liam.'

'Yes. Isn't it?'

'I was hoping it would be in the next couple of weeks if possible.'

The glass in his hand hit the table with a crash. 'What? So soon? You don't mess around, do you? You don't want to talk a bit more? At least listen to someone else's opinion?'

'And have you try to convince me against it? I don't think so. I don't need your negativity. It's a chance, Liam. I need to take it.'

For a few seconds he looked at her. Just stared at her. She couldn't read him. The man she'd thought she knew pretty much inside and out, and she couldn't even guess what he was thinking.

After a torturous silence that seemed to increase the tension tenfold, he spoke, 'Yes. Yes, you do. Take the chance, Geo.' Now he stood up and walked her to the door. Once outside he didn't wrap her in his usual goofy bear hug. Didn't graze her cheek with a kiss and a smile. Didn't give her a wink and make her laugh. 'Let me know how you get on.'

'Why? So you can make me doubt myself all over again?'

He took her by the shoulders and his gaze bored into her. 'Because I'm your friend, Georgie.'

And then she ached for him to give her one of his hugs more than anything else in the world. But he turned away. Back towards the bar and the white noise that seemed to be mingling with his words and filling her head with doubts.

What if he was right? What if this was the far side of

crazy? What the hell did she know about family anyway? About parenting? It wasn't as if she'd had any experience on either side of that particular fence. What if Malcolm didn't follow through? What if he did?

Worse, what if this rift meant that the friendship she had with Liam would be broken for ever? He was the closest thing she had to any notion of family, and the thought of not having him in her life made her suddenly feel empty and cold.

Torn and confused, she climbed into a waiting cab and watched him retreat to the bar, his dark T-shirt straining across well-defined broad shoulders, and a gait that screamed defiance.

And what the hell was going on with those pecs? The man had suddenly developed muscles of steel. Strange, too, that in the midst of all this turmoil she should even notice. That, and the shape of his lips, the way his mouth curved and softened as he smiled, which had been rare but welcome tonight. Those hormones were clearly playing havoc with her head.

But judging by the sudden strange slick of heat that hit her breasts and abdomen—which surely must be a reaction to the muggy Auckland evening—they were messing with her body too.

CHAPTER TWO

Mum's had a stroke. Had to go back to UK. Don't know for how long. Will keep you in the loop. Sorry. Can we have that meeting when I get back?

SHUTTING THE IVF clinic room door, so she could have a moment to take it all in, Georgie stared at the text, her gut clenching. Bile rose to the back of her throat. She felt dizzy.

And downright selfish.

Inhaling deeply, she pulled herself together. For goodness' sake, it wasn't the end of the world, just the end of an opportunity. That was all. There would be another chance, next month or the month after. Some time. With a different donor.

She should be feeling sorry for her boss, not herself.

No worries, Malcolm. Safe journey. Sending hugs for your mum x

And yet she felt as if her world was closing in on her, that she was fast running out of time and her dream was getting further out of reach. Scrolling through her texts, she found her conversation thread with Liam and started to type. Then stopped. She hadn't heard a thing from him for four days, and even though she knew he'd be busy, catching up on everything at work, she felt a little lost. Normally he'd text her with funny stories from his shift, jokes, stuff. Just stuff. But ever since Friday she'd been hit by silence. And it hurt a little that he knew what she was going through but didn't want to see how she was doing.

Okay, it hurt a lot.

So maybe that would be the norm from now on. She didn't want to think about that. But for the last few days it hadn't been just his absence that had been on her mind. It had been that crazy tingly feeling that had swept through her body the other night, just looking at him. And then an out-of-proportion feeling of loss that he wasn't being supportive. It was absurd. Seemed those meds made her overreact in lots of different ways.

The clinic room phone interrupted her thoughts and brought her back to reality. 'Georgie speaking.'

It was Helen, the receptionist, and Georgie's good friend. 'I have a patient here, Kate Holland. Says she doesn't feel too great. Can you see her straight away?'

'Kate? Sure, I remember her, she was in just the other day. I'll be right through.' Helen rarely showed any kind of emotion, so the anxiety in her voice made Georgie take notice. Putting her own worries aside, she made sure the clinic couch was ready, opened up Kate's notes on the laptop then collected her patient, who appeared noticeably short of breath, flushed and anxious.

'Kate. What's the problem? Are you okay?'

'No. I feel pretty rubbish, actually. My stomach hurts and I'm so thirsty.' For a toned and fit marathon runner Kate climbed onto the bed with a lot of effort.

Alarm bells began to ring. Georgie settled the young woman against the pillow, silently counting the laboured respiratory rate. 'You've been having the injections, right? Any other problems? Nausea? Vomiting?'

Kate nodded. 'Yes. Twice this morning and I feel really sick now. But so thirsty.'

Georgie took her patient's hand and measured her pulse. Fast and thready. Any number of scenarios raced through her mind. Fertility drugs had a tranche of usually mild and temporary side-effects, but when they were severe they could be life-threatening. 'Peeing okay? If you can do us a sample, that'd be great.'

'Not much at all. But I'll try.'

'Okay, when you next need to go, yell out.' Giving Kate a quick examination and piecing together her patient's history, Georgie reached a preliminary diagnosis. It wasn't what either she or her patient wanted to hear. 'How long have you felt like this?'

'The past couple of days or so. I started feeling really sick yesterday.' Kate gripped Georgie's hand, her flushed face tight and scared. 'But please don't tell me we have to stop the injections. Please say we can do this. It's our last chance.'

Georgie gently encouraged her to lie back down, not wanting to upset her even more but realising that time was of the essence. 'I know, Kate. I know. But don't get ahead of yourself. I'll quickly get the doctor to come check you over, he'll probably suggest you have a short stay in hospital, just a few days or so, to check everything's okay...'

After the doctor had confirmed Kate's diagnosis, Georgie arranged the next few steps. 'Because you're publicly funded, we'll transfer you to the General Hospital gynae ward, that's the closest to your home. They'll look after you. I promise.'

'What about the IVF? Will that happen now?'

Georgie took her hand again. 'Sweetheart, you re-member the doctor saying you had something called OHSS? That's our medical shorthand for ovarian hyper-stimulation syndrome. That means your body has reacted very strongly to the drugs. You have too much fluid in your abdomen, which is why you're out of breath. You're dehydrated, but we need to watch how much fluid you drink because we don't want you overloaded. You have a swollen red calf, which might mean you have a blood clot. We've arranged for some scans and a few more tests at the hospital. You need to rest and let your body heal before you do any more.'

'We can't afford any more. This is it, our last chance. Mark will be so disappointed. He's been really positive this time round, we both have. We talked about a Christ-mas baby, he got so excited. He wants to be a dad so much.' Fat tears rolled down Kate's red cheeks and Georgie's heart melted.

Some people, such as Kate, were lucky enough to be eligible for publicly funded treatment for a limited num-ber of cycles. Having already waited for months and had one failed attempt, this was indeed Kate's last chance. She and her husband Mark had a low income and there was no way could they afford the high costs and even more time off work for private IVF. Life was so unfair sometimes.

Georgie dealt with these scenarios in her job every day, and she'd always managed to keep a professional emotional distance, but today it felt deeply personal. She knew how desperate it was to have a ticking clock. And a chance that could be blown for any random reason. 'We'll do the best we can for you, Kate.' But she wouldn't make any promises. It wasn't her style to give her patients false hope, no matter how much her heart ached in sync with them. 'In the meantime, you have to get better.'

If anything, it made Georgie more determined to grab her chance as soon as she could. Deciding to go through with it was the first step on what she knew was going to be a long road. She had no illusions as to the prospect of being a single pregnant woman, then a solo mother. It would be immensely rewarding. It would be hard. And with no one else to help shoulder the burden she knew there would be times she'd find it difficult to cope. But she would. She'd been on her own her whole life. She didn't need anyone else. But needing and wanting were two different things.

On days like these she'd usually ring Liam and have a whinge. Often he'd suggest a drink or a movie or something to cheer her up. But as he'd gone AWOL and she didn't fancy another grim conversation, she'd do things differently tonight. He certainly wasn't the only friend she had in the world.

'Okay, that's me over and out. See you in the morning,' Liam called to his secretary, then grabbed his work bag and made his way through the crowded ER to the exit. It had been one hell of a day, dealing with staff shortages, bus-crash casualties and the usual walk-ins. What he needed now was a sundowner at the local and an early night.

The hospital doors swept open and he took his first breath of fresh air for eleven hours. It was tinged with a familiar fragrance that had him turning his head. She was standing way over to his left, half-hidden by a tall confident-looking man, and Liam would have missed her and walked by if he hadn't caught that sweet, flowery scent.

For some reason, as he saw her deep in conversation

with a stranger, his heart hammered. Mainly, he suspected, because he'd bawled her out the other day and hadn't had the chance to make things right. 'Georgie. Hi. What are you doing here?'

She whirled round, her cheeks reddening, her green nursing scrubs making her look younger somehow. Vulnerable, which she'd hate. There was a ripple of tension as her shoulders straightened, but she masked it. 'Oh. Hey. I'm dropping off a patient's bag. She had to be admitted unexpectedly and left it at the clinic by mistake. This is her husband, Mark.'

'Liam. Hi, I work here.' As he shook hands with the guy the heart-hammering slowed a little. Was it wrong to feel relief that his friend wasn't sick, but that another man's wife was? Damn right it was. But relief shuddered through him anyway. 'Is everything okay?'

'Mark's wife, Kate, has OHSS, so she's feeling a bit fragile. Mark's on his way up to see her on Ward Three.'

'Ah, yes. I remember seeing her name on the admissions board. She'll be okay, mate. She's in good hands.'

The man nodded grimly and headed through the main entrance. Leaving just Liam and Georgie and a weird sense of displacement. Georgie played with the handle of her handbag, looked at her feet. 'I should probably go.'

Not without some kind of resolution, he thought grimly. This was painful. They'd never had this kind of weird, tense scenario play out before. 'Wait. Are you okay?'

What he meant was, *Are we okay?*

'Yes. Thanks. You?' She raised her head and looked at him. She looked tired, drawn. The edges of her eyes were ringed with black. Which was a far cry from the last time he'd seen her when she'd been brimful of excitement, and he'd stomped all over her happy mood.

Was the dark look just for him or had something else happened to her?

Okay, stop guessing and cut the crap. 'Look, Geo, I didn't mean to pee all over your parade. I'm sorry about the other night. I was tired and just caught by surprise.'

'Clearly. And you've been too busy to send a text?' But the iron-clad barriers seemed to give just a little with his apology. 'Or did they get lost in cyberspace, along with your good manners?'

'As it happens, things have been manic here. I've done four long days with the last vestiges of jet-lag messing with my brain.' She didn't need to hear all that. 'I did think about texting you more than a few times. But I wasn't sure whether you'd slap me or eye-stab me with one of those killer looks you save for especially annoying people that drive you mad on purpose. And I wasn't up to taking the risk.'

That, at least, got a smile. 'Aw, Liam, I'd never eye-stab you. How could you say such a thing?'

'I know what you're capable of, my girl. Downright scary at times.' He walked with her towards the car park, feeling a little more relaxed. 'Er…done the deed yet?'

'By which you mean the assisted fertility?' Georgie slowed and gave him what he had come to recognise as one of her false smiles. Her mouth flipped up into the usual grin, but her eyes didn't shine. In fact, nothing about her was shining tonight. Even her *caramel* hair—it was just plain weird that he'd started to notice things that he'd always glossed over—seemed dulled. 'Malcolm's had to go away due to a family crisis, so I've put off asking him.'

'Oh. I see.' And with that news he really should have been cock-a-hoop but he wasn't. Strange emotions rippled through him, mainly disappointment for her. It was what she wanted. She'd been so excited and determined the other day, to the point that he'd been unable to talk any sense into her.

Now she looked like she needed bolstering. 'Okay. So you've got plenty of time. I'm sure you'll be fine waiting just a little while longer. Have you had any thoughts about asking anyone else? What about the donor lists?'

She frowned. 'Yes, well, it's far from ideal. And, like I said, time is something I don't have a lot of.'

'You sound like you're waiting for the guillotine or something. Just a touch dramatic, Geo?'

'You think so?' As they closed in on her car they stopped. She pointed up to the second floor of the hospital with a taut finger that was definitely capable of eye-stabbing if she so wished. 'That lady in there has been trying to get pregnant for five years. And nothing. Zilch. Nil. She's had one chance at IVF, which came up with disappointment, and now everything's on hold until she gets better from the side effects of trying to stimulate her ovaries. I expect that if she gets the go-ahead again she'll have to pay megabucks…and even then it might not work for her.

'I do not want to be that lady, possibly looking at years of pressure and stress. I've got to start the ball rolling and damn well soon. Otherwise when and if I'm finally in a committed relationship with someone who loves me, it might be too late. I have a window of opportunity in my cycle coming up very soon. And I'm disappointed that I can't take advantage of it. Dramatic? If you say so. But, then, you're not the one staring down the barrel of a ticking time bomb.'

'Wow. See? Scary.' He stepped back. 'I'll just make sure I'm out of eye-stabbing range.'

She stalked off to her car, then stopped abruptly and

turned on him, gravel scraping underfoot. Never before had he seen such passion and anger and determination and spirit in anyone. 'For once in your life, Liam, take me seriously.'

'I do. All the time. I was just trying to make you feel better.'

'Well, you didn't. You know what? I bet we could spend the next few weeks going round in circles with this and you'd never understand.'

Oh, he understood all right. He'd been thinking about it for days, ever since she'd brought the subject up. In fact, that ludicrous idea that had flitted through his head had taken seed and would not let go.

But the ramifications were huge.

She glared at him, her eyes fierce, curls springing loose and free around her face. Her mouth taut and determined. She looked magnificent and terrifying, like the time she'd pushed him into Resus for that baby. And many times since when she'd been hell-bent on partying hard or just grasping life in her hands and making the most of it. She'd been like that since he'd known her—reaching, grasping, dreaming. Making her life full, taking what she wanted. Because she'd had so little for so long she hadn't wanted to waste a moment, and she defied anyone who stood in her way.

She was strong and staunch and loyal and in that second he knew that if *his* back was against the wall, she'd do anything for him. Anything.

And so here they were at an impasse. All he had to do was offer her what she wanted.

Great to help out a friend, but at the same time he was held back by…abject *fear*. Fear, that was it. The increased heart rate, sweaty palms, gut clench. He was scared as hell at the prospect of it all, of letting everyone down. Of not loving enough. Or, worse, loving too much. And he knew damned well how that panned out. He wouldn't be able to function around a child or be part of her cosy family. But if he didn't do it then she'd be forced to choose someone she didn't know or give up altogether—and he knew, too, that that was not part of her dream.

Despite all the late-night musings and the words going round and round in his head, he knew it was the most stupid idea he'd ever had.

But the words lingered. Lingered still as he saw her shrug her shoulders. As she turned her back to him and opened the car door. Lingered as he watched her swipe her hand across her face to stop a rogue tear. She wouldn't even allow herself to show her bitter disappointment. That almost broke him in two.

It would cost him little in time and effort. Not overtly anyway. He'd have to deal with the ramifications later. But right now his friend was hurting and there was something he could do to help. One singular thing. He could be that guy. The one he wanted to be, the one who took an emotional risk and helped a friend in need, whatever the personal cost.

Before he'd had a chance to second guess himself the words were tumbling out. 'Georgie, wait. I'll do it.'

Her voice was small and he could hear the pain, and yet deep down there was some hope as she turned to face him. 'Do what?'

'I'll be the donor.'

'You? *You?* Why?' Her laugh was bordering on sarcastic.

He took a step forward. 'Because I'm taking you seriously. This is what you want. What you deserve.'

She wagged her finger, fast. 'Oh, no. No. No. No. No. No. No. Not happening.'

'Unless you have a particular aversion to passing along my DNA? If I were to look objectively I'd say I was pretty okay. I'm a doctor, so not dumb. Oh, and my compassion knows no bounds. Apparently you like that in a father figure. I'm funny—always a winner.' He pointed to his abs, which he sucked in for effect. 'And pretty much the most devastatingly good-looking man in town.'

And bingo—his aid work meant he'd be out of the country for most of the rest of his life if he wanted. So he wouldn't be forced into any emotional attachment. This was a purely altruistic act. Which begged the question—what the hell did he want?

This wasn't about him, he reminded himself. It was about Georgie. 'How could you not want to use my *sperm*?' He whispered the last word as reality started to seep through his feel-good fuzzies.

The sarcasm melted away and the laugh was pure Georgie. 'Yeah, right. That's objective? Don't get above yourself. For one, you have a slightly crooked nose.'

He ran his down his ethmoid bone and he gave her his profile view. 'Rugby injury, not genetic. Besides, you can hardly see it.'

She cocked her hip to one side as she perused him. 'You have particularly broad shoulders.'

'Great for tackling and giving great hugs.' And he should know. He'd done it often enough. Usually as he was patting women on the back and wishing them well. *It wasn't them, it was him.*

She frowned. 'But not great for wearing halter-neck tops.'

'Ah shucks, and now you've spoilt my dress plans for tomorrow.' Funny, but it felt strange, being analysed in such a way by a friend.

'On the other hand, you do have…long legs.' Her voice cracked a little as her gaze scanned his trousers. Her pupils did a funny widening thing. A flash of something—and then it was gone. Two red spots appeared on her cheeks. 'Ahem, big feet.'

'And we all know what that means.' He winked. 'Any boy would be happy with the MacAllister brand of DNA. If you bottled it you'd get a fortune.'

'Oh, yeah? No girl wants big feet. Bad for shoe buying.' She gave him a final once-over glance. Then her voice softened. 'Really, it's a lovely offer and I'd be stupid not to take you up on it. But what about you? You don't want this. You really don't want this.'

'But you do, Georgie.' There was a long beat while he tried to put into words the weird feelings he was experiencing. He could give her the chance she wanted, on one condition. 'But we'll need a contract. I don't want any involvement.'

'Oh.' Giving the minutest shake of her head, she held her palm up. 'You'll be the baby daddy but don't want to be *the* daddy?'

'Yep.'

'Oh. Okay. Then I'm utterly shocked that you've offered. Why would you do that?'

Not wanting to dig up something he'd pushed to the darkest part of his soul, he gave her the scantest of explanations. 'Happy families isn't my style. But a happy Georgie is. I'll do it. Just agree before I change my mind.'

'Oh, this is fast and so out of left field.' She put a hand to his shoulder, ran her fingers down his arm. And in the cool late summer evening goosebumps followed the trail of her warm skin against his. 'Can I think about it? Get used to the idea?'

'Sure.' He needed time too, his chest felt blown wide open.

'It would mean a lot of changes. For us.'

'I know. I realise that.' And if it hadn't been Georgie's dream on the line, no way would he ever contemplate something like this.

She looked hesitant, shocked, but hopeful. 'So…well, we could have a contract similar to the clinic's standard donor document. We can use that as a blueprint. If that's what you really want?'

'That's what I want. No involvement, nothing.'

'I won't ask you for anything else. Ever. Trust me.'

He did. Absolutely. He just wasn't sure how much he could trust himself. 'Yes. Definitely. A contract will be best.'

'And it'll mean tests. Soon. Like this week.'

'Whatever it takes.' Although the altruistic vibe was fast morphing into panic.

'Oh, my God, is this really happening?' She reached round his waist and pulled him into one of her generous hugs. His nostrils filled with her perfume and he fought a sudden urge not to let go.

Her body felt good close to his. She was soft in his arms and her head against his chest made his heart hurt a little. He'd missed her these last few weeks. Especially these last few days. They never argued.

And this…was just a hug. Nothing strange there. She gave them all the time. And yet… He was aware of the softness of her body, the curve of her waist… He swallowed.

Nah. She felt just the same as always. Just the same old Georgie. She turned her head and looked up at him, her dark eyes dancing with excitement, the evening sun catching her profile. For a second she just looked into his eyes. One. Two. He lost count. She had amazing eyes. Flecked with warm gold and honey that matched her hair. His gaze drifted across the face he knew so well, and a shiver of something he didn't want to recognise tightened through him.

She pulled away quickly and the connection broke.

Thank God, because he was getting carried away in all her emotion. And that was definitely not something he was planning on doing. Emotional distance was the only thing that stopped him wreaking any more damage on those he loved. Hell, he was his father's son after all. Emotional distance was what MacAllister men did better than anyone else. But somehow he didn't think that that admission would go down well on Georgie's tick list.

'Thank you. Thank you so much. It means a lot to me.' She placed a gentle kiss on his cheek. Again with the goosebumps. This time they prickled all the way to his gut and lower. 'I'll mull it over and…um…let you know? Soon as possible?'

'Okay, and I'll get the turkey baster sorted for when you say yes.' Now he needed to ignore the strange feelings and off-load some of this ache in his chest. He saw a damned long run in his immediate future.

Her demeanour changed. She brushed a hand down over her scrub trousers, all business and organisation as she took a shaky little step away from him. 'Like I said, we'll do it the clinic way.'

'For sure. Any other way would be just too—'

Her head tilted a little to the side. 'Ick?'

He grinned. 'Is that a technical term?'

'Absolutely. For that weird feeling you get when you think about sleeping with your best friend? Like sex with your cousin? Right? Weird.' Shuddering, she looked to him for reassurance.

Which he gave unreservedly. 'Right. Yes. Ick's the word.'

The notion of them having sex had rarely arisen. Back in the early days he'd caught himself looking at her and wondering. She'd walked through his dreams many nights. He'd tried to imagine what kissing her would have been like. How she would taste. How she would feel underneath him. Around him. But he'd never put any of that into words for fear she'd run a mile. He'd never asked more from her than what they'd already had and, frankly, he'd believed that any kind of fling would inevitably ruin the great friendship they'd built up.

She was worth more to him than just sex. And seeing as that was the only thing he ever offered to women, he'd never wanted to risk doing something so pointlessly stupid and losing her.

Plus, while Georgie was funny and loyal, she'd never made a move or seemed interested in him in that way. They'd had an implicit agreement that anything of a sexual nature could never happen. So he'd sublimated those imaginings until he'd stopped having them. Had lost himself in other women.

Which made it all the more nonsensical that he'd started noticing things again…like her smell, the colour of her hair, her eyes. Surely it could only mean some sort of nostalgia for the younger Georgie in his past when the present was shifting out of his control?

CHAPTER THREE

Eight months ago...

Hey, stranger. Thought you'd want to know that your genius sperm has done what it was designed to do... I'm pregnant!

Great news. Congratulations.

FINALLY, AN ANSWER. Biggest news she'd ever had and not one exclamation mark. Not one. No cheers or fanfares. No questions. Was he not just a little curious? Pleased for her? Maybe it was the whole emotionless text thing stuffing up the sentiment of his message, but hadn't the man heard about emoticons?

Disappointed, Georgie texted him back.

I'm so excited! :) Catch up soon?

Sure. Things are a bit busy right now. Packing. South Sudan. In two days. I'll try come over to say bye.

Okay, your call.
He was heading off again and he'd try to come and

see her? *Try?* What the hell…? Packing didn't take two whole days. He was the world's lightest traveller.

And, actually, it was her call just as much as his. Worrying about contacting him had never been an issue before and it shouldn't be now just because she was carrying his baby. *No. Her* baby. He'd made that very clear. But surely they could still be friends? She wasn't going to allow this to change what they had. Why should pregnancy make a difference?

But it did, she realised. Not just to her relationship with Liam, but to her. She was going to be a mum. *A mother.* With a family. Something she'd never had before. She was going to be part of something…more.

She put a hand to her very flat, very *un*pregnant-looking stomach and her heart did another flip. It was still so early, too early to grow attached; any number of things could go wrong. But it was already too late. Her stomach tumbled as she closed her eyes, imagining.

Hey, there, little one. Nice to meet you.

And that was about all she dared say. She felt something tug deep inside her. These days she seemed to be so emotional about things. About the baby. About Liam…

Well, if he wasn't going to make an effort then she damn well would. She wanted to celebrate and send him off on his travels with no tension between them. Georgie stabbed his number into the phone and left a message: 'Hey, step away from your backpack. Let's do something. I won't take no for an answer. I get the feeling you're avoiding me. But if you are, please don't admit it. Just say you've been busy. Mission Bay? Six-thirty. I'm hiring bikes. No excuses.'

'Are you bonkers or just straight up certifiable?' Three hours later his voice, behind her, although irritated and loud, made her heart jig in her chest. He'd turned up at least, and for that she was grateful. 'Cycling? In your condition? Seriously?'

'Oh, for goodness' sake, I'm fine. How many times have we done this?' She turned and pretended to scowl, but her scowl dropped the moment she set eyes on him. He was wearing a scruffy old T-shirt that hugged his toned muscles and was the same vibrant blue as his eyes. Faded jeans graced his long legs, framing his bum…and, no, she'd never really studied it before, but it was deliciously gorgeous. No wonder he had a queue of women trying to encourage him to commit.

Heat hit her cheeks and shimmied down to her belly, where it transformed into *What would he be like in bed*?

And that was just one of too many thoughts about him recently that were way out of line.

To distract herself from staring too long at the man who had suddenly become a whole new fascination for her, she clipped on her helmet and prepared to use up some of this nervous energy. Pregnant, yes. Petrified, indeedy. Strangely excited just to see her long-lost best mate? Very definitely. And that made her legs twitch and her stomach roll.

'I needed some fresh air. It's such a beautiful evening and it's the weekend tomorrow. Freedom! We could get fish and chips and eat them on the beach later.'

He frowned and pointed to her helmet. 'Take it off, Georgie. It's too dangerous. We haven't been cycling for years, you could fall off. Why you suddenly want to do it now I don't know.'

'Because it used to be fun and I don't know why we got out of the habit of doing it. I want the fun back.' She shook her head in defiance. 'And stop being ridiculous. You're a doctor, you know very well that at this stage in pregnancy it's perfectly fine to exercise. Come on, I'll be fine, it's not as if I'm bungee jumping. Although, there is a free slot at the Skytower at eight. So if we hurry…' She handed him his helmet and stood, arms crossed over her chest, until he'd put it on over that grumpy face. 'Breathe, Liam. Breathe. It was a joke. And do try to keep up!'

The sea air was filled with salt and heat and the smell of a distant barbecue. Overhead, seagulls dived and squawked, making the most of a bright summer evening's scavenging. Mission Bay was, as always, filled with smiling people, cycling, blading or running along the seaside promenade. On the right, beyond small beach inlets and a turquoise sea dotted with anchored yachts, the mighty volcanic Rangitoto Island stood verdant and powerful. On the left they cycled past coastal suburbia, higgledy-piggledy candy-coloured houses clinging to the steep hillside.

Georgie pedalled hard, keeping him in her slipstream, ignoring his concerned cries. She could do this. She needed to do this to show him—and herself—that she was still the same old Georgie. And if she could also purge those weird fluttery feelings that seemed to happen whenever she saw him, that would be even better. Because this new Georgie who kept popping up with hot thoughts about Liam was unsettling in the extreme.

Usually he raced ahead, screaming over his shoulder for her to go faster, but today he seemed happy to pootle behind. She had the distinct feeling that, in his own way, he was keeping watch over her.

After a few kilometres, pedalling towards towering city skyscrapers, she turned and cycled back to the row of Victorian buildings flanking a children's playground and large fountain. Toddlers kicked and splashed in the spraying water, watched over by attentive parents.

Georgie braked, imagining being here some time in the future, showing her little one the exciting new world. Making everything a game, lining up her pram with the others, chatting to parents about nappy changing, bedtimes and the terrible twos. Her heart zinged. It seemed that, despite all her best efforts, she was starting to see everything through a different, pregnancy-coloured lens. With a heavy heart she glanced at the young dads splashing around and on the reserve, throwing balls to their sons, cheering, encouraging and, most of all, laughing.

Liam had been definite in his refusal to be a father. She understood that some people didn't have the need for kids in their lives, but that didn't mean she liked the idea. How could someone not want to know their own flesh and blood? It had been a question burning through her for her whole life. How could you just walk away and not want to be found, not want to make contact? What the hell ever happened to unconditional love?

It went against everything she knew about him. He was gregarious, funny, and cared deeply about the people he helped. But if he really meant he wasn't going to be involved she'd have to be Mum and Dad to her child. After all, in the children's home where she'd eventually settled, one parent was always better than none at all.

As Liam approached she flicked the bike into gear and cycled on to a small caravan advertising fish and chips and ice-cold drinks. 'Usual? Snapper?'

'Of course. And a large portion of chips. Tomato sauce...' He grinned, pointing to a can of cola. 'And all the trimmings.'

'I don't know where you put it all.' His belly was hard and taut. Body lean. Again with the full-on flush as she looked at him, this was becoming an uncomfortable habit. 'If I ate half of what you ate I'd be the side of a house.'

'You can't exactly worry about putting on weight now, can you?' He laughed and gave her a look she couldn't quite decipher.

Having returned their bikes to the hire shop, they walked in step down to the beach and found a spot on the sand in the warm, soothing last rays of the day. Liam sat beside her and they ate out of the paper in companionable silence, pausing every now and then to comment on the food. The fish was divine, as always, the chips hot and salty, the cola too cold and too fizzy. Everything seemed exactly the same as it always was, except that it wasn't. She didn't know how to begin to have any kind of conversation that referred to being pregnant without causing another rift between them.

In the end she decided that rather than going over and over things in her head she was just going to say what was bothering her. She waited until he met her eyes. 'I wanted to say thank you, thank you, thank you for what you did.'

'It's fine. Honestly. Congratulations. You must be pleased.' He didn't look fine, he looked troubled as he leaned in and kissed her cheek, long eyelashes grazing her skin. 'You're looking good. Feeling okay so far?'

'Feeling a little numb all round, to be honest. It's real and happening and I can't quite believe it. I'm so lucky for it to have worked first time round. But it does happen.' She ran her palm across her tender breasts. 'No morning sickness yet, but my boobs are pretty sore.'

'Yeah. It happens. Wait till the varicose veins and heartburn kick in then you'll really be rocking.' He gave her a small smile, smoothing the tiny lines around his eyes, and for a second she was ten years younger, meeting him for the first time. All über-confident medical student who had been knocked sideways by the tiniest of beings—so small she'd fitted almost into the palm of his hand. Never had Georgie seen anyone look so frightened by something so frail, the cheery self-assurance whipped from him as if he'd been sucker-punched.

He'd been honest and open and warm. And since then she'd stood with pride at his graduation, cheered him on the sidelines at rugby games, dragged him kicking and screaming to ballet performances and musical theatre, entirely happy with what he'd had to give her. Just a simple, uncomplicated friendship.

But now his eyes roved her face and then his gaze dipped to where her hand was over her breast. Suddenly she felt a little exposed and hot again under his scrutiny. She kept her eyes focused on the top of his head but eventually he looked back at her as if he was going to speak. A flash of something rippled through those ocean-blue eyes. Something that connected with her, something more than warm, which made her belly clutch and her cheeks burn. Heat prickled through her, intense and breath-sapping.

Her fingers ached to just reach out and touch his cheek. Just touch it. To see what his skin felt like. To feel his breath on her face. Her mouth watered just looking at his lips. Open a little. Just a little… Her breath hitched. He was so close. His familiar scent of male and fresh air wrapped around her like a blanket.

Close enough to—

He shook his head as if confused and disorientated. Then he shifted away and focused on the remainder of his food. Meanwhile, she breathed out slowly, trying to steady her ridiculously sputtering heartbeat. Had she imagined that flash of heat? Those feelings?

Yes.

It was all just her stupid clunky imagination.

She would rather die than ask him and be laughed at… or worse. That kind of conversational subject was explicitly off limits and would only cause tension. It was bad enough that she'd created this difficult atmosphere in the first place. But now, to… Oh, my God. The thought flitted into her brain and rooted itself there, so obvious, so immense, so downright out of this world… *No*. Surely not. She didn't. Couldn't.

She fancied him? Fancied the pants off Liam MacAllister? The guy she'd got drunk with, thrown up on, told her deepest dirty secrets to? She wanted to kiss him? Really? Truly? Her heart thudded with a sinking realisation. Things between them were complicated enough, not least because he was going halfway across the world in less than twenty-four hours and she had no idea when she would see him next.

She couldn't want him, and he certainly wouldn't want her, especially with a baby in tow. Not now. Not ever. End of.

Hell, no.

Georgie was wearing a soft white lacy bra.

That was all Liam could think of. Not how amazing it was that she was pregnant. Although that was pretty amazing. Foolish and foolhardy and well beyond his comprehension too. But she did have a kind of warm glow about her, a softness he'd never seen before. He was no longer even registering how far beyond stupid she'd been to race along the pavement on two thin wheels when anything could have happened to her.

No, the only thing that took up room in his thick head was that her small perfect breasts were covered in lace.

As she leaned forward to take another hot chip, her top gaped a little more and he caught a glimpse of dark nipples. Cream skin. He swallowed. Dragged his gaze away and looked out at the boats bobbing on the turquoise water. What the hell was wrong with him?

Why, when he needed to put distance between them, had that whole concept suddenly become too hard to contemplate? He'd gone from not thinking about her in that way to not being able to stop thinking about her in the matter of a few weeks. He'd kept away, making excuses not to see her, just to get his head around everything. And it had failed spectacularly because the moment she'd told him she was getting on a saddle he'd thundered down here with a distinct determination to convince her not to. He'd always teased her, had fun with her, joked around with her, but never until now had he had this need to protect her. Even if it was from herself.

And he was damned sure it wasn't just because she was pregnant. But he wished to hell it was. Because that was none of his business. Because that he could distance himself from.

Couldn't he?

Man, his life was changing in a direction that was beyond his control and it was taking a lot of getting used to. His life, yes. But another life, a new life, was growing inside her and he was struggling to get past that.

After finishing her dinner and crinkling up the paper into a tight ball, she spoke. 'You didn't have to sneak into the clinic during my lunch hour, you know. I would have given you some space.'

'It just didn't feel right.' He looked everywhere but at her. The finer details of how he'd provided the sperm were definitely not for this conversation. Even more, he'd really not wanted to alert her to the fact he'd been in her workplace, doing the deed in a side room. 'Man, they ask a lot of questions.'

'Tell me about it. They always ask a heap of stuff about

your parents too. Any genetic conditions, inherited diseases. Has either parent had cancer, heart problems, high blood pressure? It kills me just a little bit to not know. In some ways it's a whole clean slate and I don't know about any inherited illnesses that may be hanging over my head. But in other ways it's a jigsaw, trying to piece bits together.' She shrugged, trying for nonchalance, but Liam knew just how much she'd ached to know just something about her mum and dad. 'I don't even know who I got my eye colour from, for God's sake.'

He wanted to say it didn't matter. Because even if you did know who your parents were, it didn't mean a damned thing. It sure as hell didn't mean they loved you. Or maybe that was just his. But, then, how could he blame them? 'Well, at least you know little Nugget there will have big beautiful blue ones, to break the girls' hearts.'

'Or brown. She could have my brown ones.' She glanced over at him with a curious look and he immediately regretted mentioning any kind of pet name. He was not going to get involved. He would not feel anything for this baby. Which was currently only a collection of cells, not a baby at all. Not really.

His chest tightened. Who was he trying to fool? He could barely look at Georgie without imagining what was growing in her belly.

Who. Who was growing in her belly. *His baby.* He was going to be a father. And what had seemed such a simple warm-hearted gesture to help out a friend a few weeks ago had taken on a whole new meaning. This was real. This was happening. She was having his baby.

For a moment he allowed himself the luxury of the thrill of that prospect, let the overpowering innate need to protect overwhelm him.

Then he remembered a very long time ago, as a young

boy of eight, the excitement deep in his heart as he'd felt a baby's kick. His hand on a swollen bump. The soft, cooing voice. A new life.

Then it was gone.

Ice-cold dread stole across him like a shadow. It didn't matter how far you ran, your nightmares still caught up with you.

He quickly tried to focus on something else. 'So, plans for the weekend? After the bungee is it whitewater rafting? Paragliding? How about base jumping? All perfectly suitable under the circumstances.'

'First I thought I'd go running with the bulls, then perhaps a little heli-skiing.' She threw the rolled-up paper ball at him. Missed. Completely. 'Idiot!'

He threw it back at her. 'Bingo. On the head. Your aim is appalling.'

'Show-off!' She threw it towards him. Missed by a mile. Went to grab it. He reached it first and held it high above her head. Way out of her reach. She jumped to get it. Failed. Jumped again. Then she playfully poked him in the stomach so he flinched. 'Ouch!'

'Yes! Got it.'

He grabbed her arms and pulled her into a hug. Tickled her ribs until she yelped for mercy. Felt the soft heat of her breath on his skin. The way she moulded into him. Warm. 'Play fair.'

'Says the man with elastic arms. You have a natural advantage.'

'And you…'

Grinning and breathless, she pulled away, but not before he'd got a noseful of her flowery scent. She smelt like everything good. Everything fresh and vibrant and new. Something spiralled through him. A keening need. Rippling to his heart, where it wrapped itself into a ball of content, then lower to his groin, where content rapidly turned into a fiery need.

He let her go as his world shifted slightly. This could not be happening.

She sat back down, pink-cheeked but smiling. 'Actually, I thought I'd rip up the carpet in the spare room and see what's underneath. I'm hoping it's going to be one of those miracle moments—*Ooh, look, the last owner covered a perfectly intact parquet floor*—like on the DIY TV shows. But somehow I doubt it.'

'So do I. You'll be lucky if there's a decent layer of concrete there. Thinking about your dilapidated house makes me laugh. Either that or I'd cry. It needs serious work.' And thinking about something tangible and solid made a lot more sense than thinking about the searing lusty reaction he'd just had that had thrown him way off kilter. 'Don't get your hopes up. I've seen that old scabby carpet. The walls. The roof. My guess is that the previous owners only spent time covering up just how badly falling down the place was.'

'Aw, you know it was all I could afford. And it's a nice neighbourhood, good school zone, so will be worth a lot more by the time I've finished. Worst house on the best street and all that. And the roof is sound, it just needs some TLC.' She pouted a little and his gaze zeroed in on her mouth. Plump lips. Slightly parted. The tiniest glisten of moisture. He leaned over and dabbed a drop of ketchup away from her bottom lip. His thumb brushed against warmth. And his body overreacted again in some kind of total body heat swamp, accompanied by a strange tachycardia that knocked hard against his rib cage. The beach seemed to go fuzzy out of his peripheral vision as she blinked up at him, surprised by the sudden contact.

Her lips parted a fraction more and if he leaned in he could have placed his over them.

And now he was seriously losing his mind.

Clearly he needed to get laid and quickly. With someone else.

Georgie moved away, frowning. She might have said his name. He didn't know. He willed his breathing back to normal.

Where were they? Oh, yes. The house. For God's sake, he needed to get up and go. This was crazy. This irrational pointless need thrumming through his veins. Crazy and sudden and he didn't know what the hell he was doing any more. Or where this had come from. But he wished it would go as suddenly as it arrived. 'It'll be great when you're done. Lots of potential.'

'So you said when I bought it. But now I've got to capitalise on that. I've chosen some paint. I thought a soft cream would be nice and I'll add colour with blinds and cushions, nursery furniture. I saw a great changing table in a second-hand shop down the road from work—all it needs is a lick of paint, I'm not going to be one of those mums who—'

'A bit early for nesting, surely?' He gathered all the wrappers up then stood, offering his hand to pull her up.

She threw him a look filled with hurt, brushed her clothes down and reached for her bag. 'Well, I've got to start somewhere. Nine months flies by, believe me. I see it all the time at work—people often don't even come up with a name in that time.'

Ignoring his hand, she stood without help and looked out at the ocean. Her shoulders taut, back rigid. Her jaw tightened.

He'd meant that she shouldn't be too sure that this early pregnancy would last the course, that she needed to wait before she spent money on things. Invested. But saying that would be crass. Distasteful. Working at the fertility clinic, she was well aware of all the pitfalls and rewards of pregnancy. And judging by the way her eyes glittered with any baby talk, she was very invested already.

When she turned back to him her eyes were blazing. 'You remember that first night in my house, Liam? When we sat on packing crates and talked all night about the plans I had for renovations?'

'Of course I do.'

'I'm still the same person. I still have that dream. It's going to be a fabulous place. Then I will sell it and climb that property ladder, baby in tow. We'll be zillionaires by the time I've finished. It just needs a bit of imagination, more time and a few willing hands.'

There was a long pause in which he felt sure she was waiting for him to offer to help with the decorating.

He'd returned from Pakistan planning on doing just that. But if he got involved in doing up her house that would mean more time spent with her and that was diametrically opposed to his plan. Which had been to ease himself out of her and her baby's lives. Gently. Without her really noticing. Just longer absences that she could fill with her antenatal classes, nursery shopping, other pregnant friends—because she must have them. Everywhere he looked these days there were blossoming bellies and tiny squawking babies.

But now, seeing her pregnant and the immediate emotions that instilled in him, his plan seemed like a crock full of madness.

So all the more reason for him to get out quickly. He couldn't be ruled by emotions, he never let that happen

in his professional or his personal life. It was too dangerous to do otherwise.

'Anyhoo…' Her eyes were clouded now as she blinked
away. She rooted in her bag and pulled out a folder of papers, clearly trying to keep her voice steady. Goddamn,
everything he did hurt her. She cleared her throat. 'Here's
your signed copy of the contract from the clinic. Helen
was supposed to mail it to you, but I offered to bring it
along here instead. As you saw, it's pretty standard stuff.
You get no claims, no guardianship or visitation rights,
you're not a legal parent, you have no parental rights….
yada-yada. Just what you wanted.'

'Oh. Okay. Great. Thanks.' In black and white it
seemed so cold-hearted. And yet it absolved him of everything. No responsibilities. He took it and shoved it
in to his backpack. He didn't need to reread it. He was
signing every right to this child away.

Truth was, his thoughts about this baby were so
blurred now. He'd thought it would be easy to walk away.
But…well, it wasn't easy at all. He felt like he was giving
his child the same fate he'd had—a life with little contact
with his father. A life wanting something…guidance,
truth, recognition. He couldn't give his child that. He just
couldn't. But what could he give? What did he have left?

Georgie peered up at him and everything he knew
about her was in that guarded look in her eyes. She understood his pain, but was equally angry. She was putting her needs first. And she needed to, he didn't blame
her a jot for that. 'That's what you really want, isn't it,
Liam? You don't want to help me get a nursery ready—
that is clear. Or choose decor. Or talk about baby things.
You don't want me to be pregnant. You don't want any
of this…'

'Look, Geo, that's not it. I'm thrilled for you. I am. It's

what you want and you look so happy, how could I not be pleased for you? I thought this was what you wanted.'

'Me too. But I don't know how you can do it. The more I think about it, the more I don't understand you. I've known all along that you cut yourself off from any kind of decent meaningful human connection…' She twisted in the sand and stepped towards him. 'So just explain to me one thing: what are you so afraid of?'

'I'm not afraid of anything.' And that was the biggest lie he'd ever told. He was afraid of the responsibility of another baby's life, of not being able to protect it from harm. Of loving too much. Of dealing with the utter heartbreak if something went wrong, because he didn't think he could live through that again. His heart raced as blood drained from his head, from his face. 'Nothing.'

'I watched you, Liam…that day in Resus, when your whole world crumbled at the sight of a sick baby. I know you are carrying some terrible burden and, through knowing you for ten years, I think it has something to do with your family. Your sister Lauren?'

He railed around, wishing he didn't know her so well, wishing she couldn't see through the barriers he'd erected. 'It has got nothing to do with anyone.'

'If you choose to let whatever happened colour everything you do for the rest of your life then I can't help you. And I want to, I really do. But I can't bear that every time I mention my baby—*our* baby—you flinch. So I'm going to do this my own way. I'm sorry if that doesn't work for you. Just go off to the South Sudan and do your precious job.'

'What?' His heart thumped harder, fast and furious. 'Is this about my job now as well? You don't like it that I'm going to be leaving all the time, is that it?'

'It's about everything, Liam. About your attitude,

about your refusal to admit what's bothering you, the damned contract that means you will willingly let our friendship irrevocably change and allow a baby to be fatherless, and, yes, it's about your job. It's dangerous, and scary for those of us left behind.'

He shoved his hands in his pockets. He could barely look at her. By donating his…by delivering the goods, he'd done what he'd thought was the right thing—he *had* done the right thing—but the fallout kept coming. 'That job keeps me sane.'

'And drives me mad with worry. But I don't know why we're even bothering talking about this. You've got your contract, you can go off unhindered by any kind of sense of responsibility.'

Responsibility? That was the one single thing that drove him to do what he did. Every damned day.

She whirled around and stalked away, but paused, momentarily to turn back. Scraping her hair back from her face, she glared at him, her body language so at odds with her words. 'Stay safe.'

CHAPTER FOUR

Four months ago...

'ONCE THE PAIN relief kicks in you can take him to X-Ray. Let's see exactly how far up the little tyke stuffed the ball bearing, shall we? Depending on where it is, he might need a sedative for us to get it out. But we need to know more before we do anything else.' Through the fog of his sleep-deprived brain Liam offered the concerned mum a smile. Just a little shut-eye between his plane hitting the tarmac and coming into work would have been nice. Still, boys would be boys, and stuffing things up nostrils was par for the course for a four-year-old.

Hopeful images of a little boy who looked a lot like him flashed through his head. He batted them away. He'd call Georgie and talk to her *later*, explain his plan, what he wanted…once he'd worked out exactly what it was he was going to say. Theoretically it made sense to have some contact with his baby. He'd be responsible for finances and guidance, provide things. No emotional involvement. No day-to-day stuff—he didn't want to tread on Georgie's toes. But enough that his child would be able to identify him as his father. He was responsible, for God's sake.

All very good in theory, but in practice he had no idea.

Maybe this was just another of his ludicrous plans that would be fraught with endless fallout. But somehow he did not like the idea of being a dad and not having at least some contact with the child.

The little boy's mum laughed, but Liam could see by her lined forehead and forced smile that she was still anxious. It didn't matter what befell a kid, their parent always worried.

'I don't know why he decided it needed to go all the way up his nose. I just wish he hadn't found it at all. I'll kill his dad when we get home. Leaving little things on the floor is so dangerous.'

'I guess having kids means big changes. It takes a bit of getting used to.'

That thought had been running over and over in his head since he'd left. Would he be like that with his child? Worried sick if it stuffed something up its nose? Would he refuse to let them play outside in case they injured themselves? He'd seen extremes in this job. Neglect that almost tore his heart in two, and the worried well who caused a fuss over nothing. Where children were concerned, it was difficult to get the balance right. But generally it didn't matter where he was—flooded Pakistan, drought-ridden Africa—parents were the same the world over. They loved. They gave their children what they could. They worried.

He tried to find the wee lad a smile.

The boy grinned back. With sticky-out ears beneath sand-coloured hair he was pretty cute. And now, with the analgesic kicking in, clearly unbothered by the metal ball in his left nostril. 'I liked it. It was silver. I wanted to smell it.'

'Oh.' Kids said the strangest things. Stupefied by his inadequacy where children were concerned, Liam wondered whether you should talk to them like adults or use special kiddy words. He stuck to plain and simple. 'Metal ball bearings don't have a smell, buddy. Now, don't put anything else up your nose. Not even your finger. Off you go.' He turned to the mum and relaxed a little. It was far easier to talk to a grown-up. 'See you when you get back from X-Ray.'

The kid laughed at Liam's grumbling stomach, clearly unfazed by whichever way Liam spoke to him. 'What's that funny noise?'

'It's…er…' Not often he was lost for words. 'I'm hungry. My tummy's asking for lunch.'

'Metal balls don't smell and tummies don't talk.'

'No. Well, I don't suppose they do. But they growl, like mine, so go on and get your picture taken so we can see inside you. Skedaddle.'

And lunch was supposed to have been six hours ago. But since then he'd had a steady stream of minor emergencies on top of a few pretty major ones. Now, shift almost over, he could finally go home. Looking forward to getting something into his stomach that wasn't yet another Sudanese stew or tasteless plane mush, he strode across the ER floor, past the whiteboard. And stopped. Turned. Refocused on the names. *What the…?*

White noise filled his ears, his appetite replaced by an empty hole deep in his gut as he hot-footed it back to Minors and threw the cubicle curtain open. Sure enough, she was there, head in her hands, making soft snuffling noises.

'Georgie? What the hell—?' Four months he'd lain sweltering in a too-hot tent and she'd been tattooed onto the back of his eyelids as he'd gone to sleep, their last conversation going over and over in his head. Making things right hadn't seemed possible from the dodgy dirty-walled internet cafés he'd visited sporadically, so his emails had been short and perfunctory.

He'd spent weeks wondering what he'd say when he saw her in person, how he'd feel when he saw her carrying his baby. How he'd feel when he saw her, period. He hated it that she had put a line under their friendship, ending everything so abruptly. But none of that mattered now, none of it.

He tugged her into his arms, hauled her head against his chest and stroked her back. 'Hey, don't cry. It's okay. It's okay. Whatever's happened we'll fix it. It's okay.'

Firm hands pressed on his chest and gripped his shirt. Her voice was low but not upset. In fact…was she laughing? 'Oh, my God! Liam. You're back! When?'

He'd finally stopped shaking enough to concentrate. Goddamned ER doctor and he'd crumbled the second he'd seen her name. *Georgie. The baby.* He didn't know which thought had come first—one had been so quickly followed by the other. And if that wasn't the most bizarre sequence of mind mess he didn't know what was.

And now she was here, damaged somehow—because this was where damaged people came. And that was just the staff. Worst-case scenarios flitted through his doctor's brain, fuelled by his own awful experiences. 'Early this morning. I was going to call you once I'd had a sleep, but they needed me here urgently. I didn't even get the chance to go home. But what the hell—?'

'Don't get carried away. And, no, I'm not crying.'

'What happened? The baby?' He took a step back and surveyed her belly with quick observations. She had a rounded-out bump now, small and perfect, but the rest of her was thin. Too thin. Grimy, dusty. None of this added up. 'Is the baby okay?'

'Yes, everything's fine. Except…' She finally let him go and moved her hand away from her face. 'I hurt my eye.'

Her right eye was weeping, closed and puffy. Her cheek was swollen. 'Whoa. Great job. What did you do?'

'I smashed a wall through and got dust or shards of chipboard or plaster or something in it. It hurts like hell.' She grimaced, swabbing at her damp face with a dusty fist.

Thank God she was okay. Thank God the baby was okay. Unfamiliar feelings sliced through him, accompanied by a strange lumpy sensation in his throat that made words hard to find. 'You were knocking a wall through? On your own? Are you mad?' He hauled in air. 'Don't answer that. I know the answer. Which one?'

'The kitchen-lounge one. I thought it'd be nice to have one big sunny room all finished in time for Christmas. Imagine what fun it'll be to have dinner in there.'

'The legendary Georgie Taylor Christmas, with enough liquor to sink a ship. And enough food to feed an army. But couldn't it have waited until you got help? Christmas is months away.'

'I've got to be prepared, Liam. This renovating lark takes time and I want Christmas to be perfect this year. I have grand plans.' With her one good eye she glared at him. 'If all you're going to do is tell me off, I'll ask for someone else to deal with my injury.'

'Go right ahead, missy. I think you'll find I'm the most experienced doctor here but, please, feel free to find someone better. I'll take you on a tour if you like. See if any one takes your fancy.' He thumbed the teary trail across her cheek. As he touched her an immediate heat suffused his body. He took his hand away, shaken by such an intense response. 'Oh, sorry, I forgot, you can't see.'

'Excuse my bluntness, Dr Mac, but your bedside manner is slipping. You're supposed to be nice to people when they come and see you with an injury. Basic ER doctoring.' She stuck her tongue out and if she'd felt any electric surge at his touch she didn't show it. He'd thought he'd purged her from his heart, that if he'd worked harder, faster, later then he wouldn't care so much. *Feel* so much. Too bad it hadn't worked. He didn't want to feel anything at all.

'Looks like I suck at interpersonal skills.' He picked up her chart and feigned calmness. 'That was meant to be an apology, by the way.'

'Must try harder. See me after class.' Her lips pressed together tightly. She took a breath and let it out slowly. She definitely looked thinner than the last time he'd seen her, cheeks a little more hollow. Her hair, T-shirt and jeans were covered in bits of wood chip and plaster, but her eyes…well, her good eye had darkened shadows round it. She gave him a reluctant smile that had him craving more. 'Oh, Liam, I've missed you. Missed this.'

Me too. 'Okay. So sit still and let me have a good look.' He tipped her chin towards him. And, yes, it would break every damned oath he'd ever made but, hell, if those lips weren't made for kissing. Which would be a pretty dumb move all round, because things would never be the same again. 'Trust me, I'm a doctor.'

She laughed. 'The old ones are the best. I bet you use that on all incapacitated women?'

'Only the bloody foolish ones who are hell-bent on being so independent they do themselves a mischief. You tried to knock down a wall on your own?' He focused on her eye, not her lips. Damaged or downright sexy. Either way his heart hurt.

'And who else could help me? I'm hardly going to pay someone.'

'You could have waited for me.'

'We both know that that wasn't an ideal option. I didn't know when you were coming back or if we were still friends. Are we?'

The heart hurt intensified. 'Come on, we'll always be friends, whatever happens. Now, let me look.'

'Okay. Give it your best shot.' She managed to open her eyelid a tad but blinked so rapidly he knew it was painful. It slammed closed again, tears rolling down her cheek.

He grabbed a tissue and wiped them away, unwilling to risk a skin-on-skin encounter again. 'Hey, it's okay. I forgive you.'

One eye widened in disbelief. 'What? You? Forgive me? But you were the one—'

'Seriously, no need to cry over me.'

Her lips pursed. Pouted. 'I'm not crying over you, matey. I just can't stop it watering.'

He looked away and began writing on her charts, mainly because it was far easier to do that than look at her. At least he didn't want to kiss the charts better. 'Well, whatever you've done, you've made an almighty mess in there. We're going to need to give you an eye bath to get the gunk out and then get an ophthalmic opinion.'

Her shrugging shoulders confirmed her agreement. 'So you'd better get it organised, then. You must be busy with more needy people than me. I don't mind seeing someone else. That would be if I could see at all.'

'Actually, I'm finishing my shift very shortly. I've got one patient to review then I'll sort out your referral while you have an eye bath. As soon as I'm done I'll wait with you.'

She shook her head. 'No need, honestly. If you don't want to.'

'Of course I want to.' He wasn't letting her go that easily. 'I know I made you angry and for that I'm sorry. I know I can be blunt and unthinking at times, but I realise there are two of us in this friendship…'

'Three now,' she hissed at him, rubbing her belly. His heart gave a little jerk. *His baby.* At once he felt proud and anxious. Excited and terrified.

Protective. Should he say something now?

No. She was damaged and he needed to deal with that, get things on a firmer footing. And work out exactly what it was he wanted to say. What kind of involvement he wanted. He rubbed his hand across his forehead. 'Come out with me for dinner, like old times. We could do fish and chips with extra grease, your favourite. Or curry. Thai, Chinese?'

'Urgh. Please. Don't mention—' She held up her hand then covered her mouth. 'I should have… Oh. No.' She grabbed the back of her chair and stood. Swayed a little.

'Should have what?'

She murmured through her fingers, 'Eaten something. I'm sorry, I have to—'

Then she was ripping back the curtain and staggering across the corridor to the toilet, leaving grubby handprints along the wall. He was beside her in a millisecond. Maybe she'd hit her head too and forgotten to mention it? Concussion? 'What's wrong?'

'Morning sickness? *Morning?* Yeah, right. Liars. Allday sickness, more like. Switches on at the thought of food. Goes away when I eat. In all this excitement I forgot to eat.' She pushed him back away from the bathroom door. 'Wait. Please, wait here. Before I chuck on your shoes.'

And he got a distinct impression that she probably didn't care if she did. 'No, Georgie, you can't see a thing. I will not wait. I will stay here and make sure you're okay.'

'Go do your patient review. You're not the boss of me.'

'How old are you?' He'd spent ten years getting to know that no one could ever be the boss of Georgie. He could hardly leave her and go back to ball-bearing-in-nostril kid when she was like this. 'You infuriating woman—'

But he stopped arguing as she slammed the door open and crouched down while he held her hair back in a thick makeshift ponytail. Her body shook. He held her steady.

This was his fault. He'd allowed this to happen. He'd facilitated this. He ran his hands across her back, felt the knobbly bones of her spine through her loose-fitting T-shirt. Jeans hanging off her hips. She was definitely thinner. This pregnancy was taking a toll on her and she was so damned proud she would never think of mentioning it. She needed a good meal. To be looked after. Someone to take care of her while she grew her baby, instead of believing she could do it all on her own. 'Does this happen a lot?'

'Enough.' She rocked back on her heels and wiped her mouth with toilet tissue.

Putting his hands under her arms, he hauled her up, made sure she was steady on her feet, watched her wash her hands and splash her face, wincing as cold water hit her eye. 'You're losing weight.'

She looked at him in the bathroom mirror, dried her hands and threw the paper towel in the bin. Peered at her eye in the glass. The swelling had worsened. Her one good eye pierced him. 'So are you.'

'South Sudan can do that to a guy.'

'Don't tell me you gave half your food away again?'

'I can survive. They don't have enough. I had plenty even with half-rations.'

'So how was it?'

'Messy. Murky. Complicated.' Like the rest of his life. 'But I'm back here and I want to know about you. How long have you been vomiting and how many times?'

'Simmer down. A few times a day. Counting wasn't helping. Let's just say, too much. It's perfectly normal. It's supposed to go once I hit the second trimester, so it'll be gone any day now. I'm fine.'

Fine? She was a mess. 'And in between the vomiting you're working full time and then taking out your frustration on your house walls? When do you rest?'

She threw him a smile that stopped way short of her dark eyes. 'Well, you know what they say about giving a job to a busy person. That's me! I like being busy.'

'No, you don't, Georgie. You like getting drunk in grungy bars playing loud eighties rock anthems, you like blobbing on the couch and watching reruns of your favourite soaps until you can say the dialogue better than the actors, you like strawberry ice cream, but not berry swirl. You like doing nothing at all if you can help it. You do not like to be busy.'

Uh-oh. Hip-planting was occurring. Both hands fisted. Bad sign. 'Well, you can add doing renovations when pregnant to that list. Go figure, you learn something new about people every day.'

'You know what they say about people like you?'

'No.' She turned to him and swayed a little, her cheeks drained of colour. Her eyes fluttered closed as she steadied herself, leaning against the sink, hands flopped to her sides. She looked exhausted. He wanted to swoop her into his arms, wrap her up in bed and look after her. As if she'd ever let him. 'Tell me, Liam, what do they say?'

'That only the pig-headed, wilful, independent and stubborn will not listen to anyone else. To the detriment of their health. You can't get sick, this baby needs you to be well. You need to stop and rest.' And he was not going to stand by and let anything bad happen. Period.

But contrary to everything he expected from her, she didn't rally. Her shoulders sagged as she gripped the sink, her voice so small he had to strain to hear her. 'Okay, okay, I get it. I'm done arguing. Whatever you say, you're the doc.'

Things must be bad. Never in all the years he'd known her had she so much as uttered a single word that would make her appear less than über-confident and capable.

He took her by the shoulders and steered her out into the waiting room. Found her a chair. Sat her in it. Put a finger over her mouth to hush any complaints.

She needed him and he wasn't going to let her get sick on his watch. It wasn't as if she could call a relative to come look after her—she didn't have any. No one to look out for her, to give her a break when she needed it. To take the baby for a few hours when she needed sleep. To babysit. Did she really have a clue how hard this parenting was going to be? 'You're going to start taking it easy. Doctor's orders.'

CHAPTER FIVE

'LET ME HELP YOU. Be careful, you have a nasty corneal abrasion.'

'So you keep saying. Urgh. So I'll play pirates and keep wearing the eye patch, me hearty.' Georgie had to confess that even though the thick white cotton wool patch didn't help much with healing, and made her look a lot like a numpty, it protected her eye from the glare of her house lights and made her think seriously about wearing safety goggles in the future.

But one thing she'd be reluctant to confess out loud was that the moment Liam had said she needed to take things easy it had felt as if a huge weight had been lifted from her shoulders. Because it was all very well trying to be big and brave and bold but sometimes, just sometimes, she tired of having to rely solely on herself for everything.

A deep breath escaped her lungs as Liam pushed the front door open. She was home. She could relax. At least in theory. It was a little harder in practice, having him in her space, being big and bold for her. Why had he suddenly come over all macho? Why did that make him even more desirable?

For that matter, why hadn't her desire dampened down over the last few months? And why was a man in combat kit and biker boots infinitely more attractive than anything else? She turned on the doorstep. Pregnant and now injured, this was not a good time to be finding her friend attractive. 'Thanks for getting me home. I'll be fine from here. Maybe we could catch up tomorrow when we're both feeling better.'

'Hey, what's the hurry? Are you scared about what I'll do?' He shook his head, eyes glittering with tease as he surveyed her body. If she wasn't mistaken, tension of a very sexual kind rippled between them.

Air whooshed into her lungs as she gave a sharp intake of breath. She wasn't afraid of Liam at all, she was more scared about what *she* might do, suddenly alone with him and very, very hot. 'No…er…I—'

'Don't panic. If it's a total mess I won't get mad. I'm here to help.'

He was talking about the state of her house. Not…*of course not*…anything else. 'I'll be okay. Honestly. Go home, you look beat, Liam. You must be jet-lagged and knackered.'

'Listen to yourself, Geo. You're not letting me help. You don't have to do everything on your own.'

'Of course I do. And I like it. That way I don't have to compromise on anyone else's plans, don't have to work to their timetable, I can just please myself.' She placed her hand against the wall and kept him on the doorstep.

He shook his head. 'Has anyone ever told you that you're the most stubborn person in the world?'

'You? Many times. But you're saying it as if I might care. And I don't.'

'Well, today you're my responsibility and I promised the discharging medical officer I'd take care of you.'

'But you were the discharging medical officer.'

'Go figure. So I'll fix you some dinner, have a look at the damage you've inflicted on your poor house. Make sure you're OK. Then, once I'm satisfied, I'll leave.' He went to squeeze past her, but she blocked his way.

'Promise?'

He frowned. 'If that's what you want.'

She wanted him to be happy about the baby—the single most important thing, and which he'd hardly mentioned. That was all. Well, and to hold her again. Possibly kiss her. Make out, maybe… But that would be a wish too far. 'What do you want, Liam?'

'To make sure you're safe, crazy lady. That's all.'

As he peered through the dust and grime he scratched his head, fluffing his short dark hair into little tufts. 'Bloody hell, Georgie. It's worse than I imagined.' He stepped in, walked across the floor, leaving large thick footprints in the grey film that coated everything. 'What the hell have you done?'

She hid a smile as she followed him into the house where she'd half knocked through the wall, making her downstairs pretty much open-plan. She had grand plans for this room, plans she'd been aching to share with someone. Him, mainly.

And even though she'd been beyond angry with him for the last couple of months, it was good to be able to see him—through her one useful eye—and talk to him. Because she'd been honest when she'd said she'd missed him.

She hadn't expected to have those strange feelings rattling through her again, though. She'd put it down to a cluster of hormones, but when he'd held her, cradling her head like she was something very precious, her heart had done a little leap. More, her body had started to hum with something dangerous. It was a bad idea, having him in her space. 'Personally, I think it's looking great. That old partition wall made everything dark and dingy. Just needs a little bit of cosmetic work and it'll be fine.'

'Plus finishing off. Cornices, a new floor.' He tapped along what remained of the plasterboard wall. 'You go and sit down in the lounge, if you can find the sofa under all this mess. I'll finish this off, clear up, then sort out something to eat.'

'You're hardly dressed for it.'

He looked down at his ex-army fatigues. 'They're old. I don't care. You just sit tight. That is, Miss Independent, if you know how to let someone else do the work.' He picked up the hammer and his forearms tightened. Capable hands, plus mussed-up hair already, and he hadn't even lifted a finger. How was she going to cope?

For a few minutes she lay back on her couch, closed her eyes and let relaxation take hold. It was lovely to lie there, listening to the crash of the hammer. The crumble of plaster, his deep male grunts as he swung and hit. He worked for a while then there was silence.

It stretched.

Suddenly interested in what was happening—or not—Georgie opened her eye and peered across the settling dust.

Oh, good Lord. Her stomach contracted as she inhaled a mouth full of dust. He'd taken off his shirt and was now measuring across the space with an industrial tape measure. Defined muscles stretched and contracted as he moved. Tight abs ridged down to his trouser waistband, a sexy smattering of dark hair pointed to a promised land. The man had no business looking like that, all sunburnt and muscular and just too damned hot. She swallowed, her mouth suddenly dry. Her throat was tight. Her breathing came quick and fast.

Staring was rude.

She reclosed her eye.

No good.

She wanted to look again. It was like watching bad reality TV: she knew she shouldn't watch, but she couldn't help herself. The man was gorgeous. And, heck, she'd always known what his body was like. Days spent with him at the beach had had little effect on her in the past. But now... Wow. He'd developed strength and solidity and muscles. Filled out into those broad shoulders. Her body hummed with need.

He turned to face her. 'You okay? You need anything?'

Not the kind of thing he'd want to give her. 'I'm just fine, thanks. But I wanted to let you know I'm sorry that you left and we'd fallen out. I was worried about you, you know, the whole time.'

He winked at her. 'Forgiven. Just about. I hate this arguing. It's not like us. We don't argue.'

So many firsts for them. 'You do realise that not once have you asked me for any details about the baby? About when it's due. Or if I've had any scans. Which I have.'

'I didn't know where to start.' Dropping the hammer to the floor, he looked lost. Shame faced. Terrified. 'This is all so new. It's pretty intense to get my head round.'

He was a long way behind her in this. For the last few months she'd been wondering whether her child having a father around mattered. Whether, in the long term, it would matter to him.

God, there were so many things she hadn't thought of when she'd gone hurtling into this process. Things she should have talked to him about. Things that could make or break their friendship for ever. It was already spinning out of control.

She pulled a scrap of paper from her purse, taking another risk at rejection. If he baulked at this then she'd reconsider. She got up and walked over to him. 'Here, have a look. An early scan. More of a blob really, but there she is.'

'She?' He took the paper in a shaking hand but didn't look at it. His face paled, he swallowed. And again. 'Too early to talk about gender, isn't it?'

She shrugged. 'I just think of her as a girl. Don't know why.' She pushed the paper closer to him. 'Take a look.'

His fingers closed over the top corner of the paper. He took a deep breath and looked down. No sound. No emotion. Nothing flickered across his face. Nothing to register that this was his child. That she was carrying his baby. Then he raised his head and gave her the scan picture back. 'My God.'

His voice was hollow and raw and she wondered what he was thinking. Maybe he was happy that she was happy but didn't know how to show it.

Her throat filled. 'I don't know what to say or do to make this easier…or less complicated. I know this is going to sound very selfish, but I want everything, Liam. I want this baby, but I don't want to lose your friendship.'

'And I…'

She thought he was going to say more but he didn't. His hands dropped to his sides as he shook his head and turned away.

Despite his doubts, he'd given her this gift. How could she have been so angry with him? He looked so empty and confused that she stepped forward and wrapped her arms round him, pulled him to her, and he responded by holding her close.

Her hands ran over muscles, dips and grooves of naked hot skin, slick with a light sheen of sweat. Her heart began to pound as awareness surged through her. His smell of surgical soap, aftershave and pure male heat filled the air. She inhaled it. And again.

His face was inches from hers. His breath feathered her skin. But she daren't move. Something stirred inside her deep and low. Her breasts tingled for his touch. Was he feeling this too? She hoped...but then what? This whole crazy messed-up situation didn't need complicating further. If he knew what was running through her brain right this second he'd probably walk away and never come back. For all she knew, he was probably planning that anyway.

Keeping her eyes tightly closed, she held her breath, felt him relax against her, felt his grip on her lessen. She didn't want him to let go. She wanted...

'Thanks for that, you old bat,' he whispered, lips pressed against her cheek, his scent intensified along with the tingling through her body, pooling in her groin. She couldn't think of anything but him, being in his arms, how good this felt.

Heat swamped her. There was no point pretending that what she felt for him wasn't real, that this was just a hormonal response. For goodness' sake, she'd been struggling with these weird emotions for months now. And, yes, she wanted to kiss him. She had to know what he tasted like. How he would feel.

With every risk of him leaving—and with no thought for the consequences—she turned her head, met his mouth. Felt his surprise resonate against her lips. Then a groan. A growl. A need.

Liam registered the first touch of Georgie's lips as his heart slammed loud and thunderous in his chest. For one split second a dark corner somewhere in his brain considered that this was the far side of madness—but then that thought was gone and he was left with nothing but heat and need raging through his veins.

Cupping her face in his hands, he opened his mouth to her. Felt her shaking body, heard the guttural moan from her throat, felt her tight fists grip his trouser waistband as he dragged her closer. And each of her responses fed his need. She tasted wet and hot and soft. Of salty tears and fresh pure joy. He closed his eyes at the sweet sensations she instilled in him.

Her hands made a slow trail to his backside as she clamped her body to his and she moaned again as she felt him harden at the press of her hips. He liked the way she felt against him. Liked the feel of her fingers on his body. The thrill of her touch.

As his hands slid down her back he brushed against her bra strap and the memory of those perfect nipples covered in lace made him ache to touch them. Slipping his hand under her T-shirt, he worked his fingers to her breast, felt the hardening nipples beneath silk. He wanted to feel them against his skin. Naked. Wanted to suck those dark buds into his mouth. To taste her everywhere. Wanted to feel her around him.

'Oh, God, Liam.'

'Georgie…' He opened his eyes, and immediately registered the harsh reality. *Damn.* This was Georgie. She was injured and pregnant and he was supposed to be looking after her.

Not taking advantage of her. This was Georgie. His best friend. The hands-off friend.

Who was pregnant.

With his child.

And, yes—ever since he'd held that picture in his hand and felt the deep singular ache in his heart he'd known that he'd fight heaven and earth for his baby. This was something that was a part of him and he couldn't turn his back on that.

He'd been about to tell her his plan. About the financial help he'd decided he wanted to give. About giving his son or daughter the best. Because they deserved it, Georgie did too. But…when it had come to it, after holding the scan in his hands, he'd panicked. He needed to be sure.

And then…this…had blown his heart wide open.

My God. Kissing Georgie.

In the cold stark light of day that dark corner of doubt started to flourish. Another person he would let down. His life was littered them. He sure as hell didn't want to include Georgie and the baby in that line-up.

The shock of what they were doing made him break away. He did it with little finesse and immediately saw the embarrassment or disappointment or just plain confusion flash across her gaze.

What the hell just happened? He coughed, cleared his throat, tried to sound a lot less shaken up than he felt. 'Well, that was unexpected. And not at all like kissing my cousin. But, then, Mike never was much good at tongues, apparently. You, however…'

'Always the joker.' She twisted away and stalked back into the lounge area, wringing her hands in front of her, clearly trying to work out how they'd gone from friends to…this. And what the heck they were supposed to do now they'd crossed an unspoken line. 'I'm sorry. I shouldn't have done that.'

'No.' He followed her but couldn't find it in him to sit down. His first and only instinct was to get the hell out. But running out on a woman who was sick and confused would make him a jerk and a coward. Although he couldn't help feeling that he'd already started to put distance there. He wasn't sitting down and talking reasonably, he was edging subconsciously closer to the door. He made himself stand still and focused on her. '*We* shouldn't have done that.'

'No, Liam. *I* kissed you. Embarrassment totally one hundred per cent complete.'

And he'd kissed her back—without any encouragement. What happened to reining in his libido, like any other decent man would? But something a lot like a mind meld had happened, pushing him to continue, and he'd been unable to stop.

Her lips were a little swollen, her good eye misty, hair messy, as if she'd just scrambled out of bed. She looked sexier than anyone he'd ever seen. Sexy and very off limits.

Actually, sexy, off limits and torn. 'Really, Liam, I think you should go.'

'Yes. I'll come back and finish this off another time.' He went to get his T-shirt, shook off some of the debris stuck to it before pulling it over his head. 'I should order you a pizza or something. You need to eat. Regularly and properly.'

'I can manage a phone quite well.' Waving her hand in front of her, she gave him a brief smile that was laced with hurt. 'Please, just go. You're officially off the hook. Go, and let me die a thousand embarrassed deaths in peace.'

He didn't know what was running through her mind, but he'd take a big guess that it wasn't him actually agreeing with her and leaving. The last thing she needed right now was uncertainty. But everything was messed up and muddied; there he was tangling her pregnancy with his feelings. He was having a hard time separating the baby issue from his attraction to Georgie. If they didn't get everything out in the open, this would be hanging over them for ever. 'But shouldn't we talk about what just happened?'

'No. That's not going to get us anywhere but deeper in trouble. It's pretty clear from your face that you're shocked. Please. Please. Just go.'

'I'll be back tomorrow to help you.'

'Off the hook, I said. I can manage. Please…' She was biting her bottom lip and looking so regretful that he did her bidding. She didn't want him around. And the truth was he didn't much feel like staying when his head and his body were so much at odds and he was at risk of making things worse. Or, even more catastrophic in the long run, helping to make her feel better in the only way he wanted to right now, which would be a one-way ticket to the far side of stupid.

CHAPTER SIX

MORTIFIED. JUST DOWNRIGHT mortified. Georgie was surprised her cheeks hadn't burnt a hole right through her pillow. Twelve hours later and she was still…utterly mortified. Half peering, half feeling her way around her house, she went downstairs to the kitchen, finished wet dusting all the surfaces, popped the kettle on and contemplated pushing two pieces of wholegrain bread into the toaster. Then gave up on the idea. Ruining friendships had sent her appetite running and hiding along with her pride.

And, okay, so he'd kissed her back, and appeared to have been enjoying it, but the moment he'd cut loose and let her go she'd seen doubt and fear and confusion run across those eyes. Eyes that had turned, once again, a darker shade of navy.

But, man, he'd tasted so good. *Felt* so good. Until the moment he'd jerked away and she'd wished she could have been swallowed up in the house's perennial dust cloud and whirled back to five minutes previously. Before the kiss that had probably, finally, broken their friendship.

And it was all her fault. She'd pushed him in one direction to give her his sperm, acknowledged he didn't want to go there at all but had done it anyway, and then had pulled him to her in a selfish moment of unwarranted and uninhibited need. Putting her head in her hands, she leaned against the grey kitchen bench, dusty again already, and groaned. Stupid. *Stupid*.

God knew where they'd go from here.

The doorbell rang quick and sharp and then Liam was calling out, and then standing in her lounge, muscled arms filled with brushes and buckets and tools, which he put on the floor in the corner of the room.

'Morning.' He stopped short and frowned, and her stomach contracted. 'Holy cow, you look awful.'

'Thanks a bunch. So do you. Why don't you come right in and make yourself at home?' She tried to make her voice sound nonchalant instead of shaky, but it all just came out weird and high-pitched. She was a little bit relieved to see that he looked like he'd just finished night duty—tired, paler and shadowed with a perfectly stubbled jaw. Which inevitably made her stomach contract again, but this time for a totally different reason.

She peered up at him, trying to measure his mood while at the same time trying to quell the nausea in the pit of her stomach. And she knew it was nothing to do with her morning sickness and everything to do with kissing her oldest mate—and even now, despite the mortification, wanting to do it again. The hot spots on her cheeks reappeared. 'I thought I said you didn't have to come and help. I know you have little time off as it is without bothering about me. I can manage fine.'

'And leave you here knowing what disaster was lurking behind this door? No way. No doubt if I left you in here with a hammer for any length of time you'd be completely blind and crippled within the hour. So basically I'm doing my colleagues at A and E a favour by keeping you out of their hair.' He made no effort to hide his smile. 'I thought we should go out for a while first, take a walk to the French market. Get out of this dust bowl and clear your lungs.' AKA not wanting to be in a confined space with her. She understood, loud and clear. 'You don't need an asthma attack added to your medical history.'

'My lungs are perfectly clear, thank you.' *Unlike my head*, she thought, which was filled with grimy confusion. 'The dust settles downwards all over the surfaces rather than floating upwards to my bedroom.' And at the mere mention of where she slept, usually near-naked, she had an unwelcome image of him also naked, in her sheets. Okay, so not unwelcome…in fact, very welcome indeed. Just unrealistic. And never going to happen. 'So…er… how are you? Good sleep?'

And maybe it was the mention of her bed that did funny things to him too, because all of a sudden his bravado slipped, he shoved his hands deep in his pockets and his gaze was not at her, but beyond, or around, or anywhere else but meeting her eyes. *Eye.*

An awkward unspoken tension hovered between them as he shifted from one foot to the other. 'I'm fine. How are you feeling? How's the eye? Using the drops as prescribed?'

'Yes, Dr MacAllister.' She patted the new patch gently, knowing that, added to the sleepless eye bags and the uncombed hair, it gave her a pathetically ill look. Still, having managed perfectly well for twenty-eight years pretty much on her own, she was far from fragile, but it did feel nice to have someone ask how she was feeling, even if it was just to avoid talking about the kiss or what the heck they should do now. 'The prickly headache's gone. I feel okay, a little sore, but raring to get going in here.'

'Well, first brioche and espresso are calling. Then you can go and do whatever you want to do for the day and leave me in peace to get this place sorted. I've got more stuff in the car—plaster, rollers, cornices, skirting, protective goggles and face masks. It'll keep me busy for a few...' His fingers speared his hair as he looked at the room, the magnitude of the utter mess they'd made clearly dawning. *And not just the house.* She'd made a mess of everything. 'Weeks.'

And he was also playing the *let's not talk about it* game. She could do that too. And perhaps, by the time they'd got to the market normality would be restored and her appetite would come out of hiding. 'Okay. Well, I'll just drag a brush through my hair and grab a jumper. Give me a minute or two.'

The sky was a brilliant cloudless cobalt blue as they strode down the hill, past rows of perfectly maintained colonial-style houses, just like hers was going to be...possibly next millennium. Luckily the market wasn't far so they didn't have too many moments of difficult silence to fill before they got there.

They walked through the car park to the stalls dotted around the forecourt of a large open-fronted building selling everything French. Colourful Provençale earthenware sat next to tins of *foie gras* and jars of bright thick jams; soft linens and dainty sprigs of lavender graced traditional wooden dressers; blue and white chequered tablecloths covered a hotchpotch of mismatched tables. People sat around, chatting and eating and laughing.

A stack of antique furniture sat in one corner of the building, rickety tables and chairs, kitchen and bedroom heirloom pieces. Georgie spied a quaint rocking bassinet in need of a little care and attention, adorned with the softest cream-coloured blankets and the cutest coverlets, and her heart did a little jig. It was perfect. But, as with most things here, it was also too far out of her price bracket.

She sighed, dragging herself away from such beautiful things. Buying would have to happen when she could afford it, not when it took her fancy. Liam noticed her gaze drift back to the bassinet but, then, he would. Annoyingly, he knew her through and through. Her heart jig went into a serious funeral dirge. It seemed everything was an issue between them these days. He nodded at the bassinet. 'Planning ahead?'

'Window shopping. At least that's free. I have to get my priorities straight. Firstly, I have to provide a decent place to sleep. Then I have to provide something to sleep in.'

'Babies cost a lot, eh? So much to think about, it's mind-blowing.' His forehead crinkled as he frowned. He looked as if he was about to say something, then changed his mind and tugged her to the juice bar instead. 'Okay, now you're going to have a fresh juice. Then we'll get a decent coffee and something to eat.'

'But—'

He placed a gentle palm against the small of her back and manoeuvred her towards the juice stall. 'No buts. And we're going to be the same as we always are when we come here. We're going to *ooh* at the cheese and hold our noses at the smell. And buy way too much and not eat it all. And then we'll have to fumigate your kitchen-diner-lounge room thing, whatever you want to call it.'

'I call it my living area, and it's going to be fabulous. But unfortunately I'm not going to eat any unprocessed soft cheese there or anywhere else. Along with alcohol, pâté and most kinds of processed meat that I love, stinky cheese is out for a while. Remember?' She patted her stomach. Damn the man, she was going to mention her pregnancy. It was part of her. Soon it would be most of her, plumping her out like a huge fat cushion. And then there'd be no denying it. Whether he liked it or not.

To her surprise, he grinned.

'Okay, so you're going to look at the cheese section and be downright miserable. Walk straight past the pâté, giving it a cold hard stare. Cast eye-daggers on that devilish salami and *jambon*. And then order a double helping of *pain au chocolat* and a *chocolat chaud* with lashings of cream, and still wallow in what you can't have instead of what you've got. Which, in my book, is three helpings of chocolate and it's not even ten o'clock.'

He stopped at the juice stall and ordered a freshly squeezed OJ for himself and a 'Brain Booster' for her, like always.

'Which is why you need this vitamin blast to counteract the sugar rush. And now we're going to talk about what happened last night, and when we've stopped cringing we're going to laugh about it. We will laugh. Eventually.'

At her shocked face he smiled again, but this time it was softer and more tender. And she liked it that he was trying to make things normal, that he was making sure she had the right things to eat, and that she was as content as she could be under the circumstances. This was the Liam she'd grown to love. Whoa. *Love?*

Platonically, yes. She loved him as any friend would love a friend. And fancied him, just a little bit. Which was understandable, because a lot of women did. He was just the type that appealed—dashing doctor with a great sense of humour and nice hands. Looking lower, she admired other parts of him too.

Okay, if he kept on staring at her and smiling like that she could definitely fancy him a lot.

'Na-ah.' Georgie shook her head as her cheeks heated

again. 'I'm not going to talk about it, I'm just pretending it didn't happen.'

'Well, I'm not. That's not going to work. It's going to be the big elephant in the...market, stomping around with us for ever. So we'll acknowledge that it happened. We'll agree it was—'

'A mistake,' she butted in, before he could say anything else. Because that's what it had been. A huge silly mistake.

'Here you go, you two. Your usual. Beautiful day...' The juice lady passed over large plastic cups of vividly coloured juice with perfect timing. Georgie took hers and handed Liam his. Then she wandered through the stalls, perusing the locally grown fruit and vegetables, the huge bowls of oily olives and myriad savoury dips, and feigned interest in everything apart from this conversation.

He was by her side in a moment. On any other day she wouldn't have paid much attention but today all her body seemed interested in was getting closer to that smell, in being near him, in having his lips on her skin again. His mouth was dangerously close to her ear. 'I was going to say it was nice. More than nice. In fact, it was a bloody revelation. I didn't think you'd be so...unleashed. But if you want to say it was a mistake, go ahead.'

She twisted to see him, his eyes glinting with tease. And heat. 'It was a mistake. And I'm so-o-o embarrassed.'

His arm snaked across her shoulder and he wrapped her in a sort of guy-style headlock hug thing. Which shouldn't have been remotely sexy but was the biggest turn on since her lips had touched his last night. 'It's okay, Geo. We can move on. It is possible.'

'You think?' Wiggling from his grip, she faced him. 'I kissed you! In fact, I almost attacked you!' The clatter of teacups reverberated around the space, and then ended in an abrupt silence. People stared and then turned away and pretended not to stare, which made everything ten times worse. She lowered her voice and her words came out a lot like a hiss. 'But, then, you kiss so many women you probably didn't even think much about it.'

Hadn't he? Had it been really not special? Had she not turned him on while she'd been burning up? By saying they could move on, was he trying to say that he didn't want her? Which was what she wanted, wasn't it? An end to these weird feelings? So why did she feel as if she'd been stabbed through the gut?

'To be honest, it's all I've been thinking about for the last twelve hours.' He steered her to a table and sat her down, grinning. He was enjoying this. Well, of course he was, this was Liam, the great non-committer. 'But what I need to know, Geo, is why?'

'Well…' If she knew that, she'd be up for a Nobel prize or something. The secrets of the universe. The chemistry of attraction. The laws of inconvenience and mortification. All started and ended with the *but why?* of that kiss. 'Haven't you ever wondered about…you know…us? What it would be like? What we would be like?'

He shrugged his gorgeous shoulders, but a tiny muscle moved in his jaw. 'I seem to remember you used the descriptor *ick* the last time we talked about this. So, honestly, it wasn't something I imagined could happen. Then, suddenly…*wham.*'

'I attacked you. I did—*do*—think it's an ick idea. But, then, for some reason last night I felt really connected to you. I'm sorry.'

'Stop apologising. Never apologise for kissing like that.' The waitress brought their order and he took a bite from his *croque monsieur*, which oozed melted cheese over the plate and looked almost as delicious as the man sinking his teeth into it. He swallowed and took a sip of espresso. 'Do you think it's because of the baby? Is this all because I'm the father? Because, frankly, you never gave me any reason to think you liked me…in that way. And, yes, we're going to keep talking about it like we talk about everything, so take your hands away from your face.'

'No. Yes. No. I don't know. It's all become too complicated. I felt weird when I saw you that day in the bar after you came back from Pakistan. Something was different. You seemed different, I felt different. Maybe it was the fertility drugs.' But that was a lame excuse. Lots of women took them and didn't go around kissing inappropriately. She finally had the courage to look up at him. Yes, something was still very definitely different. The feeling hadn't gone, it had got worse. 'Anyhoo, I got it out of my system last night, and we both know that nothing can happen, don't we…?'

'Absolutely. Understood.'

What she wanted him to say she didn't know. Except, possibly, that he wanted to do it again and again. That he fancied her in just the same way. Okay, she wanted the whole dang fairytale—but Liam had never been much of a Prince Charming, and she definitely didn't suit the Cinderella role, apart from the having no money bit. In that part she was absolutely typecast.

Placing his cup slowly into the white bone china saucer, Liam looked like he was carefully choosing the right words. 'We are in no state to start anything. Imagine if we did the sex thing and then fell out. Imagine if we took anything any further. Me the playboy and you pregnant and vulnerable. You need to think of the baby.'

'So I don't get to have a sex life? Women can have sex

when they're pregnant. Numpty.' Her eyes almost pinging out of her head, she picked up her fork and pointed it at him. 'And I am not vulnerable. Dare to say that again and I'll fork you to death.'

'No, never. Please. Anything but that.' His voice rose a teasing octave. Then got serious. 'You are one of the strongest people I've met. It was the wrong choice of words. Your situation makes you vulnerable. But you need someone who'll stick around. Someone who—'

'Wants me?' She closed her eyes wishing to hell she hadn't said that. It sounded so needy, and she wasn't. Just uncertain. And frustrated. Because she wanted to kiss him, she wanted to take him to her bed and tangle in the sheets, like she'd imagined. She wanted him…in a way she hadn't known could be possible. But he didn't want her. And he was trying so hard to put it gently and nicely and in a friendly way. It was humiliating that he even thought she needed the gentle treatment.

A sharp twist of pain radiated through her solar plexus. Even her own mother hadn't wanted her and had left her in a box on steps outside a church hall with nothing except a small cream woollen blanket and the clothes she'd been wearing. No one had ever claimed her. And bureaucracy and mixed-up paperwork had meant she hadn't been put up for adoption until she'd been too old, so she'd never belonged. Period. No one had ever wanted her.

And to a certain extent Liam was right. He didn't stick around anywhere for long, his job took him to some of the most dangerous parts of the world, and for the most part she thought it was exciting, glamorous even. But in reality it was dangerous. He ran a serious risk of being killed, caught or tortured. Did she want that kind of anxiety to infiltrate her life and that of her child's from here on?

His warm hand covered hers. 'You know I wouldn't do

anything to hurt you, right? But we can't put our whole friendship under threat because of curiosity. Things would inevitably change. They couldn't not change. Everything would come under the spotlight—past partners, broken promises, how we fill the dishwasher, whose turn it is to empty the bins. And everything we've ever done with other people will come under scrutiny too, what we've said, what we've done. There'll be expectations, and I'm not good with that. You know that. I don't want things to get complicated.'

Too late, mate. 'Like me having your baby?'

'Yeah. That. It's complicated already, without getting things involved sexually too. Not that I don't want to… wouldn't…you know…mind. That kiss wasn't ick. It was good. Very good.' He shook his head. 'God, this is awful. I think I preferred your way of pretending it didn't happen. Let's go back an hour, shall we?'

Or twelve?

He held her gaze for a few seconds and smiled apologetically. Then his smile melted. As if distracted by something over his shoulder, he turned away. When he looked back he didn't give her eye contact at all. Just stared down at his cup. 'And…'

'And?'

His head jerked up, and he looked spooked and shocked. 'Nothing. Forget it. Just that. I can't give you what you need.'

'I don't need anything. It was only a kiss.' But the caution in his eyes told her he had been about to say something else. Had broken off before he'd dared say it. What the hell? Her heart began to rattle against her rib cage. 'Wait a minute. What are you hiding?'

'Nothing. I don't know what you mean.'

'You look edgy and worried and I've seen that look on

your face many times. Right before you give your poor
sap of a girlfriend the old heave-ho.'

He looked down at his hands and dragged in a breath.
'Georgie, there's something else. Something I've been
meaning to say since I got back, but haven't...quite found
the right words.'

The chocolate croissant felt like a hard lump in her
churning stomach. Things had become really messed
up. 'I won't jump you again, if that's what you're worried about.'

'Of course I'm not worried.' No? Well, he just looked
it, then. 'I'm going to help you renovate your house, I
promised I'd do that. And I will.'

She knew a man was stalling when she saw it. 'And
then, when you've done your dutiful bit and fulfilled the
promises, you're going to adhere to the baby daddy contract and do a runner.'

'Far from it. In fact, just the opposite.' He stood up,
took her by the arm and began to walk back through the
market. 'Not at all. Georgie, I know it's taken me a long
time to outright say it, but I wanted to make sure. I was
trying not to mess you around.'

'What? What is it?' *You've met someone. Someone
important.* Words clogged in her throat, thick and fast.
'Spit it out, man. I'm on tenterhooks here.'

He gave her a sideways smile. 'Thing is, I do want to
be the father of this child. I want to provide, I want to
take responsibility for my baby.'

'What? *Your* baby? Your baby? Whoa. That's a surprise.'

'Yes. My baby. It's got my DNA. Just like we agreed.
Like you wanted.'

'But you said...' All her ideas tumbled around in her
head with a sharp mix of frustration.

All she'd known about him for ten years suggested he didn't want a child. He didn't want a family. He'd signed a damned contract, made that the only condition. So instead of being the far side of elated, her gut felt churned up. Would he change his mind again?

And again?

And then there was the small matter of the kiss, which coloured everything.

His involvement was what she'd wanted ever since he'd offered to be the donor, but this was not how she'd imagined it would make her feel.

Irritated, she shook her arm free from his. Shoppers jostled against them as they headed back towards the house. The busy street was so not the place to be having this conversation. 'I know it's what I wanted, but I thought you didn't…weren't…aren't…' She pulled herself together and chose bluntness and honesty. 'Why now? Why this all of a sudden? How can I trust that you'll take this seriously? You're so confusing.'

Unlike her, he seemed far from irritated, his voice steady and determined. 'It's not confusing at all. This is the most serious and the most single-minded I've ever been about anything.'

'And you decide to tell me now? Here, on Parnell Road?'

'Okay, I have to admit my timing's lousy.'

'You can say that again.' She whirled round to face him, her head woozy at the sudden and fundamental change in her life. She didn't know how she felt about this. He hadn't exactly declared his overwhelming love for the baby, and she didn't know how she *felt* about him—except that he'd just completely blindsided her and everything was getting more complicated by the second.

And more, she had to be sure this wasn't some passing

phase he'd move out of next week, next month, next year. 'Is this some kind of misdirected duty thing? Because you don't get to do that. You don't get to mess around with other people's lives just because it makes you feel better. Here one minute, changing your mind the next.'

'I won't change my mind.'

She tried to stay calm. 'A contract has been signed, Liam. You're legally bound, remember? Clause number six? *"You will have no paternal rights whatsoever over the child, and will have no authority of any kind with respect to the child, or any decisions regarding the child."'*

'Whoa. Really? Off by heart?' He stared at her openmouthed.

'What? I counsel about this exact dilemma every damned day, Liam. So I know the wording. Okay?'

'So you'll remember clause ten, then? You can agree to me having social contact—at your discretion.'

He'd certainly read it. He'd taken the time and effort to read and research. He was serious. 'Yes, I can, if I think contact will be good for the child. But what do you know about bringing up a child? About being a father? What's changed for you?'

Love, she thought. She hoped.

Because love for her child, even though it was still so small and so precious, had changed her fundamentally.

But Liam's expression turned thunderous. 'This is ridiculous. I don't want to mess anyone around, I want to be involved—the two things are completely different. I knew you were going to react like this. You just don't want anyone butting in on your little family of two.'

'How dare you? I would love my baby to have a father, you know that. You know I want that more than anything.' She shook her head. Amazing that he could think that. 'Is that what you think of me? That I'm selfish? That I want to keep this child purely for myself, like some kind of…toy?'

'Of course not. But surely, as the father, I have a say in things?' He really meant it. He wanted to be part of this. But could she trust him to be wholly there for them?

'No. Actually, you don't. You signed your rights away. All I know is that not many months ago you demanded a contract and now you don't want that. Maybe next month you'll want the contract again.'

He stopped short, breathing hard, dragged a wad of paper out of his jacket pocket. 'Here. Here's the contract.' He held the papers up and tore them in half. Then half again. Then again. Pieces of ripped paper fluttered to her feet like large bits of confetti. Only this was the severing of something, not celebrating the uniting of something. 'I want to be a father. The father of the child you are carrying. My child.'

And the word 'love' is still not there.

She'd listened hard and it was still missing. No matter how much she wanted it to be there, no matter how much she strained to hear it in the cadence of his words, in the silence between them.

He wanted to be a father, but he didn't want to be a daddy. That was the fundamental difference. He wanted the label but not the emotional involvement. That was Liam through and through.

But, on the other hand, if he was truly serious and did want to be involved, she couldn't deny him that, couldn't deny her child the right to know its father.

Why did this have to be so complicated? Why couldn't he have kept to his side of the deal? Why did she have to have developed more than friendly feelings for him? Those emotions were tainting things, making her think in a way she'd never done before. This whole morning wasn't about the kiss at all. It had never been about the kiss.

His hand was on her arm now. 'Georgie, I don't want to have this conversation here on the street and I don't want to argue. This was the furthest thing from my mind. You look upset and that really wasn't my intention. I honestly thought you'd be pleased.'

Pleased? If his intentions were genuine then she'd be delighted. How could she not want him to be a father? He was smart, funny and, if she was honest, would make a great daddy—if he stuck around long enough. And there it was again, her immediate concern: he just wasn't the staying sort of guy. For whatever reason—and she only knew half of his story—he didn't commit.

She picked the pieces of paper up and shoved them at him. Then hesitated on her doorstep. 'Can we talk later? This is pretty big for me, I need some time to think things through.'

'Yes, by all means, think it through.' He followed her up the steps and when it was clear he wasn't giving up, she took her key out of her bag. As he watched her he shook his head. 'But I need to say this now, Geo, and I need you to listen. It's tough work, bringing up a child. I don't want you to go through it on your own and I don't want our child to miss out on having a father. I know how that feels and I couldn't condemn my own flesh and blood to that kind of life. Don't you want me to be involved?'

'This is my flesh and blood too. My only flesh and blood. So I've got to be careful, make the right decisions.' At least he had a family. He might not want to have them, but he was tied to them. And now she would be tied to him for ever. Oh, why the hell hadn't she thought this through more thoroughly at the beginning? 'What exactly do you mean by "involved"? Cash? Because that's not enough. Is that why you're here? To pay us off or something?'

'It's been in my head for the last few weeks, I just didn't know how to say it. When to say it. What to say, even. But the more I see you, the more I think about it, the more it makes sense.'

'It's not about making sense, it's about how you feel. In here.' She touched her chest. It felt a little cracked open and raw. 'In your heart and your soul. You can't do something because it makes sense, otherwise we'd never do any of the rash, amazing stuff we do. Like this pregnancy thing from the start. None of it made sense, not to you or anyone else. But it did to me.'

'And it does to me now.'

His words hovered in the air as she thrust the key in the lock and threw the door open. She took several long deep breaths and tried to clear her thoughts.

Then tried to explain them to him. 'If I was going to co-parent I would expect a fully one hundred per cent committed father who was around, who wouldn't flinch during the darker times. Because there will be some, I'm sure.' And although she adored Liam, he wasn't re-liable. He was away a lot of the time, never knowing when he'd be home. And she couldn't get past the fact that he'd told her that this baby plan was the worst thing he'd ever heard.

'It's got to be for ever, you can't change your mind again. I don't want to open our child up to a whole world of hurt. I saw plenty of kids at the home whose families made promises and broke them, and in the end broke their kids' hearts and crushed their spirits.'

'I know you had a hard time, Georgie. And that's why

I'm here now. So our child doesn't have to go through what you went through.'

'You have no idea. You don't know what it means to be alone. To make up a pretend family because you don't have any. To watch others being chosen. To wish that someone, anyone, would choose you. And to try to be, oh, so brave when they didn't, when inside every part of you is crumbling.' She would never crumble again. This child inside her gave her twice the strength and three times the resolve. 'This is your last chance to decide, Liam. I'll hold you to whatever decision you make now. This is it. No going back. No coming to me in three years, six, twelve and saying you made a mistake and you've changed your mind again. You have to be in or out—for ever.'

This was something Liam could answer. Because this was the one thing he knew. He would not let his child down. He'd known that with every damned fibre of his being since the moment he'd seen her carrying his child. Since he'd seen that scan of a real living being. His child. Their child.

Every single mention of a baby, every thought of who was growing inside her, brought back the crushing pain again. And with that hurt still beating against his rib cage he knew he'd make every effort to make his child safe. Because that was his job. A father did that.

But he was also going to keep any emotions out of it. Because, hell, he needed to keep his heart safe, too. He would provide from a distance. He would have visits but he wouldn't—couldn't—put any of them at risk by allowing himself to care for them. He would treat his child with the same compassion and consideration he treated his patients, no more and certainly no less.

'I know what I said. I didn't think it through. But this

is my child and my responsibility and I will never shirk from that. I don't want your experiences for our child, or mine either. This child will know he's always wanted.' This was not how Liam had imagined this scenario playing out, but he had to go with it. He'd already stumbled too far along without saying what he felt. Although he'd been shocked by the ferocity of Georgie's reaction. He'd seriously misjudged her. She was growing braver and stronger and more independent every moment she carried that baby. 'I am in it for ever.'

'How can I be sure?' Her hands were on her hips while her dark eyes blazed.

'So tearing up the contract isn't enough for you?'

'No. Actions speak, Liam. I want actions—and not dramatic hollow ones like those shreds of paper.'

Now this was well and truly out in the open he knew there could never be any more kisses. He needed to keep a good long distance from her, too. Anything else would make things far too complicated. They could both be good parents if they were a team, a *platonic* team. Messing with that, opening a whole potential for destruction, would be a recipe for disaster.

He knew how much pain a child suffered when their parents couldn't bear to look at each other. Knew how destructive it was, watching arguments unfold, always calculating when the bomb was going to drop. Always being on guard. Always feeling, believing, *knowing* that every single ounce of friction was his fault. He couldn't put his own child through that, so if there was no intimacy there would be no chance of that damaging scenario happening. 'You'll know, Georgie, because I'll damned well prove it to you.'

CHAPTER SEVEN

Three months ago...

'IT'LL KEEP ME *busy for weeks.*'

Ha. He wished.

By Liam's reckoning it should have been finished months ago, but whenever he turned around this tinpot wreck of a house threw another job at him. Georgie had been wrong about the roof. With the winter came high winds that blew off and cracked more than enough tiles for the whole thing to need replacing.

Then there was the floor in the kitchen. Weathered and abused over seventy years, it took four consecutive weekends to sand it down enough that it was even and usable. Then three coats of varnish. A perfect parquet floor it was not, but it was now an acceptably usable one. All done on a tight budget, and fitted in between exhausting twelve-hour shifts at work. It had taken a lot of coercing Georgie to even allow him to do that.

Climbing down the stepladder from where he'd been fixing the new light fitting in the flash living area, he huffed out a long breath. He had to admit she'd had a point about knocking the wall down, the open-plan space was amazing. With the renovated floor and antique white walls it was impressively large and light, with a good flow from one area to the next. She'd managed to find, on the cheap from a trading website, a set of elegant French doors that opened the kitchen out onto the small deck. Beyond that was a riotous garden, overgrown and dingy. But he had no doubt she had plans for there too. The woman clearly had a gift for renovation.

A loud bang and a very unladylike curse came from above him. Liam was up the stairs and in the bathroom in two seconds flat. 'You okay? What the hell was that?'

'Just a little contretemps with a tin of paint. And… damn, I was so nearly finished.' From her crouched position on the floor she grimaced up at him as a pool of off-white gloop seeped across stained dustsheets. A paintbrush stuck out of her denim dungarees pockets, her face was splattered with paint and she wore a plastic carrier bag tied round her hair. She dabbed at the ever-increasing seepage with a rag, huffing and puffing a little. 'I'm going to have to nip out to the hardware store and get some more paint now. Do we need anything else?'

His eyes flickered from her to the stepladder, back to her. *Unbelievable.* 'You were painting the ceiling?'

'Um…yes?'

'After I specifically told you it was next on my list of jobs?'

'Um…yes.' This time there was no hint of apology. 'It needed doing and it was next on *my* list. I was free to do it, so I made a start.'

'Why can't you accept more than the slightest bit of help without a row? You are slowly driving me crazy. No—make that rapidly driving me crazy.' There was only so much independence a guy could take before it became downright stubbornness, and then it made him really mad. 'You were supposed to be taking a break.'

'Breaks are boring. There's nothing more satisfying

than seeing the instant difference a coat of paint can make to a room. Look, isn't it great?' She gestured at the white over the dirty green and, yes, it looked good. That was not the point.

'And risk a broken collarbone...or worse?' He didn't allow his brain to follow that train of thought. Already she was showing signs of discomfort with her growing bump—all it had needed was one wrong step. 'These ladders are unsteady, and those trainers have a slippery grip. You said so yourself.'

'I was fine.'

'Oh, clearly. So fine that you dropped the paint can?'

'No one likes a smartass.' With an irritated groan she whipped the plastic bag from her head and stuffed it into her pocket, then gripped the side of the bath to assist her to transition from sitting to standing—flatly refusing his outstretched hand. Once up she rubbed her back, which pushed out her stomach, fat and round and very obviously pregnant. Her face had filled out a little too, her long hair, which she'd piled on the top of her head in some sort of fancy clip, was glossy. Man, was it shiny, and it took him all his strength not to pull her close and inhale. Somehow the more annoying she became, the more he wanted her. Seemed he was hard-wired to protect her too.

But he'd never contemplated giving her this job and hadn't thought she'd be so hell-bent on doing what she wanted. How much did he need to do to show her he was invested too? She'd taken him at his word and had never referred to the contract again, but he knew she watched him and wondered. Every day. And every day he tried to prove to her he was up to the father job.

He just hadn't contemplated how hard it would be to keep his emotions out of the agenda.

'How about you sort out the cupboards in the kitchen

instead, like we talked about earlier? I'll do this when I've finished the lights downstairs.'

And, yes, it was like this every week. She had a problem or, more usually, the house had a problem and he had an insatiable, irrational need to fix it. Except the biggest problem was that he shouldn't be here at all. The baby wasn't due for months, so in theory he could let her get on with it. But, well, he couldn't.

Her voice had a sudden edge to it. 'You can't bear to be in the same room as me for five minutes, can you?'

'Sorry? What on earth are you on about?'

'It's just that every time I go into a room you leave it. It's been going on for weeks, it's like there's a revolving door. Me. You. Me. You. I'm getting dizzy.'

'Ridiculous.' Truth was, he couldn't bear to *not* be in the same room. Being with her was killing him. A long, drawn-out agonising death of lust. He was doing this for the sake of his child, making sure they had everything they needed. At least, that was what he told himself, and not because he didn't want to wake up every morning and not have the prospect of seeing Georgie's smiling face or inhaling her scent that pervaded everything in the house.

'Is it me? Is it seeing me like this that you don't like?' She paraded in front of him, laughing, sticking her tummy out—there was a bubble where her belly button protruded. 'Because I happen to love it.'

He laughed. 'Or maybe it's a coincidence, ever thought of that? Perhaps I just always happen to be about to leave when you come dashing in. Bad timing, maybe, and you're looking for it so you have confirmation bias?'

'Yeah, right. Never try arguing with a know-it-all doctor. I notice it because it happens, matey. And don't deny it.'

Avoiding the wet paint, he took her hands and faced

her, putting a serious tone in his voice, ignoring the immediate sharp jolt of electricity that ran through him as he touched her. 'Okay, yes, Geo, you're right. I'm sorry to have to break it to you, but you do look terrible, hideous, unsightly. In fact, I was going to ask you to cover up with that dust sheet. But now you've spilled on it I'll just have to put up with you as you are.' He laughed at her tongue sticking out of her mouth. 'Yeah, really, I can't bear being with you, and that's why I spend every spare hour here, doing your bidding.'

If only she knew how partly true those words were. It was seeing her, full stop. Seeing Georgie carrying his child, seeing her turn this dilapidated wreck into a home for her family. His family.

Every time he turned around there was something else: the piles of gifted baby clothes; the stockpile of nappies for newborns. The baby scans on the fridge—the most recent one at twenty weeks, where he could see every finger and toe. Where the ribs encased his baby's fast-beating heart. Its chubby belly. The MacAllister nose.

Liam's heart swelled, then tightened. The memories threatened to swamp him again. He rubbed his chest, but the pain wasn't physical, it was psychological. And every time he saw Georgie it got worse.

And still he kept on coming back. Because he couldn't not. Because he couldn't contemplate an hour of his life when he didn't see her.

She dropped her hand from his grip and began wiping a paintbrush on the rim of the can. 'I am grateful, really. You don't have to give up all your spare time...' Her hand went to her belly and she made a sharp noise. 'Oh!'

He knew that look. He knew most of them now, thank God, because she never complained about any of the changes she was experiencing and he knew a few of them must have taken some getting used to. A rise of eyebrows and a gentle smile meant baby movement. A frown but determined-not-to-show-it stubbornly stiff jaw meant she had backache. A fist against her chest meant heartburn. He'd never been so aware of anyone in his whole life. 'Kicking again?'

'Yes. It doesn't hurt, it just makes me jump. It's weird. though, I don't know if I'll ever get used to it—it's like a whole crowd of butterflies stretching their wings. He's a little wriggler, this fella. I think he might be a martial arts expert when he grows up.'

He nodded towards her belly, his heart suddenly aching. 'She might be a dancer? Cheerleading? Gymnast? Scottish country dancing? That has kicks, doesn't it?'

Her eyebrows rose. 'The ones I learnt at school had a lot of skipping in circles and peeling off. I don't remember kicking. Apart from hot sharp prods to my nine-year-old partner's ankles. He had no clue what he was doing and was far happier pulling faces at his friends than swinging me in a do-si-do.'

Then clearly the boy had been a prize idiot.

Clearing the paint pot and mess out of the way, Liam stood her in front of him. Goddamn, she was beautiful, all flushed and smiling. He had to admit that being pregnant suited her. She'd never seemed so content. Apart from the odd moment when he'd catch her staring out of the window into the distance, or looking at him with a strange expression on her face. 'Show me?'

'What? Scottish dancing, in a tiny bathroom? Are you nuts? Silly me, of course you are.'

'Probably.' He took her hands in his and twirled her round. 'Like this?'

'Not even remotely.' Her head tipped back as she laughed, and for the first time in for ever things were

back to normal between them. There was no baby, no
contract, no tension, just two old friends messing about,
like they'd done hundreds of times before. He twirled her
again, faster, and caught her in his arms and she squealed,
'Stop! I'm covered in paint, my hands—'

'Are fine. Now, show me what to do. Like this?' He
made a woeful attempt at a highland jig that had him
stumbling over the stepladder. 'Clearly this needs practice.'

'And a lot more space.' She sucked in air, and again,
doubling over with laughter. 'You are a lot worse than
David Sterling.'

'David?'

'My nine-year-old partner. Broke my poor innocent
heart when he kissed Amy Jenkins at the Year Four social, but at least he had rhythm.'

'I have rhythm.' And Georgie's heart was too damned
precious to be broken again. Although Liam had a feeling that when all this was done, he'd be no better than
David-bloody-Sterling.

'Oh, yeah?' She prodded him in the stomach, and he
wondered whether that was a step up or down from being
kicked in the ankle. 'I've seen your rhythm, mate, at Indigo, late at night, when you're filled with booze.'

'Bad, huh?'

'Actually, no, not at all. You're a good dancer, probably better than I am if I'm honest. But I'm not exactly
going to want to admit that, am I?'

'You, my lady, are such a tease.' Feeling suddenly way
out of his depth, he gave her a smile and it was pure stubborn willpower that stopped him from kissing her again.

'Really? You think so? I haven't even started.' She
smiled back and the air between them stilled. Her hand
slipped into his and squeezed, and she peered up at him

through thick dark eyelashes. And he was sure she was just being Georgie, but that kiss hovered between them again, in her words, in the frisson of electricity that shivered through him. In the touch of skin on skin. Her voice was raspy. 'Is it just me or is it very hot in here?'

'Hmm. You want to try peeling off? That might help. I could give you a hand. That is one thing I am very good at.' He rested his palm on her shoulder, toying with her T-shirt sleeve. Her pupils widened at his touch, heat misted her gaze and he knew then that she was struggling too. That just maybe she wanted the physical contact that he craved.

But, goddamn, he knew that was the most stupid thing to say, especially when they'd agreed to go back to situation normal between them—but it was out there now. He was tired of fighting this…and absolutely sure he shouldn't have said those words.

Time seemed to stretch and he didn't know what to do. Apologise? 'Georgie—'

'Oh. There it is again. It always takes me by surprise.' Shaking her hand free from his, she pressed her hand to her belly again watching his reaction, eyes wary now. She gave her head a little shake as she stepped away. 'And don't look so worried. I won't ask.'

'No.' She wasn't talking about his faux pas. Once she'd asked him if she wanted to feel the baby kick and he'd refused. Point blank. And she'd never asked him again, but sometimes made a point of telling him when it was happening. And, by God, he wanted to, but he knew he couldn't, that with one touch of her, and of their baby, he'd be compelled to want more. And that didn't fit in with the emotionless parenting idea. Or the platonic parenting either.

The atmosphere in this minuscule room was reaching suffocation point, he needed to cut loose. 'Okay, so break time. You go put your feet up and I'll pop out to the hardware store. We need more sandpaper anyway. I'll get more paint, and I've got to get the right bulb for the light fitting—you got screw-in instead of bayonet.'

'Oops. Sorry. And when you come back, do you think we could spend more than two minutes in the same place? You won't run out on me?'

The ten-million-dollar question. 'This house is throwing us so many problems we have to divide and rule if we're going to win. Now, get that kettle on and I'll bring back biscuits for afternoon tea.'

'Are you sure?'

'Buying biscuits isn't exactly a difficult task. Of course I'm sure.' And, yes, he knew that wasn't what she'd meant. Dodging bullets seemed the aim of today. 'Chocolate? I know, white chocolate with raspberry. Two packets.'

She threw him a huge grin. 'Oh, Liam, I do like it when you talk dirty.'

He could have been out for another few months and it wouldn't have been enough to stop the need surging through his veins. In less than an hour he was back, trying to locate her, with his peace offering of her favourite biscuits. She wasn't in the kitchen, and the contents of the cupboards were still in boxes in the same place on the floor.

Wondering if she was actually doing as he'd suggested and taking a nap, or on that damned stepladder again, he mounted the stairs two by two, in total silence, glad that he'd fixed the creaking floorboards. The bathroom was empty.

Intrigued, he walked along to her bedroom, heard the

radio, a song he didn't recognise, and she was singing along. It sounded ditsy and bright and he knew he should call out, make her aware of his presence, but something compelled him to be quiet as he approached her room. He told himself that he didn't want to make her jump.

She was standing in front of her closet, holding a black lace dress up against her body and looking in the mirror, turning from side to side, stretching the fabric across her belly. The work dungarees had gone, and now she was wearing flannel shorts and a baggy blue T-shirt. After a few seconds she frowned and threw the dress on the chair then shook her hair free from the hair slide. It cascaded down her back, a river of lush honey curls. Her breasts strained against the T-shirt. She was dusty and paint-streaked and fertile and ripe. She looked sexier than any skinny model on the front of the magazines, sexier than any woman he'd ever laid his eyes on. His heart stuttered. He took a step forward, paused.

She still hadn't heard him. Her humming continued. Taking a brush from the closet, she gathered a fistful of hair and started to brush rhythmically. And even though he knew he shouldn't be standing here, watching her do this, knew he was breaking a zillion unspoken promises they'd made in the aftermath of the single kiss, he still couldn't bring himself to speak. His throat was scratchy and raw, and his body was on fire. Each swipe through her hair was considered and resolute, her slender arm moving up and down, almost trancelike, what he could see of her face was calm and relaxed.

She was lost in thought, and still singing the upbeat, happy song. The reverence with which she took each brushstroke made his heart contract. The glossy sheen of her hair, the ridges of her back as she moved and shifted from foot to foot. Her body swayed a little, her backside bopping to and fro; and maybe it was the heat from before, the soft light in the room, the smell of her, the intimate nature of watching her, but he struggled with a powerful urge to carry her to her bed and make love to her.

He realised he was hard, that his hands were clenched against his body's strain towards her. That he had to consciously control his feet and make them still.

How could someone doing something as mundane as brushing their hair bring him to the edge of reason?

After a few moments she started to coil her hair back up onto the top of her head again—and that was it—his control was lost. In a second he was behind her, hands on hers, whispering close to her ear. 'Don't. Leave it down.'

In response to his sudden arrival she turned, shaking. Confusion racing across her face. And heat too. 'Oh, my God, Liam. You made me jump.'

'Sorry. I just…' He curled a lock of her hair around his fingers, pressed it to his mouth.

She placed her hands on his chest, that intimate gesture firing more need through him. 'What?'

'I can't do this any more.'

'Can't do what?'

'I can't keep away from you. Ever since that kiss I've been hiding out.'

She let out a long breath and her face creased into a soft smile. 'I knew it. I knew you were up to something. See. I told you. You are avoiding me. I was right. I'm always right.'

'Intuitive, perhaps. Give a guy a break. I was doing the right thing.' He touched her lips with the pad of his thumb, tracing the soft path, the delicate curve. They were pink and moist and kissable. He remembered how good she had tasted and suddenly he couldn't wait any longer. Finesse lost, he dragged her to him. 'Come here.'

She inhaled a stuttered breath, her lips opening a little, her body trembling. And made a concentrated effort to calm it. She briefly closed her eyes, opened them again. 'But I thought—'

'Shh… Thinking is overrated.' He reached his arms round her thickened waist, pulled her closer, spiked his hands through her hair and nuzzled right into it. Cupping the back of her head, he held her face close against his throat. Just held her against him until the shaking stopped. Until he could look at her again. He wanted to kiss her, but he wouldn't, wouldn't make things difficult. But he could hold her. Could feel her soft curves and taut belly pressing against him.

Breathe.

He prayed for the awareness and attraction to go, to be left here with just his old friend Georgie and nothing else, nothing complicated, because he knew that by taking those steps across the room he'd made things muddier than ever. But it was so compelling to hold her, to feel part of something so good. To be, for once in his life, actively looking forward, instead of just running from the past. To be accepted for the man he'd grown into.

Only now he knew how it felt, he didn't want to go back. Couldn't go back.

And then…the strangest of sensations. A tiny shiver against his hip, something almost ethereal…then it was gone.

His baby kicking.

Breathe.

But there was no oxygen. His chest hurt as he tried sucking in air, there was no space for anything more, emotion had filled his chest. A hard core of deep affection, a protective need, a desperate ache. And pride. His baby was moving, stirring in her belly. The shaking started again, but this time it was his body that was on the edge of control. 'Was that...?'

'The Scottish country dancer?' She pulled away a little and pressed a palm against his cheek. 'Yes, Liam. It was. There it is again.' She reached for his hand and pressed it against her bump. It was a flutter, not a whack. At least, not against his palm. The whack to his heart was mighty, though. And, God, no, he didn't want to feel this. Not this ache. Not this wanting. He didn't want to feel anything.

'Wow.' It was all he could manage. His throat was thick, his heart rampaging as all the pain came hurtling back. Pain, and yet something else, something profound that made his soul soar.

He didn't know what to think or what to say as he stepped back. He'd been trying to avoid any kind of physical contact with Georgie but he'd been unable to stay away, had been compelled to hold her. Now his reasoning had been proved right. All his emotions were getting tangled up and he didn't want that. Didn't want any emotions to get in the way of clear thinking.

Obviously sensing him detaching already, she tugged at his hand and pulled him to sit on the bed, her other hand stroking his shoulder. And it was tempting to sit with her and let her stroke the tensions away, but he couldn't sit, so instead he walked to the window and looked out at the encroaching night. Dark shadows filled the garden, like the dark shadows in his heart. He needed to find some place where he could breathe normally again.

Georgie's voice reached to him. 'I know this is hard for you. I just don't know why. I'm trying to understand, I really am, and I'm trying not to push, but I want to know. I might be able to help. Tell me about your sister, about…Lauren.'

'I can't… I don't want to.' Didn't want to spoil this moment, where *this* child was vivid and vibrant and had so much potential.

There was a long silence where the night breathed darkness into the room, and he thought she might have fallen asleep.

When she eventually spoke she sounded disappointed, and that was so not his intention. 'Some time, then. Tell me some time.'

But it was too much to ask of him. He didn't even know what words to use. Lauren…had been there, and then she hadn't been. And a huge hole had blown open in his eight-year-old heart that had never been filled with anything other than anger. At himself, mainly. At his parents.

And now… 'It'll only spoil everything.' He forced air out and inhaled again, trying to make some space in his chest, but still he felt constricted and tight. 'Let's get the hell out of here. I need to breathe.'

CHAPTER EIGHT

'THE PUDDING PLACE?'

'The right choice?'

'Oh, yes. Most definitely. These desserts are to die for. I couldn't think of anywhere more perfect.' Georgie's gaze slid over the rows and rows of chocolate éclairs, mini-Pavlovas and baked cheesecakes in the little dessert-only café, and then landed on Liam. She regarded him with caution. Whatever had been haunting him had passed. The shadows on his face had cleared a little, leaving him pale and reserved and yet trying so hard to act normal. She hadn't realised how emotionally distant he could make himself, even when he was in the same room.

For so many years his background had never mattered to her and she'd respected his need for privacy and put his quirky way with relationships down to immaturity at first, then pickiness, but now she believed it was meshed in fear. Of what, she wasn't sure. But now…now it meant everything. It meant the difference between them surviving this strange set-up they'd created or failing it.

If she could understand why he held back so much, perhaps she could help him surmount it. Because although he'd shown commitment with his time, she still didn't wholly trust that he would be there when it mattered. That he wouldn't change his mind and run. And she wasn't prepared to take that risk with her heart or her child's.

A waitress arrived and asked for their order. Georgie couldn't decide. 'I think I'll have one of each. To start with.'

'You sure that's enough?' Liam laughed, a little more carefree. 'Or are you just keeping it light until your appetite really gets going?'

'This eating-for-two business is pretty damned good. I'm going to miss it after the baby comes.'

He gave his order then turned the menu over and over in his hands as he spoke. 'In South Sudan it's not uncommon for women to have large families, sometimes up to twelve kids. Imagine the fun you'd have then: eating for two for ever.'

'I'd be the size of an elephant if I did that and be on a perpetual diet for the rest of my life.' The chocolate éclair was divine. Great choice. Thick and rich and moist. It slid very easily down her throat. 'But, listen, you never tell me properly about your trips. It's always *murky* or *dry* or *messy*. But it must be way more than that.'

Leaning back in his chair, he crossed his arms and watched her eat. His gaze wandered over her, causing a riot of goosebumps over her skin, and she stared right back. Splatters of cream paint stuck to his old grey T-shirt. Funny, she remembered buying that for him years ago at a gig she'd been to when he'd been covering the night shift. It had been a little baggy on him back then but now it barely contained his solid biceps and stretched across a chest of muscle. His hair was sticking up in odd places, and he was dusty.

His knuckles were scratched and his skin torn. He looked rugged and edgy and it was such a turn on to watch him move she could barely think straight. This was dangerous territory. Every second spent with him was pushing her closer to an edge she knew was going to be at once delicious and yet potentially soul-damagingly painful.

He took a sip of hot black coffee. He'd ordered just that, no food. With wall-to-wall dessert on offer the man was clearly mad. 'So what exactly do you want to know?'

'What kinds of things do you get up to out in the field? The people you meet. I know you usually work at the tent cities, but what are the real cities like?'

His shoulders lifted in a sort of nonchalant shrug. 'The agency gang are pretty solid— people who want to do good, but all fed with a huge dose of reality. We know our limitations, there's never enough of anything—resources, people, help—but there's no point beating yourself up about what you can't achieve, you just get on and do what you can. While we're there the team always develops a huge bond, but such intensity can also drive you completely nuts. We do what we can in desolate and desperate parts of the world. There are, sadly, too many of them. But we do make a difference.'

'Well, there's no shortage of work, judging by the stories in the papers about floods, earthquakes and war zones. There's endless need for you everywhere.' He went to them all without any hesitation and she'd never once heard him utter one word of complaint about the harsh conditions he must have to endure, and the terrible things he must have seen. He kept everything tight inside him, but she didn't doubt he made a difference. He must have saved hundreds of lives and given thousands more help and much-needed hope. 'And the people you help? What are they like?'

'Desperate. Stoic. Honest. Victims. They have nothing apart from the clothes they stand up in. No homes, nowhere to call their own. There's always a threat—if it's not soldiers and fighting, or landmines and rogue devices, it's weather. Too much rain, or not enough. They need so much more than we can give them. But we fight to save their kids' lives. It's important to have a generation of hope that can break through the cycle of poverty and suffering.'

Pride rippled through her chest, her already tender heart bruising just a little more. Between him and her baby her emotions were being bumped around all over the place. 'But isn't it desperately heartbreaking? I know when I worked on the paeds oncology ward it damn near broke my heart.'

Again with the shrug. 'Of course, but it's uplifting too. You try to keep the emotion out of it, or you'd never survive. You can't carry all that and more around with you all the time, you just get on and do the job. I've learnt to detach.'

Hallelujah. 'Oh, yes. I've seen you detach, my friend. I have personal experience. You're pretty expert at it.'

'Yeah, well. I don't like getting in too deep.' He tried for a smile, which at once made him look boyish and yet very, very sexy. 'It brings me out in hives.'

'That much is obvious. You have form. Lots and lots of form. I'm thinking Sally the medical student, Jenny from Hamilton and Hannah the interior decorator. Poor Hannah, she was nice. You really broke her heart.'

'She was talking babies, mortgages, retirement homes…' He visibly shuddered. 'She had our whole future mapped out on the first date. And she even had a cutesie name for me. Seriously, one evening spent together and suddenly I was Macadoodle-doo. No one does that.'

Georgie couldn't help but smile. 'Oh, yes, they do. It's

part of the relationship ritual. It's about creating a whole new world of two, developing a language you wouldn't speak to anyone else. I think it's endearing.'

'It isn't.'

She laughed. 'You know your trouble? You just need to let people in a little.'

'Really? My trouble?' His laugh was brief. 'My relationships have given you lots of entertainment over the years, missy, and vice versa. But I've never thought you had trouble that needed fixing. I just took you the way you are. I still do.'

'Even pregnant? Because that took a bit of getting used to, didn't it?'

His eyebrows rose and he let out a big breath. 'Yes, even pregnant. Look, things have been very weird since this whole pregnancy thing started, but I'm doing my best to deal with it.'

'I know you've been working really hard on the house. And it's been brilliant.' But he still had a damned long way to go—like talking about the baby unhindered, like being in the same room with her, like being able to look at the baby scans with joy instead of concern and fear, as if he expected pain.

Although the last day had proved he could spend some time with her. But with what consequences? She'd almost dragged him to the bed the minute his breath had touched her neck. Holding back was the single most difficult thing she'd ever had to do.

Up until now she'd been the only woman he'd never detached from and it broke her heart to think she could well end up being just another one to add to his list. One kiss and they'd been on shaky ground ever since. Every movement he made, every space he filled, she was aware of him. Too much. Way too much. And that stunt in the bedroom had her flustered all over again. She was fighting the attraction but she didn't know how long she could hold out.

'I'm sorry. You're right. It's just...I can't help noticing that when you're struggling or getting close to someone you always cut loose right at the point when things start getting interesting. Like...' She wasn't sure of the wisdom of bringing this up, but if she didn't then he probably would anyway, if the conversation at the French market was anything to go by. 'Like earlier. Weird, but I really thought for a minute that you were going to kiss me.'

'Oh. That.' His mouth had been close to hers, his raw masculinity emanating from every pore. She'd wanted him with a fierce and frightening urgency, had wanted him every day while he'd been up that ladder, flexing his arms to the ceiling, carrying timber around the house, hammering nails. Every. Damned. Nail. Each hit with the hammer had made her hot and bothered—and she was sure it wasn't good for her, or the baby, to have such a need that was being unfulfilled.

At what point, she wondered, did desire ever go away? Because for her it seemed to be getting worse by the minute, and just when she thought it was waning, he'd do something as simple as open a damned can of paint and just watching his hands move so confidently made her all hot and bothered again. Worse, the way he looked at her with such heat in his eyes made her believe he felt the same but that he was fighting it every step of the way.

But why?

Friendship. They had a decade of past and a long future hanging on the choices they made now.

There was a beat before he answered, as if he was debating what to say and how to say it, and she wished this situation hadn't made him so guarded. 'Georgie, make no mistake, I do want to kiss you, but I have just about enough self-control to hold myself back. It may not be a good idea to talk about this.'

'You did at the market.'

'That was before it had become a…habit.' He looked at his hands. They were still damned confident, even wrapped around a coffee cup, and she remembered what it had been like to feel so wanted as he'd hugged her.

'One kiss is hardly a habit.'

'Not the kiss. The wanting.'

'Ah.' Words were lost somehow between her throat and her mouth. The café sounds around her dimmed and her senses hyped up to acute overdrive. It was hard to breathe. Hard not to stare at those lips, those eyes, that face. Hard not to imagine what he could do to her and what she could do right back. Hell, he'd just admitted he wanted to do it again, so should she just kiss him anyway?

She felt like she was on a seesaw, her heart pulling one way, her head tugging the other. Up. Down. Up. Down. It was exhausting and exhilarating. With one look she could be flying, one word and she'd be hurtling back down to earth.

She struggled with her composure, but as always was falling deeper and deeper under his spell. And she could have struggled just a little bit harder, walked away, called a halt, but she didn't. Pure and simple. 'And why would you want to be so self-controlled?'

'Because it's too much to ask of us.' His eyes were burning with a sudden heat that felt as if it reached out and stroked her insides.

'We've already been through ten years. We already ask a lot of each other.'

'But now you're asking questions I don't know the

answers to. You never did that before. You're trying to fix me and I don't need fixing. I don't want to be fixed. If we continue like this, things will change. Things have changed, and I'm not sure I like it, or want it, or know how to handle it, without letting you down.'

Part of her believed that to be right. He was being chivalrous and living up to his values, being honest about where things could or couldn't go for them. There was surely no future, especially with his emotional barriers. They were utterly and completely incompatible.

The other part of her wished he'd give up on his good intentions and kiss her anyway. Because she could see neither outcome sat comfortably with him. Perhaps she should just make it easier for him. It wasn't as if she didn't know exactly what she was getting into. And if something didn't happen soon she would finally know what it was like to die from desire. *Fan the flames and let them burn out*.

'I've a feeling it's already a little late to worry about things changing between us. Don't you think? I'm not the only one here wondering what it would be like if we kissed again.' Pricking some vanilla cheesecake onto her fork, she offered it to him across the table. 'Don't you get just a little tired of being so saintly?'

'Yes. Every single moment I'm with you.' He leaned forward again and she was transfixed as he closed his mouth over the morsel of food. Heat shimmied through her as he very slowly chewed then swallowed, the movement of his Adam's apple dipping up and down strangely and compellingly sexy. Her eyes slid from his throat to his mouth, a guarded smile on a face filled with dips and curves she knew so well but had never really explored. How she wanted to trace her finger along those lips, to run her hand across his cheek and feel the rasp of his stubble against her skin. To scale the furrows of his cheekbones.

His voice was an octave dirtier when he spoke. 'My mind is working overtime, thinking of the things we could do together. But I'm sure it's just a passing phase. All interest in the new curves and stuff. I just want to touch you. It's a man thing—feral and protective and instinctive. We can't help it. Nature's a bitch sometimes. If we act on these instincts and then it doesn't work out, that's a lot of friendship down the drain. We need to co-parent on a platonic and sensible basis, not give in to rash lust and then have regret to deal with too.'

'Oh, so you mean the bigger boobs are distracting you? Interesting…' She very slightly arched her back as he lowered his gaze to her breasts. A powerful need zinged through her. She wanted him and was resorting to seduction of the clumsiest kind. But she couldn't get him out of her head. She needed to know what it would be like to be with him. If only one time. Just to hold each other as lovers, unlike the way they touched each other now, as friends. She wanted to stroke him, kiss every part of him. And if she didn't do it soon she'd go completely mad.

One day they'd look back on this and laugh. If they were still speaking to each other. 'So it's nature that's making you look at me like that?'

'Like what?'

'Sex.'

His pupils flared at the word. 'It'll wear off.'

'I sincerely hope not.' She finished the last bit of dessert in one big, almost but not quite satisfying mouthful. She had a feeling there was only one thing that could satisfy her right now, and it wasn't cheesecake. 'We should give in to our natural urges sometimes, it's bad for us to repress them all the time, apparently.'

'It's even worse to break something that's pretty solid.'

Their friendship. But that was true and lasting and proven. 'Why would it break? It doesn't have to break, not if we don't want it to. We can do whatever we want. It's our choice.' She couldn't resist stretching her fingers across the table towards his. For a few seconds just their fingertips touched. Then, without looking at her, he slid his fingers across hers, intertwined them, stroked his hand across hers. His skin was rough but his touch was soft. His heat spread through her, up her arms, to her back, down to her belly.

After a moment of such an excruciatingly sexy caress he turned her palm over and lifted it to his mouth. His kiss was hot. He licked a wet trail to her forefinger. She snatched her hand away before a moan erupted from her throat. Even so, her voice was filled with need. 'We should be getting home.'

'We? Is that an invitation?' His face cautious, and turned on at the same time, he scraped his chair back to go.

Finding him her sexiest smile, she whispered back, 'Honestly, Macadoodle-doo, since when have you ever needed an invitation to my house?'

'I think maybe this time I do.'

She hadn't answered him in words, but she'd taken his hand and led him out of the café like a woman on a mission. Thank God she lived only a short drive away because he couldn't have waited many moments longer. Liam didn't know when he'd ever been so burnt up about a woman.

They bypassed the living area and made it to her bedroom without words, without kissing. He went in first, held open the door and she walked straight in and turned to face him, a question on her face. A dare. A promise. There was space between them. It would only need one step.

Just one.

He faltered. For a few moments neither moved as they stared at each other. This was happening. Really happening. The step from friends to…to whatever this was. *Lovers* might have been doubtful, but the trajectory from restaurant to street to bed was unstoppable. The air in the room seemed to still. One second. Two. With every lingering moment heat spread through his body like a raging fire, threatening to engulf him. If he touched her now there would be no going back.

This could have been a time to leave. He almost took a sideways step, his hand lingering on the doorhandle, but faltered again.

As she watched him a slow sexy smile appeared on Georgie's lips, and if he'd had any flicker of doubt that she didn't want this it fled right then. And that was when, he supposed, he should have drawn that line, the one they shouldn't have stepped over. Or where they should have agreed what this meant. But he was too consumed by her, by this need to utter a word.

In the end he didn't know who made the first move but suddenly she was in front of him, or he was in front of her and his mouth was hard against hers. This time there was no hesitation, no coy shaking. This was pure need and desire. She tasted of chocolate and vanilla and every flavour in between. Her mouth was wet and hungry and it fired a deeper, hotter want within him. Jaws clashed, tongues danced, teeth grazed. There was nothing sophisticated about the kiss, no gentle sucking or tender caress. It was messy. Dirty. Hungry.

His lips were on her throat as he dragged her T-shirt

up around her neck, ripping it as it snagged on its journey to the floor. Finding what they wanted his hands cupped her beautiful breasts over her bra, then under her bra to the accompaniment of a deep guttural moan. She pressed against him, writhing against his thigh. 'Liam, oh, my God, I want you now.'

'I want you.' For a brief moment he acknowledged that this could be the singularly most stupid thing he'd ever done. Then that thought was gone, erased with more of her kisses and the press of her fingertips against the top of his jeans. He sucked in air as she played with his zip. And, no, he did not want to hesitate for a second—but his hand covered hers. 'You first.'

Her bra hit the floor and then her shorts, and he was walking her to her bed and laying her down on the flowery duvet he'd seen a hundred times before but never in this light, never at a moment like this. Everything was familiar and yet unfamiliar, like her. His mouth found her dark hard nipple and sucked it in. She was divine, so sexy, her nipples so responsive. *She* was so responsive as she writhed against him, nails digging into his back until he groaned.

As his mouth started its journey south, kissing carefully over the undulation of her belly, her hand stopped his and her voice was, for the first time, wary. 'Is this really stupid?'

'Without a doubt.'

'Yeah, I thought so. Dumb and then some.' Her mouth was swollen and red. He knew it had been a long time since Georgie had been kissed, and kissed like that—because he had been the last one to do it. God only knew when she'd last had sex but unless he was mistaken he could count the time in years, not months. So this was important. She'd chosen him.

He relieved her of her panties, hands skimming a belly that was plump and soft. He followed a trail of dark hair down her midline, watching her squirm as he parted her thighs and found her centre. He slipped a finger in, two, and felt her contract. She moaned, 'Oh, yes.'

'Crazy?'

'Madness.' She arched against him. 'But that feels so good.'

He kissed a slick trail to a nipple and smiled against it as she bucked in pleasure against his hand. Then he found her mouth again, her tongue tangling with his as she unzipped his jeans and took him in her hand. His gut contracted. He was so hard, so hot for her, and, damn, if he didn't have her soon he was going to explode.

She rubbed his erection against her sweet spot and he could feel the wet heat of her. Then she pushed him against the mattress and straddled him. 'I want you inside me, Liam. Now. Please don't do the whole slow build-up thing. That's been happening for days, months if we're honest. I just need to feel you inside me. Otherwise I'm going to just about die.'

'Don't do that. No. We can't have that.' And without any further encouragement he slid deep into her. She was so ready for him, he could feel her orgasm building already, her walls contracting around him as she pulsed with him. She met his rhythm, found his mouth again and he was lost in sensation after sensation of her mouth, her centre, her weight on his thighs. Her scent around him, her heat around him. Deeper. Harder.

He wanted to slow down time, to hold onto this moment but the luscious heat of her, her sexy, knowing smile made him sink deep into her. 'Oh, my God, Georgie, you're going to make me lose it.'

He fisted her hair and dragged her face to him, kissing

her long and hard until he was fighting for breath, until the pace increased, faster and faster. Her eyes closed as he felt her contract around him, her body shaking with the strength of her orgasm. *'Liam. Liam.'*

Never had his name sounded so sweet, so wanted, so precious. He was lost in her, in her voice, in her heat, grinding against her, hard and fast and deep, until he felt his own climax rising and then crashing on a wave of chaos and kisses.

For a few seconds she was quiet against him, Liam could feel her heart beating a frantic pulse against his chest. Her hair was over his face. She was covered in a fine sheen of sweat, fists still clinging to his shoulders, pinning him against the sheets. He was already hard again, thinking about a few moments' repose, then maybe a shower— preferably with her in it. It was startling, surprising and felt surreal to be here, with her, doing this.

So he wasn't prepared for her words as she bolted upright and her hand went to her belly. 'Oh, God, Liam. Oh, my God.'

The baby. For those fleeting moments he'd forgotten, blown away by the sultriness of her ripe body, of being inside her, of losing himself completely in the best sex of his life. He'd wanted Georgie the woman. Not Georgie the mother. Although she came as a package deal, he knew that.

No, he hadn't forgotten but blocked out that thought.

And then things got very murky in his head. 'What is it? Are you okay? What's wrong?'

'No, I'm not okay.' Twisting away from him, she climbed off his thighs, wrapped the top sheet across her front and curled onto the bed in a protective foetal position, her hands in front of her face. 'Oh, God, best-friend sex. Kill me now.'

'Why the hell would I want to do that?' The laugh erupting from his throat was part relief, part concern because she was right; in fact, they'd both been right. This was the most half-cocked stupid thing they'd ever done.

'I can't believe we've just done that when I look like this.' Her cheeks were red and hot. 'I've never cared how I looked to you before. You've seen me in all states of soberness and drunken debauchery, when I was sick, when I was glammed up to the nines. You've seen me lose my bikini completely in an ill-timed dive into the pool, even caught sight of me in my scaggy weekday bra and pants, and none of it mattered. Ever. But now? Now I'm so embarrassed.'

He stroked fingers down her spine, tenderness for her goofy display of embarrassment meshing with something else in his heart. This was not meant to happen. He was supposed to be creating a safe place for his child, proving he could be a good father. Making sound choices. It was okay to give in to a little sexual play with someone who had no strings attached—but they had a ten-year history and an uncertain and very shaky-looking future that involved another life. They shouldn't be playing at all. He was getting in too deep, getting himself into a situation he didn't know how to get out of. 'And maybe you're just a little bit crazy? Why do you think I care how you look?'

'Because it's suddenly important. Everything is. I didn't think it would be, but it matters.'

'I don't believe this.' Pulling her hands away from her face, he made sure she was looking right at him. Because, yes, this mattered. She mattered. Whatever else happened now—and already a thousand doubts were stampeding into his head—she had to hear what he was saying. Because she still needed to hear the truth, regardless of what he thought or felt about it. 'Is it enough for me to say that you're beautiful?'

'No. Not really. I'm six months pregnant, for goodness' sake. I'm fat. I'm getting stretch marks. My boobs are huge.'

'Really? I hadn't noticed.' He pretended to take a sneaky peek. And then wished that he hadn't. He could make light of this, but the honest fact was she was beautiful. So beautiful it made his heart ache and he wanted to kiss her again, to make her scream with pleasure. To make her realise just how much she was wanted.

'Well, you've been staring at them for long enough.'

'That's because you are amazing. Beautiful. Fertile. Vibrant.' He took her hand, gently kissed her knuckles and brought her fist to his cheek. 'And I don't care how you look, Georgie. Because, honestly, the wrapping's not what I was making love to.'

Honestly? *Honestly?* His heart banged fiercely as if protesting. What the hell were they doing? She was his friend and by doing this he'd let her down. Period. He was supposed to be the strong one, dammit.

'You know, we should really have stopped before we started.' Dragging her hand from his grip, she sat up. 'If that makes sense.'

'Things stopped making sense a while ago.'

'Yes, you can say that again.' She let out a long sigh but snuggled against him, her hair tickling his nose, baby-soft skin touching his, then closed her eyes. 'That was good, though. Damned good, Macadoodle-doo.'

He glanced towards the bedside table and saw a baby name book, a pregnancy book. In the corner of the room there was a bottle steriliser still in its wrapper next to a bundle of baby clothes. On the floor to his left was a magazine open at a page about safety in online dating. She'd gone through the questionnaire and circled a few As, some Cs, a smattering of Bs. Was she thinking about dating again? Before all this she'd have filled in the questionnaire with him and they'd have been in fits of laughter at the results. But this one she'd done on her own. In private.

Despite the post-coital warm fuzzies he realised with a jolt that he might not be a real and integral part of her new life. She was thinking about a future without him in it. That was what he'd wanted, right? That was why he'd signed the contract in the first place. So she could have her dream life—a partner would be the icing on the cake for her. A husband, two kids and a dog. The family she'd missed out on, growing up in that children's home she'd hated. Traceable DNA.

A husband who didn't keep running away. She deserved that. She deserved the very best.

And even though he knew all the reasons he shouldn't be here, he still kept batting them away, trying to find good enough reasons to stay. But he didn't have many, apart from selfish ones that meant he got the best sex with an amazing woman and then broke both their hearts.

He edged his arm out from under her neck, lay for a few minutes and watched her. She looked so relaxed, so peaceful, so hot that he couldn't bear to think of her with another man. But did that mean he had to commit? What if it fell apart? That would be all kinds of messy. A family didn't need that. He didn't need that, and she certainly didn't. From his own bitter experience he knew damned well what damage a broken family could do to a child.

Better to stay friends for ever than fall apart as lovers.

Snaking away from her, he sat on the edge of the bed

and looked around for his jeans. 'I guess I'd better get off home.'

'Oh, no. Don't you dare move, matey.' Her hands were on his shoulders, gripping them with more force than when he'd taken her over the edge, forcing him to sit back down. She picked up one of the books he'd seen and flicked through it, shoving it under his nose. 'So, I was thinking Desdemona for a girl. Albert for a boy? What do you think?'

'What? You're joking.' Not what he'd choose in a million years. What he would choose he didn't know. He hadn't allowed his mind to wander down that route as yet.

'And in the morning we need to go shopping for a breast pump. There's a new babyware shop opened up on High Street. And I know it's early but I want to get some Christmas decorations from that pop-up shop in Regents mall.'

'Christmas? Already? It's September.'

'My first Christmas in my first home. A baby on the way. I want it to be special.' Her voice was wistful. 'No harm in starting early, and they'll sell out of all the good stuff pretty quickly, you'll see.'

'What was Christmas like at the home?' He knew she tried to make a huge effort to celebrate it every year and asked everyone she'd ever met to eat around her large wooden table—waifs and strays, everyone's uncle's cat… she just didn't want to be on her own.

There was a pause as if she didn't want to go back there. He couldn't blame her. The bits she'd mentioned about growing up had been a far cry from his early experiences. Until his perfect world had imploded.

She put on her *I'm okay* voice. 'Oh, the social workers and carers tried to make it feel special, but we all knew they just wanted to get our celebrations out of the way so they could finish up and get home to their real families. It was depressing, in truth. This year I'm going to go big. I'm going to get the biggest tree and the most decorations anyone has ever had and cover the place— the tree, the walls, the outside. You know, like on Franklin Road, where every house has decorations and lights? It'll be like that, a Christmas to remember. And then next year I'm going to give Desdemona—or Albert—every damned thing they want. Because I couldn't have what I wanted. Ever.'

He imagined her, stuck in the home, wishing her little heart out and always being disappointed. Life sucked sometimes. For Georgie life had sucked a lot. 'What did you want, Geo? What did you wish for?'

'Ah, you know, the usual stuff.'

He propped himself up on his elbow and ran his fingers across her curves, down her shoulder, to the side of her breast, and stopped for a moment as she shivered under his touch. Then continued stroking her hip. 'No. Really, what did you want?'

She laughed, shyly. 'I wanted to start a collection of Beanie Babies—these little stuffed-toy things. Man, they were expensive and all the girls at school had them for birthdays or Christmas. I saved up my allowance every week and eventually bought a second-hand whale. He was my favourite.'

So he wasn't the only one here who was expert at dodging a question. 'No. Really. You're always telling me to stop hedging—but you're champion of it too. What did you deep down want?'

'Oh, God. However I say it, it's going to sound twee and crass but…well, I really wanted to be part of something. And now I am. So I got it in the end.' She laughed. 'It only took twenty-eight years.'

Did she mean him? Did she mean they were now part of something? Or did she mean the baby? *Family?* His heart started to pound. What had he done? Given her hope that she belonged to him?

Didn't she? No. No one did. No one could.

What the hell had he done? 'Oh. I see.'

'Anyway, before we go shopping I thought perhaps a big brunch in town first. That's what we'll need, right? A good sleep and then some decent food. Or maybe some food now? Are you hungry? Sex makes me hungry.'

'These days everything makes you hungry.' Okay. He got it that it would be rude and insensitive to split right now. He slumped against the pillow, trying to reconcile his head with his heart, but it seemed they were cursed to be at odds with each other for ever. 'Whatever you want.'

'Really?' Her foot dug him in the thigh. 'What I want is for you to stay. Talk to me.'

'God knows how you have the energy to talk after mind-blowing sex.' He ignored her assertion that he stay. For how long? Tonight? Tomorrow? A year? For ever? Reality was blurring dangerously with the ache in his heart.

One eye opened. 'It's not because we've just had sex, it's because *we* talk, Liam, that's what you and I do. We talk endlessly and have done for a decade. About everything. *Mostly.* We've never not known what to talk about before. How about we talk about stuff…about your work, my pregnancy, this child, your family, why you don't contact them ever? What the heck it is that spooks you so much about creating something that everyone else in the world craves. I want to know about you growing up, and I want to know about Lauren.'

The walls were closing in. It was time for evasive action, because he did not want to go there. At all. 'You know, suddenly I'm really fascinated about how breast pumps work. Talk me through—'

'No way, José. You don't get out of stuff that easily.'

'Oh, but I do. By fair means or foul…' The sheet covered most of her body, but her right foot was sticking out. He took it, leaned forward and slowly sucked her big toe into his mouth. He felt her soften against the mattress and her moan stoked more heat in him. That shower scenario was looking more and more attractive.

'Yeow. Definitely not fair.' Four vermilion-varnished toes wriggled against his chin. 'Use that mouth for talking, Macadoodle-doo.'

'Why, when it's so much better at doing other things?' His mouth hit her ankle, the back of her knee, her inner thigh, and he licked a wet trail northwards. As she squirmed he gave a wry smile. Any more wriggling was halted by his hands on her thighs. 'See?'

'But I want to— Oh, yes, that feels good. Just a little to the… Oh, yes.' Her hands fisted into his hair. 'Don't stop now, Liam…'

'I have no intention of stopping.'

'We…can…talk…later…'

Like never. 'Hush. Relax. Enjoy.'

And with that her mouth clamped shut and as he grasped her hand, she did exactly what he'd suggested.

CHAPTER NINE

WHEN GEORGIE WOKE the next morning the left side of the bed was cold. He was gone. As she'd thought he would be. It had all been too good to be true. He'd had second thoughts and hot-footed it to Afghanistan or somewhere equally unreachable. Typical Liam. Typical men. She lay back on the pillow and growled.

And then growled again, because since when had her mood been determined by a man?

Since Liam MacAllister had become…whatever he'd become. More than a friend…and with added and rather nice benefits. He certainly was very, very good at the bedroom side of things, even if he was quiet—*mute*—on the history side. But, hey, a forward-thinking man was always better than one looking back, right?

Although his past had shaped who he was, and that intrigued her. It had also created those barriers he was so keen at throwing up between himself and anyone who wanted to get close. The sex had been a really crazy idea. Lovely but crazy, and now she was even more confused than before. Ask him for clarification? Not likely. She imagined how that conversation might go and decided she didn't need to have him actually voice the rejection out loud.

After a few minutes of lying there, debating what

to do, there was a gentle tapping at the door and in he walked, topless, with jeans slouching off his hips, a tray in hand, a pot of coffee and a plate of something that smelled nice but looked a little…suspect. He gave her a smile as he placed the tray on the bed. 'Morning. Here's a sad-looking croissant I found at the back of the freezer, along with a couple of rogue frozen peas and a lot of ice. There was literally nothing else to eat. Nothing. You really do need to go food shopping.'

'The trouble is I eat it as fast as I buy it. I can't keep up.' Without his shirt *he* looked good enough to eat—did she need anything else? And he hadn't run off, he was here, making sure she ate properly. Was this a dream?

She rubbed her eyes, which she really shouldn't have done because the corneal abrasion was still healing, but it was too late and… Yes, he was still here, not an apparition. With food. And coffee. The man was a god.

The god sat on the edge of the bed. 'Well, seeing as we're having a day off renovating today, I'll make sure we fill up the fridge before we're done.' He buttered a piece of croissant, offered it to her, then waited until she'd opened her mouth and popped it in. 'Come on, get your strength up, we're going to need that soon enough.'

'Thanks. Eugh. Not such a great croissant. I can't even remember when I bought— Wait…we're having a day off? Who says?'

'You said you wanted to go shopping. And I'm tired of sanding and painting and you look like you need a decent break. I want to forget about this dust and dirt and do something else. So I've made some calls. I have a plan: your breast pump will have to wait, along with the Christmas decorations. Eat up and then we'll get going.' He got up as if to leave.

'Not so fast.' She caught his hand and he took it,

wrapped his fingers around hers and squeezed. In all the years of knowing him she'd never been aware of this tender side to him. She liked it. Goddamn, she liked it, just when she was trying to think of more reasons not to like him. Not to lose her heart or herself to someone who wouldn't want it. 'To where?'

'It's a surprise. But there'll be proper fresh air. The sea. Decent food. No dust.'

'Is this just another tactic to avoid the issue? You know…talking?'

He gave her a guilty grin. 'I feel restless. I just need to get going. Out. Somewhere.'

This was the guy who spent most of his life travelling and the last few months cooped up in her house. He never stayed anywhere for long, so she could see why he'd need to cut loose sometimes. Plus, a break would be fun. 'Then what are we waiting for?'

'Well…' He pulled the sheet down a little and exposed her breasts. Then he kissed her neck, her throat, her nipples, and she was putting her arms around his neck and drawing him to her. He whispered against her skin, 'I really need a shower before I set foot outside. You?'

'What? Me and you? In that tiny bathroom? You think we'll fit?'

'If it's big enough for a highland jig, it's big enough for a shared shower. We'll squeeze in somehow.' His fingers stroked down her back and she could see the bulge in his jeans. He was hot and hard for her.

Which made her hot in return. She couldn't resist reaching her hand to his chest. Felt his heart beating underneath her fingers. Solid. Steady. *Liam*. This was Liam. This was all kinds of surreal. She remembered his little dance in her tiny bathroom, the way he'd looked at her, the way she'd wanted to touch him then. How touching him now made her feel excited and jittery and turned on. Not solid or steady at all. 'But it wasn't big enough for a highland jig, remember?'

'We'll fit. Trust me?'

'I don't know.' That was half the problem. And, yes, he'd stuck to his words and been there for her throughout this pregnancy. Not once had he mentioned the contract again. He seemed committed to the baby, even though there were times when she caught his worried face and just knew the spooks were there, haunting him a little. But he'd surprised her with his resolve. And kept on surprising her, but could a man really change? She just didn't know. For a few minutes last night she'd thought he'd been having doubts, had felt his restless legs keen to leave, had known that if she'd let him he'd have gone. Would she always have to keep anchoring him here? Would she never be enough for his first instinct to be to want to stay?

For now, though, he was here and was asking for nothing more than to spend time with her. Time she didn't want to waste analysing things to death. 'Oh, okay. Where's there a will, there's always a way.'

'Always…' His laugh was deep and sexy and there was no way she was going to put up any kind of fight against those fingers, that mouth, those eyes. Had she been thinking about fighting? She couldn't remember. Her whole world narrowed to this single moment when she could forget everything else. 'So what are we waiting for?'

His hands closed around her fingers. 'Absolutely nothing.'

An hour and a half later, which truly could have been only thirty minutes had it not been for a lovely long shower and a very deliciously sexy start to her day, Georgie let out a yelp of excitement as Liam steered his expensive and very un-child-friendly two-seater coupé into a car ferry terminal. 'Waiheke Island? A day trip?'

'If that's okay?' He looked genuinely concerned that she was happy with his choice. 'I thought it'd be nice to do something different.'

'Yes, it's fabulous. It's a lovely idea. I haven't been there since a school trip years ago.'

He stared across at the ferry. 'My grandparents lived there, we used to go over and stay at their house every holiday when I was little. I can't remember the last time I visited.'

And there was something else she hadn't known about him. Maybe that concern on his face was really apprehension? 'Oh, I had no idea. Will it bring back bad memories for you?'

'I'm hoping to cement some new ones. It's a big enough island for me not to even go there.' A stream of vehicles appeared and queued up behind them as a crew member gestured for the cars to embark. Cranking the car into gear, Liam drove up the metal ramp and parked the car on the ferry platform. Once out, and breathing a lungful of fresh sea air, he slipped his hand into hers and whisked her towards the bar area. 'Come on, let's get a coffee and watch the world go by.'

The short journey across the Hauraki Gulf was smooth and pleasant, enhanced greatly by a pod of dolphins that came alongside to play. Diving and chasing and showing off, they added extra magic to this unexpected trip. Standing on deck, watching him walk towards her with two cups of coffee in his hands, grinning and gesticulating to the wildlife, Georgie's stomach gave a little hearty jump at the thought of a stolen day with Liam. Things were definitely changing, moving along in a direction she hadn't ever imagined. She didn't know if the changes were for the good, but she did know she would never be the same after all this.

Waiheke, famed for its vineyards and olive oil, was showing the tentative beginnings of the new spring season. After a long wet winter the hills were green, the acres of vines stretching on and on to the horizon were budding and leafy, while ewes watched over lambs in the fields adjacent to the roads. Once away from the main township they headed east along a winding road that eventually opened to vistas of clean empty beaches and blue water sparkling in the pale sunshine. Such a difference from her city house, which she adored—but stepping onto green fields would be nice for a change. Liam had been right, time out would do them both some good.

After half an hour or so he pulled left into a white gravel driveway that led towards the sea. On their right was a large whitewashed colonial house with a sign advertising wine sales and tastings. Georgie was surprised he'd pick a place like this. 'Oh? You booked us lunch at a vineyard? I assume you want to sample the wares?'

'I may have a small glass. But it's not so much the vineyard I was planning to see.' He threw the car into park and got out.

She stepped out of the door and sighed at the wisteria just starting to flower and framing the large wooden door. The soft pink against the white was startling and soothing, and like something from a film set. 'Oh? So what is it? What's the big secret?'

'It's not so big really, more a thought than a secret. Wait and see. And apparently they do a very nice lunch platter. It's huge. Which seems to be the only consideration you make these days when choosing meals.' There was a flurry of activity as their hosts found them a table out in the garden, bottled water and much-needed shade.

The garden was private and secluded, but felt somehow open rather than cloistered. Cushioned candy-striped hammocks hung between trees flanking a small neat square of grass. Palms and large ferns gave much-needed shade. There were fairy lights entwined around the vegetation that she imagined would give a pretty effect in the evenings, along with tealights in coloured glass jars on the ornate ironwork tables. It was tranquil, cool and very calming, and as they sat she felt some of the tensions of the last few months float away.

The menu was limited but sounded delicious. Suddenly she felt famished and so ordered a large mixed platter that promised fish, freshly cooked meats, a selection of local hard cheeses and lots and lots of bread. Most of which, she knew, she could eat and not worry about them having any effect on her baby. The rest she'd leave for Liam.

As they waited for the food he started to chat. 'Chris, the owner of this place, is an old school friend of mine. He inherited the vineyard from his dad and has turned it into a very successful business.'

As she listened to the sound of…nothing, except the fuzzy hum of bees and faint birdcalls, and took in the impossibly breathtaking surroundings, she felt the most peaceful she'd felt in weeks. Either that, or the sex-induced endorphins had made her limbs turn half to rubber. 'It's amazing.'

'Isn't it?'

'So what made you decide to come here of all places?'

'He sent me a link to his new website the other day. I took a look, saw the photos of the deck and the garden.'

They were momentarily interrupted as their drinks

arrived, then were left alone again. Liam took a sip of pinot gris, then put his glass down on the table. 'Then, when I was standing on your deck this morning, looking out at the garden, I thought that we really need to sort it out. The wood's rotting in places and there are nails popping up all over. It's a wreck, Georgie, and could be dangerous if we don't do something about it. The inside of your house is almost complete now so I thought we should finish things off properly. The baby's coming in the summer, and with the usual Auckland humidity you're going to want to sit outside. I thought the hammock idea would be great. And the palms give great shade. A lawn in the middle would be a pretty cool place for a baby to learn to crawl—no risk of injury.'

'Well, wow. That's really thoughtful. And, yes, it's absolutely gorgeous. I can see it working perfectly in the space I have. That's very kind of you, and especially to bring us all the way out here to actually see it.' She felt a little as if the ground was shifting. Half hope, half… what?

He shrugged, looking a little embarrassed at her enthusiasm. 'It's just a day trip, Georgie.'

But it was one of the kindest things anyone had ever done for her. Why did he have to keep getting better and better? Why couldn't he slink off and make her feel unhappy and not pine for more? In cold, harsh reality she was scared that she'd get too attached to a man who would break her heart. Because even if he did want to be involved in her family, how could she be sure he'd be in it for the long term? With her? How could she be sure he'd love *her*?

'But it's—'

'Oh, here's lunch. And here's Chris. Clearly a busy man, he owns the place, makes the wine and so, it seems, serves the food.' He stood and shook the hand of a thick-set man who looked older than Liam's thirty-two years. 'Good to see you, mate.'

'You too.' Liam's friend's eyes grazed over Georgie, down to her belly, and he beamed. 'And you must be Georgie. I'd know you anywhere, that social media's a beast, isn't it? You feel like you know people without ever meeting them.'

'Yes. Isn't it? Hello.' She may have been Liam's friend on any number of social network sites, but Georgie wondered how much Chris really knew and what Liam had said, if anything, about their unusual situation. After all, not many couples got pregnant first and then had sex. Everything was happening the wrong way round. Besides, the word 'couple' hadn't been breathed out of either of their lips.

They hadn't discussed yet what to say, if anything, to anyone who enquired about their situation. But as that seemed to be changing by the day, it was probably better that they hadn't come up with any definite description. Just Liam and Georgie, same as it ever had been.

Still, the winemaker seemed gentleman enough not to pry and diverted his gaze from her bump back to Liam. 'Look, I've got a bit of a rush on, can't stay and chat. Give my regards to your father, Mac. I hear he's retiring up north.'

Liam's eyebrows lifted. 'Oh? Really?'

It was his friend's turn to raise eyebrows. 'You didn't know?'

'I haven't caught up with him for a while.'

'No. He said as much last time he was over. He seemed a bit miffed. But, then, he always did. Are you going to pop over to The Pines?'

Liam shook his head. 'No. He sold it years ago. No point going backwards, is there?'

'I don't suppose so. Look, thanks for coming. Lunch is on the house. Good to see you.' Chris turned to leave then paused. 'Oh, make sure you try the syrah too. Delicious.'

Lunch was lovely, and as filling as Liam had promised, and Georgie ate as much as she could, managing almost the whole meal without mentioning the last conversation. But in the end it got the better of her. Her heart began to race as she brought up the difficult subject, so she tried to keep her voice level. 'So, when did you last talk to your dad?

Liam shrugged. 'I don't know. Two years ago?'

'Two?' It seemed nonsensical to have no communication with family members. If she—

'Look…' Pushing aside his empty plate, he let out a long breath. 'Please don't give me a lecture on how lucky I am to have a father and that I need to make the most of him. I know that's how you feel about families. But it isn't how I do.'

'But—'

'It's a lovely day. I really don't want to spoil things.'

'That may be a little late.' Although she knew she shouldn't have pushed it, he'd brought her out of a desire to help her, and to give her a rest. She was the one spoiling things.

For a moment she thought he was going to stamp or growl, but he fought with his emotions and put them back in that place that he never let anyone see. The man must have some ghosts, she thought, if he was so unwilling to talk. But he was tight-lipped about his work too—he kept everything tied in. Some people needed counselling, but he just wore it all in his skin, would never consider any kind of help, not even to get things straight in his head.

He saw that as a strength. 'Let's not do this today, Geo. Let's enjoy ourselves, plan the garden, take a walk, anything but this. Talking about my family tends to put a huge downer on everything.'

'Okay.' But something niggled at her. Ate away at her gut. She was genuinely trying to help. 'Or we could say everything really quickly and get it out in the open.'

He shook his head with irritation, but he smiled. 'Or say nothing at all.'

'Or I could ask Chris.'

'He doesn't know everything.'

Now she knew she could leave it and walk away and pretend this conversation hadn't happened. Or she could take it a step further...hell, he knew everything about her. Everything. 'And I know nothing. When did you last see your mother? What is The Pines?'

'Okay, so we *are* doing this.'

She took a sharp breath and threw him her most winning smile. 'I see it as my duty as a friend to annoy you until you actually get to the nitty-gritty.'

'You don't have to take that role so much to heart, Georgie. Maybe the nitty-gritty isn't what you think it is.' He placed his napkin on the table and stood, offering her his hand, but he looked impatient rather than annoyed. 'The Pines was my grandad's house and I am resolutely not going there so don't even ask. Just don't. It's a no. There is no point going over stuff, it doesn't help. You can't change the past and some of it is best not remembered. And I last saw my mother on Mother's Day. I took her out for tea. And it was awkward as always.'

'No. You were in Pakistan, or South Sudan—somewhere. Either way, you weren't here. Make it the year before.' They walked out into the vineyard. Rows and rows of vines stretched before them on and on into the distance. They wandered aimlessly down a row, inhaling the smell of freshly mown grass. 'You know, Liam, your parents will be the only grandparents our child has. Seriously, they are the only other people in the whole world with a connection to him…or her. They are flesh and blood. I really wish you could try to make things work between you all. If not for anyone else's sake, for Nugget's.'

He shook his head. 'Sometimes I wish I didn't know you as well as I do, because then I wouldn't have to put up with this. Trouble is, I do know you and I know you won't give up. At all. Digging and digging.'

'It's what makes me such a good nurse, and why you love me.'

'Love?' He stopped short and stared at her. For too long. For so long she wondered what the heck was going on in his head. She closed her heart to his shocked question…*love?* She didn't want to know his answer. Or maybe it had always been there and she'd been afraid to look. But in the end he just shook his head. 'My parents divorced when I was ten, and neither of them have shown any interest in me since well before then. The feeling's mutual.'

'Why?'

'You really do want to do this, don't you?' He ran his fingers through his hair, opened his mouth, closed it. Opened it again. 'Because Lauren died. And rightly or wrongly we all blame me.'

'Why? What on earth happened? What could you have done that was so bad?' Over the years Georgie had pondered this. She knew his sister had died, knew his parents were separated. But piecing the bits together had been like trying to do a jigsaw with no picture as reference.

They walked in silence to the very end of the row and onwards towards the ocean, found a crop of rocks in the little bay and sat on them. A breeze had whipped up, but the sun still cast a warm glow over them. Even so, Georgie shivered at the look haunting Liam's face. The dark shadows were back. His shoulders hunched a little. He'd already let go of her hand and even though they were sitting side by side it seemed almost as if he'd retreated within himself.

His voice was low when he finally spoke. 'She was a premmie, born at thirty weeks, and had a struggle, but she finally got discharged home. She was doing well. She was amazing. Really amazing. The light of our lives.'

Georgie sensed something terrible was coming. She laid a hand on his shoulder and waited, holding her breath. The sound of waves crashing onto the shore was the only thing that broke another prolonged silence. That, and her heartbeat pounding in her ears.

'I caught a winter bug. Nothing serious, just a stupid cough, fever and a snotty nose that laid me low for a few days, one of those that most kids get. Mum banned me from being near her. Very sensible, in hindsight. I just thought she was being mean.'

He looked like he wanted to continue but couldn't find words. When he composed himself enough to speak his voice was cracked and barely more than a whisper, 'But Lauren was so fascinating, such a little puzzle of noises and sounds with an achingly beautiful smile, that, as an eight-year-old big brother with a strong sense of respon- sibility and a lot of curiosity, I didn't want to keep away. So one morning when she was crying I sneaked into her room and picked her up, soothed her back to sleep. I held her for ages, I don't know how long, but long enough for her to go to sleep and for me to care enough not to wake her, so I held her some more.

'A few days later she came down with the same bad

bug, but she couldn't fight it off. She tried, though. Tried damned hard. But she just wasn't strong enough.'

He hauled in air and stood, hands in pockets, looking out to sea. So alone and lost that it almost broke Georgie in two. She imagined what it must have been like for a young boy to go through something like that, and her heart twisted in pain. He'd been doing what he'd thought was the right thing. Not knowing how wrong it could be. But the baby could have caught a bug anywhere—in a shop, at the doctor's surgery, in a playgroup. It had been bad luck she'd caught it from her brother. Bad luck that had kept him in some kind of emotional prison for the rest of his life.

At least, Georgie thought, she hadn't had something and then lost it. She just hadn't had anything at all, and in some ways that seemed almost preferable to suffering the way Liam had. Again she couldn't think of anything helpful to say, and couldn't have managed many words even if she'd known some formulaic platitudes that might have helped. Her throat was raw and filled with an almost tangible sorrow for him. 'I'm so sorry, Liam.'

'To cut to the chase, my parents were never the same after that. Eventually the grief was too much for their marriage. I got lost in the slipstream of guilt and blame. We've all rarely spoken since, doing only the perfunctory family necessities, if that. I suppose you could say it's pretty damned loveless.'

No. *He* was loveless. Losing his sister and then being neglected by grieving parents must have been almost unbearable, especially countered by a flimsy excuse that it had all somehow been his fault. He'd been a child too, for goodness' sake. How could you lay blame on someone who only wanted to give a baby more love?

Georgie knew Liam well enough to know there was

little point in trying to convince him that he was anything other than culpable. If he didn't believe it himself, and if his parents, the people who mattered, had never tried to reassure him, then what would her words mean to him?

But she stepped forward and wrapped her arms around his waist, hoping that somehow the physical sensation of her touch might convey her empathy for him in a way that words never could. 'And that's why you fight so hard year after year to save all those babies in those disaster-stricken countries.'

'They just need a chance. I can't right any wrongs and I can't wave a magic wand but I can give them real help.'

'And that's also why you don't want a family of your own.'

'Yeah, I didn't do so well with mine. Lauren dying was hard going, but you get through it. Somehow. Eventually. But what I needed most was help, support, love. And I got nothing. Families can hurt you so badly. I wouldn't want to do that to any child of mine. Worse, judging by my experiences, I'd probably do more harm than good.' He shook his head, shook himself free of her grip, and walked back towards the vines.

'No. You're going to be a great dad.'

He pulled up to a halt. 'Really? You think? After what I just told you? I don't want to go through anything like that again. I don't think I'd survive it. I don't want to…' He started to walk again. Head down. Shoulders hunched.

She kept a few feet behind him, giving him the space he clearly craved. 'To what?'

'To lose something like that again.'

'You wouldn't.'

He railed round at her. 'How can you be sure? How can you stand there and make promises no one can keep?'

It was all so clear now. His idea of family was broken.

His image of love was filled with so many negative con-notations he couldn't dare risk himself again with that emotion. That was why she'd found him so distraught that first day she'd met him—caring for a sick baby had di-minished him, reminded him of what he'd lost. But he'd taken that loss and turned it into his vocation. Not many could do that. Not many would face their fears every day.

Although he never let it get personal. He never let any-thing get to him. Ever. That was what the death of his sister had taught him, to keep everything and everyone at a safe distance. So he wouldn't feel responsible, so he wouldn't have to face the prospect of more pain if things got sticky. Hell, she'd been watching him do it for years, and had never felt how much it mattered. But now, *God*, now it mattered.

And still she was left only with questions. If that was how he felt, why had he torn up the contract? Was this all just some duty kick he was getting?

What would become of them all?

Sometimes she wished she had a crystal ball and could look into her future and see how it all worked out. But this time she was afraid. Afraid that what she'd see wasn't what she wanted.

She left him to meander through the vineyard, stop-ping to look at the tight fists of bright red buds at the end of each row, gathering strength to grow into flourishing roses, and to watch tiny white butterflies skitter past. And as they walked she noticed his shoulders begin to relax again. The sunshine and quietness chased the shadows away and eventually he came back to her, took her hand in his and walked towards a cluster of old stone buildings.

But before they left the vines Georgie paused and looked at the tiny fruit gripping tightly onto ancient gnarled wood. 'Do you think Chris would mind if we tried one of the grapes?'

He laughed. 'I think he probably would, but they're not remotely ripe anyway. They'll make our stomachs hurt.'

'But they're award winning, it said so on a big certificate on the wall back at the restaurant. Should we try? I've never had anything award winning straight off the vine before. How about you? You should try one.'

'No.' He pulled her hand away from the plant and hauled her against him. His eyes were hungry, his breathing quickened as he looked into her face, at her eyes, at her mouth. He was a complex man filled with conflicting emotions—but that didn't make her want him less. He was real and, yes, he was complicated. He was layered and that was what made him all the more intriguing.

He cupped her face and stared into it, his expression a mix of heat and fun and affection. Then he pressed his mouth to hers and kissed her hard. It was a kiss filled with need, with deep and genuine desire. This was new, this…trust, this depth, sharing his worse times and dark past. It was intense and it was raw but Georgie felt a shift of understanding to a new level. A new need. His grip on her back was strong as he held her and for a few moments she thought he would never let her go. And, holding him tight against her, she wished that very same thing with every ounce of her soul.

'Can I drive the car? Please?' Georgie grabbed the keys from Liam's hand and he let her take them. Let her run to his pride and joy and take the driver's seat, which he would never ever normally do. But, well hell, just telling her about his old life had set something free from his chest. He felt strangely lighter, freed up a little.

But then, as he climbed in beside her, his gaze flicked

to her belly and there was that hitch again, the one that reminded him that happiness was always fleeting. That love could hurt just as much as it could give joy. He'd thought he'd be able to distance himself emotionally from her, and from the baby, but in reality the feelings just kept hurtling at his rib cage, ripping his breaths away, one after the other. Hard and fast until he didn't think he'd ever be able to breathe properly again. He didn't know whether to run away from her or keep a tight grip. But staying close opened them all up to him wreaking havoc again.

'Where are you going to drive to? Palm Beach is nice. There are some good shops in Oneroa. Or we could go for a walk along Rocky Bay.'

She ran her fingers over the leather steering wheel. 'No. I remember from my school history classes that there are tunnels somewhere left over from the Second World War. Do you know anything about them?'

'Stony Batter tunnels? Sure. My grandfather helped build them actually. He was born here, camped in the fields just up past Man O'War Bay through the last years of the war.' Sheesh, he'd opened his mouth and now he couldn't stop his past pouring out. 'He used to take me up there when I was a kid.'

She flicked the ignition and drove back towards the main road. 'Do you want to take a look?'

Did he? That would mean a drive past The Pines and a whole lot more memories. The weeks they'd spent here as a real family. Complete. God, why had he decided to come here to relive everything again? Why? Because, for some reason, Georgie made him feel as if anything was possible. Even overcoming a dark and murky past. Who knew, maybe he could squeeze his eyes shut as they drove past The Pines and he wouldn't feel the dread already stealing up his spine. 'Okay. If you insist.'

'I do.'

But that was a mistake. Memories joined the swirl of pain in his chest as they closed the kilometres between the vineyard and his old holiday home. Part of him wanted to grab the steering wheel and head straight back to the ferry terminal. But it was too late.

The Pines stood tall and dark and ominous as they drove past, the short driveway leading to the front door, still painted dark blue, ancient pohutakawa trees flanking the lawn, laundry flapping on the line, all gave his gut a strange kick. Memories of happier times filtered into his head—his father swinging him round and round, his mother laughing at their antics and calling them for dinner. The long leisurely Christmas lunches filled with fun and excitement—midnight mass, waiting for Santa, opening presents on Christmas Day morning.

They had been happy, once upon a time. But once that dream had been shattered, it had never been possible to reach that state again.

He let his gaze wander, turning his head slightly as the large rambling house went out of view. Glancing at him, Georgie jerked the car to a halt. 'That was it, wasn't it? The house?'

There was no point lying. 'Yes. It looks as if someone is renovating it.'

'Do you want to go and take a look?' Her eyes were kind as they settled on him and he knew she was trying to do the right thing by making him confront his demons. But he didn't need to do that here, he confronted them most days as it was. 'I'll come with you, you won't be on your own.'

'Let's keep driving.'

'Actually, no.' She drew up at the side of the road and

before he could stop her she'd done a U-turn and they were back at the house.

'Georgie, I know what you're trying to do. It's okay. I'm fine. Things are fine.'

'Sure. If you say that enough times you might just believe it. I, however, take a little more convincing. Come on.' She stepped out, leaned against the car and wrapped her arms around her chest as she stared at the house. 'I can imagine you playing there in the garden. Causing mayhem. It's a real family home. Three generations all together. Nice.'

'It was once.' He wrenched himself out of the car and looked over at the house, fighting the tightness in his throat. 'The last time I was here was for my grandad's funeral.'

She turned to him, hair blowing wildly in the sudden breeze. 'I'm so sorry.'

'He lived here all his life, he loved the place, said he didn't need to go anywhere else.'

'It's nice that you have family history. It must be reassuring to hear about the past, thinking that your grandad walked along these same paths as you. It gives a connection, doesn't it?' Slipping her hand into his, she left it at that. But her words kept coming back to him as they walked across the road past the house and looked out over the bay towards the tiny islands dotted around the horizon.

Liam remembered his grandad telling him about the antics he and his mates had got up to here on the island— fishing, drinking, farming. How he'd courted Liam's grandmother for two years but had always known he'd marry her. How they'd devoted years of their lives to the community here. Liam had always known his ties to this place but it had been too easy to take them for granted.

Then he'd tried to put as much space between him and them as he could.

He looked at Georgie now in profile, those gorgeous lush curls whipping in the wind; she would never know if they came from her mother's side or her father's. Those soft brown eyes—a hint of Maori blood? Italian? Again, she'd never know. That staunch tilt of the jaw—well, that was pure Georgie, from years of forging her independence and stamping her place in this world. How she'd turned her life into such a success from her rocky beginnings, he would always wonder at. She had no memories of any kind of family time, good or bad, no special Christmases, no history to talk of, no stories to tell her baby.

Nugget.

Fear washed through him. Fear and hope mingling into a mish-mash of chaos in his gut. He was going to be a father.

He was going to have to create memories for his child too. A history. And a future.

See, this was why he'd been against families for so long. Because the unbearable weight of responsibility meant you had to stop hiding yourself and be someone good. Deep down good. Unselfishly open and honest. You had to let go of the past and be that person, the one everyone relied on. The one everyone looked up to. The one who knew there was danger and risk in opening his heart, but did it anyway.

Trouble was, he just didn't know if he could be that man.

CHAPTER TEN

One month ago...

TIME WAS MOVING FAST. Too fast.

The next few weeks were a blur of sensual lovemaking and laughter. It seemed, to Georgie at least, that sex could be a good mix with friendship after all. Liam was still funny and helpful, he still hammered nails and painted walls. He made her laugh and sigh with delight. They chatted and joked about pretty much everything, as ever—and it seemed almost as if something inside him had been set free.

Except...there was that nagging worry that things were rattling towards an abrupt end. And there was still a part of himself that he held back, that she couldn't break through.

Georgie's head was in a state of flux. She didn't know what he wanted, and she wasn't sure what she wanted out of this either. There'd been no discussion of expectations and she was too scared to ask him about...*what next*. All she knew was that having him in her bed and by her side made her feel the very best she'd ever felt. Although she'd never again mentioned his past, she also didn't want to discuss a future.

Because for the immediate future—which in her terms

amounted to the next eighteen years—she wanted what she had never had: a stable, loving environment for her child. She wanted her baby to feel loved and nurtured, as if it were the centre of the universe and not, like her, alone and unwanted. She wanted her child to not have to fight every day to be noticed. She wanted her child to feel completely and utterly confident and…loved. Just loved.

So, in reality, she needed to forget about any kind of intimacy with Liam, shouldn't waste precious time wondering how it was going to work out—because she should be concentrating on getting through the pregnancy and planning to bring up a child as a co-parent with a friend.

Which didn't work so well for her when she was lying next to him in bed, or trying to do the nine-to-five at her day job when her head was full of naked images of him earlier that morning.

'Georgie, did you manage to get the blood-test results for Kate Holland? She's coming in this afternoon and I want to make sure she's all set.' Malcolm had returned from settling his mum into a nursing home in Dorset and had hit the clinic with renewed vigour.

Georgie watched as he bustled around the office, ordered and officious. He was a nice guy, but had some traits that she found just a little irritating. In retrospect it was good that she hadn't asked him to be the donor for her child. What on earth had she been thinking? But, then, on the other hand, Malcolm was nice. Just nice. Not anything else. Not complicated, not sexy as all hell, not a brilliant kisser—okay, so she didn't know that, but he didn't have sexy lips.

'Georgie?'

Malcolm. He was sitting at the desk opposite her now, face masked by a computer screen. 'Oh, sorry. Yes?'

'Blood results for Kate Holland?'

'Yes, I phoned the lab to chase them again an hour ago and they said they'd email them through. They should be here…' She tapped on her keyboard and brought the work up on screen. 'There you go. I've directed them to her file. All looking good. She'll be pleased.'

'Thanks.' Her boss's head popped up over the monitor. 'Georgie, are you okay?'

'Absolutely fine, thanks.' And so far she hadn't let her thoughts interfere with her job, but they were definitely trying to filter in. Which was annoying in the extreme, because she loved this job, needed the pay, loved helping people reach their dreams, so *focus* was the watchword of the day.

'If you need to talk anything through I'd be more than happy…' Malcolm's face disappeared back behind the computer screen, but after a few moments it reappeared again. 'No pressure, though.'

'Seriously, I'm fine. Tired, but that's to be expected.' And in truth the lack of sleep wasn't all pregnancy related.

Malcolm looked hugely relieved at the prospect of not having a stressing-out employee on his hands. She hadn't mentioned to anyone at work who the father was and wanted to keep things quiet. It was far too complicated to try talking about this kind of thing here. Everyone thought they knew everything, everyone thought they understood and they were all so lovely and well meaning, but how could they understand when she didn't even understand half of it herself?

Malcolm went back to tapping on the keyboard. 'Ah, I see we have Jo Kinney arriving in ten minutes for follicular monitoring.'

'I know, I made the booking, but don't worry—I'll make myself scarce. I understand how frustrating it is to see pregnant tummies in a fertility clinic when you're struggling to get even a fraction of the way.'

Her boss's voice was concerned. 'I'm hoping the counselling sessions are helping her.'

'I think so. The last time she was in she confessed to feelings of uncontrollable jealousy if any of her friends told her they were pregnant. And she's not talking to her sister at the moment because she's carrying twins. It's all so very difficult for her.' Since she'd become pregnant Georgie had been at pains to make sure she'd been extra-compassionate with her patients. She had what many of them only dreamt about and that was something she would never take for granted. 'I do have a feeling that she'll get there in the end, though.'

'We can only hope so. Don't look so worried, I'll give her the best shot we have.' Malcolm stood to leave. 'So do me a favour and take a lunch break for a change. The sun's shining and the yachts are racing out on the gulf. Get some fresh air. And while you're out, buy some tinsel, we need to Christmas this place up a bit, and last year's decorations are looking a bit sad.'

'Now you've definitely asked the right person for that job. I don't need to be asked twice to go Christmas shopping.' Smiling, Georgie stood and took off her name badge. She had plans to meet Liam for lunch, but had kept that information under wraps. Meeting him in secret for snatched lunches added to the excitement. 'Actually, I'm also going to go and take a sneak peek at that new baby shop. They import things from Europe apparently, it sounds wonderful.'

'Don't go buying the whole place up.'

'I won't. I'm just going for ideas. After the renovations I don't have much left over for the frills.' She grabbed her bag and made a quick mental list of things she needed.

A pram, a cot, cloth nappies, a stroller. Basically, the essentials. It was only window shopping, but it was lovely to dream.

The light warm breeze was welcome after the cloistered atmosphere in the clinic. Summer was edging in and starting to make its presence felt; the shoppers and office workers on High Street had shed their thick woollen coats and knee-length boots. The shop displays had Christmassy reds, greens and silvers instead of wintry blacks and browns, Georgie noted, and that made her feel bright. Despite not knowing which way was up with Liam, there was so much she should be thankful for. She had a great house, a great job with understanding and supportive colleagues. She had a future right here in her belly. There were many not so fortunate.

She almost broke into song, with the buskers churning out the old Christmas favourites...and, strangely, hearing 'Away In A Manger' brought a lump to her throat. A happy lump.

Choosing a colour theme for her tree this year was hard, but in the end she went with traditional red and gold. A few new baubles. And a named one for her and one for Liam. And for Nugget too... Desdemona didn't fit.

The baby shop was exclusive and expensive, she could see that just from the window displays with beautiful hand-carved cots and no price tags. When she entered the well-dressed shop assistants greeted her with expectant smiles.

'Just looking, thanks,' she answered their questioning faces, and wondered whether she'd have been better walking past and on to the more affordable chain stores further down the road. But, oh, it was such an adorable place, decorated with luxury Christmas items—'Baby's

First Christmas' bibs, blankets, towels. Miniature stockings hung from a makeshift mantelpiece. She eyed a kit for a hand-sewn advent calendar and made a mental note to add it to her ever-growing list. That would all have to wait until next year. Nugget's real first Christmas, and she'd make sure everything would be just perfect.

No, this Christmas would be special too. She had the feeling that waddling around trying to feed an army would be too much for her this year, so it would be just her and Liam, if she could lure him away from that ER… for the first time in her adult life she'd have a quiet one. At the thought of just the two of them spending such a special day together she grew a little hot. She imagined waking up to a special Liam Christmas surprise…and her cheeks flushed.

But where was he?

Clearly, he'd been held up by some emergency or other, but soon she'd need to get back to work, so she headed for the exit.

'Georgie? Hey, is that you, Georgie? Wow! Look at you. I had no idea…' It was Kate and Mark Holland, hand in hand staring into the same shop window.

'Kate?' The woman looked a darned sight healthier than she'd looked before, when she'd been bloated and on bed rest and pretty damned miserable. 'Lovely to see you. How are you doing?'

Kate's eyes twinkled. 'Not as well as you, clearly. My goodness, this is a surprise. When are you due?'

Georgie resisted running her hand over her now huge bump. 'Eight more weeks, end of January. A summer baby. Believe me, I am not looking forward to waddling around in that humidity.'

'Do you know the gender? What about names?'

More things on her list. She'd been putting off talk-

ing to Liam about names again, and when she'd jokingly
mentioned it he'd ended up…well…it had been very nice
indeed. 'No, I don't know the sex, I want it to be a surprise. And names are so hard to choose, don't you think?
Picking one's hard enough, but a middle name too? That's
all kinds of heavy-duty responsibility. Imagine picking a
name and them hating it for the rest of their lives.'

'So you have some planning to do. I like the traditional ones myself. Make a list.' Kate seemed genuinely
pleased for her and wrapped her in a gentle hug. 'Lucky
you. I really am pleased.'

Georgie told herself to get a grip as her throat filled
with emotion for Kate. Her hormones were all over the
place today. 'I saw you'd booked into the clinic this afternoon—what's the plan?'

Her patient gripped her husband's hand as they both
smiled. 'My mum's given us some money for one more
round, an early and very unexpected Christmas present.
I can't tell you how amazing that is. I just can't give up.
I just can't.'

'That's great news. Really brilliant. I'll keep everything crossed for you and we'll do everything we can at
the clinic.' Georgie knew exactly how Kate felt and wondered just how hard she'd have fought to feel the way she
felt right now. Hell, she'd have kept on fighting until she'd
had no fight left. And then she'd have fought harder still.
Nothing was as precious as this child, getting this child.
Having this child. It was the first time that Georgie had
ever sensed what it would be like to be part of a family.
To belong. To love and be loved, unconditionally. And
Liam fitted into that picture too. No matter how much
she tried not to, she couldn't help but do some serious
Christmas wishing on that account.

'Thanks.' Kate bit her lip and her eyes briefly fluttered

closed. 'I'm a bit worried, to be honest. I don't want to have another major disaster like last time.'

'Okay, so the first thing you have to do is stop worrying. That's not going to help at all. We'll start you on a lower dose of stimulation drugs this time and monitor you very closely. There's nothing to say that you'll have the same experience again. Really, try to relax, that's the best thing you can do. I'll see you later and we can talk more then.'

'Okay. See you soon.'

Georgie was about to leave when she felt a prickling along her neckline. Turning, she saw Liam approaching and felt the immediate rush of bright light whenever she saw him. 'Hey. Did you forget the time?'

'I'm so sorry. Just one thing after another today.' He shook his head and pecked a kiss on her cheek. 'Did I miss the shopping? Come on, let's go. I'm starving.'

'Me too.'

He grinned. 'No surprises there. What's in the bags?'

She hid the bag of named baubles behind her back and grinned right back—he'd probably think she was just a sentimental old sook. 'Not telling.'

'Aw…come on.' As he spoke his mobile phone went off. He shook his head in irritation, dragged his phone out of his pocket and looked at the display. 'Look, I've got to get this.'

'Who is it?'

'Just MAI.'

'The agency? Why? What do they want?' She felt the colour drain from her face. He'd been home so long this time. Long nights she'd kept him to herself like a delicious secret, always knowing that this day might come but pretending that it wouldn't. Convincing herself that it wouldn't matter anyway, that she was on top of her feelings about him. She'd managed to leave herself enough space and hadn't fallen for him so completely that his leaving would damage her.

Besides, he didn't have to go. The baby was due soon. He would turn them down. He would stay. 'What do they want?'

'No idea.' He shrugged. 'Sorry again. I won't be long.'

He turned a little away from her and she stared into the shop window, half looking at the too-expensive wares, half-listening to his side of the conversation. It would be fine. She would be fine. He wouldn't run, she trusted that he wouldn't go now, not when she needed him.

'Hey. No worries. Where…? How long…? Why…? What do you need?' Suddenly his voice went quiet and the bright light inside her went out.

He stayed quiet for a few moments as he listened to the caller. Then he looked over and caught her eye. There was something about his tense expression that made her heart stumble. Guilt? Panic? He tried for a smile, but it was more regretful than reassuring. Then he closed his eyes, turned his back to her, shoulders hitched.

Something was wrong.

She strained to listen, but whether he was hiding the information from her or protecting her she didn't know.

She heard her name.

She heard 'pregnant'.

She heard, 'Yes, I'll do it.'

Then he stood stock-still.

Something was wrong. Numbness crept through her. The only things she could feel were the fast, unsteady beat of her heart and the clench of her fists around the shopping bag handles.

Something was wrong but, unlike her house, or the

garden or the zillion things that had broken over the last few years, Liam wasn't going to fix this.

Liam snapped the phone into his pocket and turned to face her, already understanding that she'd heard a little and assumed a lot. Things were careering out of control in every direction he turned. 'I'm sorry. Again.' It was inadequate, he knew, but it was heartfelt.

'So you keep saying. What for? Being late for lunch or agreeing to whatever it was you just agreed to?' Her eyes were dark, her cheeks hollowed. She knew him too well, Liam realised. He couldn't hide things from her. 'What did they want? No…more to the point, when are you leaving? Where are you going?'

'Sudan. Tonight.'

'They need you, right? There's no one else? Absolutely no one else? Tell me they were desperate. You had no choice?'

The pause he gave was too long. Long enough for her to read between the lines. They'd sort of asked and he'd sort of offered. And, yes, there were others who could have gone. He'd just fast-tracked himself to the top of the list.

Things between them had got so complicated so quickly, he was thrashing around trying to make sense of it. But he couldn't.

Yes, he loved waking up with her. Yes, he loved spending time with her. Too much. It was all too much and he was starting to want things, to feel things he shouldn't about the baby and about her. He was supposed to have kept his emotions out of all this and yet here they were washing through him. Guilt. Panic. Adoration. Need. *Fear.*

And taking that risk was a step too far. He needed to

get his head straight. To have time to think. Sudan was the perfect place. It wouldn't be for ever, but it might just be enough to get things in order again, so he could be rational and stop these gut-wrenching emotions messing with his head. 'Well...'

He could hardly look at her, but he had to face her anger.

Which was swift and fierce and almost tangible. He could see her starting to close down.

She shook her head and strode past him. 'Okay. So you've made your decision. I have to go to work. I'm going to be late.'

Liam followed her down Queen Street towards her clinic, trying to keep up. The way she'd looked at him he could have sworn she'd wanted him to say something more. Something profound. But he wouldn't lie to her, let her think one thing, believe something—*want* something—that he wasn't sure he could give. Hell, she was hearts and flowers all the way and he was, in comparison, a lost cause. He shouldn't have let things get to this point. 'For a woman who's seven months pregnant you can sure keep a good pace.'

'That's because I'm in a hurry. My clinic's due to start and you're making me late for *my* job. You're not the only one with a strong work ethic.' She was in front of him now, grumping over her shoulder. And watching her stalk ahead, all proud and indignant, made him want her more. Which gave him every reason why he should get that damn flight.

'Georgie, we need to talk about this.'

'Really? You think?' She stopped outside the clinic. 'When you've already made your decision? You jumped at the chance. No hesitation. I didn't see much talking going on between us.'

He followed her up the stairs and into a meeting room. He closed the door and went to sit opposite her across a table. The table was too big, the room too sterile.

Her words echoed off the walls. 'And you don't know for how long. You never do. It could be months.'

'Look, it'll be okay. Everything will be fine. The deck's almost finished, the garden just needs some final touches. Don't do anything until I get back.'

Those lifeless eyes regained a spark that flamed. 'So this is your idea of being in it for ever? A lifetime commitment, and this is what you're promising? You won't be here geographically—and I can probably handle that. A lot of mothers have to deal with that. But…oh, this is unfair. I'm being unfair.' She stood up. 'I knew this all along, but—'

'What? Say it… Say what you're thinking.' He reached across for her hand, but she pulled it away. She was closing down. 'Talk to me, Georgie.'

'What's the point?'

'It's what we do. Talking.'

'Not, it appears, about the important things. Not when it matters. You should have discussed it with me first. *We* should have decided.' She took a deep breath and huffed it out. 'You say you're committed, that you want to work as a team, as a co-parent, but the moment they call, you jump. *You* choose. You can say no. You can stay here. There is a get-out clause. I do know.'

It was important that he remain calm and let her anger bounce off him. 'It's my job, Georgie. I've been home for a long time.' *Home.* That thought made Liam's stomach clench— it was the first time he'd thought of anywhere as home. Georgie's home. His heart swelled in pride at what they'd achieved at her house, but simultaneously he felt as if it was being slashed into pieces. 'This will be the last time. I'll make sure I resign completely after this.'

'I'm sure that's what they all say, and I'm sure they mean it too. Besides, I know why you do it, month after month, serving your penance to Lauren. I get that. I wouldn't ask you to give it up. But now? Right now? When you have a choice and you chose them. You chose them. Unbelievable.' She began to pace the room, glancing every few seconds at the clock. Which ticked away the minutes sonorously, ominously, like a sentinel counting down.

She stopped walking. Her hands gripped the back of a chair. There was a small hole in the dark grey fabric, the edges frayed. She seemed to stare at it as she spoke. 'So you told them? About the baby?'

'Yes.'

'And you might not be here for the birth?'

'They said they'd try to make it happen.' The ache that had started in his throat seeped into his chest, getting more raw and more real.

Distance. That's what they needed, then they'd be able to think and talk and act rationally, without the sideshow of pumping hearts and that long aching need. He needed to feel about her and the baby the way he felt about everyone else, not infused with some sort of mind-melding, heart-softening drug. That way he would be able to make good decisions, act responsibly.

He walked to the window and looked out at the street below. It had started to rain. Heavy clouds spewed thick drops over the passers-by below.

Finally, she came to him and made eye contact. But it wasn't what he wanted to see. All affection had gone, all excitement and hopefulness.

Somewhere along the way all his emotions had got

locked up with her. Every day started and ended with thoughts of Georgie. As he turned to the window he caught sight of a stack of magazines and remembered the online dating article. She was hoping for something more.

She wanted a declaration, he supposed. Something that told her how he felt about her, about this. But he didn't know what to say. Couldn't express the chaos, couldn't see through those clouds, only that his heart felt raw at the prospect of not being here. Of letting her down. But it wasn't fair to make her believe a lie.

Her voice was cold. 'And they're going to try? Is that what we've got to look forward to? You trying?'

'Surely that's better than me not trying? I'll call when I get there. I'll call as often as I can. I'm sorry it's not going to work out exactly to plan.'

'We didn't have a plan, Liam. That's just the problem. We just pretended everything would be fine, and it's not. It won't be.' She shook her head, her ponytail bobbing from side to side. She looked so young. And so cross. So magnificently annoyed. 'I won't hold my breath about the calls. I know what those satellite phones are like. You've never managed it before.'

It had never mattered so much before.

She was distancing herself from him, he could see. She was systematically putting space from her emotions, he recognised it because he'd done it himself so many times—but she never had.

When she looked back at him her resolve seemed clear. The emotions were settled, she was cold and distant. Things had irrevocably changed—including the emotions whirling in his chest like some sort of dark storm cloud, whipping away the oxygen and leaving nothing in its place. An empty chasm that hurt so hard.

He was going to help those who didn't have the wherewithal to help themselves. But, bone deep, he knew he was going because he couldn't not. Because facing other people's truths was always easier than facing up to his own. 'They need me there.'

'And we need you here.'

He looked over at the shopping bags she'd dropped on the floor. 'You bought decorations?'

'Suddenly I'm not feeling very festive. You're not going to be here.'

'I doubt it.' And that was all his fault. She'd been looking forward to spending Christmas together and he'd ruined it.

He turned to face her as hurt and pain whipped across his heart.

Her arms hugged across her chest. Her eyebrows rose as she infused her voice with a brightness she clearly didn't feel. 'So go. Save some lives. Come back safe and then be a good father to your child.'

'It'll only be for a few weeks. I'll get back for the birth. I'll make it happen.' His child. It was so close now, a few more weeks and he'd be able to hold his child.

Was that why he'd taken this job? Because he was too afraid? Was he too afraid to love his child?

To love Georgie?

That idea shunted him off balance. He didn't want to look too deeply inside himself, at his motivations, so he was going by gut feeling here, because that was all he had to go on. His head wasn't making any sense. 'And what about us?'

'Oh, Liam, we want different things, I understand that now. I feel that now. I want a big messy family with two parents who love each other, with doting grandparents who want to share the joy, and you don't want any of that.' She touched her heart and a little piece of him shattered because he knew what she was saying. That this was the end. 'We just don't have the same dream.'

No. Now his heart was being ripped away. He didn't want to hear those words, to feel this hurt. But he knew that it was the only way they would ever be able to get by, to see each other and survive. Maybe one day they'd find a place where they could be friends again. 'And when I come back?'

'We'll have rewound in time to before the baby. To before you came back from Pakistan. Back to when we were just friends. When things weren't complicated. You can have your life and I'll have mine and we'll meet somehow in the middle, for this little fella. Co-parents, like we agreed.'

'But—'

'No.' Her hand flicked up to stop him speaking. 'It's what I want, Liam. What I need to get through all this. Things are going to be hard enough as they are without wondering what you want from me too, worrying if you're going to change your mind or choose something else, something more appealing. Because you do that… don't you? So it'll be better if we have no promises. No pretence. No ties between *us*. No *us*. Just this baby.'

'But—' He wanted to fight her, to fight for them, but she was right. It was easier, cleaner if they broke everything off now and got back to being friends again. If that could ever happen. Time apart would help. It had to.

'I'm used to being on my own, Liam. That way there aren't any expectations. I can't spend my life wanting people to love me if they don't. If I'm not enough, that's fine. I'll be enough for this little one.'

You're more than enough for me. For anyone. But love? That was another level he hadn't dared strive for since Lauren. Something he'd closed himself to. Love?

Nah, he couldn't trust himself to go there. 'I'll be back as soon as I can. I'm sorry, about everything.'

'No. This is all my fault, Liam. I should have listened to you in the first place. It was a beyond crazy idea. And now our friendship is ruined, we can't talk without shouting. You're leaving and we're arguing. We never did this before, we used to go to the pub and give you a good send off, and off you'd trot, with a damned fine hangover, to save the world. And we cheered from the sidelines, proud and happy that you were doing something most excellent and good.

'But look at me, I'm not cheering now. I resent you for going and that's not how it should be. You'd resent me if I asked you stay. We're caught between our own needs and wants and it's too hard to live like that. Everything's changed between us. You said it would and it has. It's me who should be sorry. I made you do this. I kissed you first. I took you to my bed. I'm sorry for all of it.'

'Never. We've created something. A child. *Our* child. We can't ever be sorry for that.' He tried to pull her into his arms, to kiss her once more. To taste those honeyed lips, to feel her, soft and gorgeously round, in his arms. To feel that sense of belonging that she gave him, that reason to stay. To make him stop running from the past and look ahead to something different, something better, something not haunted by what happened before. Something more than good. But she stepped away, out of reach.

So far out of reach he didn't know if he'd ever find a way back to her.

'I need you to leave now.' She wanted him to stay. Wanted him to want to stay with her and the baby, and make a family of three. Oh, God, she wanted him. Wanted more. Wanted so much more. Wanted a different way to describe what the two of them had shared. It didn't necessarily need paperwork—she didn't expect marriage, but she did want commitment. Not just to the baby but to her. She wanted to be part of something long term. With him. She wanted her dream.

But he was running away, and he'd given her no choice in the matter.

And, yes, he'd shown commitment to the pregnancy despite her initial doubts. Not once had he wavered when even she'd had the odd wobble about impending parenthood. Hadn't he helped her create a beautiful space for her and their child? Hadn't he designed a garden? Hadn't he made sure she was safe, that she ate the right things, that his child was cocooned in the right environment to grow?

But he had still never said the word 'love' to her. Not about her or his child. Or about anyone or anything, for that matter, ever. He was all locked up in the tragedy of his baby sister and it was desperately sad but she wanted him to love someone.

She wanted him to love her.

And he couldn't. Because if he did he wouldn't be heading off on some mission that he didn't need to go on. He'd be here, holding her hand and planning a happy Christmas, supporting her in her last couple of months of pregnancy.

Was it too much to ask? Was she expecting too much?

No. It was what every couple strove for. She wanted him to feel the same way about it all as she did. She wanted him to share that excitement she felt whenever she lay in his arms. The way her heart soared when he was inside her. The sensation of utter completeness when he looked at her, when he made her laugh. She wanted him to love her and the baby the way she loved him. Wholly. Totally. Without reservation.

And there it was. The naked, ugly truth. She'd fallen in love with him.

When she should have been putting all her attention into this baby, she'd gone and fallen for its father—the wrong kind of man to love.

No.

She tried not to show her alarm and fixed her face as best as she could into an emotion-free mask as she walked away from him, while he stared at her uncomprehendingly, his hand on the doorhandle.

No. Don't go. She wanted to shout it at him. To hurl herself at him and be a barrier between him and the door. But what would be the point? Letting him go was the right thing to do. What was the point in making someone stay, hoping they would learn to love you? Hoping…

She loved him. Completely. Devastatingly. Instead of protecting herself against more heartache, she'd allowed her life to be bowled over by a man who couldn't and wouldn't ever love her. It was a simple and as difficult as that. How stupid.

And now, even worse, she was tied to him for ever. She'd insisted on that. And he'd agreed. He'd torn up the contract in a dramatic gesture of commitment and determination that had both impressed and scared her. And despite everything she knew about him, she'd believed him and somewhere deep inside a little light had fired into life and it had grown and she'd hoped…

And now the light had blown right out.

Because, after all, she'd been the silly one in all this, she'd allowed herself to dream, had allowed herself to slip under his spell, had willingly given her heart to him. He'd always been upfront. And you couldn't be more upfront than jumping on the first plane out of Dodge.

Liam had been right all along. Love could be damned cruel. She could never let him know. 'I need you to leave. Now. I need you to go, Liam.'

'Georgie—'

'Go. I have to work.' She watched the door close behind him, and almost cried out, almost declared herself, to see if that would make a difference to him going or staying. But she wasn't about to play games, give him tests, make him say something he'd regret. Or that they'd both regret.

But, still, nothing took away from the fact that she loved him. She had probably always loved him—as a friend, as someone who she could confide in and share a joke with. He was, deep down, a good man who was conflicted, who was trying to hide from hurt, and after his experiences who could blame him? His flaws made him even more likable. Falling romantically in love with him had been the icing on the cake and she would be proud for her child to have him as a father. One day she would tell him that. When she could look him in the face again. When her heart had stopped shattering into tiny pieces.

With shaking hands she picked up her shopping bags, took out the tinsel and gaudy baubles and threw them on the table. That would be for later, for a time when she felt like celebrating. Right now Christmas loomed ahead a sad and sorry affair. A Christmas without Liam. She'd wrapped him up in her festive excitement, made him the best present a girl could have, and he'd gone. Left her, just like her mother had.

One day she'd find someone who wanted her enough to stay around.

She took a few deep breaths, swiped a hand across

her face and caught a tear. And another one. Then gave up the fight and let them flow.

My God, she thought as she looked in the staff-room mirror, she needed to pull herself together; this clinic could be hard enough without the nurses falling apart too.

'Come on, girl.' Plumped up her cheeks and dried her eyes. 'There are plenty who are much worse off.' Like the people Liam was going out to save. Like the ones she had booked in now, who looked to her for support and advice. Who didn't have a healthy baby in their bellies. Who needed her dedication and attention to get them through. She allowed herself two more tears. Exactly that. One for her, one for her baby, then she took another deep breath, put on her game face and went back out into the world.

CHAPTER ELEVEN

Two weeks ago...

LIAM LURCHED AGAINST the cold hard passenger seat as the Jeep bumped over potholes along the pitted dirt track. 'Man, these roads don't get any better. I'm going to be covered in bruises before we get to the camp.'

'Aren't you pleased to be back?' Pierre Leclerc shouted above the din of the engine, his words tinted with his French-Canadian accent and vestiges of the countless places he'd visited in his long aid career. He cracked a booming laugh and hit Liam on the thigh. 'We missed you.'

'Ah, shucks, mate, I missed you too.' Like hell he'd missed them. He'd struggled every kilometre, every minute of the interminable flight, the uncomfortable transit, the stench. The seven-day layover in Juba, getting supplies, waiting for the right documents, stuck in bureaucratic hell. The long drive out here. Every second wishing he'd had the courage to stay in Auckland with Georgie.

He just couldn't get rid of the memory of her. All grumpy and stroppy, stomping down the crowded street, the swing of her backside, the tense holding of her shoulders, the swish of her ponytail. The closed-off posture.

The truth of her words. *Our friendship is ruined.* But it was all too late.

Pierre leaned across. 'I hope you bought us something decent for our Christmas stockings?'

'I have something to help us forget, if that's what you mean.' Patting his duty-free purchases of rum and whisky, he joined in the laughter, trying to be friendly, wishing like mad he was back in New Zealand, far away from this nightmare of dry earth and flies.

I made a mistake, he thought. *I made a million of them.*

They pulled into the camp compound, the dull corrugated roof of the medical building half-hidden by a layer of brown sand whipped up by the morning wind. A thin pale grey sky stretched above them, promising little relief from the scorching sun.

Liam looked around at the thousands of tents and crudely made straw structures lining the gravel and mud path. Sun-bleached rags, tied between sticks and corrugated metal, provided the best shelter they could from relentless heat. A group of women huddled around a water tap. 'It hasn't changed at all.'

'Nothing much changes around here. It's like *Groundhog Day.*' Pierre pulled out a handkerchief and swiped it across his forehead. 'People still arrive every day seeking help, and we still struggle to house them, to feed them, to provide adequate clean water. There aren't enough toilets, the kids are all getting sick. Nothing changes at all.'

Except last time Liam couldn't wait to get here. And this time he couldn't wait to leave. 'So, what's planned for today?'

'Immunisation programme. Training the new assistants so they can go on and run it solo.'

'Okay. Let's do it.' Liam jumped down into the fog of red dust created by the Jeep wheels.

Within seconds, dozens of semi-naked children appeared screaming, laughing and singing, surrounding Liam and Pierre and clinging to their legs. Such joy in everything, even in the direst circumstances. But that was kids for you: they didn't overthink, they didn't worry or analyse, they just got on with life, running forward to the next great adventure. There was a lesson there.

Pierre steered him into the medical centre. As they squeezed past the long queue of sick people waiting to be treated Liam found himself wondering where to begin, but as always Pierre had the routine down like clockwork. And Liam easily slipped back into it.

'Okay, your turn.' He beckoned to a mother holding a small child in her arms. 'How old?'

The woman looked at him, not understanding. She offered him the child, a boy of about twelve months, scrawny and lethargic with the telltale potbelly signs of malnutrition.

'He's about one year and a half.' The base nurse translated the woman's local dialect, 'His name is Garmai. Just out of the supplementary feeding programme two weeks ago.'

Liam checked him over and measured the child's arm circumference to determine the extent of malnutrition. Garmai would probably spend the best part of his life growing up in a refugee camp, his home town too dangerous to go back to as rebels terrorised the streets and drought stole their crops. So different from the life his own child would lead in New Zealand, where water came through invisible pipes below the ground, machines worked with the swipe of a finger and food was plentiful.

And a father half a world away.

What the hell had he been thinking?

'Eighteen months old? Really?' He spoke to the nurse.

'It looks like he still has signs of mild malnutrition. He needs to go back to the feeding centre, not stay here where he's probably only going to get sick again.'

'There isn't room. They discharged him because there's too many more coming every day.'

'They'll have to make room. This child needs help and I don't want a half-hearted effort.' He turned and smiled at the mother, trying to dredge some hope when there was little. 'I'm going to have a child. To be a father.'

He'd never given any personal information to anyone here before, not even to the staff—but the words just tumbled out. Pride laced his voice as his thoughts returned again to Georgie for the umpteenth time that day, along with the familiar sting of regret and yet startling uplift of his heart. Every thought of her brought a tumbling mishmash of emotions and a fog of chaos. 'Soon. Very soon.'

The mother gave him a toothy grin and gabbled something to him, but a high-pitched scream grabbed their attention. A heavily pregnant woman half walked, half crawled into the room, clutching her stomach. She was immediately ushered back out and into the emergency area by two nurses.

Georgie? *Georgie.* Of course it wasn't Georgie. He'd left her to face her biggest challenge alone back at home. How would she cope with the pain of childbirth? Did she have a plan? Why the hell hadn't he made sure she had a plan? He'd phone her again, at least try to, tonight, and make sure she was okay. That was, of course, if she ever deigned to speak to him again. Her silence had been deafening.

Unlike the squawk of chattering voices and laughter and screams that filled the room as a huddle of women walked towards the emergency area. He looked up at the nurse for an explanation. 'The pregnant woman's sisters, here to help.'

'Great. She'll need some support.' He looked back at the boy, then jerked his head up again at another straggle of women walking through the room.

'The birthing attendants. The mother's mother. Her aunts.'

'Are they going to have a party or something? There's a lot of them.'

The nurse beamed. 'Of course. Family is very important here.'

As it was to Georgie. And she was going to be alone. And that was his fault.

Watching those people come together to help their sister, to celebrate family in all its messy glory, made his heart clutch tight and he realised that Georgie had been wrong about one thing: he did want the same dream. He'd spent the last nine months trying to fight it with his head, but his hands had worked on her house, her garden, building a home for them all, a home that he loved. His arms had held the woman he adored, cradled her belly holding the baby he so desperately wanted.

For the first time in years he saw his own needs with startling clarity. He wanted to look forward instead of back. He wanted to be a father his child would be proud of. He wanted a family.

Hell, Georgie had even got him thinking about his own mother and father. And how much, deep down, he wanted to make some kind of contact with them again. He'd make a start tonight. He'd phone them and tell them they were going to be grandparents.

He wanted to be part of something good. He wanted somewhere to call home, a community of friends. Someone to love. And to be loved. The same simple dreams as every single person in this camp. He just hadn't realised it until now.

Most of all he wanted Georgie, with such a passion it stripped the air from his lungs. But he knew her heart came with a proviso. He had to love her. She wouldn't accept any less than that.

He had to love her. *Had to?* Could he do that? He sat for a moment and that thought shook through him like a physical force. He let her image fill his brain, suffuse his body with so many wild emotions. His throat filled with a raw and unfettered need.

Man, how he wanted her. He missed everything about her. He wanted her. Dreamt about her, saw her soft beautiful eyes in everyone's here, her kindness in the gentle touch of strangers, her compassion, her independence that frustrated and endeared her to him. He missed her so intensely it hurt. He needed to touch her, to lie with her, to fight with her. And, of course, to make love to her over and over and over. And such a need and such a want could only amount to one thing.

He did love her.

He'd been fighting so hard to protect himself he hadn't seen the single most important thing that had been happening.

God. He loved her and he'd walked away. No, he'd *run* away, afraid of how much she made him feel things. He'd messed up everything and now was it too late to start again? Would she even let him in the house? Would she let him love her?

Did she love him back?

He needed to know. He needed to make things right. He needed to go home.

A scream and a healthy wail echoed through the flimsy walls. New life. New beginnings. Not just for that family in there. But for him. Being here reminded him how fragile life was, and he needed to spend the rest of it with the woman he loved.

It was time to act. He needed to get back to her. Before Christmas, before the baby came. Before he lost any more time being here instead of there. He stood up and realised that a queue of people had formed, all staring at him in this tin-roofed lean-to in a place, it seemed, even God had forgotten.

Damn. He'd made too many mistakes and being here was one of them.

But how the hell to get out of this godforsaken dustbowl and bridge the fifteen thousand kilometre gap to be home in time?

Christmas Eve...

'Kate? Is that you? Hey, it's Georgie. From the clinic.' Georgie gripped the phone to her ear and tried to keep her feelings in check. This part was always the most emotional bit of her job but she wished, just this once, that she could see Kate's face when she told her the news. Knowing exactly how her patient would be feeling at this moment, she wanted to wrap her in a hug. In fact, wrapping anyone in a hug would be lovely—it felt so long since she'd done that. One month, two days and about twelve hours, to be exact. Not that she was counting.

And the loneliness was dissipating a bit now, especially when she distracted herself. Which she felt like she had to do most minutes of most hours, because he was always on her mind. Just there. The look on his face as she'd called the whole thing off, haunting her. But it had been the right thing to do. A very right thing.

'Yes?' Kate's voice wavered. The line was crackly. 'Yes?'

'I've got the results from the blood test you came in for earlier today.'

A sharp intake of breath. 'Yes?'

'So...' Georgie read out all the numbers, knowing that this gobbledegook would mean the difference between heartache and ecstasy for this couple. 'So, all that means we have good news. Great news. You have a positive pregnancy test. Looks like you're going to have a very happy Christmas. Huge congratulations. I know how much this means to you.'

There was a slight pause then a scream. 'Oh. My God. Really? Really? Are you sure?'

Georgie couldn't help her smile. Her heart felt the fullest it had in a month. Since, exactly, the moment she'd watched Liam disappear from the clinic. 'Yes. It's very early days, obviously, and we still have to take one day at a time. But, yes, you are pregnant.'

'Oh, thank you. Thank you so much. Mark will be so thrilled. I know how much he wanted this. We both do. We can't thank you enough.'

Georgie ignored the twist in her heart at the thought of how gloriously happy this couple would be, together. Expecting a baby, making a family. Of how much Mark would be involved, and how much his love and concern for his wife always shone through his face.

It did not matter, she kept telling herself, that she was facing all this on her own. She would be fine and one day, maybe, she'd find a man who wanted her too. 'Okay, so we need to make another appointment for you for a few days' time to check the HCG levels are rising as well as we want them to, which means you'll have to come in before the New Year,' Georgie explained. 'I also need to book you an ultrasound scan...'

'Not long to go for you now?' Kate asked, after they'd finished the business end of the call. 'How are you feeling? Excited?'

'Very. There's just over a month to go and I don't feel remotely ready. I still have heaps of shopping to do, and I haven't even thought about preparing my delivery bag.'

'Get your man to spoil you rotten over the holidays, then. Make him do the fetching and carrying while you put your feet up.'

Familiar hurt rolled through her. Emails had been sporadic. Phone calls virtually non-existent. The only news she got was on the TV or radio. But even then she wished she hadn't heard anything. Too many people being killed. It was too unsafe. And all this stress just couldn't be good for the baby, so in the end she'd switched the damned TV off and played Christmas music to calm her down. 'He's overseas at the moment. I'm not sure when he'll be back.'

'That's a shame. What are your plans for Christmas?'

'Oh, just a quiet one at home.' She thought about her Christmas tree with the lavish decorations that she'd eventually found the motivation to finish last night. The small rolled turkey she'd bought and the DVDs of old Christmas movie favourites stacked up waiting for her to watch in the evenings. It was going to be an old-style Christmas, just her and Nugget. Not what she'd hoped for. And that was fine. It really was.

'Well, have a good one. *Kia kaha.*' *Stay strong.*

'Yes, thanks. Bye.' Georgie smiled as she put the phone in the cradle. Broken heart or not, she fully intended to.

Six hours later she was standing on the deck, adding the final touches to the outside decorations to the jolly and earnest accompaniment of carol singers blasting through her speakers. The deck may not have been quite finished, but the garden looked beautiful, with the candles flickering in the darkness. Liam had been right, the winery garden idea had worked well—just a shame that the edges still needed to be finished off.

But tomorrow's forecast was for sunshine and she had no intention of sitting inside when she had such a fairy-tale place to spend the day. The hammock had her name on it, along with a glass of cranberry and raspberry juice, a large helping of Christmas pudding and a damned good romance novel.

There was just one more string of lights to hitch onto a branch to make everything perfect. Standing on tiptoe, she reached up and tried to throw the lights around the branch.

Missed. *Damn.*

She tried again. Missed again. Stretching forward, she flung the lights towards the branches, the weight of her baby tummy dragging her forward and off balance.

Stepped out into…air.

She felt the scream before she heard it, rattling up through her lungs, into her throat that was filled with panic. The one single word that came to her, the only thing she wanted right now. 'Liam!'

Then she flailed around like a windmill as there was nothing and no one to stop her fall into darkness.

Now…

Pain seared up her leg with even the slightest movement. She was sure she'd broken her ankle—it was twisted at such a strange angle caught in the gap between splintered wood and the garden wall. A bad sprain anyway, too sore for her to put her weight on, and she was too wedged in to be able to lever her big fat belly upwards.

So she was stuck. *Damn.*

And hurting. *Double damn.*

And how long she'd lain here calling for help, she didn't know, but the moon was high in the sky now. Typical that she'd left her phone in the house. Typical that the neighbours had gone to their holiday home by the sea. Typical that it was Christmas and she was on her own. And the music she'd been playing seemed to be on repeat and if someone didn't turn it off soon she'd go down in history for being the first woman to have been turned clinically insane by Rudolph and his damned red nose.

And it hurt. Everything hurt. Including her heart, because she felt stupid and sad, here on Christmas Eve, alone and stuck. And for some reason her usually capable mind set had got all mushy and she felt a tear threaten. And more than anything she missed Liam.

That was it. She loved him and she missed him with every ounce of her being. And he wasn't here and he never would be. Not in the way she wanted.

She tried again to wriggle free but her ankle gave way and she didn't want to put more pressure on it. Thank God it was summer and the night was warm. At least she could be grateful for that small mercy.

No. She wasn't grateful, she was angry. With herself, with Liam, with everyone and everything. Was she going to be stuck here all damned holiday? 'Hey! Anyone? Lady with a baby here. Stuck. Help?'

Rudolph with your nose so bright...

'Shut up! Please. Someone. Help.'

Once she'd calmed down a little she tried pulling herself up again. This time she managed an inch. Two...

but then nothing more. She was about to call out again when a sudden searing pain fisted across her body. And her feet got wet.

Her heart hammered just a little bit more. No. Surely not?

The baby? Now? She pressed a hand to her belly and spoke in the softest voice she could muster. 'No, Nugget! Don't you dare make your appearance here. You've got five more weeks to cook. You stay exactly where you are.'

She waited, biting back the pain from her foot. Trying not to cry. Maybe it had been a Braxton-Hicks contraction? Maybe it was all just practice?

No such luck. More pain rippled across her abdomen, sapping her breath and making her grip tight onto the side of the deck. That one had hurt. A lot. 'You are just like your father, you hear me? You have lousy timing.'

How could she have a baby here, when she couldn't even lift her leg up half an inch? Never mind that it was five weeks early. What was she going to do? Her lips began to tremble.

No. She wasn't going to cry. She was going to be fine.

More contractions rippled through her. Faster and more regular and every time they hurt just a little bit more. Time ticked on and she wanted so much to move, to free herself. To walk, to bend, to stretch.

And then more contractions came and the night got darker.

To cope with the pain she tried to conjure up an image of Liam, pretending he was here with her. Pretending he was helping her. Pretending he loved her. Because only that would be enough.

Think. Think. What could she do?

She didn't want to think. She wanted someone to do that for her, for a change. She wanted to be tucked up in bed, her head on Liam's shoulder, wrapped safe in his arms. She wanted— 'Owwwww. This is all your fault, Liam MacAllister. I hate you. I hate…*youoooooww.*'

'I'm sorry. Is this not a good time?'

And now she was hallucinating, because through all this thick soupy darkness and Rudolph on repeat and searing pain she could have sworn she'd heard his voice.

She decided she was going to go with it. Maybe she was already clinically insane after all. 'Yes. You bet your damned Christmas socks it isn't a good time. I'm caught between a deck and a hard place. My foot's broken and I'm having your baby.'

'Right now?'

'Yes, right now.' She spoke to the Liam-shaped smudge that appeared so real it was uncanny. And to her endless irritation her heart did a little skipping thing. She didn't want it to skip. She wanted it to stay angry because that was the only way she was going to get through this. 'What the hell are you doing here anyway? Aren't you supposed to be healing the sick? Giving alms to the poor?'

Then he was there, really right there, with his scent and his capable hands, and he wasn't panicking like she was, he was talking to her in a soothing, very understanding voice. 'Let's get you… Oh.' His hands shoved under her armpits and he tugged. 'You're stuck.'

'Give the man a medal. Yes, I'm stuck. I've broken my ankle and Desdemona's about to make her— *Owwwwww.*' Pain ripped through her again. The contractions were coming faster now. More regular and more intense.

But he was here. Like some goddamned guardian angel, he was here. For her. He'd come back. For her?

Or was it just for the baby? She couldn't think about any of that right now. He was here.

His voice soothed over her again. 'You're going to be fine, really, but I think we need the fire brigade or someone else to help lift you out. I don't want to hurt you…'

You already have. 'No way. No way are you getting those good people out of bed on this special night just to come with their special lifting equipment and heft me out of— *Oowwwwww.*'

'Contractions are that regular, eh? We've got to get you out. How about if I…?' He put his foot against the wall and heaved her upwards, and if he hadn't been tugging at her she might have melted into his embrace just for a moment. Just held on tight, just for one solitary moment, to absorb some of his strength and his heat. Just held right on. 'Twist left a bit…wait…slowly…'

'Whoa. Watch it…' Then she was somehow shrugged up and sitting on the deck and her foot was throbbing and her stomach contracting and she gripped onto his old T-shirt while sudden enormous pain rattled through her. 'It hurts, Liam. It all hurts.'

He grimaced a little, she thought. She could just about make him out. The candles had blown out hours ago and she hadn't managed to even plug the fairy-lights in. Some other time she might have thought this was romantic. It wasn't. It hurt.

But then he pushed her hair back from her face and rubbed his thumb over her cheek and she bit her lip to stop herself from crying because he was here and she wanted him so much. But he didn't want her.

He looked right into her eyes. 'I know, darling. I know it hurts. It'll be fine. Honestly. It'll be okay.'

'No, it won't. This baby can't come yet, it doesn't have anywhere to sleep…and I haven't had my baby shower,

I want my party. I want to play games—I don't want to do this.'

And I don't want you here to torment me and be the macho hero and loving father when you'll go and break my heart a million times over every time I see your face.

'This. Is. Not. My. Birth. Plan. I want gas and air. Pethidine. *Drugs.*'

'Roll with it, Geo. Looks like you're going to have a special guest of honour at that party. Because this baby is coming, whether you want it to or not. I get the feeling it has your genes when it comes to independence.'

'Oh. Oh. *Owww.*'

'Let's get you inside. It's too dark. I don't know how to help if I can't see.' Half carrying her, half walking her, he managed to get her inside and onto the lounge floor. 'The bedroom's too far. Okay. I'm calling back-up. This baby's in a hurry.'

After stabbing numbers into a phone, he rattled off information and only then did she hear the anxiety in his voice. When he turned back to her she saw him in full light. My God, he was breathtaking. But he looked concerned. No, more than that. He looked haunted. *Lauren.* 'It won't happen again, Liam. It will be fine.'

'I know, I know. Everything's okay.'

'And I think I want to push—'

Everything was not okay.

Liam consciously regulated his breathing, but there was nothing he could do about his pounding heart rate and his overwhelming sense of dread. There was every chance that this could go wrong. This was a prem scenario. The one nightmare he wanted to avoid. It was happening all over again.

He tried to shake away the image of tubes and an incubator and a tiny pink thing that grew into his crying wailing sister, but had looked so quiet and so sick that it had almost broken his heart. And of the tiny coffin that had barely filled the space in the dirt.

So, no, everything was not okay.

He inhaled sharply and took Georgie's hand and waited until she'd stopped screaming and screwing up her face. 'That's it. It's all good. You're doing well.'

How many babies had he delivered? He'd lost count. Out in the field where there was little help and lots of disease, when mum and baby had less than a good chance of surviving. And he'd never panicked. Not once. But right now he'd never wanted so much for medical equipment. For back-up. For the pain in his heart to dislodge so he could think straight. For the woman and the child he loved to be okay. 'You're doing good. Now breathe… breathe…'

At what point had he so hopelessly and completely fallen in love with her? Maybe right then that second as she stared up at him with such fear and love and relief in her eyes that it made his heart jolt. Or maybe when she'd told him to leave and he'd seen the same love shimmering in her face, even though she had been trying so hard to hide it from him. Maybe when he'd found her in the ER with a damaged eye. Or when she'd told him she was pregnant.

Or even that very first day in the sluice room ten years ago when she'd taken no nonsense and told him to harden up.

But in the last few days that thought had taken hold of him and he just couldn't shake it off. Damn fine time to realise you loved someone, right when you had a chance of losing them. But whatever happened he had to love her now, from this minute on, and protect her and care for her. And help her. And be brave for her. 'I can see the head, Geo. Breathe for me. Just a second. Breathe.'

'I don't hate you.'

A smile flowered in his heart—enough to take him past the fear and into a place of calm. They'd get through this together. 'I know. I know you don't hate me, Geo. Concentrate on the breathing.'

'Really, I'm sorry. I don't hate you— *Owwwwww.*' Then with an ear-splitting scream a slick baby slithered into his arms. The doorbell rang. Footsteps pounded into the room. Georgie cried. The baby cried. The cord was cut, a murmur of voices. A hearty chorus of congratulations!

And, able to finally breathe again, he was left staring at this miracle. His son. All ten fingers and ten toes and a hefty set of lungs. Who was managing just fine on his own. And suddenly Liam's heart was blown wide open with a different kind of emotion. A searing riotous joy and a feeling that life was just about to get gloriously messy.

Then he looked at his son's mother, who was the most red-faced, tear-stained disaster he'd ever seen. And his heart swelled some more, shifting and finding more space for love for her. And he knew in that moment that nothing would ever be the same because he'd allowed these people into his heart and that was where they were going to stay. For ever. 'You are amazing, Georgie Taylor. He is amazing.'

'It's a boy? Yes?'

'Yes. He's doing fine. Just fine.' He passed the baby to her to hold, watched as the tiny bundle nuzzled towards her nipple. 'A boy, with great instincts and a particularly well-defined MacAllister package, if I do say so myself.'

'One minute old and you're assessing his genitals?'

'It's a guy thing.' Unable to resist kissing her any longer, he lifted his head and pressed his mouth to hers. 'I love you. I love you, but I need to explain—'

'Whoa? Really? Now?' She nodded towards the team of busy paramedics. 'I've just had a baby and we have an audience, and you want to do this now?'

'Yes. Now, and always. My timing is legendary, didn't you know? I don't care who hears it, I love you, Georgie.'

Her eyes widened but she put a hand between them to create space. 'It's the hormones. You'll grow out of it in a day or two. Then you'll be hot-footing it back to South Sudan at the first opportunity.'

'No. It's taken me a decade to come to my senses, but I love you. I want to be with you. Nowhere else in the world has you, so I want to be here, to make you happy.' His throat caught a little. 'And now we have this one.'

Those wide dark eyes brimmed with tears. 'No. It's because of him that you're here. Not me. You don't love me. You want to. Oh, how you want to. But you don't.'

'Are you for real? I've called in every favour I've ever had and flown halfway across the world. Dashed straight to you. Which part of *I love you* don't you believe?'

She bit her lip and as always her stark honesty was there in her face, in her words. 'I'm scared, Liam. I want to believe it all. Wow, that would be such an awesome dream to have come true, really. I couldn't think of a better thing I could have. But you don't have to get carried away. I get that you don't like connection.'

She was rejecting him? He hadn't factored that into his plan. 'I have spent every available waking hour for the last eight months here. I have pimped your house, transformed your garden, been at your beck and call. I've been your friend through thick and thin. I am still your friend, Geo. That is the best part about all of this. We are friends first. Doesn't that prove that I love you?'

'I want your heart. Not your duty or your responsibility, or some friendship loyalty thing. I want your true love.' It was there in her face and mirrored in his heart, unfettered, truthful, raw. He needed to make her believe him. She clearly took some persuading. 'I want your true love. For me. I won't take anything less.'

'Wait. Wait right there.' He dashed out to the car, grabbed his things and dashed back. 'The paramedics are waiting outside, they want to take little Nugget—we need a name. Really, we need a name. Just to be checked out at the hospital. And to get your foot sorted. But I want to give you this first.'

He dragged the cot into the lounge and placed it next to the biggest, brightest Christmas tree loaded down with the most garish baubles he'd ever seen. 'Here. I got this.'

Her hand went to her mouth. 'You bought the cot from the French market? And you've painted it? That's very sweet, very kind of you. He'll love it. I love it.'

'And I love you. I bought this for you back then, the day after you fell in love with it. Because you wanted it so much. Because it makes you happy. I just want to do things that make you smile. I love you. Please believe me.'

'Oh, Liam.' Georgie shuffled across the sofa, trying to avoid the pain in her nether regions, her foot, and just about everywhere on her body. But it all faded just a little bit. He loved her? Did he? She'd listened out for it for so long, but he'd never used the words. She'd wanted to hear it, had waited so patiently for someone somewhere to say those three words to her. She had believed that a declaration of love could only be spoken. The deeds, though—they'd been plentiful. He'd shown her his love instead of declaring it. Every day for ten years.

For some reason she couldn't breathe, her lungs were filled with nothing, her throat choked with a lump of emotion. 'I don't know what to say.'

'Well, don't, then. Don't say a thing. Just listen. I didn't want to fall in love because love can be damned painful. I pushed everyone away to protect myself. I didn't want a family, I didn't want those things you craved. But you've shown me how to make it work, how to take a risk. That fighting for the people you love is the most important thing of all. I love you. Because you are you. You're funny and weird and you laugh at my jokes and your smile warms my heart every time I see it. But best of all we can get through anything—hell, we've stood by each other ten years already. I'm ready for another thirty, forty, eighty… You?'

'Yes. Yes, of course.' She wrapped him into her arms, with a slight protest from the little fella. 'Thank you. Thank you so much. I love you too. Really. Truly.'

'And if you want me to give up the aid work, I will. I'll find something else.'

She shook her head. 'Enough with the crazyville talk. I know how much you need to do that work. Just maybe shorter stints? And we'll definitely discuss it, right? You won't just decide.'

'Of course not. We're in this together.' And the way he was looking at her convinced Georgie that he really did mean it. He planted a kiss on her cheeks, then laughed. 'Hey, it's Christmas Day, you realise? We'll have to think of something festive to call him. I'm sorry, but Nugget doesn't cut it.'

She looked over at the twinkling lights on the tree, at the three baubles centre stage with their names on. At the stack of DVDs and the romance novel. This was not how she'd intended spending Christmas Day, but she couldn't think of a better way. Two guys to look after. Two guys to love her. A family. A proper family—now that had always been at the top of her Christmas wish list. 'There's always Noel or Gabriel…Joseph, maybe? We could call him Joe?'

'Or…Rudolph? Rudi?'

That damned music was still playing in the background. 'Not on your life. Come here and kiss me again.'

His nose nuzzled into her hair. 'I can't think of anything else when I kiss you, my mind goes to mush.'

'That's the plan, I don't want any more suggestions like that. Besides, we've got plenty of time to think of a name, but way too many kisses to catch up on…'

He did as requested. When he pulled away it wasn't as far as he usually went. She liked that. Liked the way he was intent on staying. Liked the way he loved her.

'Happy Christmas, darling.'

'Happy Christmas, Macadoodle-doo.' She gave her man another kiss. Then snuggled into the baby snuffling in her arms. 'Happy first Christmas, Nugget.'

And many, many more to come.

* * * * *

LUCY & THE LIEUTENANT

HELEN LACEY

For Robert…to the moon and back.

Chapter One

Brant Parker grabbed the T-shirt stuffed in the back pocket of his jeans and wiped his brow.

It was cold out, but he'd been working for four hours straight without a break and it was quite warm inside the closed-up rooms of the Loose Moose Tavern. He'd spent the best part of three weeks stripping out the old timber framing and flooring that had gone through a fire eight months earlier.

Most people said he was crazy for buying the place, like it had some kind of hoodoo attached to it. But he didn't believe in hoodoo or bad luck, and he wasn't swayed by anyone telling him what he should or shouldn't do. The Loose Moose had been a part of Cedar River for over thirty years and he believed the old place deserved another chance.

Maybe he did, too.

Brant dropped the piece of timber in his hands,

stretched his back and groaned. It had been a long day and he wanted nothing more than to soak under a hot shower and to relax in front of some mindless TV show for an hour or two. But first he had to go to the veterans home to visit his uncle, as he did every Tuesday and Friday.

Uncle Joe was his father's oldest brother and a Vietnam veteran who'd lost a leg in the war. He also had a heart condition and suffered from the early stages of Parkinson's disease. He lived in full-time care at the home adjacent to the small community hospital. Brant cared deeply for his uncle. The older man knew him. Got him. Understood the demons he carried.

He headed upstairs to the small apartment and took a shower, then dressed in jeans and a long-sleeved shirt. It was snowing lightly, a regular occurrence in South Dakota in winter, but quite unusual for mid-November. He shouldered into his lined jacket, pulled on woolen socks and heavy boots, and grabbed his truck keys. The home was a ten-minute drive in good weather from the main street in town and since snow was now falling in earnest, he knew the roads would be slippery. Brant took his time and arrived about fifteen minutes later. It was late afternoon and the parking lot was empty, so he scored a spot easily and got out of the truck.

The wind howled through his ears and he pulled the jacket collar around his neck. It promised to be a long and chilly winter ahead. But he didn't mind. It sure beat the relentless, unforgiving heat of a desert summer like the last one he'd endured in Afghanistan. The light blanket of snow made him feel as though he was home. And he was. For good this time. No more tours. No more military. He was a civilian and could lead a normal life. He could get up each morning and face a new day. And he could forget everything else.

Brant headed for the front doors and shook off his jacket before he crossed the threshold. When he entered the building, heat blasted through him immediately. The foyer was empty and the reception desk had a sign and a bell instructing to ring for attendance. He ignored both and began walking down the wide corridor.

"Hi, Brant."

The sound of his name stopped Brant in his tracks and he turned. A woman emerged from a door to his left and he recognized her immediately. *Lucy Monero.* He cringed inwardly. He wasn't in the mood for the pretty brunette with the lovely curves and dancing green eyes, and tried to stay as indifferent as possible. "Good afternoon, Dr. Monero."

"Please," she said just a little too breathlessly. "Call me Lucy."

He wouldn't. Keeping it formal meant keeping her at a distance. Just as he liked it.

Instead he made a kind of half-grunting sound and shrugged loosely. "Have you seen my uncle this afternoon?"

"Just left him about ten minutes ago," she said, smiling. "He said he's feeling good today. The nurses left food on the tray, so perhaps see if you can get him to eat something."

"Sure."

She didn't move. Didn't pass. She simply stood there and looked at him. Examined him, he thought. In a way that stirred his blood. It had been too long since anything or anyone had stirred him. But Lucy Monero managed it with barely a glance.

And he was pretty sure she knew it.

"So, how's the shoulder?" she asked, tossing her hair in a way that always made him flinch.

A trace of her apple-scented shampoo clung to the air and he swallowed hard. "Fine."

He'd dislocated his shoulder eight weeks earlier when he'd fallen off his motorbike. She'd been one of the doctors on duty at the hospital that night. But he'd made a point of ensuring she didn't attend him. He hadn't wanted her poking and prodding at him, or standing so close he'd be forced to inhale the scent of her perfume.

"Glad to hear it. I was talking to your mother the other day and she said you plan to reopen the tavern in the next few months?"

His mother had made her opinion about Lucy Monero clear on numerous occasions. She was Lucy's number-one fan and didn't mind telling him so. But he wasn't interested in a date, a relationship or settling down. Not with anyone. Including the pretty doctor in front of him. Her dark brows and green eyes were a striking combination and no doubt a legacy from her Italian heritage. She wore scrubs with a white coat over them, and he figured she'd just come from the emergency room at the hospital where she worked. But he knew she was also filling in at the veterans home a couple of times a week while one of the other doctors was on leave. Uncle Joe thought the world of her, too. And even his older brother, Grady, had extolled her virtues after she'd attended to his youngest daughter when the child had been taken to the ER a couple of months ago with a high fever.

Brant did his best to ignore her eyes, her hair and the curves he knew were hidden beneath the regulation blue scrubs. "That's the plan."

She smiled a little, as though she was amused by his

terse response, as though she had some great secret only she was privy to. It irritated him no end.

"I'm pleased your shoulder is okay."

He wished she'd stop talking. "Sure, whatever."

Her eyes sparkled. "Well, see you soon, Brant."

She said his name on a sigh. Or at least, that's how it sounded. There was a husky softness to her voice that was impossible to ignore. And it *always* made him tense. It made him wonder how her voice would sound if she was whispering, if she was bent close and speaking words only he could hear.

Brant quickly pulled himself out of the haze his mind was in and nodded vaguely, walking away, well aware that she was watching him.

And knowing there wasn't a damned thing he could do about.

Lucy let out a long sigh once Brant Parker disappeared around the corner of the ward. His tight-shouldered gait was one she would recognize anywhere—at the hospital, along the street, in her dreams.

He'd been in them for years. Since she'd been a starry-eyed, twelve-year-old mooning over the then-fifteen-year-old Brant. She'd lived next door to the Parker ranch. The ranch he'd left when he was eighteen to join the military. She'd left Cedar River for college just a couple of years later and put the boy she'd pined over as a teen out of her thoughts. Until she'd returned to her hometown to take a position at the small county hospital. She'd seen him again and the old attraction had resurfaced. He had been back from another tour of the Middle East and they'd bumped into each other at the O'Sullivan pub. Of course he hadn't recognized her. The last time they'd crossed paths she had been a chubby, self-conscious teenager with glasses. He'd seemed surprised to see her, but had said little. That had been more than two years earlier. Now he was back for good. Just as she was. He had left the military after twelve years of service and bought the old Loose Moose Tavern.

He could have done anything after high school—maybe law or economics—as he was supersmart and was always at the top of his class. One of those gifted people who never had to try hard to make good grades. He spoke a couple of languages and had been some kind of covert translator in the military. Lucy didn't know much about it, but what she did she'd learned from his mother, Colleen. The other woman regularly visited Joe Parker and also volunteered at the hospital where Lucy specialized in emergency medicine.

She'd known the Parkers since she was a child. Back then her parents had owned the small ranch next door. When she was fourteen her dad had died unexpectedly from a stroke, and then within a year her mother had sold the place and moved into town. A few years later her mother was killed in an accident. By then Lucy was ready for college, which would be followed by medical school, and had left town. The house her mother had bought in town was now hers and it was conveniently located just a few streets from the hospital. She was back in Cedar River to give back to the town she loved.

And maybe find her own happiness along the way.

Because Lucy wanted to get married and have a family. And soon. She was twenty-seven years old and had never had a serious romantic relationship. She'd never been in love. The truth be told, she'd never really been kissed.

And she was the only twenty-seven-year-old virgin she knew.

In high school she had been a geek to the core and had mostly been ignored by the boys in her grade. She hadn't even managed to get a date for prom. And by the time she was in college, her dreams about dating quickly disappeared. Three weeks into college and her roommate was assaulted so badly Lucy spent two days with the other girl at the hospital. It was enough to make her wary about getting involved with anyone on campus. She made a few friends who were much like herself—focused kids who studied hard and avoided parties and dating. By the time she started medical school the pattern of her life had been set. She was quiet and studious and determined to become a good doctor. Nothing else mattered. Though she'd gotten more comfortable over time in social situations, she was known as a girl who didn't date and, after a while, the invitations stopped.

One year quickly slipped into another and by the time she'd finished her residency she'd stopped fretting about being the oldest virgin on the planet. Not that she was hanging on to it as though it was a prize…she'd just never met anyone she liked enough to share that kind of intimacy with. Of course her closest friends, Ash, Brooke and Kayla, thought it amusing and teased her often about her refusal to settle for just *anyone*. She wanted special. She wanted a love that would last a lifetime.

She wanted…

Brant Parker.

Which was plain old, outright, what-are-you-thinking-girl stupid, and she knew it deep within her bones. Brant never looked at her in that way. Most of the time he acted as though he barely even *saw* her. When they were kids he'd tolerated her because they were neighbors, and in high school he had been three years ahead and hadn't wasted his time acknowledging her in the corridors. By the time she was in college he was long gone from Cedar River.

Her cell beeped and quickly cut through her thoughts. It was Kayla reminding her that she'd agreed to meet her and Ash and Brooke at the O'Sullivan pub for a drink and catch-up that evening. It had become something of a Friday-night ritual since she'd returned to town. Kayla had been a friend since junior high and worked as curator of the small Cedar River historical museum and art gallery, and Ash was a cop with the local police department. Brooke, who was Brant's cousin, was pure cowgirl and owned a small horse ranch just out of town.

All four women were good friends and she thoroughly enjoyed their company…most of the time. But she wasn't really in the mood for drinks and conversation tonight. She'd had a long morning in the emergency room and had been at the veterans home for the past few hours. She was tired and wanted nothing more than to go home, strip off and soak in the tub for a leisurely hour or so. But since her friend wouldn't take no for an answer, she agreed to meet them at the pub at six, which gave her an hour to get home, feed the cat, shower and change, and then head back into town.

Lucy ended the call and walked toward the nurses' station. She handed in her charts to the one nurse on duty and signed out. She had another two weeks at the home before her contract was up and then she'd return fulltime to the hospital. But she'd enjoyed her time working with the veterans. And with Joe Parker in particular. He was a natural storyteller and entertained everyone with his charm and easy-going manner.

Pity his nephew didn't inherit some of those manners or charm.

Lucy wrinkled her nose and headed down the hall to

the small locker room. Brant made her mad the way he ignored her. It wasn't like he was some great catch or anything. Sure, he had a body to die for. And the sexiest deep blue eyes. And dark hair that she'd often imagined running her fingers through. But he was a moody, closed-off loner who didn't seem to have time for anyone. Except his closest family members. She'd seen him in town one morning with his young nieces and the girls clearly adored him. It had made her think about how he'd probably make a great dad one day. And the idea of that quickly had her womb doing backflips.

Idiot...

She shrugged off her foolish thoughts, hung up her white coat and grabbed her bag.

The cold air outside hit her like a laser blast when she walked through the hospital doors. She quickly made it to her Honda and jumped inside. Snow was falling lightly and she watched the flakes hit the windshield. She loved snow and everything that went with it. Skiing, snowballs, log fires and the holidays... It was her favorite time of year. And one day she hoped she'd have a family of her own to share it with.

If only she could get the silly and impossible dreams of Brant Parker out of her head.

She popped the key into the ignition, started the car and drove off. The roads were slick, so she took her time getting home. When she pulled up in the driveway it was past five o'clock and she spotted her ginger cat, Boots, sitting idle in the front window. The image made her smile, and she was welcomed by the demanding feline once she'd dusted off her shoes and entered the house.

The place was small and very much in need of a complete renovation. She'd painted the walls in the living area and main bedroom when she'd returned to town for good, but since then she'd been so busy at the hospital, anything else had been put on hold. The kitchen required a complete overhaul as the cupboards were decades old and styled in old-fashioned laminate paneling and bright orange trim. It was retro in the truest sense and not to her taste. But she couldn't really afford to get someone in to do the work until the following summer and wasn't skilled enough to tackle anything more than painting herself. So, it would have to wait.

She dropped her bag, fed the cat and quickly checked her email before she headed to the shower. Within half an hour she was dressed in her favorite long denim skirt, emerald green shirt and mid-heeled boots. She pulled her hair from its ponytail, applied a little makeup and grabbed a small handbag for her wallet and cell phone. She texted Kayla as she was leaving, grabbed her coat and headed outside. She dusted the thin layer of snow off the windshield before she got into her car. The vehicle took a few turns of the key to start, but she was soon on her way.

The O'Sullivan pub was in the center of town and possessed a kind of richly authentic Irish flavor. It was actually a hotel, with fifteen luxurious rooms, two restaurants, a bar, an outdoor garden for private functions and several conference rooms available for rent. The O'Sullivan family was rich and well-known. Although the old man, John O'Sullivan, had retired and his eldest son, Liam, now ran the place, he still walked around with his chest puffed out like he ruled the town and everyone in it. No one crossed the O'Sullivans. No one would dare. The hotel was one of the main draws in the town and that had a lot of pull with the mayor's office. Tourists came to see the old mines, the occasional rodeos, the horse and cattle ranches, and many used the town as a stopover before they crossed the state line. Since the O'Sullivan's hotel was the poshest place to stay, few people objected to paying for their amenities.

She did wonder if that's why Brant had bought the Loose Moose—as a way of sticking it to the O'Sullivans. There was certainly no love lost between the two families. Brant's older brother, Grady, had been married to Liz O'Sullivan, and Lucy knew her parents had never thought a rancher was good enough for their beloved daughter. When Liz died a few years ago things had gotten worse and, according to Colleen Parker, the feud between the two families was now quite intense.

It was early, so she found a spot outside the hotel and parked. She got out, grabbed her coat from the backseat and tossed it over her arm. A few people milled around the front of the hotel, and she recognized a couple of nurses from the hospital and waved as she made her way through the wide doors.

Kayla, Brooke and Ash were already seated at a booth in the bar when she arrived, with a pitcher of sangria between them. The O'Sullivan pub certainly wasn't the average run-of-the-mill kind of drinking establishment. If you wanted beer and a game of pool you went to one of the other cowboy bars in town like Rusty's or the Black Bull. She slid into the booth and raised a brow at the quarter-empty pitcher on the table. "You started without me?"

Brooke tossed her straight blond hair a little and grinned. "You're late. So, of course."

Blue-eyed Ash, whose bobbed hair was the color of copper, smiled and nodded. "I'm off duty."

"And being a museum curator is thirsty work," Kayla said and laughed. "Although I'll be stopping at one drink. But we got you a glass."

Lucy chuckled and stared at her friend, who was easily the most beautiful woman she'd ever known. Kayla's long blond hair and dark brown eyes stopped most men in their tracks.

She lifted the half-filled glass and took a small sip. "Thanks. Are we staying for dinner?"

"Not me," Brooke said. "I have a foal due within days and with this weather coming in…" She sighed and grinned. "You know how it is."

Yes, they all knew Brooke lived and breathed for her horses.

"Nor me. I only have a sitter until seven thirty," Ash replied and inclined a thumb toward Kayla. "And this one has a date."

Lucy's gaze widened. "Really? With whom?"

Kayla laughed again. "Assignments. Marking papers for the online class I'm teaching through the community college."

"Gosh, we're a boring group," Lucy said and smiled. "Just as well I have a cat to get home to."

"You could always ask Hot Stuff over there to take you to dinner," Kayla suggested and laughed again.

Lucy's eyes popped wide. *Hot Stuff?* There was no mistaking who she meant. Her friend had been calling Brant that name for years, ever since Lucy had admitted she was crushing on him when she was a teenager.

"He's here?"

"Yep," Kayla replied. "Over by the bar, talking to Liam O'Sullivan."

Lucy looked toward Ash for confirmation. "She's right. He was here when we arrived. Looks like he's not too happy about it, either. I don't think he's cracked a smile in that time."

Nothing unusual about that, Lucy thought. She itched to turn around and see for herself, but didn't want to appear obvious. But she was curious as to why he was with Liam O'Sullivan, considering the family history.

"You know, he's not a complete killjoy," Brooke said about her cousin and gave a little grin. "And if you like, I could ask him for you?"

Lucy almost spat out her sangria. "Don't you dare," she warned. "You know how I feel about—"

"Yes," Brooke assured her and chuckled. "We've known how you feel about him for well over a decade."

God, how foolish that sounded. And, if she were being completely honest with herself, a little pathetic. She certainly didn't want friends thinking she was still *pining* for Brant Parker after so many years. "Well, I *won't* be asking him to take me to dinner," Lucy assured them.

"Pity," Kayla said and chuckled. "Because he hasn't taken his eyes off you since you've been here."

Lucy's cheeks heated. So, he watched her. It didn't mean *anything*. She might be unkissed, untouched and naive, but she was savvy enough to know when a man *wasn't* interested. Even though there were times…well, *occasionally* she had thought that she'd seen interest in his blue eyes. But mostly she thought it simply *wishful thinking* and then got on with knowing he'd never look at her in that way.

She turned her head a little and spotted him. Handsome as ever, he was talking to Liam and she experienced the usual flutter in her belly. His dark hair, strong jaw and blue eyes never failed to affect her on a kind of primal level.

"You're imagining things," she said dismissively and poured another quarter of a glass of sangria to keep her hands busy.

"I know what I saw," Kayla said, still smiling. "I wonder what he's doing talking with Liam."

"I'm sure you'll find out," Lucy said with a grin.

Kayla sighed heavily. "For the last time, I am *not* interested in Liam O'Sullivan."

Ash and Brooke both laughed. "Sure you aren't," Ash said.

"We're just working together on the gallery extension plans, that's all," Kayla insisted.

Lucy was pretty sure there was more to it, but didn't press the issue. She was more interested in knowing why Brant was consorting with his brother's mortal enemy. But since neither things were any of her business, she concentrated on the cocktails and enjoying her friend's company.

Except, Brooke didn't drop the topic. "At least he hasn't wrecked his bike again."

"Not for a couple of months," Lucy said and frowned. "He was lucky he wasn't seriously injured," she added with quiet emphasis.

His last visit to the ER was his third in seven months and had landed him with a dislocated shoulder and cuts and scrapes. The first was another flip from his motorbike. The second was when he'd climbed Kegg's Mountain and taken a tumble that also could have killed him. Why he'd risk his life so carelessly after surviving three tours of the Middle East, Lucy had no idea.

"I guess he's just adventurous," Brooke said, and Lucy saw a shadow of concern in her friend's expression. This was Brant's cousin. Family. Brooke knew him. And clearly she was worried.

"Maybe," Lucy replied and smiled fractionally, eager to change the subject.

Ash bailed at seven fifteen to get home to her eleven-year-old son, Jaye. Lucy hung out with Kayla and Brooke for another ten minutes before they all grabbed their bags and headed out. Brant had left half an hour earlier, without looking at her, without even acknowledging her presence. Kayla managed a vague wave to Liam O'Sullivan before they walked through the doors and into the cold night air.

Lucy grabbed her coat and flipped it over her shoulders. "It's still snowing. Weird for this time of year. Remind me again why I didn't accept the offer to join the hospital in San Francisco?"

"Because you don't like California," Kayla said, shivering. "And you said you'd miss us and this town too much."

"True," Lucy said and grinned. "I'll talk to you both over the weekend."

They hugged goodbye and headed in opposite directions. People were still coming into the hotel and the street out front was getting busy, so she took some time to maneuver her car from its space and drive off.

The main street of Cedar River was typical of countless others in small towns: a mix of old and new buildings, cedar and stucco, some tenanted, some not. There were two sets of traffic lights and one main intersection. Take a left and the road headed toward Rapid City. Go right and there was Nebraska. Over three and a half thousand people called Cedar River home. It sat peacefully in the shadow of the Black Hills and was as picturesque as a scene from a postcard. She loved the town and never imagined living anywhere else. Even while she was away at college, medical school and working at the hospital in Sioux Falls for three years, her heart had always called her home.

Up until recently the town had been two towns—Cedar Creek and Riverbend—separated by a narrow river and a bridge. But after years of negotiating, the townships had formed one larger town called Cedar River. Lucy had supported the merger... It meant more funding for the hospital and the promise of a unified, economically sound community.

Lucy was just about to flick on the radio for the chance to hear the weather report when her car spluttered and slowed, quickly easing to little more than a roll. She steered left and pulled to the curb as the engine coughed and died.

Great...

A few cars passed, all clearly intent on getting home before the snow worsened. Lucy grabbed her bag and pulled out her cell. She could call her automobile club for assistance, but that meant she'd be dragging mechanic Joss Culhane out to give her a tow home. And Joss was a single dad with two little girls to look after and had better things to do than come to her rescue because she'd forgotten about the battery light that had been flashing intermittently all week.

Better she didn't. She was just about to call Kayla to come and get her when she spotted something attached to one of the old buildings flapping in the breeze. A shingle. Recognition coursed through her.

The Loose Moose. Brant's place.

A light shone through one of the front windows. He was home. She knew he lived in the apartment above the tavern. Of course she'd never been up there. But Colleen Parker had told her how he was renovating the tavern while residing in the upstairs rooms.

Lucy got out of the car and wrapped herself in her red woolen coat. Surely, Brant would help her, given the circumstances?

She grabbed her bag and locked the car before she headed toward the old tavern. The old adobe front was boarded up, apart from the two windows, and the heavy double doors were still blackened in spots from the damage caused by the fire eight months before.

Lucy knocked once and waited. She could hear music coming from inside and discreetly peered through one of the windows. There were trestle tables scattered with power tools and neat stacks of timber on the floor near the long bar, and the wall between the remaining booth seats and the back room that had once housed pool tables had been pulled down. She knocked again, louder this time, and then again. The music stopped. By the time the door swung back she was shivering with cold, her knuckles were pink and her patience a little frayed.

Until she saw him. Then her mouth turned dry and her knees knocked for an altogether different reason.

He wore jeans and a navy sweater that molded to his shoulders and chest like a second skin. His dark hair was ruffled, as though he'd just run a hand through it, and the very idea made her palms tingle. His blue eyes shimmered and his jaw was set tightly. He looked surprised to see her on his doorstep. And not one bit welcoming.

But, dear heaven, he is gorgeous.

She forced some words out. "Um, hi."

"Dr. Monero," he said, frowning. "It's a little late for a house call, don't you think?"

She swallowed hard, suddenly nervous. There was no welcome in his words. She jutted her chin. "Oh, call me Lucy," she insisted and then waved a backward hand. "My car has stopped just outside. I think it's the battery. And I didn't want to call for a tow because my mechanic has two little kids and I thought it was too much to ask for him to come out in this weather and I was wondering if… I thought you might…"

"You thought I might what?"

Lucy wanted to turn and run. But she stayed where she was and took a deep breath. "I thought you might be able to help. Or give me a lift home."

His brows shot up. "You did?"

She shrugged. "Well, I know it's only a few blocks away, but the paths are slippery and the snow doesn't seem to be easing anytime soon."

His gaze flicked upward for a second toward the falling snow and then to her car. "Give me your keys," he instructed and held out his hand.

Lucy dropped the keys into his palm and watched as he strode past her and to her car. He was in the car and had the hood up in seconds. Lucy tucked her coat collar around her neck and joined him by the vehicle. He closed the driver's door and moved around the front, bending over the engine block. Lucy watched, captivated and suddenly breathless over the sheer masculine image he evoked. There was something elementally attractive about him...something heady and fascinating. Being around him felt as decadent as being behind the counter in a candy store. He had a narcotic power that physically affected her from the roots of her hair to the soles of her feet. And she'd never responded to a man in that way before.

Not even close.

Sure, she'd crushed on several of the O'Sullivan or Culhane brothers back in high school. But Brant Parker had never been far from her thoughts. Returning to Cedar River had only amplified the feeling over the years. Being around him made her realize how real that attraction still was. She liked him. She wanted him. It was that simple. It was that complicated.

"Battery's dead," he said, closing the hood.

Lucy smiled. "Well, at least that means I remembered to put gas in the tank."

He didn't respond. He simply looked at her. Deeply. Intently. As if, in that moment, there was nothing else. No one else. Just the two of them, standing in the evening snow, with the streetlight casting shadows across the sidewalk.

"I'll take you home," he said and walked back toward the Loose Moose.

Lucy followed and stood by the doors. "I'll wait here if you like."

Brant turned and frowned. "I have to get my jacket and keys, and my truck is parked out back. So you might as well come inside."

He didn't sound like he wanted her in his home. In fact, he sounded like it was the last thing he wanted. But, undeterred, she followed him across the threshold and waited as he shut the door.

"You've been busy," she said as she walked through the room and dropped her bag on the bar. "The renovations are coming along."

"That was the idea when I bought the place."

Lucy turned and stared at him. He really was a disagreeable ass. She wondered for the thousandth time why she wasted her energy being attracted to him when he made no effort to even be nice to her.

Not one to back down, she propped her hands on her hips. "You know, I was wondering something... Is it simply me you dislike or people in general?"

His jaw tightened. Hallelujah. Connection. Something to convince her he wasn't a cold fish incapable of response. His gaze was unwavering, blistering and so intense she could barely take a breath.

"I don't dislike you, Dr. Monero."

She shook her head. "My case in point. I've asked you half a dozen times to call me Lucy. The very fact you don't speaks louder than words. I know you *can* be nice because I've seen you with your mom and brother and nieces. At least when we were kids you were mostly civil…but now all I get from you is—"

"You talk too much."

Lucy was silenced immediately. She looked at him and a heavy heat swirled between them. She wasn't imagining it. It was there…real and palpable. And mutual. As inexperienced as she was, Lucy recognized the awareness that suddenly throbbed between them.

Attraction. Chemistry. Sex.

All of the above. All very mutual.

And she had no real clue what to do about it.

Chapter Two

Lucy Monero was a walking, talking temptation. And Brant wanted her. It took all of his willpower to *not* take her in his arms and kiss her like crazy.

But he stayed where he was, watching her, noticing how her hair shone from the light beaming from above. Her dazzling green eyes were vivid and suggestive, but also filled with a kind of uncertainty that quickly captivated him. Lucy had a way of stopping him in his tracks with only a look. So he didn't dare touch her. Didn't dare kiss her. Didn't dare talk to her, even though there were times when he thought he'd like nothing else than to listen to her voice or to hear her breathless laughter.

When they were kids she'd hung around the ranch, often watching him and his brother break and train the horses from the sidelines, her head always tucked into a book. She'd been quiet and reserved back then, not trying to grow up before her time by wearing makeup or trendy clothes. When her dad died, her mom had sold the small ranch and they'd moved into town, so he hadn't seen her as much. His own dad had died around that time, too, and with twenty-year-old Grady taking over the reins at their family ranch and Brant deciding on a military career midway through senior year, there wasn't any time to spend thinking about the shy, studious girl who never seemed to be able to meet his gaze.

Not so now, he thought. She'd grown up and gained a kind of mesmerizing poise along the way. Oh, she'd always been pretty—but now she was beautiful and tempting and had firmly set her sights on what she wanted.

Which appeared to be him.

Brant wasn't egotistical. But he recognized the look in her eyes every time they met. And he wasn't about to get drawn into *anything* with Lucy Monero. She was pure hometown. A nice girl who wanted romance, a wedding and a white picket fence. He'd heard enough about it and her virtues from his mom and Brooke. Well, it wasn't for him. He didn't do romance. And he wasn't about to get involved with a woman who had marriage on her mind.

"You're staring at me."

Her words got his thoughts on track and Brant felt heat quickly creep up his back and neck. His jaw clenched and he straightened his shoulders. "So, I'll just get my jacket and take you home."

"Is everything okay?" she asked quietly.

"What?"

She tilted her head a little and regarded him with her usual intensity. "You seem…tense."

It irritated him to no end that she could see through him like that. "I'm fine," he lied.

Her brows came up. "I'm pretty sure you're not."

"Is there a point you're trying to make?"

She shrugged one shoulder. "You know, most times we meet, you barely acknowledge me. At first I thought it was because you were just settling back in to civilian life and that small talk was really not your thing. But then I've seen you with your family and you seem relaxed and friendly enough around them. And you were with Liam O'Sullivan earlier and didn't end up punching him in the face, so that interaction must have turned out okay. So maybe it's just me."

Brant ignored the way his heart thundered behind his ribs. *It is you.* He wasn't about to get drawn into her little world. Not now. Not ever. He had too much going on. Too much baggage banging around in his head. Too many memories that could unglue him if he let someone in.

"Like I said, you talk too much."

She laughed, the sound wispy and sort of throaty and so damned sexy it sucked the air from his lungs. He was tempted to take the three steps he needed to be beside her. Maybe kissing her would get her out of his system. Maybe it was exactly the thing he needed to keep her out of his thoughts. But he stayed where he was, both irritated and fascinated by the relentless effect she had on him without even trying. And he knew the only way around it was to stay out of her way. To avoid her. To ignore her. To keep himself separate, as he had for the past eight months, and not get drawn into the land of the living where he would be forced to take part. Instead he'd stay on the sidelines, pretending everything was fine. Pretending *he* was fine. So his mom and brother didn't work out that he was now a shadow of the man he'd once been.

"So, I'm right. It *is* just me?" she asked, stepping a little closer. "Why? Are you worried that I might work out that underneath all your brooding indifference there's actually a decent sort of man?"

"Not at all," he replied quietly. "*Dr. Monero*, the truth is I don't think about you from one moment to the next."

It was a mean thing to say. He knew. She knew it. And he hated the way the words tasted in his mouth. He wasn't cruel. He wasn't good at it. He felt clumsy even saying the words. But he had to try to keep her at a distance.

"I see." Her eyes shadowed over for a second. She looked...hurt. Wounded. And the notion cut through him like a knife. He didn't want to hurt her. He didn't want to have any feelings when it came to Lucy Monero. "Okay. Fine. You've made yourself perfectly clear. Now, I think I'll find my own way home."

She was past him and by the door in seconds. As she rattled the doorknob, Brant took a few strides and reached her, placing a hand on either side of the jamb. She turned and gasped, looking up, so close he could feel her breath on his chin.

"Lucy..."

The sound of her name on his lips reverberated through him, sending his heart hammering and his blood surging through his veins. She was trapped, but didn't move, didn't do anything but hold his gaze steady. And this, he thought as he stared down into her face, was exactly why he needed to keep his distance. There was heat between them...heat generated by a sizzling attraction that had the power to knock him off his feet.

"Don't...please..." she said shakily, her bottom lip trembling fractionally.

Brant stepped back and dropped his arms instantly. "I'm not going to hurt you."

She nodded. "I know that. I didn't mean I thought you would. It's just that...being around you...it's confusing."

She was right about that!

"It's like you ignore me as though I don't exist," she

went on to say. "But sometimes you look at me as if… as if…"

"As if what?" he shot back.

"As if you do…like me."

"Of course I do," he admitted raggedly, taking a breath, hoping she couldn't see how messed up he was. "But I'm not in the market for anything serious. Not with you."

There…it was out in the open. Now she could move on and stop looking at him as though he could give her all she wanted. Because he couldn't. He didn't have it in him. Not now. He'd been through too much. Seen too much. He wasn't good company. He wasn't boyfriend or husband material. He was better off alone.

"Why not?" she asked.

Nothing…

Brant sighed heavily. "I'd prefer not to get into it."

"Oh, no," she said and crossed her arms, pushing her chest up, which instantly grabbed his attention.

God, her curves were mesmerizing. He looked to the floor for a moment to regather his good sense and hoped she'd stop talking. But no such luck.

"You don't get to make a bold statement like that and then think you're off the hook. What's wrong with me?" Her brows rose again. "I'm honest, intelligent, loyal and respectable, and have good manners. I even have all my own teeth."

Brant laughed loudly. God, it felt good to laugh. There was something so earnest about Lucy it was impossible to remain unaffected by her. During the past few weeks he'd often heard her soft laughter through the corridors of the veterans home and wondered how it would feel to be on the receiving end of such a sweet, sincere sound. And he wanted to hear it again.

"Well, I guess if I was buying a pony, all bases would be covered."

Her chuckle started out soft and then morphed into a full-on, loud guffaw. By the time she was done there were tears on her cheeks. She wiped them away and thrust out her chin.

"Wow…you do have a sense of humor." Her eyes shimmered. "Your cousin was right, you're not always a complete killjoy."

"No," he said easily. "Not always."

"So, this being a jerk thing…that's something you save especially for me?"

Brant's mouth twitched. "I have to get my keys," he said, ignoring the question. "Wait here."

Her eyes sparkled. "Aren't you going to invite me upstairs?"

To his apartment? His bedroom? "Not a chance," he said and strode off without looking back.

Lucy wrapped her arms around herself and wandered through the tavern. Every sense she possessed was on red alert. By the door he'd been so close…close enough that she could have taken a tiny step and been pressed against him. The heat from his skin had scorched hers. The warmth of his breath had made her lips tingle with anticipation. It was desire unlike any she'd known before. And she wanted it. She wanted him. She wanted his kiss, his touch. She wanted every part of him to cover every part of her.

And she shook all over, thinking about her false bravado. She'd never spoken to man in such a blatantly flirtatious tone before. But being around Brant was unlike anything she'd ever experienced. As *inexperienced* as she was, flirting and verbally sparring with him seemed to have a will and a power all of its own.

"Ready?"

He was back, standing by the steps that led upstairs. Lucy swallowed hard and nodded. "Sure. Thanks."

He shrugged loosely. "My truck's out back."

"No motorbike?"

He raised a brow and began to walk toward the rear of the building. "Not in this weather."

He was right, but the idea of being behind him on his motorbike, holding on to him, being so close she'd be able to feel his heartbeat, made her pulse race.

"So you're only reckless with yourself. That's good to know."

Brant stopped midstride and turned. "What?"

Lucy held out three fingers. "That's how many times you've been in hospital in the past seven months. Twice off your bike because you were speeding and once when you thought it was a good idea to climb Kegg's Mountain—alone—and without the proper gear, I might add."

"You're still talking too much," he muttered and then kept walking.

Lucy followed him down the long hallway, past the kitchen and restrooms, and then through the rear door. He waited for her to walk outside and locked the door. It was still snowing lightly and she took quick steps toward the beat-up, blue Ford pickup parked outside. He opened the passenger door, ushered her inside, strode around the front of the vehicle and slid into the driver's seat.

"What's your address?" he asked.

Lucy gave him directions and dropped her bag into her lap.

She expected him to immediately start the truck and drive off. But he didn't. He put the key in the ignition but placed both hands on the steering wheel. And then he spoke.

"I wasn't speeding. My bike blew a tire the first time and the second time I swerved to avoid hitting a dog that was on the road."

It was meant to put her in her place. To shut her up. To end the conversation.

But Lucy wasn't one to be silenced. "And the mountain?"

"I was unprepared. Not a mistake I would make again." He started the engine and thrust the gear into Reverse. "Satisfied?"

Lucy's skin tingled. The idea of being satisfied by Brant Parker had her insides doing flip-flops. Of course, he wasn't being suggestive, but Lucy couldn't help thinking how good a lover he would be. Not that she would have anything to make a comparison with. But she had a vivid imagination and she had certainly fantasized about being between the sheets with the man beside her.

She smiled sweetly. "I guess I didn't hear the whole story because I didn't attend to you the night you were brought into the ER."

He shifted gears again and turned into the street. "I thought my mother would have kept you updated. You and she seem to have become quite the twosome."

"I like your mom," Lucy replied. "She's a good friend."

"Yeah, my mom is a good person." He turned left. "She also likes to play matchmaker."

Lucy's mouth twitched. She knew that. Colleen had been gently pushing her in Brant's direction for months. "Does that make you nervous?" she asked, turning her gaze. "I mean, now she's got Grady settled and engaged to Marissa, do you think you're next?"

She watched his profile. Impassive. Unmoving. Like a

rock. But he was trying too hard. The pulse in his cheek was beating madly. He wasn't so unmoved. He was simply reining his feelings in…as usual.

"She's wasting her time."

Lucy tried not to be offended and managed a brittle laugh. "Considering how happy your brother is now, you can't blame your mom for wanting the same for you."

"I'm not my brother."

No, he wasn't. She knew Grady Parker. Oh, he still had the Parker pride and was a teeny bit arrogant, but he was a good-natured, hardworking family man with three little girls to raise and had recently found love again with Marissa Ellis. The wedding was only a couple of weeks away and Lucy knew Brant was standing as his brother's best man. She'd been invited, more to please Colleen Parker than anything else, she was sure. And since Brooke and Ash were both going and she liked Marissa and Grady, she was delighted to be part of their special day.

"Have you got a speech prepared?" Lucy asked, shifting the subject. "For the wedding, I mean. I hear you're the best man. That should be a fun gig…even for you."

He pulled the truck up outside her house, set the vehicle into Park and switched off the ignition. Then he turned in his seat and looked at her, his jaw set rigid. Boy, he was tense. And the intensity of it crackled the air between them. Lucy met his gaze and held it. Felt the heat of his stare as though he was touching her, stroking her, caressing her. She shuddered and she knew he was aware of the effect he had over her. A tiny smile tugged at the corner of his mouth, as though he knew he shouldn't react but couldn't resist.

If he moved, if he so much as lowered his defenses in any way, Lucy would have planted herself against him and begged for his kiss. She wanted it. Longed for it. But he continued to look at her, into her, making her achingly aware of the intimacy of the small space they shared.

"Even for me?" he intoned, his deep voice as intense as a caress. "I do know how to have a good time, despite what you think."

Lucy's bravado spiked. "Really?"

He inhaled heavily. "What is it you want, Dr. Monero?"

The million-dollar question. Bravado was fine when it wasn't challenged. But under scrutiny, Lucy quickly became unsettled. "I'm not… I don't…"

"You want something. Is it me?" he asked bluntly. "Is that what you want?"

Color smacked her cheeks. "I just want—"

"Why?" he asked, cutting her off. "Why me? You could have anyone you—"

"Chemistry," she said quickly, dying inside. "Attraction."

"Sex?"

Lucy stilled. She didn't want to think her reaction to him was merely physical. But since she did find him more attractive than she'd ever found any other man, perhaps she was blinded by those feelings? Maybe her daydreams about getting to know him, being around him and spending time with him were exactly that. Dreams. And foolish remnants of an old teenaged infatuation. She'd spent college and medical school wrapped in a bubble—wary of involvement with anyone because of what had happened to her roommate. But once she was back in Cedar River—more confident and older and able to meet his gaze head-on—Lucy had believed she would somehow be able to capture his attention.

But that hadn't happened. He'd ignored her. Despite her smiles and friendly attention.

And the more he ignored her, the more she wanted

him. His indifference became fuel for her teenaged fantasies and starved libido. So maybe it was just sex and she was simply too inexperienced to recognize it for what it was.

"What's wrong with that, anyway?" she shot back as heat climbed over her skin.

His gaze narrowed. "What's wrong with sex? Nothing... if that's all you're after." He reached out and touched her hair, trapped a few strands between his fingertips. It was the first time he'd touched her and it was electric. "But you don't strike me as the casual-sex kind of girl, Doc Monero. In fact, I'd bet my boots you are the white-picket-fence, happy-ever-after kind."

God, if he only knew, he'd probably run a mile.

"That's quite a judgment. And what are you? Only casual, no happy-ever-after?"

"Close enough," he said and returned his hands to the wheel.

"Back at the tavern you said you...liked me...so which is it?"

"Neither. Both. You're wasting your time with me. I'm not marriage material. So, good night."

Humiliation coursed through her veins and Lucy grabbed her bag and placed it in her lap. She got the message loud and clear. He was awful. Just awful. She swallowed the lump in her throat. "Are you going to walk me to my door?"

"This isn't a date," he said quietly.

He was such a jerk, and he was right about one thing: she was seriously wasting her time being attracted to him. Lucy set her teeth together and opened the door. "Thanks for the lift. I'll get my car towed in the morning. Good night."

"Good night...Lucy."

She got out, shut the door and stomped up the path and to the front door. While she was opening the door she realized he was still parked by the curb. So maybe he did have some chivalry in him. Ha—but not enough. As she got inside and peeked through the lace curtains to watch him finally drive away, Lucy decided she was going to forget all about him and spend her nights dreaming of someone else. Anyone else.

And the sooner she started the better.

Brant had been visiting his mother's home for lunch nearly every Saturday since he'd returned from his last tour. Colleen insisted they have a family catch-up and he didn't mind. He loved his mom, even though she drove him nuts with her attempts to interfere in his personal life. He knew there were only good intentions in her meddling, so he usually laughed it off and ignored her. But today—the morning after the whole Lucy-Monero-and-her-broken-down-car thing—Colleen was onto him the moment he stepped foot into her kitchen.

"I went into town early to get eggs and milk and saw Lucy's car outside the tavern," she said, her wide-eyed gaze all speculation and curiosity.

Brant walked around the timber countertop, grabbed a mug from the cupboard and poured coffee. "Her car broke down. I gave her a lift home."

And acted like a total horse's ass.

"She didn't spend the night?"

Color crept up his neck. His mother looked disappointed. Boy, sometimes he wished he had one of those parents who didn't want to talk about every single thing. "No, Mom, she didn't."

Colleen smiled. "You know, it wouldn't hurt you to encourage her a little. She's a nice girl. Smart. Pretty.

Sweet. And she has a kind spirit. I think she'd be a good match for you."

Brant sighed. "Are we really going to do this every Saturday?"

She grinned. "Every Saturday? I don't think I mentioned it last weekend."

"Oh, yeah, you did." Brant sugared his coffee and sat at the table. "I'm not in the market for a relationship right now," he said for the umpteenth time. "I need time to—"

"I know that's what you think," she said gently, cutting him off. "But I'm concerned about you."

"I know you're worried about me, Mom, but I'm okay," he assured her.

"You went through a lot over there," she said, her eyes glittering. "More than any of us will probably ever know. You're my son and I'm always going to be looking out for you, regardless of how old you are. When you have a child of your own you will understand what I mean."

"She's right, you know."

They both looked toward the doorway. His brother, Grady, stood on the threshold.

Brant frowned as his brother came into the room and sat. "You said you wouldn't encourage her," Brant reminded him.

Grady shrugged. "When she's right, she's right. I don't think it would matter how old my girls are, I'll always be on hand to make sure they're all right."

"See," Colleen said and smiled. "At least one of my sons had the good sense to listen to me."

Brant groaned. "Just because you meddled in his life and got him on the way to the altar, don't think you are going to do that with me. I have no intention of getting married anytime soon."

"You're thirty years old," his mom reminded him quietly. "And a civilian. You can have a normal life now, Brant."

No, he couldn't...

But he wasn't about to go down that road with his mother and brother. They didn't know much about what had happened before he'd left Afghanistan for good. He hardly dared think about it, let alone consider sharing it with his family. If they knew, they'd close ranks, smother him, give him sympathy and understanding when he deserved neither. In his mind, despite how hard he tried to get the thought out of his head, he was still a soldier. Still standing on the ridge. Still hearing the gunfire and the screams of the men in his unit who'd lost their lives that day.

"So where are the girls this morning?" he asked his brother, shifting the subject.

"With Marissa, getting their hair done." Grady grinned. "It's a practice run for their wedding-day hair."

Brant admired his brother. He'd raised his three young daughters alone since his wife, Liz, had died a couple of years earlier. Brant admired Marissa, too. His soon-to-be sister-in-law adored his nieces and had effortlessly stepped into her role as stepmother to the girls since she'd accepted his brother's proposal. Grady was a good man. The best he knew. And Brant was pleased his brother had found happiness again.

"O'Sullivan increased the offer," Brant said and drank some coffee.

Grady tapped his fist on the table. "Son of a bitch!"

"I didn't accept," he said when he saw his brother's swiftly gathering rage. "And I won't."

"Liam O'Sullivan believes he can have and do whatever he wants, just like his old man," Grady said and scowled. "The whole bunch of them think they're so damned entitled. No wonder Liz couldn't wait to get away from them. He only wants the Loose Moose because he doesn't want the competition. I heard he's been sniffing around Rusty's again, too. When Ted Graham finally does decide he wants to retire, O'Sullivan will be circling like a hyena."

"I told Ted I'd be interested in Rusty's if it comes on the market. He's not foolish enough to let the O'Sullivans get hold of the place. He hates them as much as you do."

Grady grunted. "You want two pubs? That's ambitious."

Brant shrugged. "Gotta make a living doing something."

"I thought you might want to come back to the ranch where you belong."

"I'm not much of a cowboy these days," he said, grinning.

"You're good with horses," Grady said generously. "Would be a shame to waste that skill entirely."

"You know I'll always give you a hand if you need it. But not full-time."

Grady nodded. "What about school?" his brother queried. "You said you were thinking of studying business at the community college."

"I still might."

"You could teach French at the night school, too," Grady suggested.

"I could," Brant replied, thinking about his options. "If I wasn't so busy with the Loose Moose."

"How are the renovations coming?"

"Slow," he said. "But I knew it would take a while. Doing the majority of it myself saves dollars but takes more time."

"If you need money to—"

"It's fine." Brant waved a hand. "I don't need your money."

"It's family money," Grady corrected. "The ranch is just as much yours as mine. And I would consider the tavern an investment. Dad and Uncle Joe and Granddad used to love the old place, remember?"

He did remember. It was one of the reasons why he'd been so keen to buy the tavern. "I'll let you know," he said, trying to fob his brother off as gently as he could.

Grady had a good heart but still acted as though he had to shoulder the brunt of all family issues. It was an "older brother thing," he was certain. When Grady had taken over the ranch he'd made it into one of the most successful in the county. Brant admired Grady's determination and commitment to the family, but he needed to do this alone. He needed to forge a life for himself that was of his own making.

"So, about this thing with Lucy Monero?" Grady asked.

"There's nothing going on between us," he assured his brother and looked toward their mother, who was cracking eggs into a bowl at the counter and pretending not to listen. "So, drop it. That means both of you."

"Can't," Colleen said and grinned. "Not when one of my kids is troubled."

Brant looked toward his brother for a little support, but Grady was nodding. Great. Suddenly, Saturday lunch had turned into some kind of intervention. Next, his mom would be suggesting he visit the shrink at the local veterans home.

"I was just talking to Dr. Allenby the other day about…"

Yep, right on schedule, he thought, and pushed his mother's words out of his head as she rattled on. He didn't need a shrink. He'd seen too many of them after Operation Oscar had gone down so badly. Three of his team had lost their lives. It had been two days of hell he wanted to forget. And he would, over time. If only his mom and brother would let up.

"I don't need a shrink."

His mother continued to whisk the eggs. "Then what about talking to someone else. Like me? Or your brother? Or even Lucy?" she suggested. "She's a doctor...and a good one."

Brant expelled an exasperated breath. "Mom, I'm fine. You gotta let this go, okay? I am happy," he lied. "I have you guys and the Loose Moose... For the moment, that's all I have room for. Working on restoring the tavern keeps my head clear, if that makes sense. And it's all the therapy I need."

That was the truth, at least. Sure, he was lonely, but better to be lonely than to bog someone else down with the train wreck his life had become. He probably just needed to get laid. It had been a while. He did the calculation in his head and inwardly grimaced. Man, he seriously needed to get out more. He still had friends in town, but going out with his old high school buddies, drinking beer, playing pool and talking smack didn't really cut it anymore. He wasn't twenty years old. He wasn't blinded by youth or ignorance. He'd seen the world and life at its darkest and would never be able to escape who he had become. Finding someone to share that with seemed impossible. The occasional one-night stand was all he allowed himself. And since Lucy Monero was not a one-night-stand kind of woman, he knew he had to keep avoiding her.

By the time he left his mother's it was nearly two. He headed to the hardware store to pick up a few things and spent the remainder of the afternoon working on the walls in the front part of the tavern. Turning in to bed around ten, he woke up at six on Sunday morning to get an early start, planning to spend the day sanding back the long cedar bar. But at one o'clock he got a call from Grady to say Uncle Joe had been taken to the hospital and was in the emergency room. It took him five minutes to change and head out and another fifteen to get to the hospital. He called Grady again once he was out of the truck and headed for the ER.

By the time he reached Reception he felt as though his chest might explode. The woman behind the counter said she'd inquire after his uncle and told him to wait.

Great. Exactly what he didn't want to do.

He knew Grady was on his way to the hospital, so he paced the room for a few minutes and then finally sat. The hospital sounds reverberated in his eardrums. Phones, beepers, gurneys, heels clicking over tiles. Each sound seemed louder than the last.

He sat for five minutes, swamped by a building helplessness that was suffocating.

When he could stand it no more he got up and headed back to the counter. "Is there any news about my uncle?"

The fifty-something woman scowled a little and flicked through some charts on the desk. "No, nothing yet."

"Then can you find someone who might know something?"

She scowled again and Brant's impatience rose. He wasn't usually a hothead. Most of the time he was calm and in complete control. Twelve years of military training had ingrained those traits into him. But he didn't feel calm now. He felt as though he could barely stand to be in his own skin.

"Brant?"

He knew that voice.

Turning his head, he saw Lucy and relief flooded through him. In some part of his mind he wondered how she had the power to do that, to soothe his turbulent emotions. Just knowing she was there somehow made things easier. Better. He swiveled on his heels and watched as she walked toward him, wearing scrubs and a white coat. Brant met her gaze and swallowed hard.

"You're here."

"I'm here," she said and smiled fractionally. "What do you know?"

"Not much," he said and shook his head. "What happened?"

Her eyes gave it away. It was serious. "He had a heart attack."

A heart attack? Fear coursed through his blood. "Is he…is he dead?"

The second it took for her to answer seemed like an hour. "No."

Brant fought back the emotion clogging his throat. "Is he going to make it?"

She nodded slowly. "I think so."

"Thank God," Brant breathed and, without thinking, reached out and hauled her into his arms.

Chapter Three

Lucy melted.

She'd never pegged Brant as a hugger. Nor did she want to think about what was going on in the minds of the two nurses at the reception desk. Cedar River was a small town. She was a doctor on staff and the most gorgeous man on the planet was holding her so tightly she didn't dare breathe.

There might be talk. Innuendo. But she didn't care. In that moment he needed her. Wanted her. It might be fleeting. It might be the only time she would ever get to feel what it was like to be in his arms. She heard his heart beating and felt the steady thud against her ear. His chest was broad, hard, the perfect place to rest her head, and all her plans to get him out of her mind quickly disappeared.

When he released her she was breathing deeply, conscious of the sudden intimacy between them. He pulled away and dropped his arms, watching her, his gaze so intense it weakened her knees. There was something in his eyes, a kind of wary vulnerability that tugged at her heartstrings.

"Sorry," he said quietly, clearly aware they were being observed by the two women at the desk. "That wasn't appropriate."

Maybe not, she thought, but it sure felt good. It wasn't the first time she been embraced in the waiting room. Relatives of patients had done it before when they had received news, good and bad. But this was different. This was Brant. Lucy forced some movement into her limbs and gathered her composure. She was a doctor and needed to act like one.

"It's fine, don't worry about it. I can take you to see your uncle now."

He nodded. "Thank you."

"We've done a few preliminary tests and it looks as though he has an arterial blockage. So he may need surgery," she explained as she used her key card to open the doors that led to the small emergency room. "We'll keep him here under observation tonight and then he'll be transported to the hospital in Rapid City tomorrow. They have excellent cardiology and surgical departments there and he'll be in really good hands."

He walked beside her through Triage, his expression impassive and unreadable. Lucy linked her hands together and headed for the cubicle at the far end of the room. She eased the curtain back. Joe Parker was resting and she leaned a little closer toward Brant to speak.

"He's asleep. I know his pallor looks a little gray, but that's not unusual after an episode like he's had. We'll let him rest for a while and do his OBS again in half an hour. You can sit with him if you like."

Brant nodded and sat. "Thank you."

Lucy lingered for a moment. "We'll do our very best for him. He's a special man and, despite his age, he's quite strong."

"Yeah, he is."

She knew how much the older man meant to Brant. She'd witnessed his affection for Joe Parker many times when he'd come to visit him at the veterans home. And Colleen had told her about the special bond they shared. They were both soldiers. They'd both fought for their country and had seen war and destruction and death. It was easy to understand why Brant cared so much for his uncle and had such a strong connection to him.

"I'll come back in a little while," she said and lightly touched Brant's shoulder. He tensed immediately and she quickly pulled her hand away.

She left the cubicle and pulled the curtains together. There were three other patients in the ER. A woman with a nasty burn on her arm, a toddler with a fever and a teenage boy with a fishing hook through his thumb. She checked on the baby and was pleased that his fever had gone down fractionally, and then instructed one of the triage nurses to get the teenager prepared so she could remove the hook. By the time she was done a little over half an hour had passed and she headed back to Joe Parker's cubicle.

Grady and Colleen were both there, bending the rules since regulation stated only two visitors were allowed at a time. But Colleen was well-known at the hospital and sometimes rules needed to be broken. Colleen was sitting in the chair and her sons flanked either side of the bed. Joe was awake and smiled broadly when she pulled back the curtain.

"Here she is," he said. "My guardian angel. She's been looking after me since I got here."

Lucy grinned. "Well, you're a model patient, so it's been easy."

"Never a more beautiful girl have I ever seen," Joe said and chuckled. "Makes me wish I was forty years younger."

Lucy smiled at his outrageous flirting and glanced toward Brant. He was watching her with blistering intensity and she quickly shifted her gaze. "How are you feeling?" she asked, grabbing the chart from the foot of the bed.

"Better for seein' you, Doc," he said and winked.

"Joe," Colleen chastised her much older brother-in-law gently. "Behave yourself."

Joe Parker smiled again, wrinkling his cheeks. "Ha! There's no fool like an old fool, right, Doc?"

He made a breathless sound and Lucy stepped toward the bed and grasped his wrist. He was overdoing it. She urged him to lay back and rest. She checked him over and scribbled notes in his chart. When she was done she asked Grady to walk with her outside the cubicle. The eldest Parker son had his uncle's medical power of attorney and she wanted to keep the family updated on his condition.

"It was a mild-range heart attack," she explained once she and Grady were out of earshot. "But I'm concerned enough to send him to Rapid City for a full set of testing. He may need surgery sooner rather than later, but the cardiologist there will make that call. For the moment he is stable and out of pain."

Grady nodded and she was struck by how alike the brothers were. Same color hair, same eyes, same tough jaw. Grady was a little taller than his brother, but Brant was broader through the shoulders. And Grady always looked happy...like he had some great secret to life. Whereas Brant...? Lucy only saw caution and resistance in his gaze. For the moment, though, her only concern was Joe Parker's welfare. She explained the procedure for transporting him to the larger hospital and when she was done asked if he had any questions.

"No," Grady replied. "I do know Brant will want to go with him. They're very close."

She nodded. "I can arrange something." She turned to walk away when Grady said her name. "What is it?"

He shrugged loosely. "About Brant. I know this might not be the right time to say anything...but do you think you could talk to the counselor at the veterans home about perhaps having a word with him...kind of on the down-low, if you know what I mean?"

Lucy's skin prickled. "Do you think he needs counseling?"

"I think when he was a solider he went through some bad stuff and doesn't want to talk about it," Grady said and sighed. "Not even to me or Mom."

Lucy thought that, too. She knew enough about PTSD to recognize the signs. His isolation, irritability and moodiness could definitely be attributed to something like that. Of course, she had no idea what he'd witnessed in service to his country. But if his brother was concerned, that was enough for Lucy to do what she could to help.

"I could have a quiet word with Dr. Allenby. He comes to the home once a week and he's trained to deal with veterans, particularly combat soldiers."

Grady nodded. "Yes, my mom has mentioned him. That's great. I'd really appreciate it if you could do that. But we might want to keep this between us, okay?"

Going behind Brant's back didn't sit well with her conscience. This was a conversation the Parker family needed to have together. But she could clearly see the concern in his brother's eyes and that was enough to get her agreement for the moment. "Don't think there'll be a problem with that. Your brother hardly talks to me."

"Self-preservation," Grady said and grinned.

"What?"

His grin widened. "You know how guys are. We always do things stupid-ass backward. Ask Marissa how much I screwed up in the beginning. Ignoring her was all I could do to keep from going crazy."

Lucy's mouth creased into a smile. "You know he'd hate the fact we're out here talking about him, don't you?"

"Yep," Grady replied. "Just as well we're on the same side."

Lucy's smiled deepened. "I'll see what I can do."

Grady returned to his uncle's bedside and Lucy headed to the cafeteria for a break. She ordered tea and a cranberry muffin and sat by the window, looking out toward the garden, an unread magazine open on the table in front of her. The place was empty except for the two people behind the counter and a couple of orderlies who were chatting over coffee in the far corner. She liked days like this. Quiet days. It gave her time to think. The hospital was small but catered to a wide area and some days she didn't have time for breaks.

"Can I talk to you?"

Lucy looked up from her tea. Brant stood beside the small table. "Oh…sure."

He pulled out the chair opposite. "Can I get you anything? More coffee?"

"Tea," she corrected and shook her head. "And I'm good. What can I do for you?"

It sounded so perfunctory…when inside she was churning. He looked so good in jeans and a black shirt and leather jacket. His brown hair was long, too, as it had been in high school, curling over his collar a little—a big change from the regulation military crew cut she was used to seeing when he came back to town in between tours. There was a small scar on his left temple and another under his chin, and she wondered how he'd gotten them. War wounds? Perhaps they were old football injuries or from school-yard antics? Or when he used to work horses with his brother? He'd always looked good in the saddle. She had spent hours pretending to have her nose in a book while she'd watched him ride from the sidelines. At twelve she'd had stars in her eyes. At twenty-seven she felt almost as foolish.

She took a breath and stared at him. "So…what is it?"

"My uncle is seventy-three years old, and I know he has health issues and might not have a lot of time left. I also know that he trusts you."

"And?" she prompted.

He shrugged one shoulder. "And I was thinking that once he gets to the hospital in Rapid City there will be a whole lot of people there who he doesn't trust poking and prodding and making judgment calls and decisions about him."

Lucy stilled. "And?" she prompted again.

"And he'd probably prefer it if you were around to see to things."

She eyed him shrewdly. "*He* would?"

His other shoulder moved. "Okay… *I* would."

"You want me to go to the hospital with him?"

"Well…yes."

"I'm not on staff there," she explained, increasingly conscious of his intense gaze. "I couldn't interfere with his treatment or be part of his appointments with specialists."

"I know that," Brant replied softly, his attention unwavering. "But you could be there to explain things… you know, to make sense of things."

Lucy drank some tea and then placed the paper cup on the table. "With you?"

He shrugged again. "Sure."

"Won't that go against your determination to avoid me and my wicked plans to ensnare you with my white picket fence?"

His eyes darkened. She was teasing him. And Brant Parker clearly didn't like to be teased.

"This is about my uncle," he replied, his jaw clenching. "Not us."

The silly romantic in her wanted to swoon at the way he said the word *us*. But she didn't.

"I do have the day off tomorrow," she said, thinking she was asking for a whole lot of complications by agreeing to his request. But she did genuinely care about Joe Parker.

"So…yes?" he asked.

Lucy nodded slowly. "Sure. I'll arrange for the ambulance to leave here around nine in the morning and we can follow in my car."

"I'll drive. We'll take my truck."

Lucy gave in to the laughter she felt. "Boy, you're predictable. Clearly my little Honda isn't macho enough."

"I need to get some building supplies from Rapid City," he shot back, unmoving. "I don't think the footrest for the bar that I'm having made will fit in your *little Honda*, Dr. Monero. Besides the fact that your car is unreliable."

"I had my car towed and the battery replaced yesterday, so it's as good as new." Her cheeks colored. "And I thought we agreed you were going to call me Lucy?"

A smile tugged at the corner of his mouth. "Did we? Okay, *Lucy*, I'll pick you up around nine."

His uncle looked much better the following day, but Brant was still pleased he was going to be assessed in Rapid City. He was also pleased that Lucy Monero had agreed to go with him. He knew it was a big favor to ask. But she'd agreed, even when she had every reason not to. He'd acted like a stupid jerk the night she'd broken down outside the tavern.

He waited in the foyer while his uncle was being prepped for the trip in the ambulance, and Lucy sidled up beside him around two minutes past nine. She looked effortlessly pretty in jeans, heeled boots, a bright red sweater that clung to her curves and a fluffy white jacket. Her hair was down, flowing over her shoulders in a way that immediately got his attention.

"You're late," he said, grinning fractionally.

"I've been here for ages," she replied and crossed her arms, swinging her tote so hard it hit him on the behind. "Oh, sorry," she said breathlessly and then smiled. "The ambulance is about to leave, so we should get going."

Brant rattled his keys. "Okay."

It was cold out, but at least the snow had stopped falling and the roads were being cleared.

"Once you've finished renovating the Loose Moose," she said when they reached his truck and he opened the creaky passenger door, "you might want to consider giving this old girl an overhaul."

Brant waited until she was inside and grabbed the door. "Are you dissing my ride?"

She laughed. "Absolutely."

He shut the door and walked around the front. "That's cruel," he said once he slid in behind the wheel and started the engine. "I've had this truck since I was sixteen."

"I know," she said, and fiddled with the Saint Christopher magnet stuck on the dash. "You bought it off Mitch Culhane for two hundred bucks."

Brant laughed, thinking about how Grady had gone ballistic when he'd come home with the old truck that was blowing black smoke from the exhaust. The truck hadn't really been worth a damn back then, but he'd fixed it up some over the years. "How do you know that?"

She shrugged. "I think Brooke told me. We're friends, remember?"

He nodded. "I know that. She's another fan of yours."

"Another?"

"My mom," he replied, smirking a little. "Patron Saint *Lucia*."

Her eyes flashed. "How do you know my real name?" she asked as if it was something she didn't like.

"I think Brooke told me," he said then shrugged. "We're family...remember?"

"Funny guy," she quipped sweetly. "And I didn't think the Parkers and Culhanes were friends."

"Grady and I used to get into some scrapes with the Culhane brothers," he admitted wryly. "But since we shared a mutual dislike of the O'Sullivans we were friends more often than not."

"He still shouldn't have sold you this crappy old truck," she said. "You took Trudy Perkins to prom in it."

That's not all he'd done with Trudy on prom night, he thought, but he wasn't about to say that to the woman beside him. Trudy had been the wildest girl in their grade back then. And she'd had him wrapped around her little finger. He'd been a typical teenage boy and at the time Trudy had been his every fantasy.

But he'd changed. He didn't want that now. He wanted…well, he didn't have a damned clue what he wanted. All he knew was that there was nothing crass or easy about Lucy. She was kind and innocent. The kind of girl his mother approved of. Hell, the kind of girl his mother kept pushing him toward.

"I wonder what happened to Trudy," he said as he drove from the parking lot.

"She lives in Oregon. She married some rich banker and had three kids. I guess she could be divorced by now."

Brant glanced sideways. "How do you know this stuff?"

She shrugged. "I'm a doctor. People tell me things."

"Clearly."

"Except you wouldn't, right?" she said and leaned back in the seat. "You keep everything to yourself."

"Not everything."

"Everything," she said again. "Say, if I asked you what you were doing talking with Parker enemy number one, Liam O'Sullivan, the other night, you'd shrug those broad shoulders of yours and say it was *just business*."

"Well, it was."

She laughed softly and the sound hit him in the solar plexus. "When everyone knows he's trying to buy you out because he hates the idea of competition."

"Everyone knows that, do they?"

"Sure. He told Kayla and Kayla told me."

"Kayla?" he inquired. "That's your friend with the supermodel looks?"

"The one in the same. Every man notices Kayla. She's the original blonde bombshell."

Brant made a small grunting sound. "I've always preferred brunettes myself."

She glanced at him and then looked to the road ahead. "Could have fooled me."

Brant bit back a smile. "It's true."

"Trudy was blond," she said, frowning a little. "Remember?"

"She was brunette," he replied. "Trudy dyed her hair."

She snorted. "I'm pretty sure that wasn't the only fake part."

Brant wasn't one to kiss and tell, but the disapproval in Lucy's voice about the other woman's surgically enhanced attributes made him smile. "You could be right."

Lucy Monero had a habit of doing that. Whatever transpired between them, however much he desired her, wanted her, imagined kissing her, there was something else going on, too. Because he *liked* her. She was sweet and funny and good to be around. A balm for a weary soul. Something he could get used to, if he'd let himself. Not that he would.

"Incidentally," he said, speaking without his usual reserve. "Don't confuse my reluctance for disinterest."

"You really do talk in riddles sometimes," she said and then gave a soft laugh. "But I least I have you talking."

She did. In fact, he'd done a whole lot more talking with Lucy than he had with anyone outside his mother and brother and Uncle Joe for the past six months. "Communicating is important to you, isn't it?"

"People are important to me."

"I guess they have to be, considering your profession. Is that why you chose to become a doctor?"

She didn't answer and he glanced toward her and saw her gaze was downcast. She was thinking, remembering. Lost in some secret world of her own for a moment. She looked beautiful and just a little sad.

"No," she said finally. "It was because of my mom."

Brant could vaguely recall Katie Monero. She'd spoken with an Irish brogue and had taught dance lessons at the studio above the bakery in town. She'd married an Irish/Italian rancher who'd had no idea about cattle and horses, and who had died when Lucy was an adolescent. The crash that had taken her mother's life a few years later was a tragic accident. Katie had lost control of her car while a seventeen-year-old Lucy had dozed beside her. Katie had been flung from the car and Lucy had survived with barely a scratch.

"Because of the accident? It wasn't your fault, though."

"No," she said and sighed. "But my mom was alive for over ten minutes before the paramedics arrived. I didn't know what to do. I went numb. If I had put pressure on the main wound she might have had a chance. But I didn't know...and I vowed I'd never be in that position again. So I decided to go to medical school and become a doctor. I wanted to know that if I *was* ever in that position again that I would be able to do things differently."

"I understand," he said. "But you might need to let yourself off the hook a little."

"I can't," she replied. "I was there. I was the *only* person there that night. My mom needed me and I couldn't help her."

Brant's chest tightened. There was guilt and regret in her words. And he knew those things too well. "Sometimes you can't help," he said quietly. "Sometimes... sometimes in an impossibly bad situation, there's simply nothing you can do. You have to live through the moment and move on."

"It sounds like you know what that feels like."

"I do," he said soberly.

"But you don't like talking about it, do you?" she asked quietly. "The war, I mean."

Brant shrugged loosely. "No point rehashing the past."

"Sometimes talking helps."

He shrugged again. "For some people. Anyway, your mom…she'd be really proud of you."

Lucy sighed. "I hope so. I hope she'd think I was a good person."

"How could she not? You're incredible."

Heat crawled up his neck once he'd said the words. But there was no denying it. Lucy Monero was one hell of a woman.

"You better stop being nice to me," she said softly, "or I might start polishing my white picket fence again."

The heat in his neck suddenly choked him. "Look, I'm sorry about that, okay? I shouldn't have said it. I must have sounded like some kind of egotistical idiot…and I'm not. I think I've just forgotten what it's like to be normal. For years I've been driven by routine and rules, and now I'm living an ordinary life, talking about everyday stuff, and it takes practice. And time."

"I know that," she said and smiled. "I can't imagine even some of what you've been through."

His stomach clenched. "I had it easy compared to some. I got to come home. And in one piece."

"I'm glad about that."

He was, too. Most days. Until the guilt got him. The unforgiving, relentless guilt that reminded him that while he was home and healthy and physically unscathed, so many of his friends had not made it.

Survivor's remorse. He'd heard about it. Read about it. Hell, he'd even had an army shrink tell him about it. But he hadn't wanted to believe it. He longed to be grateful that he was still alive. But there were times when he couldn't be. And there were times when he felt as though a part of him had died up on that ridge that day.

"So am I."

He tried to think of something else to say, some way to convince her that her mother would be very proud of the woman she had become, but she spoke again.

"Your brother thinks you have PTSD."

Brant flinched. "I don't—"

"You might," she said, cutting him off. "It can show itself in various ways. Do you sleep through the night?"

"Mostly," he lied.

"There are other symptoms," she went on to say, calmly, relentlessly. "Bad dreams, fatigue, isolation. I know Dr. Allenby would be available to talk to you. I can give you a referral if you like. Or make you an appointment."

Great, she thought he was a head case. A nut job. Weak. And he was pissed that his brother had been interfering. "Grady had to know I wouldn't be happy he'd said that to you."

She shrugged lightly. "I might have told him I wouldn't tell you."

"But you did."

She sighed. "I thought it was more important I tell you the truth than him."

"Why?"

Brant felt her stare from his hair to the soles of his feet. But he didn't dare look at her, because her next words should have rocked him to the core. But they didn't.

"Because it's not your brother I like, is it?"

Chapter Four

Lucy never imagined she would be sitting in his truck and telling Brant Parker she liked him.

Admit it...you more than like him.

To his credit, he didn't overreact. In fact, as the seconds ticked by, he didn't do anything. He simply drove, hands on the wheel, eyes and concentration directly ahead. Nothing about him indicated he was affected by her words in any way.

But as the seconds turned into minutes, her gratitude quickly turned into irritation.

Am I so completely unlikable in return?

She sucked in a breath, felt her annoyance build and crossed her arms. "Well...thank you."

"What?" he said and snapped his head sideways for a moment.

"Thank you for making me feel about as desirable as a rock."

More silence. But this time it was filled with a thick, relentless tension that she felt through to her bones. Okay, so he wasn't unmoved. But he wasn't saying much, either!

"Don't be stupid."

Lucy's jaw tightened and she glared at him. "Now I'm a *stupid* rock?"

"You're deliberately twisting my words to get some kind of reaction," he said, still not looking at her, still staring at the road ahead. "It's not going to work."

Lucy laughed humorlessly. "You know, Brant, you can be a real horse's ass sometimes."

"Around you?" He sighed heavily. "Sure seems that way."

"Okay… I take it back. I *don't* like you. Not one bit."

"Good," he quipped. "Let's keep it that way."

Lucy clenched her hands around her tote. "Fine by me."

Silence stretched between them like elastic. Lucy was about to shift her gaze sideways to stare out the window when she heard him chuckle.

"Something funny?" she asked.

"Yeah," he replied. "You are. We are."

"But there is no *we*," she reminded him. "Remember? I'm a hometown girl with picket-fence dreams and you're not marriage material… Isn't that how it went?"

His jaw clenched but she caught a smile teetering on his lips.

"Are you going to constantly remind me of every stupid thing I say, Lucy?"

"Probably."

"Don't know how we're ever gonna become friends if you keep doing that."

Lucy's breath caught. "Friends? You and me?"

He shrugged loosely. "Why not? It would sure beat

all that wasted energy I've put in trying to ignore you for the past six months."

She almost laughed out loud. Now he wanted to be friends after months of snubbing her very existence? The nerve of him. "So, you admit it?"

"Totally."

His honest reply quickly diffused her rising temper. "And now all of a sudden you want to be friends?"

"I want my mother to stop matchmaking," he replied. "I figure that if we're friends and she knows it's strictly platonic, she'll get off my back."

Lucy clenched her jaw. "Boy, you sure know how to make a girl feel good about herself."

"It wasn't meant as an insult," he said quietly. "On the contrary, I think having you as a friend could be the best move I've made in a long time."

She tried to smile. Friends? Sure. Whatever. "Okay, we'll be friends. To please your mom, of course."

"You're making fun of me," he said, his gaze straight ahead. "That's becoming something of a habit of yours."

"You could probably do with being brought down a peg or two."

He laughed and the sound filled the cab. "You think I need bringing down?"

"Sometimes. But I guess since you look the way you do…" Her voice trailed off.

"What does that mean?" he asked.

Lucy shrugged, coloring hotly and digging herself in deeper with every word. "You know…because you're so…so…"

"So?"

"Hot," she said quickly. "Handsome. Gorgeous. And if you had mirrors in your house you'd know that already."

"I don't spend time gazing at my own reflection," he said wryly.

Lucy smiled, pleasantly surprised to discover that beneath the brooding, indifferent facade he actually had a good sense of humor. "Here I was thinking all you pretty boys were the same."

His mouth twisted and then he laughed again. "You're making fun again. See," he said easily, "this 'being friends' thing is working out already."

Lucy laughed. "Yeah...it's a breeze."

The conversation shifted to more neutral topics other than their fledgling friendship and by the time they pulled into the parking lot at the hospital Lucy was in a much better mood. And it didn't take a genius to figure out that he had somehow diffused her temper with his deep voice and quiet small talk. So, he was smart. She knew that. It was one of the things she found attractive about him. There was an understated intensity about Brant Parker that captured her attention every time he was within a twenty-foot radius.

And now he wanted to be friends. That's all. And she'd agreed.

I'm an idiot.

What she needed to do was to stay well away from Brant Parker and his deep blue eyes and sexy indifference. Otherwise she was going to get her heart well and truly crushed.

They walked into the hospital side by side and once they reached reception Lucy quickly asked for directions to Joe Parker's room. Brant's uncle was sitting up in bed, pale and tired, but in good spirits.

"You're certainly keeping good company these days," Joe said to Brant and winked toward Lucy. "'Bout time."

Brant managed to look a little uncomfortable. "Dr.

Monero is here in case you have any questions about the tests you'll be having."

Joe patted the edge of the bed, inviting Lucy to sit. "Is that what he said, Doc?" He winked again, then glanced at his nephew. "Using a sick old man to get a date... shame on you."

"Uncle Joe, I hardly—"

"I insisted," Lucy said, smiling, certain that Brant didn't appreciate his uncle's teasing. "So this isn't really a date. I wanted to make sure you were okay."

Joe's eyes crinkled in the corners. "That's nice to hear. But all this seems like a big waste of time. I don't want a whole bunch of people sticking me with needles and poking at me. I feel fine."

"You had a heart attack, Uncle Joe," Brant reminded him seriously.

Joe waved a hand. "It was nothing, just a—"

"Mr. Parker," Lucy said gently as she perched herself on the edge of his bed. "You trust me, right?"

The older man nodded. "Well, of course, Doc."

Lucy patted his hand. "You're here because I thought it was the best thing considering what happened yesterday. And I'll be close by if you have any questions. So, promise me you won't cause a fuss and will do everything the doctors say."

He shrugged and looked toward his nephew. "She certainly has a way about her, doesn't she? Is she this bossy with you?"

Brant's mouth twitched. "Absolutely."

Joe laughed and it made Lucy smile. She knew Brant was watching her and feeling his gaze made her skin hot. She wished she wasn't so affected by him. It would certainly make getting him out of her system a whole lot easier.

Two doctors and a nurse arrived, and she shuffled off the bed and introduced herself and Brant. It took a few minutes for them to explain the testing and observations they would be doing over the next few hours and once Lucy was assured Joe was in good hands, she and Brant left the room.

"Should we stay?" he asked as they headed down the corridor.

"No," Lucy replied. "The less distraction your uncle has, the better. We'll come back in an hour or so. In the meantime, you can buy me a cup of herbal tea at the cafeteria."

Brant grinned slightly. "Sure, *Saint Lucia.*"

She frowned. "I thought we agreed you were going to call me plain old Lucy."

"You're not old," he said as they reached the elevator. "And you're not plain."

Lucy's eyes widened as they stepped into the elevator. "Is that a compliment?"

He shrugged. "An observation."

She waited until the door closed and pressed the button. "Smooth," she said and crossed her arms. "But you obviously don't remember when I used to be a chubby teenager with braces and glasses."

The elevator opened and he waited while she stepped out before following her.

"I remember," he said, walking beside her as they headed for the cafeteria.

"And here I was thinking I was invisible back then."

When they reached the cafeteria he ordered her some tea and a coffee for himself and quickly found them a table. He pulled a seat out for her, waited while she settled in, then placed his jacket on the back of another chair and took a seat. "Are you always this hard on yourself?" he asked quietly.

Lucy frowned. "What?"

"You're smart, successful…" His words trailed off for a moment and he rested his elbows on the table. "And beautiful. Why would you think anything less?"

"I don't," she said quickly, feeling heat rise up her neck. "I mean…not that I think I'm beautiful…because I'm obviously not. Well, not compared to someone like my friend Kayla. But I know I'm—"

"Being tall and blonde isn't a trademark stamp of beauty, you know," he said, meeting her gaze with a burning intensity that left her breathless. "There's also beauty in curves and green eyes and freckles."

I'm dreaming…that has to be it. There's no other way Brant Parker would be telling me he thinks I'm beautiful.

She swallowed hard and took a breath. "Wow, you really can be charming when you put your mind to it."

He chuckled. "I figure I have some making up to do."

"You mean because you behaved like an idiot the other night?"

"Yes."

She laughed softly. "You're forgiven, okay? I'm not the kind of person to hold a grudge anyhow."

"That's very generous of you. My mother was right."

Lucy's expression narrowed. "She was?"

He half shrugged. "She said you were kind. And sweet."

"Wow, how dull does that sound," Lucy sighed.

Brant's eyes darkened and he stared at her with a kind of hypnotic power. Awareness swirled through the space between them and she couldn't have broken the visual connection even if she'd tried.

"Tell me something," he said so quietly that Lucy had to lean forward to hear him. "Why don't you have a boy-friend?"

Brant had no idea why he was asking Lucy Monero about her love life. He didn't want to know. The less he knew about the bewitching brunette the better. But he couldn't help himself. She looked so alluring with her lovely hair framing her face and her sparkling green eyes meeting his gaze with barely a blink.

She sat back, looking surprised. "A boyfriend?"

Her reaction was dead-on. It was none of his concern what she did or with whom. "Forget I—"

"No one's asked me out."

Impossible. Brant didn't bother to hide his disbelief. "No one?"

She raised a shoulder. "Not for a while. And I guess I wasn't all that interested in dating when I was in medical school. Since I've been back home I've been too busy at the hospital. You know how it is…it's easy to get caught up in work and forget everything else."

He *did* know how that was. Brant had deliberately fo-cused on renovating the Loose Moose for the past month or so to avoid any entanglements. But something in her expression made him think there was more to it. "So there was no college boyfriend you left behind with a broken heart when you went to med school?"

"No," she replied. "I was a geek in high school and stayed that way in college."

He smiled, remembering how she'd always seemed to have her head in a book when she was a teenager. "Don't geeks date?" he asked quietly.

"Generally other geeks." She gave him a half smile.

"You know…when we're not sitting around doing calculus for fun or asking for extra homework."

He grinned. "You really were a geek."

"One hundred percent," she said and smiled at two nurses who passed close by their table. "It's how I got through high school," she said once they were alone again. "I hung out with my equally geekish friends, studied hard, avoided gym class and tried not to get upset when I didn't have a date for prom."

Her admission made him think of Trudy Perkins and the ordeal she'd put him through about prom. There was the dress, the suit, the limo she'd wanted him to hire and her displeasure at being forced to arrive at the event in his battered old truck—she'd made him crazy with her expectations and complaints. A week later they were done. He'd enlisted in the army and she didn't want to be with someone who wasn't going to be around. And he'd been happy about it. The last thing he'd wanted was to leave a girl behind when he went off to war. Not that Trudy was the love of his life. Sure, he'd wanted her…but it was little more than that. And she hadn't seemed heartbroken when they'd broken up.

Only sometimes, when he'd returned home in between tours or on leave, he'd wondered what it would be like to have someone waiting…to have warm arms and soft words to greet him. But there never was. He'd made a point of steering clear of anything serious. Hometown girls were off-limits. And now it was a complication he didn't need.

"Prom is overrated," he said and sugared his coffee.

"Easy for you to say," she replied and sipped her tea. "You probably had every cheerleader hanging off your every word during senior year in the hope you'd take them to the prom." She grinned slightly. "But in the end Trudy won your heart."

Brant smiled. "My relationship with Trudy had less to do with heart—" he saw her expression grow curiously "—and more to do with another part of my anatomy...if you get what I mean."

He watched, fascinated as color rose up her neck. She embarrassed easily, but wasn't shy about showing it. "Us geeks generally missed that class," she said, grinning.

Lucy had a good sense of humor and Brant liked that about her. He was discovering that he liked most things about her. She had a husky kind of laugh, for one, and it seemed to reverberate through him. And her green eyes always looked as though they held some sort of secret. There was an energy surrounding her, a magnetic pull that Brant found difficult to deny.

Over the past few months he'd deliberately steered clear of her. Of course, that hadn't stopped his attraction for her from growing. But he'd kept it under control, dismissed it, put it out of his mind most days. However, being around her now, sharing her company and listening to her soft voice, made it impossible to ignore the fact that he liked her. A lot. And it was messing with his head and his intentions. He'd suggested they be friends when it was the last thing he wanted. But if he made a move for anything else, he knew he'd make a mess of it. She was a nice woman. Too nice to fool around with. He wasn't a saint, but he wasn't a complete ass, either. If he asked her out, if they dated and started a relationship, she'd want more of him than he could give. And he wasn't ready for that. The truth was, Brant wasn't sure he ever would be.

"Thanks for coming today," he said and drank some coffee.

Lucy smiled. "No problem. I like your uncle. I like you, too," she admitted. "Even though you can be an idiot."

Her bluntness amused him and Brant grinned. "So… friends?"

"Isn't that what we already agreed?"

"Just making sure we're on the same page."

"I don't think we're even in the same chapter," she said. "You're something of an enigma, Brant. You're a good guy when you want to be, but underneath all that, I don't think you really allow anyone to see the real you at all."

She was so close to the truth he fought the instinctive urge to get up and leave. But he stayed where he was and met her gaze. "Is that your professional opinion?"

She shrugged lightly. "That's my honest opinion."

Brant drained his cup and looked at her. "If you've finished your tea we should probably get back to see how my uncle is doing."

"You see, that's exactly my point. I've pushed a button by getting personal and now you want to bail." She pushed her chair back and grabbed her bag. "You should talk to your mom and your brother," she said frankly as she stood. "They're genuinely worried about you."

He knew that. But he wasn't ready for an intervention. He wanted to forget. "I don't—"

"You can tell me to mind my own business," she said, cutting him off. "But your mother trusts and confides in me, and I like her too much to dismiss her concerns. And your brother is concerned enough that he asked me to talk to you. If you don't want to discuss it with the people who care about you, at least make an appointment to speak with Dr. Allenby."

She walked off before Brant had a chance to respond.

By the time he was on his feet and out of the cafeteria she was halfway down the corridor and heading for the elevator. When he reached her he was as wound up as a spring. He grasped her hand and turned her around.

"Have we stepped into some dimension where you get to tell me what to do?" he asked.

She didn't move, didn't pull away. Her hand felt small in his, but strong, and when her fingers wrapped around his, Brant experienced a pull toward her that was so intense he could barely breathe. The sensation was powerful and all consuming. He met her gaze and felt the connection through to his bones.

"Brant..."

She said his name on a sigh and he instinctively moved closer. Her eyes shone and her mouth parted ever so slightly. It was pure invitation and in that moment all Brant wanted to do was to kiss her. Only the fact that they were standing in a hospital corridor and people were walking past stopped him.

"I'll sort things out with my family, okay?" he said more agreeably than he felt as he released her.

"And Dr. Allenby?" she asked, relentless.

"I don't need a shrink," he said and pressed the elevator button.

When the elevator door opened she walked inside and Brant stepped in behind her.

"You know he specifically works with veterans, right?" she reminded him. "You were in a war, Brant. And you went through things a civilian like me couldn't possibly understand. But one conversation with Dr. Allenby doesn't mean you're his patient."

Brant ignored her remark and once they rode the elevator up two floors they walked out. Lucy's shoulders were tight and he knew she was upset with him. But he wasn't about to open up about anything. Not the war. And not what he went through. It was over. Done. It was the past and Brant was determined to live in the present… it was the very least he owed the men who had lost their lives on the ridge that day.

His uncle was awake and seemed happy to see them. Lucy discreetly grabbed the chart at the foot of the bed and glanced over it for a moment.

"As you can see, I've been poked and prodded." Joe grinned and then winked at Lucy. "Although I would've much rather you do the prodding, Doc."

"Uncle Joe," Brant said, frowning "That's not really appropriate to—"

"Oh, settle down," his uncle said and laughed. "I'm not seriously trying to cut in on your action with this lovely woman."

Brant shifted uncomfortably as heat rose up his neck. Uncle Joe had a wicked sense of humor and most days Brant found him amusing and enjoyed listening to his stories. But he wasn't in the mood for Joe's levity at the moment.

"Good," he said, seeing Lucy's brows rise slightly.

The cardiologist returned before any more was said and they spoke at length about his uncle's tests scheduled for that afternoon. Considering his history, the cardiac specialist made it clear that he would be keeping Joe at the hospital for a couple of days for further testing and monitoring, and to determine if he required surgery. Lucy asked several questions and Brant listened intently, thinking how grateful he was she was there.

Once the doctor left, Joe spoke again. "Now, I need a nap, so take this lovely young woman to lunch and let me rest."

He nodded. "Sure. I have to pick up some materials

for the Loose Moose while I'm in town, so we'll head over to Home Depot and come back later."

Joe already had his eyes closed and a minute later they were back in the elevator.

"If you have an errand to run I can hang out in the cafeteria," she said as they headed toward the ground floor.

"You'd prefer to be alone?" he asked as they stepped out of the elevator.

"Well…no, but I—"

"Let's go, then," he said and kept walking.

When they reached his truck, Brant opened the passenger door and stood aside for her to climb inside. He waited while she strapped into the seat belt and then closed the door. Once he was in the driver's seat, he started the truck and drove from the parking lot.

"Do you mind if we make a stop before lunch?" he asked. "I have the kitchen going in in the next couple of weeks and want to make sure the contractor has everything that I asked for."

"I don't mind."

Brant took a left turn. "So, how did my uncle seem to you?"

"Good," she replied. "The testing this afternoon will confirm how much damage was done to his heart from his attack yesterday. If he needs surgery he'll probably go in during the next few days. And if he does, then we'll speak with the surgeon together so you'll know exactly what will be done."

Her words calmed him. "Thank you. I appreciate your help with this."

She shrugged lightly. "I like Joe. He's a good man."

"Yeah," Brant agreed. "He's the best."

"He loves you a lot."

"It's mutual."

"You're lucky," she said quietly. "I mean, to have such a caring family."

"I know." Brant glanced sideways and noticed her hands were bunched tightly in her lap. He thought about her words and then realized how alone she was. "You must miss your mom."

"I do," she replied. "Every day."

He looked straight ahead. "I think… I think that sometimes I take my family for granted."

"You probably do," she returned bluntly. "But when you've always had something, it's easy to forget its value."

Brant bit back a grin. "That's very philosophical of you."

"I'm a deep-thinking girl."

She was a lot of things. Beautiful. Smart. Funny. Annoying. And kind. Lucy Monero was just about the nicest person he'd ever met. And if he had any sense he'd stay well clear of her and her knowing green eyes.

Yeah…that's what he should do.

That's what he *would* do.

Starting tomorrow.

Chapter Five

Tuesday was a long and emotionally tiring day in the ER and by the time Lucy pulled up in the driveway it was past six o'clock. Boots was in his usual spot in the front window and meowed loudly once she opened the front door and walked inside. She dropped her bag and keys on the sideboard in the hallway and walked into the kitchen. She needed a cup of strong tea, a shower and about an hour or two to unwind in front of the television.

Lucy filled the kettle, fed the cat and headed for the bathroom.

I look tired, she thought as she stared at her reflection in the bathroom mirror. Not surprising. Some days were harder than others. And today had been as hard as any ever got for a doctor.

Fifteen minutes later she was showered and dressed in gray sweats that were shapeless but comfortable. She pulled her hair into a messy topknot, shoved her feet into sheepskin slippers and wandered back into the kitchen. She made tea and left the bag in while she perused the contents of the refrigerator, quickly figuring she should have stopped at the grocery store on the way home. She was just about to settle on a noodle cup when her cell rang. It was Brooke.

"Hey, there," her friend said cheerfully. "How's everything?"

"Fine," she lied, thinking she didn't want to get into a discussion about her day. "Same as usual. You?"

"Okay. Spent the day repairing fences. And I had a dress fitting."

Brooke was a bridesmaid at Grady and Marissa's upcoming wedding. The event was only a couple of weeks away and Lucy knew her friend had been helping with the preparations. "Sounds like fun."

"It was more fun than I'd imagined," Brooke said then chuckled. "You know I'm not much into frills and frocks. I don't suppose I could get you to give me a hand with my hair and makeup on the day of the wedding? And Colleen wanted me to ask you if you'd help out getting the girls ready."

She meant Grady's three young daughters who were all flower girls. "Of course," she said and laughed. "Anything you need."

"Great," Brooke said, sounding relieved. "This is my first gig as a bridesmaid and I don't want to screw it up."

"You won't," she assured her friend who she knew was more at home in jeans and a plaid shirt than satin and high heels. "You'll do great. And just remember that—" She stopped speaking when her cell beeped, indicating an incoming call. "Hang on a minute, I have a call coming in. It might be the hospital." She put her friend on hold and checked the incoming number, realizing it wasn't one she recognized. "Hello?"

"Have you eaten, Lucia?"

Lucy stilled as Brant's deep voice wound up her spine. "Ah…no. Not yet."

He was silent for moment. "Feel like sharing a pizza?"

Pizza? With Brant? Was he asking her out on a date? *Maybe I'm hallucinating?*

"Oh…I…okay. But if we're going out I need to change my clothes so I'll—"

"No need, I'm outside," he said then hung up.

Seconds later there was a knock on her door. Lucy pushed some life into her legs and headed down the hallway. She opened the door and saw Brant on the other side of the security screen, dressed in jeans, a soft green sweater and his leather jacket, a pizza box in one hand and a six-pack of beer in the other. She fumbled with the cell phone and took Brooke off hold.

"I gotta go," she said quietly and opened the screen door.

"Everything all right?" Brooke asked.

"Fine," she said as he lingered on the threshold. "I'll call you tomorrow."

Once she ended the call, Brant's gaze flicked to the phone. "Am I interrupting something?"

"No," she replied. "I was just talking to Brooke. Um… what are you doing here?"

He held up the pizza box. "I told you. Dinner." His eyes glittered. "With a friend."

Lucy wasn't entirely convinced. "So this is not a date?"

She couldn't believe the words actually came out of her mouth.

He shook his head. "No, just a pizza and drinks. But

only if you like beer," he added. "I wasn't sure. I can duck out and get wine instead if you'd prefer?"

"I like beer," she said and stepped aside. His cheeks were pink, she noticed, as if he'd been standing out in the cold night air for a while. "You look cold," she said and ushered him inside and then closed the door.

"I'm okay."

"At least it's stopped snowing," she said and started walking down the hallway. "But the air has a real bite to it tonight. I think we're in for a long and cold winter."

"You're probably right," he said and followed her.

"I have a fireplace in the front living room that usually gets a workout every winter."

When they reached the kitchen he paused in the doorway. Lucy noticed his expression narrow as he raised a brow. "Well, it's all very circa 1975 in here."

She managed a grin. "I heard that retro is making a comeback."

"Not to this extent," he said about the gaudy color scheme and old-fashioned timber paneling. "It's very bright."

"It's awful," she admitted. "But I can't afford any renovations until next summer, so it has to stay like this until then. Wait until you see the bathroom," she said and laughed a little, feeling some of the tension leave her body. "It's baby pink, all over. My mom loved all things retro so she was very much at home here. Me…not so much. I've painted a few walls in the living room and bedrooms, but the rest will have to wait."

He grinned and placed the pizza box on the table. "I hope you like pepperoni."

Lucy smoothed her hands over her full hips briefly. "Do I look like a fussy eater to you?"

He laughed and the sound warmed her blood. God, he

had the sexy thing down pat. Even though she was sure he didn't know it. She'd accused him of being egotistical, but didn't really believe it.

"You look fine."

Fine? Lucy glanced down at her baggy sweats and woolen slippers. Good enough for friends, she suspected. Since he'd made it abundantly clear that's all they were.

"So, were all your other friends busy tonight?"

He stilled. "What's that supposed to mean?"

She shrugged. "Merely curious about why you're really here."

"I told you," he said, taking two beers and popping open the tabs. "Pizza with a friend. But if you need a more complicated reason…let's call it a thank-you for your kindness toward my uncle yesterday."

Lucy nodded slowly. "Did you see him today?"

"Yes, this morning. He's scheduled for bypass surgery on Friday."

"I know," she said and sighed. "I called the hospital this morning. I thought I would go and see him Friday morning before his surgery."

"I'm sure he'd like that," Brant said quietly. "I could meet you there. Or pick you up."

That meant more time in his company.

Being around Brant Parker was quickly becoming a regular occurrence.

Spending six hours with him the day before had worn down her defenses. Of course, she'd convinced herself the day had been all about his uncle. And it had been… on the surface. But after he'd finished his errands and they'd had lunch at a café a few blocks down from the hospital, Lucy knew there was a whole lot more going on. She still liked him. Too much. Despite his sometimes moody ways and indifference toward her over the past few months.

"Sure," she said vaguely. "I'll let you know. So, where do you want to eat? Here, surrounded by this lovely decor?" she asked, waving a hand toward the gaudy cupboards. "Or on the sofa in the living room?"

"The sofa," he replied.

Lucy grabbed the pizza box and read the writing on the top. "JoJo's? My favorite."

JoJo's Pizza Parlor was something of an institution in Cedar River. In high school she'd hung out there most Monday nights with her calculus club. Kayla had also been part of her group. The token swan among a group of ugly ducklings. The rest of the group had moved on or moved away, but she and her friend had never strayed too far. Once Kayla finished college in Washington State, she'd returned home, and Lucy followed a few years later.

"It's all in the secret sauce," he said and followed her down the hall.

Lucy smiled fractionally. "Do you remember how Joss Culhane got caught trying to swipe the recipe from old Mr. Radici one night after the place was closed up? He used to work there after school and told me how he wanted to get the recipe and duplicate it."

"I didn't realize you were so friendly with the Culhanes."

"I'm not," she said. "But Joss was hoping that since I was half-Italian I'd be able to help with the translation."

"And did you?"

"Not a chance," she replied. "My Italian is about as good as my Latin. He should have asked you," she said, placing the pizza box on the coffee table. "You speak a couple of languages, don't you?"

He shrugged lightly. "A little French."

She knew it was more than a little. Colleen had told her he was fluent. But he was being modest for some reason of his own. "Your mother told me that from your years in the military you also speak Arabic."

"I speak some," he said casually and came around the sofa. He placed her beer on the table and sat, grabbing up the remote. "There's a replay of a game I missed on Sunday. Interested?"

Football? She'd rather stick a pencil in her eye. But she shrugged agreeably. "Sure."

Pizza, beer and football.

They really were just friends.

If they were more than that, the conversation would be very different. She'd be in his arms, feeling his strength and comfort seep through her as she told him about her awful day. But she wouldn't…because they weren't.

Lucy positioned herself on the other side of the sofa and flipped the lid off the pizza box while he surfed channels with the remote. It seemed all too civilized. Like they'd done it countless times before. But inside she was reeling.

"You were a translator in the army, right?" she asked as she took a slice of pizza.

"Something like that."

Her brows rose. "Secret stuff, huh?"

He carefully looked at the TV. "I prefer not talking about it."

"I'm not trying to get into your head," she said. "Just making conversation."

He sighed softly and rested the remote on his knee. "Okay…then, yes. When I was in the military part of my job was to translate intelligence."

"I thought they used civilians for that kind of thing."

"They do," he replied. "But there are times when the

front line is no place for a civilian. Part of my training included learning the local language and a few of the dialects."

"Because you have an aptitude for languages?"

"I guess," he said and fiddled with the remote.

"You were one of those people who breezed through high school without really trying, right?" she asked.

A pulse throbbed in his cheek. "You could say that."

"You would have made a good geek," she said, lightening the mood a little. "Well, except for the blue eyes and broad shoulders."

He turned up the volume a little and took a slice of pizza. "But I sucked at math," he admitted. "I still do. So I would never have made your calculus team."

Lucy shook her head, as if mocking him. "Shame... you missed some really exciting get-togethers where we discussed differential and integral calculus. Of course, you would have also missed out on having a date for the prom."

He groaned. "Are we back to that again? I told you, prom is overrated."

"Ha," she scoffed and took a bite of pizza. "So you say, Mr. Popularity."

He laughed and the sound filled her insides with a kind of fuzzy warmth that was so ridiculous she got mad with herself. *Just friends*. Remember that, she said to herself. She glanced sideways and observed his handsome profile. It was strange being with him...and yet, absurdly easy.

"I think you're confusing me with someone else."

"Really?" she queried. "Let's see, weren't you the quarterback with the pretty cheerleader girlfriend?"

"Are you trying to make the point that I was a cliché?"

"Nope," she replied and took another bite of pizza.

"You were too smart for that. But you did have a cheer-leader girlfriend."

"It was over the week after prom," he said quietly.

"Was she mad at you for joining the army?"

"Kind of," he replied. "How'd you know that?"

Lucy shrugged. "Girls like Trudy are easy to read."

"But not girls like you," he said and drank some beer. "Right?"

She settled deeper into the sofa. "I've never considered myself easy on any level."

"No," he said, meeting her gaze. "You certainly aren't."

Lucy stayed silent as the space between them seemed to suddenly get smaller. There was such a sense of companionship in that moment…as if he knew her and she knew him. She took a deep breath and tried to concentrate on eating. And failed. She'd had such a bad day. One of the worse kinds of days for a doctor. A day when she couldn't do a damned thing to stop something terrible from happening.

"Lucy?"

His voice stirred her senses. "Yes," she said, not looking at him but staring straight ahead at the television.

"Are you okay?"

She shrugged and swallowed hard. Because he seemed to know, somehow, that she was barely hanging on. "I'm fine."

"I don't think you are."

She took a deep breath. "Today was just…a trying kind of day."

The volume of the television went down almost immediately and she glanced sideways to see he'd propped his beer and pizza on the coffee table. "What happened?" he asked quietly.

"You didn't come over here to hear about my bad day."

"No," he said honestly. "But I can listen if you want to talk about it."

Not in any stratosphere had she ever imagined that Brant Parker would be the kind of guy to simply sit on the couch and *listen*. She didn't want to think about how tempted she was to take up his offer. She *did* need to talk. Talking always helped. But this was Brant…and he wasn't the talkative type.

"I can't really—"

"Would you rather I leave?" he asked.

"No," she replied quickly, feeling emotion fill her chest. "I could probably use the company."

"Okay," he said and turned up the volume a couple of notches. "I'll stay. And we can eat pizza and watch football. Or you can talk if you want to."

There was something so earnest and at the same time so comforting about his words that she had to swallow back a sob. They were becoming friends. And friends shared things. After a moment she drew in a long and weary breath and spoke.

"The thing is… I'm a doctor. I'm trained to harness my emotions and, most days, I can cope with the bad things that happen," she admitted, twisting her hands in her lap. "But today…today was one of those hard days… when I have to wonder if I'm making a difference at all." She shifted on the sofa to face him and saw that he was watching her closely.

"What happened?" he asked soberly.

Lucy swallowed hard. "A woman came in to the ER today, six months pregnant, and I knew within minutes of examining her that she would lose her baby. There was no heartbeat and there was nothing I could do or say to comfort her and her husband." She stopped, took a breath and relived the moment again. "It was the third baby they had lost in less than three years. So, I'd witnessed their heartbreak before. And her husband…he begged me to do something…to help his wife…to save his son. And I couldn't do anything."

Heat burned her eyes and the tears she hadn't dare allow that day suddenly came as though they had a will of their own. She didn't stop them. She couldn't have even if she'd tried.

"Lucy." He said her name softly. "Sometimes you can't do anything. Sometimes bad things just happen." He grabbed her hand and held it, enclosing her fingers in a way that warmed her through to her bones. "You know that. We both know that."

"I know it in here," she said and tapped her temple with her free hand. "I know that, logically, I gave her the best medical care possible and nothing would have prevented their baby from dying. But it hurt so much to see their profound sadness. Her husband was hurting so much…hurting for the woman he loved and for the child they both desperately wanted. And I felt their pain deep down. I kept thinking, *This could be anyone…this could be me*. And then I felt like such a fraud because I've been trained to *not* feel."

His gaze was unwavering. "You know, I think your innate ability to feel compassion and share that sadness is what makes you a great doctor. I saw the way you were with my uncle—and that kind of caring is genuine and heartfelt." He squeezed her hand. "You're not a fraud, Lucy…you're kind and compassionate and amazing."

And that was enough to send her over the edge.

She began to sob and suddenly she was in Brant's arms. And he held her, tighter than anyone had ever held her. Lucy pressed her face into his chest, heard his steady, strong heartbeat, and slowly felt her sadness seep away. He pulled her against him and sat back into the sofa so she was lying across his lap, her hands on his shoulders, her head against his chest, her face pressed against the soft green sweater. She closed her eyes, took a shudder-ing breath and relaxed—in a way she never had before.

Brant had no idea what had made him land on Lu-cy's doorstep with a pizza and a six-pack. Or why he'd suggested they watch football in front of the television. Or why he'd taken her into his arms. But for the past half hour he had stayed still, holding her gently. She hadn't stirred. She lay perfectly still, her one hand rest-ing against his chest, her head tucked beneath his chin. He was pretty sure she wasn't asleep, but she wasn't mov-ing, either. Just breathing softly.

I should get up and hightail it out of here.

But he didn't. She felt too good in his arms. Her lovely curves fit against him in a way that was both arous-ing and oddly comforting. She was soft and womanly, and even though his arm was numb he didn't move. He couldn't remember the last time he'd sat with a woman and talked the way he'd been talking with Lucy. Maybe never.

She finally lifted her head and met his gaze.

"Okay now?" he asked softly.

She nodded and the scent of her apple shampoo as-sailed his senses. "I'm fine," she said as she pulled away. Brant released her instantly and she sat up. "Sorry about that."

He frowned. "Sorry for what?"

"Falling apart." She shrugged and crossed her arms. "I'm not normally so fragile."

"You had a bad day," he reminded her. "It happens."

She shrugged again. "Yeah…but I'm a doctor and I should be able to keep it inside. But thanks for understanding," she said and picked up the untouched beer bottle. "So, about this football game. Explain it to me."

"Explain football?"

"Sure," she said and drank some beer. "Why not? I mean, I'm not much into sports, but I'm willing to learn new things."

Brant smiled. "Actually, football should be right up your alley."

"How?"

"You like math, right?"

She nodded slowly. "Uh, sure. Geek to the core, remember."

Brant flicked up the volume and briefly explained some of the player's positions. "You see that guy there? He's the quarterback."

"Yeah…and?"

"And he's tracked by the percentage of completions attempted and made, along with completion yards. Plus, the distance he throws the ball and from which side of the field he throws it."

She raised a brow. "Still not following."

"These numbers are then used to develop a mathematical model of the quarterback, for statistical comparison with other quarterbacks. Just like the receiver who catches the pass is judged on the number of passes thrown to him and the number of catches. It's all about statistics," he added. "Math."

She grinned. "Gee, if I'd known how important math is to sport I would never have spent so much time trying to ditch gym class."

Brant laughed softly. "Wait until summer. Baseball is even more rooted in stats and averages."

"Good to know," she said and smiled as she took a drink. "Although, I'm not particularly athletic. I don't think I've ever swung a baseball bat."

"There's a practice net at Bakers Field, so if you want to learn, I could show you."

"I'll probably get stuck on first base."

The moment she said the words the mood between them shifted. He was certain she hadn't meant it to sound so provocative, but in her husky voice and with their close proximity, it was impossible to avoid thinking about it.

About her.

About getting to first base with Lucy Monero.

That was exactly what he wanted to do.

He wanted to kiss her sweet mouth more than he'd ever wanted to kiss anyone...ever.

"You know, I'm pretty sure I could get you off first base, Lucy."

He watched, fascinated, as color crept up her throat and landed on her cheeks. Despite her bravado, there was a kind of natural wholesomeness about her that was undeniable, magnetic and as sexy as hell. Her lower lip trembled and he fought the urge to see if her lips tasted as sweet as they looked.

He knew she was thinking it, too. Her green eyes shimmered with a sudden sultry haze that wound his stomach in knots and quickly hit him directly in the groin. He shifted in his seat, trying to get the thought from his mind.

"Wouldn't that...?" Her words trailed off and then she tried again. "Wouldn't that nullify the fact we're only friends?"

"Absolutely."

"And since you only want to be friends..."

"Yeah," he replied when her words faded. "That is what I said."

Her eyes widened. "Have you changed your mind?"

"About you? About us?" Brant dug deep because he had to. "No. Friends is best. Uncomplicated. Easy."

"Strange," she said as she placed the beer on the table and pushed back her hair. "This doesn't feel the least bit uncomplicated."

"You're right," he agreed. "I guess I'm new to this 'having a woman as a friend' thing."

She cocked her head. "What? You've never had a female friend before?"

He shook his head. "I don't think so. I mean…in the military? Yeah, for sure. But that was work. As a civilian? No."

"What about Brooke?"

"She's family so it doesn't count."

"Marissa?" she asked.

He shook his head. "She's my brother's fiancée and I'm just getting to know her."

"So, if you meet someone you like or were attracted to you'd what…sleep with her and then not see her again?"

Brant nodded slowly. "I guess."

She was frowning. "Sex means that little to you?"

Discomfiture straightened his back. He didn't want to talk about sex with Lucy Monero. He didn't want any part of his life to be under the microscope. "It's just a moment…a few hours…maybe a night. Little more."

She met his gaze. "Well, that explains why you're lonely."

Brant's back stiffened and he sat straighter. "I'm not—"

"Sure you are. Isn't that why you're here with me?"

Chapter Six

First base. Second base. Third base. Lucy was pretty sure Brant would have all the bases covered. The conversation was heading way out of her comfort zone. His, too, from the expression on his face. However she wasn't about to back down. He'd turned up on *her* doorstep, not the other way around.

"I am, too," she admitted. "Sometimes. I know I have my friends and my job, which I love…but the nights can get lonely. Or a rainy afternoon. Or a Sunday morning. You know, those times that people who are part of a couple probably take for granted."

He was watching her with such burning intensity it was impossible to look away. "I guess I don't think about it too much."

She didn't believe him. Despite his loving family and how close he was to his brother and uncle, Lucy knew he'd kept very much to himself since he'd returned to town. "Well, I do," she said and grinned a little. "I want to get married. I want to have a family… I mean, doesn't everyone need someone?" She stopped speaking for a moment and met his gaze. "Well, except for you, of course. You don't need anyone, right?"

The pulse in his cheek throbbed. "It's not about… needing someone. It's about knowing what I'm capable of at this point in time. And having a serious relationship isn't a priority."

"Define 'serious'?"

His mouth twitched. "The usual kind. Marriage-and-babies kind of serious."

"What if you fall in love with someone?" she asked, feeling herself flush again.

"I won't," he replied flatly. "I'm not looking for love, Lucia. Not with anyone."

Not with you.

His meaning was perfectly clear. And even though she was humiliated by the idea he thought she was imagining they had some kind relationship starting, Lucy put on her bravest face.

"Just as well we're only friends, then," she reminded him and focused her attention on the television.

"Just as well," he echoed and hiked up the volume.

He stayed for another half hour and when he left, the house felt ridiculously empty.

I'm such a fool.

Fantasizing about Brant was only going to lead to heartbreak. He'd made it clear he wasn't interested. So they'd spent a little time together and shared a pizza and a football game. And maybe she did collapse in his arms and hold on as if her life depended on it. And maybe he did hold her in return and give her the kind of comfort she'd only ever imagined existed. It wasn't real. *It wasn't anything.*

I'm not looking for love, Lucia. Not with anyone.

His words were quickly imprinted in her brain. Exactly where they needed to be. And what she needed to do was to stop daydreaming and forget about him.

Still, as she lay in bed later that night, staring at the ceiling, she couldn't help but remember his kindness. There was so much depth to him. More than he allowed people to see. He was strong and sincere and oozed integrity. But there was vulnerability, too. And pain…she was sure of it.

Something had happened to turn his heart to stone. She didn't doubt he'd experienced something terrible while he was deployed. Something he'd been keeping from everyone, even his brother and mother. And despite knowing it was madness to dig herself in any further, Lucy wanted to know what it was. She remembered how Grady had asked for her help. Clearly, Brant's family was genuinely concerned about him and Lucy had said she'd do what she could. Getting him to talk about what he'd been through in the military wasn't going to be easy. But the doctor in her felt a pull of responsibility to do what she could. And the woman in her wanted to understand his pain.

Her shift didn't start until eleven the following morning, so she slept in an hour longer than usual, then showered and dressed. Once she had a late breakfast she headed into town at nine-thirty to meet Kayla at the museum.

"You look tired," her friend said as they sat in Kayla's small office and began sipping on the take-out lattes Lucy had picked up from the Muffin Box on her way over.

"I didn't sleep much last night," she admitted, feeling the caffeine quickly kick in.

Kayla immediately looked concerned. "Bad dreams?"

She shrugged. "Just a long day," she said, deciding not to dwell on what had happened at the hospital the previous afternoon. "And then Brant dropped over with a pizza."

Kayla's eyes almost popped their sockets. "Really?"

"Yeah," she replied. "But don't read any more into it. We're just friends."

Kayla chuckled. "Sure you are."

"It's true," she said. "He's made it abundantly clear that he's not in the market for a relationship and I—"

"Won't meet anyone else if you keep hanging out with Brant Parker," Kayla reminded her.

"I know," she admitted. "But I like him. I have no idea why, of course. He's temperamental and indifferent and sometimes downright unfriendly. But…" She paused. "There are other times when he's such a great listener and he's really smart and funny and—"

"Oh, no," Kayla said, cutting her off. "I know that weepy look. You're actually falling for him. For real. This isn't high school, Lucy…you could really get your heart broken here."

"I know," she said as if they were two of the hardest words she'd ever said.

"Then stay away from him," Kayla suggested. "I mean it. He's quicksand for a girl like you."

"Like me?" she echoed. "You mean the oldest virgin on the planet?"

Kayla, Ash and Brooke were the only people who knew she'd never had an intimate relationship. Her friend smiled gently. "So, all that means is you haven't met the right man yet."

But I have.

"Why don't we talk about your complicated love life instead?" Lucy suggested. "What's going on with you and Liam?"

"Nothing," Kayla assured her. "My father would disown me, for one. And I don't like Liam O'Sullivan in the slightest. He's arrogant and opinionated and thinks way too much of himself. We're working on the museum extension plans together because he's on the committee and putting up most of the funding."

Lucy grinned. "Yeah, and I wonder why he's doing that?"

Kayla's cheeks colored hotly. "Because he knows how important the museum is to the town."

"Or because he wants to keep you in town," Lucy suggested. "Which probably wouldn't happen if the museum was forced to close down. You'd have to leave to get a job in a big city and Liam would be devastated," she teased.

Kayla waved a hand dismissively. "Enough about me. We're talking about you…and how you get your mind off Hot Stuff."

Lucy laughed. "Don't worry about me," she assured the other woman. "I'll be fine. After Friday I probably won't see him much at all and—"

"Friday?" Kayla asked.

"His uncle is having surgery," she explained. "I said I'd be there."

Kayla tut-tutted. "See…quicksand."

"I know what I'm doing."

I have no idea what I'm doing.

"I hope so. I'd hate to see you get hurt. And this thing with you and Brant has been going on for a long time and—"

"It's nothing," she assured Kayla. "Look, I know I was

all starry-eyed about him back in high school, and maybe I have talked way too much about him since I moved back to town. But I'm *not* pining after Brant Parker," she said firmly. "I promise."

Kayla's eyes widened. "So, if someone else comes along you'll give him a chance?"

She smiled at her friend. Kayla had been her wannabe matchmaker since they were kids. "Sure. As long as you do the same."

Kayla grinned. "No question about that. I'm a free agent."

"Yeah," Lucy agreed. "Except for being secretly in love with Liam O'Sullivan."

Kayla rolled her eyes dramatically. "Ha! Good try. I heard that his brother Kieran is coming to Grady and Marissa's wedding. He's a doctor like you...now that's worth thinking about. You guys used to work together in Sioux Falls, didn't you?"

"Yes. But no doctors," Lucy implored. "Too many long working hours."

Lucy stayed for another ten minutes, where they talked about Thanksgiving and the upcoming wedding. Lucy usually worked the holidays and this year was no exception. She would celebrate in a low-key way with her colleagues who'd either volunteered to work the holidays as she had or were unavoidably rostered. She really didn't mind working the holidays. It certainly beat sitting around her house alone.

For the first few years after her mother's death she'd tagged along with Kayla's family and they'd welcomed her wholeheartedly. But as she'd gotten older her need for inclusion waned and she was content to work and free up the time for her colleagues who had families.

But this year she felt more melancholic than usual.

When she got to work Lucy quickly forgot about her lonely life. A double vehicle accident on the highway meant half a dozen people were brought into the ER, two with serious injuries and another four with minor cuts and abrasions. She spent five hours on her feet and didn't take a break until it was close to five o'clock. She headed home a couple of hours later and pulled into her driveway at seven thirty just as rain began splattering the windshield.

Lucy grabbed her bag and made a quick dash for the house and was soaked to the skin by the time she got inside and shut the door. She shrugged out of her coat and flipped off her shoes, dropped her bag and keys in hall and headed for the bathroom. Fifteen minutes later she was clean, dry, and dressed in flannel pajamas and her favorite sheepskin slippers. She was just heading for the kitchen when she heard her cell pealing in her handbag. Lucy hot-footed it up the hall and rushed to grab her phone without registering the number.

"Hello?"

"You sound breathless," a deep voice said. "Everything okay?"

Heat rolled through her belly. "Brant, um, hi. Yes, I'm fine. You?"

"I'm okay. I'm calling to confirm Friday with you," he said evenly. "My uncle is really grateful that you'll be there."

Lucy's insides lurched. "Yes…well, I'm happy to do it if it reassures him. Only…"

He was silent for a moment when her words trailed. "Only?" he prompted finally.

She took a steadying breath. "I'd like you to do something for me in return."

The strained silence between them stretched like a

brittle elastic. "And what is that?" he asked after a moment, his voice raspier than usual.

Lucy knew she'd probably only get one chance to ask for what she wanted. So she went for it. "I'd like to make an appointment for you to speak with Dr. Allenby."

Brant fought the instinct he had to end the call and never dial her number again. But he didn't. He stayed on the line, grappling with his temper.

A shrink. Great.

And cleverly done, too. No demands, no subtle manipulation...just asking for what she wanted. He'd bet his boots she also had a great poker face. But since having her at the hospital was important to his uncle, he'd do what he had to do.

"Sure," he said easily, his heart pounding.

"Oh...great. I'll make an appointment for you."

"No problem," he said, ignoring the churning in his gut. "I'll pick you up Friday."

"Fine. See you then."

Brant disconnected the call and leaned back on the workbench. Damn, she wound him up! He shoved the phone into his shirt pocket and took a long breath. Lucy Monero was the most irritating, frustrating, demanding woman he'd ever known. He really needed to stop spending time with her before she got too far under his skin.

Too late.

He shook his tight shoulders, pushed himself off the bench and grabbed the circular saw. He had plenty of work to do before the plumbing contractors arrived on Monday. By his reckoning he had at least eight weeks' worth of work to do before he could open the tavern. In that time he had to think about hiring staff, including a chef and a barman. He wanted the place to be family friendly with good food and service at reasonable prices. Not as rustic as Rusty's nor as highbrow as O'Sullivan's, but somewhere in between. A place where he would be too busy to dwell on the war, the friends he'd lost or how he was irrevocably changed by all he'd experienced there.

And he longed to be so busy he wouldn't spend time thinking about Lucy Monero.

He turned around, plugged in the circular saw and picked a timber plank from the floor. All the booth seats needed replacing and he'd been steadily working his way through the task for the best part of three days. Brant measured out the timber he needed, grabbed the saw and began cutting through the plank. Within seconds the safety clip on the circular saw flipped back and the tool vibrated, jerked out of his grasp and bounced against the side of the work table. He quickly turned off the power switch, but not before the blade sliced through the skin on his left forearm.

Brant cursed loudly, dropped the saw and placed a hand over the wound. He was reaching for the small towel on the main bench when his cell rang. He grabbed the towel, quickly wrapped it around his arm, wiped most of the blood off his hand and pulled the phone from his pocket.

"Brant, it's me," said a breathless voice.

Lucy.

"Oh…hi."

"I just realized we didn't make a time for tomorrow."

He looked at the blood seeping through the towel. "I can't really talk at the moment. I'll call you back in a—"

"Why not? What are you doing?"

He was pretty sure she didn't realize how nosy she sounded. It made him grin despite the pain in his arm.

"Because I'm bleeding and I need to get a bandage on this—"

"You're bleeding?" The pitch of her voice went up a couple of notches. "What happened? What have you done this—?"

"An accident with a power tool," he said and then made a frustrated sound. "Look, I'll call you back when I—"

"Stay still and keep pressure on the injury," she said quickly. "I'll be there in five minutes."

Then she hung up.

It was actually six minutes before he heard a car pull up outside and about another thirty seconds before she tapped on the front door. Once she'd crossed the threshold he closed the door and looked at her. She carried a bright yellow umbrella, wore a brightly colored knitted beanie on her head and had a brown trench coat tightly belted around her waist. Letting his gaze travel down, he saw the pants she wore had tiny cats on them and she had slippers on her feet.

"Pajamas?"

She shrugged and rested the umbrella against the doorjamb. "I was in a hurry." She held up a black bag and looked at his arm. "I need to see what you've done," she said and glanced around. "And not here around all this dust. Upstairs. Let's go."

Right. Upstairs. He'd lived at the tavern for a couple of months and had not invited a single soul into the three-roomed apartment upstairs. Not even his mother and brother. It was sparsely furnished and other than the new bed, sofa and television he'd bought, about as warm and cosy as an ice-cube tray. Still, it served his purpose for the moment. He hesitated and then saw her frown and realized he wouldn't win an argument while she was in such a mood.

He nodded and walked toward the stairwell. "Don't expect too much."

"You're an idiot," she said as she followed. "I don't care where you live. Besides, you've seen my retro abode."

Retro and shabby maybe. But there was a warmth and peacefulness to her house that had made it very hard for him to leave her company the night before. It was even easier to recall how good she'd felt in his arms.

Once they reached the landing he stood aside to let her pass. She took a few steps into the living area and stopped. She clearly had an opinion about the place but unexpectedly kept it to herself. The room was spacious, clean and freshly painted, and was a combined living and kitchen and dining area. But he rarely used the kitchen other than to make coffee or to heat up something in the microwave. There was a small dining table and she immediately headed for it.

"Come here," she instructed once she placed her bag on the table and opened it. "Sit down."

He did as she asked and rested his arm on the table. She pulled a few things from the bag, including surgical gloves, and quickly put them on. He watched, fascinated as she gently removed the towel and examined the gash on his arm. Her touch was perfunctory and methodical. But having her so close made Brant achingly aware of every movement she made.

"So, how did this happen?" she asked as she stepped back, undid her belt and slipped off the trench coat.

Her buttoned-up pajamas were baggy and shapeless and did nothing to highlight her curves. But he was pretty sure she wasn't wearing a bra and the very idea spiked his libido instantly. And she smelled so good…like apples and peppermint. He cleared his throat and tried not think about how one layer of flannel stood between him and her beautiful skin. "I had a problem with a circular saw."

Her mouth twisted. "You certainly did. It's deep and needs a few stitches."

"Can you do that here?"

"Sure," she said. "But I don't have any local anesthetic so you'll have to be a tough guy for a few minutes."

Good. Pain would help him stop thinking about her skin and curves. She was so close that her leg was pressed against his. She'd ditched the beanie and, with her hair loose, her baggy pajamas and silly slippers, she was more beautiful, more desirable, than any woman had a right to be. And it aroused him. Big-time. He swallowed hard and concentrated on the pain in his arm instead. "No problem."

It took her less than ten minutes to stitch up the wound and wrap a bandage around his arm. "Try to keep it dry. And let me know if there's any irritation with the stitches. Seven days should do it before they need to come out."

"Okay, thanks."

"Is there anything else?"

She sounded mad. Annoyed. Angry.

And he was sure of it as he watched her clean up and thrust equipment back into her bag.

"Lucy?"

He gaze snapped toward him. "What?"

"You're mad at me?"

Her mouth tightened. "Yes, I am," she replied honestly. "It's like you have some kind of death wish. Motorbikes, mountain climbing, dangerous power tools… What's next, Brant? White-rapid canoeing? Skydiving?"

He laughed loudly and stood. "A defective power tool is hardly my fault."

"What about the other things?" she snapped.

"Haven't we been through this already? I told you about the bike accidents. And admitted I was an idiot to climb Kegg's Mountain without the correct gear." He grabbed her hand and stepped closer. "I don't have a death wish, Lucy. I promise you."

She looked up and met his stare head-on. God, he loved how she did that. Eye to eye. As though, for that brief moment in time, there was no one else in the world but the two of them. It felt like tonic. Like salve. As though her green-eyed gaze had the power to heal.

Of course she didn't…that was crazy thinking. But the more time he spent with her, the more difficult it was to keep denying how much he wanted her. Because wanting might turn into *needing*. And needing was out of the question. He couldn't afford to need anyone. And not someone as sweet and lovely as Lucy Monero.

"Are you sure? Your mom's worried you're… She's scared because she thinks you take too many risks. As if you don't care."

Brant's stomach tightened. His knew his mother frequently talked to Lucy, and it would be naive to think he didn't regularly turn up in their conversations. But he hated the idea that his mother was worrying about him unnecessarily. "What are you saying? That my mom thinks I'm reckless?"

"That's part of it."

His stomach continued to churn. "And what else… suicidal?"

She shrugged as though she didn't want to acknowledge the idea. "Maybe. It happens to soldiers all the—"

"I'm not," he said, cutting her off as he squeezed her

fingers. "I'm very happy to be alive and plan to stay that way for a long time."

"I hope so," she said, whisper-quiet.

Brant tugged her closer. "I promise I'm not depressed *or* suicidal."

She didn't look entirely convinced. "Depression can show itself with varying symptoms. Do you sleep well?"

"Mostly," he replied, hating that he was suddenly under the microscope but inexplicably unable to move away from her.

Her expression narrowed. "I don't believe you."

The truth burned his tongue. "Okay, so sometimes I don't sleep...sometimes I pace this room for hours or stare at the ceiling. That doesn't mean I'm depressed *or* suicidal."

"No," she replied. "Not on its own, but when you combine insomnia with other things, it can manifest itself into more."

"There are no other things."

"No?" she queried. "What about moodiness? Solitude?"

"If I was as disagreeable as you seem to think, I wouldn't be reopening the tavern."

"I didn't say you were disagreeable," she shot back quickly. "In fact, you're very charming and easy to talk to most of the time—like you were last night. I needed someone and you were there for me."

It didn't sound much like a compliment. Still, he didn't release her. And she didn't pull away. "But?"

"But you rarely, if ever, talk about yourself," she replied. "And that can be harmful to a person's well-being."

"So, I'm not much of a talker. That doesn't make me a head case."

She flinched. "Now you're angry. Being vulnerable

doesn't make you weak, Brant. Something bad happened to you over there, didn't it?"

His tone grew hard. "It was a war zone...bad things happened all around me and to a lot of people."

"I know that," she said, reaching up to touch his face. "But it's you I care about."

Her fingertips were warm, her touch electric.

His stomach dropped. Damn, she just about undid him.

Brant groaned. "Lucy...stop."

She didn't move her hand. "I can't," she said and then fingered the small scar on his chin. "How did you get this?" she asked, moving her fingertip to the scar at his temple. "And this?"

"I don't remember," he said vaguely and stared into her face.

Her cheeks were ablaze with color. Combined with her glorious hair and bright green eyes, it was a riveting combination. And he was immediately drawn into her gaze. Into the very space she possessed.

Brant moved his free hand to her nape and gently rubbed the skin at the back of her neck with his thumb. Her eyes widened immediately and a rush of soft breath escaped her. He couldn't have moved away even if he'd tried. She was pure temptation. Pure loveliness. And he wanted her. Brant wanted her so much it was making him crazy.

He said her name again, watched as her lips pouted a little in pure, sweet invitation.

Her hair tangled between his fingers and his grip tightened. She was looking at him, all eyes, all longing, and when he dipped his head, his intention clear, Brant heard a tiny moan escape her.

Her mouth was warm against his as their lips met.

She shuddered, half resistance, half compliance, as if in that moment she wasn't quite sure what she wanted. But it only lasted a second and then she relaxed against him. Brant instinctively pulled her closer. Her lips parted fractionally and he deepened the kiss, felt her shudder again before she opened her mouth to let him taste the softness within. It was the sweetest kiss he'd ever experienced, almost as though it possessed a kind of purity that had never been matched, or never would.

Brant suddenly felt as if he'd been sucker punched. Because he'd known, deep down, that kissing Lucy was always going to be incredible. Everything about her had been tempting him for months. Every look, every word, every touch, had been drawing them toward this moment. Toward each other. In that instant there was no denying it, no fighting it, no way he could have stopped himself from getting pulled deeper under her spell. And she felt it as much as he did, he was certain.

Her hands were now on his chest and then his shoulders, and he wrapped his arms around her, feeling her soft curves press fully against him. Her breasts, belly and hips pressed to him so perfectly her body was suddenly like a narcotic, drugging him mindless as the kiss continued and she tentatively accepted his tongue into her mouth in a slow, erotic dance that felt so good his knees weakened.

He pulled back when he needed to take a breath and stared down into her face. She was breathing heavily, as if she'd just run a marathon. And her green eyes were luminescent and shimmering with a kind of longing that heated his blood even further. He fought the urge to kiss her again. And again. Because he knew where it would lead. He wanted to make love to her so much he could barely think straight. He wanted to take her into his bed and peel off her silly pajamas and make love to every inch of her, over and over. He wanted to drug her mindless with kisses and to caress her skin until she begged for him to be inside her and then lose himself in her body for all eternity.

And knowing that she'd allow it was suddenly like a bucket of cold water over his libido.

He wasn't about to confuse her picket-fence dreams any more than he already had.

Brant released her abruptly and stepped back. "You should leave."

She moved unsteadily and gripped the table with one hand. "Brant… I…"

Her hurt expression cut through him, but he ignored it. "I mean it. Go home, Lucy," he said coldly. "I don't want you here."

Chapter Seven

It took Lucy about three seconds to grab her things and leave. She didn't bother getting back into the trench coat and instead had that and her bag clutched between her hands as she raced out of the room and down the stairs. She picked up her umbrella on the way and was out the door and back in her car so fast she was out of breath and had a pain in her chest. She took a few deep breaths to calm her nerves as she buckled up and started the ignition.

And cursed Brant Parker the whole drive home.

Jerk.

She wasn't going to waste one more minute thinking about him.

I don't care if he is a great kisser.

Ha! She didn't have anything to compare it to anyhow. Perhaps he was a lousy kisser.

Yes...he's a terrible kisser and I never want to see him again.

Only…his kiss was incredible and the very idea of never seeing him again made her ache inside. And it confirmed what she'd suspected for weeks…she *was* falling for him. And it scared her to death. Because it was plain he would never return her feelings. He'd closed off that part of himself that was about emotion. It was a coping mechanism, she was certain. He'd experienced some trauma, something that had made him shut down. She'd seen it before firsthand…in herself. Right after her mother was killed and then in college when her roommate was raped. For years afterward she'd walked around wrapped in a kind of protective armor, never getting close to anyone, never letting anyone in. It had taken six months of therapy to help her heal and *only* once had she'd been able to self-reflect and realize she needed help. Brant was nowhere near that point. She knew it. And it made her ache for him.

Her lips tingled when she remembered their kiss. All her adult life she'd imagined that first kiss…what it would mean and who she'd share it with. In her most secret dreams she'd held on to the hope that Brant would sweep her off her feet and kiss her senseless. And for that brief moment he had…wholly and completely. And despite knowing it would probably never happen again, she couldn't and wouldn't regret it. Being with him, feeling his heart beat wildly beneath her palm, knowing he'd been as caught up in the moment as she had been, had fulfilled her every fantasy.

Still, she hurt all over thinking of his parting words.

Her cell rang and she let the call go. It beeped a few seconds later, indicating she had a message. By the time Lucy pulled into her driveway it rang again. She ignored it, got out of the car and headed inside. It took fifteen minutes to lock up the house, brush her teeth and hair and climb into bed. She stared at the cell phone for a good couple of minutes before she finally pressed the message button.

Brant's deep voice was instantly recognizable.

Her heart seemed to skip a beat. And then another.

"Hey…it's me." There was a pause. "I just wanted to make sure you were okay. And I'm… I'm really sorry about tonight. If you still want to come to the hospital on Friday I'll pick you up around nine." Another pause. "Thanks for the stitches. So…good night."

The message ended and she quickly let the next one play.

"It's me again." Another pause, longer this time. "It's just that a guy like me…can hurt a woman like you without even trying. Good night, Lucia."

Tears welled in her eyes a she ended the message and propped the phone on the bedside table. It was impossible to hate him. Even though good sense told her she should.

When she awoke the following morning she was weary and mad with herself for allowing him to invade her thoughts so much. She had an eight-hour shift at the hospital ahead of her and didn't need thoughts of Brant Parker distracting her while she was on the job. She had plenty of work to keep her busy and, when she had a chance, she made Brant an appointment with Dr. Allenby. She sent him a text message with the details and left out anything remotely personal. He replied with a brief thank-you text and she didn't respond further.

Thankfully it was a quiet afternoon in the ER and when she took a lunch break around two o'clock she spotted Colleen Parker sitting in the cafeteria. Colleen volunteered at the hospital a few times a month and was on the fund-raising committee. Lucy purchased a pot of tea and a savory muffin and walked across the room.

"Hello, there," the older woman said and welcomed Lucy toward her table with a friendly wave. "How are you?"

Lucy nodded, knowing she must look haggard and sleep-deprived. "Great. You?"

Colleen smiled warmly. "Very well."

"How's your brother-in-law?"

Collen nodded. "I saw Joe yesterday and he seems to be doing well, considering. I haven't seen you around much this week. Everything okay?"

Lucy shrugged and then nodded. "I've been busy."

Yeah...busy making out with your son.

"Not too busy for a cup of tea and a chat, I hope," Colleen said, motioning to the chair opposite.

Lucy sat. "Of course not. How's the fund-raiser going?"

Colleen waved a hand over the stack of files on the table. "I've been doing the rounds. We desperately need new recliners for the maternity rooms. You know, the ones that allow the new moms to nurse easily and new dads to sleep." She grinned ruefully. "But each one is a couple of thousand dollars and trying to raise that kind of money around the holidays is almost impossible. I may have to put aside my pride and ask the O'Sullivans to make another sizable donation."

Lucy knew Colleen had little time for the wealthiest and most influential family in town, given that they had treated her eldest son so poorly while he was married to Liz O'Sullivan, and often still did two and a half years after her death. But since they shared three grandchildren, she also knew Colleen remained civil and supported Grady's decision to keep his daughters in their lives.

"Maybe the holiday season will increase their generosity," she suggested.

Colleen made a face. "Nice idea. At least I only have to deal with Liam now and not the old man."

Lucy made a mental note to have a word with Kayla. Her friend seemed to have some influence with the older O'Sullivan son, despite her protests. "I'm sure it will work out. I'd like to believe that people *are* more generous at this time of year, so perhaps some of that holiday spirit will rub off on the O'Sullivans."

"Yes," Colleen replied, smiling. "You're probably right. So, how's your car? Brant said you had some trouble with it last week."

It was a subtle change in conversation and Lucy bit back a smile. Her car troubles seemed like an age ago. "Fine. I got a new battery and that fixed the problem."

Colleen's expression narrowed. "And I believe you're coming to the hospital tomorrow?"

"Yes," she replied, coloring when she realized Brant and his mother had been discussing her.

"That's very kind of you. Grady and I will be there, too. Marissa is watching the girls at the ranch."

Lucy would be surrounded by Parkers. But it didn't make her uneasy. She liked them all very much. Although the idea of seeing Brant again was tying her belly into knots. "I'm sure your brother-in-law will be fine."

"I hope so," Colleen said and looked unusually pensive. "Joe is a lot older than my husband and they were more like father and son than brothers. When Alan died," she said of her late husband, "Joe became both a father and uncle to my boys. He means the world to them, and to Brant in particular. I know he'd be devastated if anything happened to his uncle. And after what he went through on his last tour in the military… I'm scared for what this might mean."

Lucy saw the older woman's chin quiver. Usually, Colleen Parker came across as strong and self-assured and able to handle anything. But believing her youngest son was troubled was clearly more than she could cope with. And Lucy instinctively offered comfort.

"He'll be fine," she said and patted Colleen's hand. "Brant's been talking to me, starting to open up," she said, exaggerating the truth a little since Brant hadn't really told her anything. But Colleen needed reassurance. "He's strong, like you, and I truly believe he'll be okay."

"I hope so. And I'm glad he's been talking to you," she said, looking a little relieved. "As a child he was always much quieter than his brother...more serious. But he feels things deeply and that makes him sensitive, which is why he's such a good listener and a good friend to the people he's close to. When he chose a military career I knew he would give it one hundred percent of himself. I only hope he hasn't gotten completely lost in the process."

Lucy smiled. Yes, Brant was a good listener. "Like I said, I'm sure he'll be fine."

She wasn't about to discuss his upcoming meeting with Dr. Allenby. If Brant chose to tell or to not tell his family, then it was his business. She was a doctor, and although he wasn't her patient, she still had a moral and ethical responsibility to respect his privacy.

Lucy finished her tea and muffin, steered the conversation toward the upcoming wedding for a few minutes, and then left to return to the ER.

The next few hours were busy as a young man with a suspected spinal injury was brought in after he'd fallen off a horse at one of the local dude ranches while on vacation. He was immediately transferred to Rapid City for tests. Once he was on his way, a girl of eight with chronic asthma and very concerned parents came into Triage. As her shift was finishing she stitched up another boy who'd torn his earlobe on a fence.

She left around six. Once she was home Lucy fed the cat, showered, changed into sweats and made a toasted cheese sandwich for dinner.

She sat in the living room, crossed her legs lotus-style and grabbed her cell. She'd made a decision while showering to drive herself to the hospital in Rapid City the following morning. She didn't want to spend time with Brant in the close confines of his truck. The less time they spent together, the better it would be for her peace of mind. She sent him a text message to say she'd take her own car and then flicked on the television.

There was no point in pining over what could never be. *I don't want you here.*

She didn't need to hear that again anytime soon.

He didn't want her in his apartment. Or his arms. Or his life.

And the sooner she accepted it the better.

For everyone.

Brant pulled into the hospital garage in Rapid City just after nine-thirty on Friday morning. His brother and mother were about twenty minutes away. They could have travelled together, but he was in no mood for chitchat and had opted to drive in by himself. Without company.

Without Lucy.

He headed for the surgical ward and stopped at the nurses' station to ask what bed his uncle was in. When he entered the room he discovered Lucy sitting on a chair beside Joe's bed, smiling at something his uncle was saying. He lingered by the door, watching her. She looked so effortlessly pretty in a bright green sweater and jeans. Her hair was down, framing her face. Her cheeks were flushed and her mouth looked fuller, softer... Just the idea of her lips against his made his gut churn. Recollections of kissing her, of holding her, bombarded his thoughts. Nothing had ever felt better and there was no way to erase the feel of her against him or the taste of her kiss from his memory.

She looked up as if she'd felt him standing there and their gazes clashed. It was electric. Powerful. If he'd had any doubts he'd been somehow pulled into her vortex over the past week, they disappeared. She was under his skin and in his thoughts. And he knew he was right to have sent her away the other night. If she'd stayed, they would have ended up in bed together, he was sure of it. They would have made love and then he would have been in so deep, Brant knew he would have no hope of pulling away from her without breaking her heart. Or his own. He didn't want that to happen. The closer they got, the more she'd dig away at him, which was out of the question. He didn't want anyone digging. He didn't want to see query and then sympathy in her eyes.

Because he would. She'd get him talking—that was her way. Everything he'd been through in Afghanistan would be out of the shadows and under the microscope. He'd be back out on the ridge again. Only this time he'd have no cover, no one watching his back, no one taking a bullet meant for him.

"You plannin' on hanging around the doorway all morning?"

His uncle's voice jerked him back into the moment. "No," he said and stepped into the room. "Of course not."

"Looks like you haven't slept for a couple of days," Joe remarked and frowned. "Everything all right?"

Brant nodded and didn't dare look at Lucy. "Fine. What time are you heading into surgery?"

Joe shrugged. "Anytime."

"The surgeon will make a final decision within the next half hour," Lucy said, pointing to the chart at the foot of the bed. "If the OBS are good, then it will go ahead as planned."

Brant moved toward the other side of the bed. Damned if he couldn't pick up traces of her apple shampoo in the air. He ignored it and started a conversation with his uncle, blindingly conscious of every move she made.

Grady and his mother arrived a few minutes later and he was grateful for the reprieve. His brother began talking to Lucy and while his mother chatted to Joe, Brant hung back and tried to ignore the sudden pounding at his temples.

Forty-five minutes later his uncle was wheeled from the room and taken into surgery. Grady and his mother took off for the cafeteria and Brant remained in the waiting room with Lucy. The room was small with half a dozen chairs, a small table covered with dog-eared magazines, a tea and coffee machine, and a water cooler. Brant sat at one end, Lucy at the other.

"Are you okay?"

Her soft voice echoed around the room. He watched as her gaze flicked from his face to his tightly clenched hands. Feeling her scrutiny, he relaxed his hands. "Sure."

"I know you're worried," she said quietly. "But the bypass procedure your uncle is having is fairly standard. I'm certain he'll pull through it without any problems."

Of course her words were comforting. That's what she did. She was a doctor—she knew how to phrase comfort and offer a soothing hand. But no matter how much he was tempted, Brant wasn't about to get drawn even further into her web.

"I'm sure you're right," he said flatly.

"And he wants to get out of here as soon as possible," she went on to say. "That's often the best motivator for a swift recovery."

"Sure," he said again and sat back in his seat.

Her expression narrowed. "How are the renovations coming along?"

Brant looked up. She was persistent, that's for sure. "You don't have to do this."

"Do what?"

"Try and take my mind off things. I'd prefer not to talk."

A spark seemed to fly from her gaze, as if she had an opinion but held it inside. He knew he was being a jerk. And that she was probably hurt by his words but was too stubborn to show it. It made him bite back a smile. Lucy Monero was full of opinions and passion and a kind of captivating intensity.

"Okay...fine," she said and pulled her cell phone from her tote as she shifted her eyes from his. "No talking."

Brant eased back into the chair and stared directly ahead. Within five minutes there was enough tension in the room to fill a stadium. He grabbed a magazine off the table and pretended to flip through the pages, but he was suddenly so restless he had to fight the urge to get out of his seat and pace. He could feel her, edgy and ir-ritated just a few seats away. Her perfume lingered in the air and the way her fingers fiddled with the phone made him want to feel those hands on his skin. His at-traction to her was relentless. Powerful. And certainly well out of his control.

"All right," he said, still not looking at her. "Let's talk."

She sighed sharply. "You're such a jerk."

He stilled. "Yeah... I know. I'm sorry. I guess I'm just worried about my uncle and–"

"I know that," she said, cutting him off as she dropped the phone back into her bag.

Tension tightened his shoulders. "So, did you switch a shift so you could be here today?"

Her head turned. "I start night shift tonight for a week so I didn't need to."

"When do you sleep?"

"Tomorrow," she replied.

He had a thought. "You're working over the Thanksgiving holiday?"

She nodded. "I usually do." Her gaze sharpened. "The other two doctors have families. So I work."

Brant considered her words. She had no family and gave up the holiday so that her colleagues could spend time with their loved ones. Her thoughtfulness made him like her even more. "That's very generous of you."

She shrugged lightly, but he wasn't fooled. She seemed a little sad. Strange, he thought as he looked at her, how quickly he'd gotten to know her moods. Like she'd gotten to know his. They'd developed a fraught, tense friendship over the past week and even though good sense told him otherwise, Brant felt compelled to get to know her even better. Despite her intriguing mix of strength and resilience, there were times when she seemed hauntingly vulnerable. And naive. Almost…innocent. Brant couldn't quite define it…couldn't work out what it was about her that drew him like a magnet. It wasn't just a physical thing. He'd been attracted to women before. But Lucy Monero was different. When he was around her it *felt* different. When he was around her *he* was different.

No…that's not it.

He was himself. Without armor. Without pretense. Without anything to hide behind. And that's why he'd avoided her since he'd returned home. The moment he'd met her again Brant had experienced a kind of heady awareness, deep down, that shattered all his plans to steer clear of involvement with anyone. When his mother had started matchmaking it was all the excuse he'd needed to act like a compete ass. And he had, again and again. On most occasions over the past few months he would barely acknowledge her when they were in the same room. Like a jerk. And a fool. And a coward.

"Lucy?"

She looked at him. "What?"

"I'm sorry about the other night." Face to face, the words were harder to say. "I didn't mean to, nor did I want to, hurt your feelings."

She shrugged. "You didn't. It was just a kiss, Brant. Nothing."

For a moment he thought she meant it and part of him was glad. But then she blinked and he saw the shimmer in her eyes. And in that moment he was done for.

Lucy was determined not to let him see her cry. She blinked a couple of times and willed the tears back. This wasn't the time or place to get all weepy. So they'd kissed and then he'd behaved badly.

Welcome to the world of being a grown-up.

"I did say that guys like me can hurt women like you without even trying," he reminded her. "And I'm not saying that to let myself off the hook. I genuinely don't want to see you get hurt. And if we get involved…you will."

Humiliation coursed over her skin. Was her sexual inexperience so obvious? Of course he must have noticed. No doubt he'd kissed many women over the years…like Trudy with her overt sexuality and bedroom eyes. No sweet wonder he'd acted like he'd wanted to run in the opposite direction after their kiss…he'd probably figured out she was a greenhorn in the bedroom department.

"Don't forget your appointment on Monday," she reminded him, quickly shifting the subject.

"I haven't," he said quietly. "Not that I think it's necessary. But I'll do it because I gave you my word that I would."

"He's a good counselor," she said. "He talks to a lot of the veterans at the home, including your uncle. So try to go with an open mind, okay?"

"I said I'd go," he replied. "And so you know, I have talked with a shrink before."

"Me, too."

His expression narrowed. "You have? Why?"

A week ago she wouldn't have dreamed of having such a conversation. But things had changed. They'd changed. Even without the kiss, things had altered between them. "It was a few years ago. I found myself withdrawn and spending way too much time alone. I knew I hadn't moved on from the accident and my mom's death and what happened in college so I—"

"What happened in college?" he asked, cutting her off.

Lucy took a deep breath. "Three weeks after first semester started my roommate was assaulted."

"Assaulted?"

"Raped," she explained and felt a familiar heaviness weigh down on her shoulders. "I found her and got her to the hospital and stayed with her for two days. She didn't press charges. She didn't tell anyone. She never went back to class and left school a month later."

She watched Brant's hands clench. "And the individual responsible?"

"He went about his life as though nothing had happened. I used to see him on campus and he always had a smug kind of sinister look on his face. He knew *I* knew what he'd done."

Brant got up and sat in the seat beside her. His back was straight, his shoulders tight. After a few seconds he spoke again. "Did he ever come near you?"

She shook her head. "I made sure I was never alone around him."

He looked relieved...as if the idea of someone hurting her was unthinkable.

She didn't want to imagine what it meant. She couldn't. Wouldn't. She was already halfway in love with him... Imagining he cared about her even a little was a catastrophe waiting to happen.

"And your friend?"

She shrugged. "We lost contact when I went to med school. I was still mourning my mom's death and with my course load and everything else... I don't think I had enough of myself to give. I think about her sometimes and wonder if she has had a happy life. Or if she let that one terrible thing outline the rest of her life. I hope not. I hope she managed to pull through and find some happiness. I still feel guilty, though... I still feel as though I could have done more to help her."

He grabbed her hand. "I'm sure you did everything you could."

Lucy's insides fluttered. Being so close to him wreaked havoc with her determination to keep him at a figurative distance. It was impossible when he was touching her. She wanted to pull her hand away but couldn't. "I hope so. But it reminded me of my mom all over again," she admitted, feeling a familiar pain seep into her heart. "I experienced the same helplessness, the same guilt. And yet, in a way, it confirmed my decision to go to med school."

He linked their fingers and held tight. "And look where you are now."

She glanced around. "In this room, you mean?"

"I mean," he said quietly, "that you're helping people again...because that's what you do."

Lucy's gaze flicked to their joined hands now resting on his jeans-clad thigh. "Looks to me like you're the one doing the helping."

"Don't kid yourself," he said and smiled so intimately it sent a shudder running through her. "The only reason I feel as if everything will work out with my uncle today is because of you."

As an admission it spoke volumes. This man, who she instinctively knew had been through hell and back and didn't want anyone to know it, trusted her.

"You know, it's hard to admit when we need help. Going to see a therapist was one of the most difficult things I've ever done," she said, feeling him flinch a little. But he didn't move his hand. The doctor in her suddenly made her cautious to get any more involved with him on a personal level. But the woman in her... She wanted to hold him in her arms and never let him go. "But I went because I wanted to feel whole again."

He expelled a heavy breath. "Whole? I don't even know what that means anymore."

"It means sleeping through the night," she said gently, looking straight ahead. "It means not waking up in a cold sweat at two o'clock in the morning. It means talking about what happened...it means sharing your fear."

"I can't."

Lucy heard the pain in his words but pressed on. "Why not?"

Silence stretched between them. Finally he spoke.

"Because I can't go back there."

Her insides constricted tightly. "Back where? To Afghanistan?"

He shook his head. "To that day. To that moment. To that second."

Lucy turned in the chair and grasped his arm. His muscles bunched beneath her touch. "Why can't you?"

"Because," he said quietly. "It will break me."

A sound interrupted them and they both looked toward the door. Grady stood in the doorway, two foam cups in his hand. Brant released her immediately and Lucy's hand dropped. She knew how it must have looked, being so close, their hands linked and her fingers digging into his arm. It would have looked impossibly intimate. Brant got to his feet and moved away, dropping into a seat by the water cooler.

"I brought coffee," Grady said as he entered the room. "It's not so great, but it's better than what comes out of that machine," he said and pointed to the equipment on the small counter. "Mom is walking around one of the gardens." He passed the coffee around and sat on one of the chairs. "So, what's new with you guys?"

Brant laughed first, because the question sounded so absurd considering Grady had walked into the room and caught them holding hands like a pair of guilty teens.

Lucy shook off her embarrassment and got to her feet. "I think I'll join Colleen in the garden."

She left the room and knew she would be the hot topic of conversation between the two brothers. But she didn't care. They could talk about her all they wanted. It wouldn't change the fact that she was falling in love with a man who was clearly so weighed down by his past he didn't have any room in his life…or his heart… for anyone.

By the time Joe came out of surgery it was past three

o'clock. Once she was certain he was out of danger and had come through the anesthetic, Lucy said goodbye to the Parkers. She was in the foyer, just about to walk through the automatic doors, when she heard her name being called.

Brant was about fifteen steps behind her.

"What?" she asked sharply, suddenly breathless.

"I wanted to thank you for being here."

"No problem," she said and clutched her tote.

"It means a lot to my uncle."

Lucy's brows came up sharply. "Is that the best you can do? Really?"

He thrust his hands into his jacket pockets. "Okay... if you need to hear it...it means a lot to me."

"Anytime," she said and managed a tight smile. "Make sure your uncle follows the doctor's orders. And good luck with your appointment on Monday."

She turned and began walking.

"Are you going to be there?" he asked.

He wanted her there? Did she dare? Her heart begged her to say yes. But her head told her not to make it too easy for him. Lucy nodded and tossed her hair. "I'll be around."

And then she walked out.

Chapter Eight

I'll be around...

Brant had been hearing those words in his head for three days.

Even with a busy weekend, traveling back and forth to the hospital to visit Joe, and then immersing himself in the renovation for the tavern, he couldn't get Lucy from his thoughts. He'd said too much. Admitted too much. And he couldn't believe he'd asked her if she was going to be at the appointment with him. No wonder she thought he was a head case who needed a shrink.

He lingered outside Dr. Allenby's small office at the veterans home five minutes before his appointment. He knew the doctor reasonably well and respected his abilities as a counselor. But that didn't mean he wanted to bare his soul to the other man. There was no one else in the office other than the middle-aged receptionist who kept glancing his way every time he moved.

Just over an hour later he was forced to admit that it hadn't been as bad as he'd expected. Dr. Allenby didn't try to force him to talk about the war. Instead Brant spoke about his uncle and the tavern and what it was like being back in Cedar River after so many years away. Of course, he wasn't entirely fooled. It was about gaining trust. Therapists employed tactics just as soldiers did. But at least Brant didn't break out into a cold sweat or completely shut down to the idea of conversation.

And he knew why.

Lucy.

He'd made a promise and he didn't want to disappoint her. Over the past week he'd seen enough hurt in her eyes and it was almost unbearable. Thinking about what she'd been through made him want to wrap her in his arms and protect her from the world. Of course he couldn't. He wouldn't. She wasn't his to protect. Besides, it sounded old-fashioned and foolish. She was a smart, independent woman who could obviously look after herself. Still…the thought lingered because imagining her hurt or in trouble somehow switched on something in his brain and made him feel protective and stupidly macho at the same time.

When he walked out of Dr. Allenby's office he saw Lucy sitting by the door, her head down, flicking through a magazine. He stopped in his tracks when she looked up and met his gaze.

"Hi," she said and placed the magazine down on the small table in the middle of the waiting area.

"Hi, yourself."

She got to her feet. "How did it go?"

He briefly raised one shoulder. "Okay."

She was just about to respond when the receptionist spoke. "Mr. Parker, will you be making another appointment to see the doctor?"

Brant's instinct was to reply with a resounding no. But he looked at Lucy and saw her gazing at him questioningly. As though she expected him to say no but hoped that he'd say yes. And, foolishly, he didn't want to disappoint her.

"Sure," he said, ignoring the heat filling his chest at the idea of another session under scrutiny. "How about the same time next week?"

Once the appointment was confirmed Brant thanked the receptionist and walked toward the door. He held it open and allowed Lucy to pass, catching a trace of her perfume as she moved ahead of him.

"So, it was okay?" she asked as they walked down the corridor.

"It was okay."

"I'm glad."

Brant slowed his stride a fraction. "I didn't think I'd see you here today."

"I said I'd be around," she reminded him.

His skin tightened. "I thought you were on night shift this week?"

"I am," she replied. "I changed at work and came straight here. I'll sleep this afternoon. How's your uncle?"

"Good," he replied. "He'll be home by the end of the week. Unfortunately not in time for Thanksgiving, but we'll celebrate with him over the weekend once he's back here. My mom is all about the holidays, so no doubt she'll make sure he gets some of her turkey and pumpkin pie."

"Sounds delicious," she said, smiling as she walked.

Lucy's heels clicked over the tiled floor. She wore a blue dress, shorter than usual, and her bare legs were impossible to ignore. Her hair was loose, flowing over her shoulders, and she wore a short denim jacket that accentuated the flare of her hips. And she had boots on, the short cowgirl kind with fringe on the side. For a moment he was poleaxed. He stopped walking and stared at her.

When she realized he wasn't beside her she came to a halt and turned around. "What?"

His gaze slide over her. "You look…really pretty."

"Oh…thanks."

Brant wondered if she knew how sexy she looked in her short dress and boots. Probably not. Most of the time he was pretty sure she had no idea how beautiful she was. "I appreciate you coming here today. It was very thoughtful of you. Especially considering that I haven't done much to deserve it."

Her cheeks colored and she smiled tightly. "No problem. Ah…how's your arm?"

"Good. No problems. You're something of a whiz with a needle."

"Yeah," she said almost breathlessly. "Shame I can't cook."

"Nice to know you have some flaws, Lucia."

The air between them crackled and he knew she felt it as much as he did.

"Well, I have to go," she said and swung her tote around her hips.

Disappointment foolishly rushed through him. "Hey, I was thinking we could have a late breakfast at—"

"I can't," she said, cutting him off. "I have a date."

A date?

He frowned. "Like an appointment?"

He watched her expression harden instantly. "No. Like a *date*. I'm not completely undatable, you know, Brant… despite what you might think."

"I've never said you were—"

"Goodbye. Have a good day."

How was he supposed to have a good anything when

she was out on a date with someone else? He reached for her and grabbed her hand. "Lucy...wait."

Her fingers felt soft and warm enclosed within his. He met her gaze, saw her lip tremble a fraction and felt an inexplicable urge to pull her close.

"That's just it, Brant," she said, wriggling her hand free of his. "I'm tired of *waiting*."

He watched her walk down the corridor, hips swaying, head held high, and fought the need to chase after her. He knew what she meant. It was a direct hit. She wanted more...and he didn't know what the hell he wanted. Suddenly tired of his own company, Brant left the building, got into his truck and drove to his brother's ranch.

The Parker Ranch was one of the largest in the area. His brother had been successfully running cattle for a decade and also worked as a county brand inspector. He'd always admired Grady's work ethic and integrity. His brother was one of the most decent human beings he'd ever known. He'd been through a lot, too, with losing his wife more than two and half years earlier, and raising his three young daughters. Since finding love with Marissa Ellis, Brant knew his brother was truly happy again.

Grady was in the stables with Rex, the ranch foreman. Who, as it recently turned out, was also Marissa's father. It was a long and complicated story, but Rex had returned to Cedar River after twenty-six years and discovered he had a daughter. Marissa's mom had since passed away and Marissa had lived in New York, returning a couple of times a year to see her aunt and her best friend, Liz— Grady's first wife. Yeah, complicated didn't half cover it. Rex had stayed in town, gotten a job on the ranch and hoped he'd get a chance to connect with his daughter once in a while. Of course when Grady and Marissa had fallen in love, it had added a whole other level of complexity to the mix. But everything seemed to be working out. Marissa and Rex were getting to know one another, Grady's daughters were delighted by the idea of having a new mom, and his brother was head over heels in love with a woman who clearly adored him and his children.

Yeah…some people really did get a happy-ever-after.

Brant ignored the twitch in his gut and met his brother by the stable doors.

"Good of you to drop by," Grady said and clapped him on the shoulder. "The girls were complaining they haven't seen you for a while. You bailed on Saturday lunch at Mom's."

Brant shrugged. "I had stuff to do."

And he hadn't wanted to answer the inevitable barrage of questions he'd get from his mother about a certain brunette.

"Brooke's inside watching Tina," Grady said. "Coffee's on. I'll be a few minutes here."

Brant nodded, left his brother to his work and headed for the house.

He never ceased to be amazed by the sense of peace he felt whenever he walked into the ranch house. It was wide and sprawling, with verandas all the way around and shuttered windows. There was a love seat on the front porch area that he was pretty sure had been there for an eternity. Out the back was a pool and patio that Grady had put in a few years earlier.

The front door was open and he headed down the hall. His cousin Brooke was in the kitchen, chatting to Grady's youngest daughter, Tina. Brooke Laughton lived about as solitary a life as he did. She owned a small ranch out of town and had once been the queen of the rodeo circuit. That was before her parents were killed, her brother ran off and her fiancé left her for another woman. He liked Brooke, though—she was candid and easy to get along with.

As soon as the toddler spotted him she dropped the sippy cup in her hands and raced across the room. Brant scooped her up and held her close. She was a precious, loving child, and he adored her and both her sisters.

"Wow," Brooke said and smiled. "That was quite a welcome."

"I can be charming when I want to be."

She laughed and looked at the child clinging to him. "You know, that's a good look on you."

Brant shook his head. "Don't you start, too. I get that enough from Mom."

Brooke shrugged. "Just saying."

He dismissed his cousin's words. Mostly. But as he poured himself a mug of coffee and sat at the table while Tina proceeded to stack a pile of stuffed toys around him, he let the idea linger for a moment. Having a child was the biggest commitment a person could make. And yet he'd watched his brother do it seemingly effortlessly for years and a part of him had envied that ability. But every time he tried to see that future for himself the image always appeared blurred...as if he wasn't ready. Sometimes he wondered if he ever would be.

And then, deep down, a feeling suddenly stirred, a restless thought that quickly turned into something else... a picture...an idea. And if he closed his eyes for a second he could see it clearly...a woman and a child, both with dark curly hair and deep green eyes.

"Brant?"

His cousin's voice jerked him back into the present and he quickly dismissed the image in his head.

"How are things at the ranch?" he asked casually.

Brooke managed a smile. "Okay, I guess. I have creditors snapping at my heels and the land rezoning issue is still a problem. But I'm still there."

Brant knew his cousin had some serious financial concerns. "If there's anything I can—"

"There's not," she said quickly and then grinned. "So…you and Lucy, huh?"

"What?"

She shrugged lightly. "I hear things."

"You mean from Mom. I wouldn't believe everything you—"

"From Kayla, actually," Brooke said matter-of-factly. "She said you were there last week having dinner. Besides, Lucy is my friend…"

"And?"

Brooke's forehead wrinkled a little. "And don't break her heart, okay?"

Discomfiture spiraled up his spine. "I have no intention of doing any such thing."

"I hope not." His cousin half grinned. "Although you may have missed your shot."

"What?"

"Your shot," she echoed. "With Lucy. I spoke to her last night and she said she had a coffee date with Kieran O'Sullivan today. He's back in town for the wedding this weekend…you know how he's a friend of Marissa's. Anyway, he called Lucy last night and asked her out. I mean, it makes sense, I suppose, since they're both doctors so they'll have a lot in common. And they worked together at that hospital in Sioux Falls a few years back."

Kieran O'Sullivan. Great.

Not only did he have to think about the fact she was on a date, she was on that date with one of the Parkers' enemies. Well…maybe that was a stretch. Kieran was okay, considering he came from that family. They'd gone to school and been on the football team together. But *a date*.

The very idea twisted at his insides. But he didn't dare show it. "She's an adult. She can see who she wants."

Brooke laughed. "Gosh, you're a rotten liar. You're about as crazy as a bear in a trap just thinking about it." His cousin put up a hand. "But I won't say anything more about it. You're gonna have to figure this one out for yourself."

"What's he figuring out?"

Grady's voice from the doorway made them both turn.

"Lucy," Brooke supplied, still grinning.

His brother walked into the room. "Ah, the pretty green-eyed doctor with the heart of gold. Is he falling in love with her or something?"

"Looks like it," Brooke said and chuckled.

Brant jumped to his feet. "Would you two stop talking about me as though I'm not in the room? I am *not* falling in love with Lucy Monero," he insisted. "We're just friends."

"You looked pretty cozy together the other day at the hospital," Grady said then looked at Brooke. "They were holding hands. It was very sweet."

Brant's blood boiled. "We were *not* holding hands."

"Sure you were," Grady said and grinned as he winked toward their cousin.

"Sometimes you can be a real pain in the—" His words were immediately cut off when he remembered there was a child in the room. "I have to go. I'll see you both Thursday."

He bailed quickly, angry and so wound up he barely made it to his truck without tripping over his own feet. Sometimes families were nothing but trouble. He drove down the driveway and hit the main road into town.

By the time he'd settled his temper he'd pulled up at the back of the Loose Moose. And he got to work. It was still early, barely noon, and by three o'clock he'd finished building the new booths at the front of the tavern and was ready to start painting.

Is he falling in love with her or something? His brother's words kept slamming around in his head as he worked.

No. Absolutely not.

He was not falling in love. He didn't know how to. Lust, for sure. He wanted her like crazy. But love… That was out of the question. It was about sex, that's all. He wanted to make love to her. And, sure, he liked her. How could he not? She was smart and funny and kind and he enjoyed her company. But that was all it was. *Lust* and a little *like* thrown into the mix.

Not love.

That would be plain stupid.

Lucy enjoyed her coffee date with Kieran O'Sullivan. She liked Kieran and they'd always worked well together at the hospital in Sioux Falls. He was handsome and charming and had just enough of the O'Sullivan arrogance and confidence to make him good company. Of course, he'd never so much as made a blip on her radar. And they'd often joked about how they'd be perfect for one another—except for the fact they weren't attracted to each other in the least.

She left the café after accepting a chaste kiss on the cheek from her date and headed home. Once she was inside she fed the cat, changed into her pajamas, pulled the curtains closed to block out the light and dived into bed. She managed a few hours' sleep and by the time she roused it was past four o'clock. She ate a sandwich, had a cup of tea and spent an hour on her laptop paying bills and budgeting for the next month. She started her shift at seven and was just about to leave half an hour before when her cell beeped to indicate she had a text message.

Lucy grabbed the phone and checked the screen.

How was your date?

She sucked in a breath. Right. Suddenly, Brant Parker was Mr. Curious? She waited a few minutes and replied.

It was good. I had a soy latte and pecan cookie.

A minute passed and the phone beeped again.

Are you seeing him again?

Lucy stared at the screen. He had some nerve, that's for sure.

Maybe. Do you have a problem with that?

She waited for a minute, well aware that her provocative question would niggle him. *Well, he deserves a little niggling.* When a few more minutes passed and she didn't get a response, Lucy grabbed her bag, put on her shoes and headed out. It was snowing again and she covered her head with her coat as she raced to her car. She was just about to shove the key in the ignition when her cell beeped. She fumbled through her bag and pulled out her phone.

I think I do.

Lucy grinned foolishly.

I am seriously falling for this guy.

But she wasn't about to start imagining a few texts meant anything. Lucy fought the urge to write something in return and instead tossed the phone back into her tote. Then she drove into town and headed for the hospital.

It was a quiet but long night in the ER and when she got home at six the following morning she fell into bed after a quick shower and slept until noon. It usually took a couple of days for her body clock to kick in when she started a block of night shifts and this rotation proved to be more difficult than usual.

On Tuesday as she was getting ready to leave for work when her cell pealed.

It was a message from Brant.

How's work?

For a moment she considered ignoring him, but temptation got the better of her. She mulled over her response for several minutes and then replied.

Not busy. Which is good. Great to see you're keeping away from the place, too.

She grabbed her jacket and keys, and finished locking the house up. And waited for a reply.

Motorcycles and icy roads don't mix. Told you I wasn't reckless.

Lucy petted the cat, got into her coat, switched off the lights and headed outside. When she was inside her car she sent another message.

I guess you're not such a bad boy after all.

Ten seconds later he replied.

Lucia, I'm good. I promise you.

Even to her naive eyes the innuendo couldn't be missed and her body turned hot all over. She had so little experience flirting—*if* that's what they were doing—and didn't know how to handle the feelings running riot throughout her system. Of course she knew she wanted him. That one kiss had ignited her libido and she wanted to feel it again…and more. She wanted passion and sweat and heat and all the things she imagined were shared between two people who were lovers.

Because she wanted Brant Parker as her lover…no doubt about it. Only, she wasn't sure if that's what he wanted, too. Oh, he'd certainly kissed her that night in his apartment as if he was interested. But he'd also sent her packing. His hot then cold approach was confusing. And annoying. And *unacceptable*, she decided with a surge of confidence and gumption.

So by the time Wednesday evening came around and she was dressing for work, Lucy was almost back to being furious at him for behaving like such an impossible jerk.

Until her phone rang. She recognized the number and said his name almost on a sigh. "Brant…hello."

He was silent for a moment, and then spoke. "Lucia… I was wondering something… Do you think anyone would notice if I skipped the best man speech on Saturday?"

Lucy smiled to herself as the sound of his deep voice wound through her blood. She knew he'd never let his brother down like that.

"Yes," she said, laughing softly. "And you're an idiot for thinking it."

He chuckled. "Ain't that the truth."

Lucy dug deep. Making it too easy for him wasn't on her agenda. "Did you want something?"

She heard his hesitation. "No… I mean… I just wanted to say…that I think… I actually think I'm missing something."

Lucy's nerve endings twitched. Talking was much more intimate than texting and she could feel her nerves fraying. She took a deep breath. "Missing something in the speech you mean?"

"Not exactly."

"Then what do you mean?"

She heard him draw in a hard breath. "I miss… I think I miss…you. I mean, I think I miss talking to you."

God, he was impossible. "You think?"

There was more silence. "It's not…easy for me to say."

No…nothing was easy when it came to Brant.

She sucked in a breath, galvanized her nerves and spoke. "You're talking to me now."

Silence stretched again. "I guess I just wanted to see how you were."

"I'm fine. But I'm getting ready for work so–"

"Okay," he said quickly. "I'll let you go. Goodbye, Lucy."

She inhaled heavily. "Goodbye, Brant." She held the phone close to her ear. "And Brant…if you want to talk you know where I am."

By the time she got to work and swiped in, she was as coiled as a spring. Brant had a way of invading her thoughts like no one else. But she couldn't let anyone see that or allow her personal issues to impact her job. So she sucked in a few steadying breaths and got on with her shift.

She was about to take her first break around eight o'clock when Kayla unexpectedly turned up. Lucy met her by the nurse's station and gave her a hug.

"What brings you here?" she asked.

"I had a late meeting and was driving past and thought I'd stop by on the chance you might want to grab a coffee and have a chat."

A few minutes later they were in the staff lunch room, sipping coffee and tea.

"Don't forget my mother insists you stop by on Friday and have some Thanksgiving leftovers. She's pretty miffed you're not coming over again...you know how much my folks adore you."

Lucy was touched by Kayla's kindness. "I have to work a double shift. But I'll do my best to stop by, I promise. So, how are things?" she asked.

Kayla shrugged. "Same as usual. How's it going with Hot Stuff?"

"Would you stop calling him that?"

"I've been calling him that since the ninth grade," her friend reminded her. "I probably won't stop now. Is it true you were holding hands at the hospital last week?"

Lucy almost spat out her tea. "What?"

Kayla laughed. "Grady said something to Brooke. She told me. The great circle of life," she said and grinned.

"Circle of gossip more like," Lucy said, frowning. "And it wasn't *that* kind of hand holding."

"How many kinds are there?" Kayla asked, still grinning.

"Plenty," she replied. "We're friends and sometimes friends hold hands during a—"

"This is me, remember?" Kayla reminded her. "Your *best* friend. What's going on?"

"Honestly," Lucy said and let out an exasperated sigh. "I have no idea. Some days I feel like I'm back in high school again, as though I'm idly wasting my days doodling hearts with Brant Parker's name inside. Metaphorically speaking," she added. "I'm not really doodling. But I am spending way too much time thinking about him when I should be concentrating on my work, my home and my friends."

Kayla's perfectly beautiful face regarded her inquiringly. "And is he thinking about you, too?"

Lucy shrugged. "It's impossible to tell. Oh, he's civil to me now and we have spent quite a lot of time together lately and there's been a bit of texting this week so I—"

"Texting?"

"Yes," Lucy replied. "Texting."

Her friend chuckled. "That's kind of romantic."

"It's kind of confusing," she corrected. "And I can't allow myself to imagine it means too much. Even if I hadn't kissed him I probably wouldn't let myself believe it was—"

"Whoa," Kayla said, cutting her off as she waved a hand. "Back up. You kissed him?"

Lucy's skin heated. "Well, technically he kissed me," she explained. "And then I kissed him back."

Her friend's eyes widened. "And when were you going to share this tidbit?"

"Do you tell me every time you kiss Liam O'Sullivan?" Lucy teased.

Kayla groaned. "I don't kiss Liam. But enough about that—tell me everything… Was it fabulous?"

"Yes," she admitted and smiled. "You see, this *is* high school."

Her friend shook her head. "It's life, Lucy. So what happens next?"

She shrugged. "I have no idea. I'm new to all this, as you know. He keeps insisting he's all wrong for me— that I want a picket fence and he's not that kind of man. There's a part of him that's broken...or at least that's what he believes."

Kayla's eyes softened. "And can it be fixed?"

"I'm not sure he wants it fixed," she replied, exhaling heavily. "It's as if he's stuck somewhere...in some place, some moment in time, that he believes has suddenly come to define him. I don't know what it is and he's not talking. But I feel it whenever we're together. In here," she said and put a hand to her heart. "I feel as though he thinks he has to hang on to this thing from his past or he'll be *redefined*...somehow changed." She sighed and drank some tea. "Anyway, I really shouldn't be talking about him like this."

"Why not? It's only talking."

Heat filled her chest. "Because it doesn't feel right."

"Conflicting loyalty, hey?"

She nodded. "Something like that."

Kayla sat back in her chair and regarded her intently. "Lucy, have you considered that the reason you want Brant is because he *is* broken? Unfixable? Which also makes him unattainable?"

"That doesn't make sense."

"Sure it does," her friend said gently. "And it really means only one thing."

"And what's that?" she asked.

Kayla met her gaze. "That you're falling in love with him and it's scaring you to bits."

Lucy met her friend's stare head-on and knew she couldn't lie. "Yes...that's it exactly. I'm falling in love with a man who doesn't want to fall in love with me in return. And I'm terrified."

Kayla reached across the table and patted her hand. "So what are you going to do about it?"

Lucy sat back in her seat and tried to ignore the ache in her heart. "Nothing," she replied. "He has to figure this out for himself."

Chapter Nine

Brant stared at the huge cooked bird on the kitchen counter and impossibly bright vegetables piled onto a tray, and watched as his mother managed to attack three separate tasks at once without skipping a beat. Her skill in the kitchen never ceased to amaze him. She baked and grilled and sautéed like a head chef at a top-end restaurant and he suddenly had an idea.

"You know, Mom," he said and snatched a green bean from the plate. "You could come and work for me once the tavern opens. I'm still looking for a chef."

Colleen looked up from her task and smiled. "And have you bossing me around all day? I don't think so. Besides, I'm too busy to work. With the quilting club and volunteering at the hospital, I wouldn't find the time."

"It was worth a shot," he said playfully. "If you know of anyone worth interviewing, let me know."

Colleen grinned. "I hear chefs are a temperamental

lot. What about Abby Perkins? Didn't she study cooking in New Orleans for a year or so?"

"She works for O'Sullivan, remember?" he reminded his mother. Although he liked the idea of having a chef the caliber of Abby at the Loose Moose, he didn't like his chances of trying to poach her away from the O'Sullivans' five-star restaurant at the hotel. Abby had married Trudy's brother a year or so out of high school.

Brant had a couple of chefs lined up for interviews the following week and hoped to find someone from that. "So, how's the fund-raising coming along?"

"Slow," she acknowledged. "Although I did get a sizable donation from Liam O'Sullivan this week. Sometimes I think he's not as disagreeable as he likes to make out."

"Sure he is."

Colleen laughed. "Well, his brother is back in town for the week, so maybe that has something to do with his generous mood. Kieran always has been the peacemaker in that family."

Brant's shoulders twitched at the mention of the other man's name. "Yeah…maybe."

His mother looked at him oddly. "Everything all right?"

"Fine," he said, taking another green bean. "What time are the troops arriving?"

"Six o'clock," she replied. "You're the one who's here early."

"I had some time."

Her expression narrowed. "Something on your mind?"

Brant shrugged. "Not a thing."

"You're a worse liar that your brother," she said and smiled gently. "Grady will at least try and make a joke when he doesn't want to talk. So, have you seen much of Lucy?"

No...

And it was making him crazy. His brain was still scrambled by the idea of her being on a date with Kieran O'Sullivan. Texting her daily wasn't doing him any favors. Neither was calling her and saying he missed talking to her. He really needed to cut all contact to give himself a chance of getting her out of his thoughts. But he liked knowing what she was doing each day. He liked her sense of humor and how she didn't cut him any slack. He liked that they could share a joke or flirt or both and how it felt like the most normal thing he'd done since forever.

"Ah...not much," he said finally. "She's working over the holidays."

Colleen nodded. "Yes, I know. She's such a committed doctor. Everyone adores her at the hospital. But," his mother said, stirring the cranberry sauce simmering on the cooktop, "it's a shame she'll miss out on a real Thanksgiving dinner."

There was a gleam in his mother's eyes and Brant swallowed the tension suddenly closing his throat. "I'm sure they put something on at the hospital."

"Well, yes," Colleen said and nodded. "But it's not like a real home-cooked dinner with all the trimmings, is it?"

Brant didn't have a chance to respond because there was laughter and happy squeals from the front door that echoed down the hall. Within a minute his brother's family was bursting into the kitchen, with Grady behind them, his hands laden with bags. Marissa placed a Crock-Pot on the counter and moved around to help Colleen as the kids raced back and forth between Brant and Colleen, giving hugs and showing off sparkly nail glitter. Marissa's father, Rex, arrived minutes later and the kids quickly transferred their attention. There was lots of cheering and laughter and a kind of energetic happiness in the room that was palpable, and everyone looked incredibly content.

Everyone but him, he realized.

Grady slapped him on the back. "All set for Saturday?" his brother asked.

"Since it's your wedding," Brant reminded him, "shouldn't I be asking you that question?"

"I'm solid."

Marissa laughed. "Don't let him fool you. He's been a bag of nerves all week."

Grady groaned, swept her up into his arms and dropped a kiss to her forehead. "That is so not true. Don't believe a word she says."

As Brant watched their interaction, something heavy lodged in his chest. Although he was thrilled that Grady had found happiness, a part of him was almost envious. He'd never experienced envy before and couldn't understand it now. He certainly hadn't felt that way when Grady was married to Liz and had started a family. But things seemed different now. Back then Brant had been absorbed with his military career and hadn't had any time to think about relationships or having a family of his own. And, logically, he still didn't. However, in that moment, Brant didn't feel very logical. He felt…alone.

Lonely.

Which was plain stupid considering he was surrounded by the people he cared about most in the world. Still, the thought lingered as his mother shooed him and his brother and the kids to the living room while she finished preparing dinner. Marissa stayed to help in the kitchen and Brooke arrived about ten minutes later. It seemed strange not having Uncle Joe around on Thanksgiving, but he wasn't being released from hospital until the following day and the older man had insisted they all have their usual holiday celebration and not worry about him. Of course they all planned to visit him when he returned to the veterans home, but Brant missed Joe's corny jokes and craggy smiles.

By seven his mother called him in to the kitchen to carve the turkey and tossed an apron toward him when he entered.

"And slice it thinly," she instructed. "Not great chunks like your brother did last year."

Marissa laughed. "Don't let the master of the grill hear you say that, Colleen."

They all laughed and Grady popped his head around the doorway. "Too late."

Brant ignored the twitch in his gut. He should have been laughing along with the rest of his family, but he couldn't switch off the uneasiness running through his system. By the time the bird was carved and the table set, he felt so cloistered and uncomfortable he wanted to grab his keys and bail. Only his mother seemed to notice and once they were alone in the kitchen she asked what was wrong.

"I'm not sure," he replied honestly. All he knew was that he wanted to be somewhere else. He *needed* to be somewhere else.

Her expression narrowed. "Are you sleeping okay?"

Brant ignored the question and placed his hands on the counter. "Mom," he said quietly, "do you mind if I have dinner to go?"

"To go?" she echoed then frowned instantly. "You're leaving? But it's Thanksgiving."

Brant sighed. "I know and I'm sorry. But I think I need… I *feel* like I need to be somewhere else."

"Somewhere else?" Colleen's eyes widened and then her mouth slowly curved with a little smile—and a flash of understanding. "So, this dinner to go…is it for one or two?"

He swallowed hard, dismissed the heat in his face and spoke. "Two."

There was snow falling outside and enough cold air blasting through the hospital doors every time someone entered to remind the staff that winter was on its way. Thankfully it was quiet in the ER and even though they were on skeleton staff, by eight o'clock Lucy was ready for a mug of hot chocolate and fifteen minutes of watching a rerun of some mindless show on the television in the staff room.

She was just about to head that way when she was paged. Answering the call, she was told someone was waiting for her in the foyer. Thinking it was most likely Kayla coming to spread some holiday cheer, Lucy clipped the pager to her coat pocket and walked out of the ER and down to the general administration area. The place was deserted except for one of the maintenance staff pushing a janitor's trolley. She said hello as she passed.

And then she came to a standstill.

Brant stood beside the information desk, dressed in jeans, boots, a navy plaid shirt and sheepskin jacket. He had a Stetson on his head and carried a wicker basket. He turned as though sensing her arrival and immediately met her gaze.

"What are you doing here?" she asked, moving closer.

He held up the basket. "I thought… Thanksgiving dinner. For two."

"You brought me dinner?" Her legs suddenly stopped

working. "But shouldn't you be at your mom's? I know she was planning a big family—"

"I'm here," he said quietly. "With you."

Lucy almost burst into tears. It was the most utterly romantic thing anyone had ever done for her. Maybe even the kindest thing. She fought the burning sensation behind her eyes and tried to smile. "Oh, I…thanks."

His mouth twisted and when she stepped closer she noticed how a tiny pulse beat in his cheek. He looked wound up. On edge. Way out of his comfort zone.

And it made Lucy fall in love with him even more.

"Can you take a break?"

She nodded. "Sure. I'll just let the other doctor on duty know I'll be out of the ER for a while."

Lucy snatched up the closest telephone, put in a call to the nurse's station in the ER and said she'd be back in half an hour. When she turned her attention to Brant he was directly behind her and she quickly felt the heat emanating from his body. The edge of his jacket brushed her elbow and she looked up, caught in his gaze and without a hope of denying how pleased she was to see him.

"Where should we go?" he asked and looked around.

Lucy scanned their surroundings. The foyer was empty but still reasonably well-lit; there were a couple of vending machines against one wall and a small bench seat in between them.

"That looks like as good a spot as any," she said and headed to the other side of the room and sat.

He followed and sat beside her, placing the basket between them.

"It's quiet here tonight," he remarked, opening the basket.

Lucy peered inside and nodded. "It will probably get busier later tonight. Right now most people are eating dinner and celebrating. It's the MVAs or bouts of food poisoning that mostly keep the ER busy around the holidays."

He met her gaze. "Well, hopefully there's nothing poisonous in here."

She chuckled. "What are we having?"

"Turkey sandwiches on cranberry bread, sweet potato casserole and iced pumpkin cookies for dessert."

"Sounds delicious," she said and licked her bottom lip.

He pulled a few things from the basket and handed her a small stack of sandwiches wrapped in a gingham cloth. Lucy unwrapped the food and laid it on top of the basket while he bought sodas from the vending machine.

He sat, twisted the caps off the soda bottles and handed her one. "Happy Thanksgiving, Lucia," he said and clinked the bottle necks.

Lucy felt a surge of emotion rise up and fill her heart. "Happy Thanksgiving, Brant. And…thank you. I was feeling a little more alone than usual today."

"Me, too," he admitted and drank some soda.

Lucy passed him a sandwich. "But weren't you with your family tonight?"

Brant smiled warmly. "You can be in a room full of people and still feel alone."

He was right about that. "I feel that way, too. Sometimes when I'm at a party or out to dinner with friends, I get this strange feeling of disconnect. I especially felt that way after my mom died. For a long time I couldn't stand to be in crowds or around too many people at one time."

"It's a coping mechanism," he said softly. "But I understand what you're saying. You must think about your mom a lot around the holidays."

"I do," she said and sighed deeply. "She loved the holidays so much. And Christmas especially. She would decorate the house with a real tree and hang ornaments everywhere. And she and my dad would kiss under the mistletoe. There were always lots of gifts under the tree… Nothing extravagant, of course, since we didn't have a lot of money, just small things. Like, my dad would make her a footstool or she would bake his favorite cookies or knit him a pair of gloves that never really fit right. There was never much money but always a lot of love. And I miss that. One day I hope I'll have that again…if I get married and have children, that is."

"I'm sure you will," he said softly. "You're a marryable kind of girl."

Her cheeks burned. "I hope I am. I mean, I hope there's someone who will want to marry me one day. Someone who will want to have children with me and grow old with me."

"Someone like Kieran O'Sullivan you mean?"

He sounded jealous and it made her grin. "I'd never marry a doctor. They work terrible hours. Besides, there's no blip."

"'Blip'?" he repeated.

"Blip," she said again and took a bite of her sandwich. "You know, on the radar."

His gaze narrowed and she could see he was trying to work out what she meant. "I believe a blip is a malfunction or a problem."

"Well, thank you, Mr. Walking Dictionary," she said, drinking some soda. "But falling in love *can* be a little problematic, don't you think?"

"I don't really know," he muttered and ate some food.

"I thought smart guys like you knew everything."

He glanced at her. "Who says I'm that smart?"

Lucy chuckled. "Oh, you're smart all right. Your mom

told me you've been asked to teach French at the high school in the evenings, for the adult classes."

He looked faintly embarrassed. "Yeah... I'm still thinking about it."

"Why are you so uncomfortable with the fact that most days you're probably the smartest person in the room?"

He shrugged again. "I could say the same thing to you."

"Oh, no. I had to study long and hard to get good grades. And I was hopeless at French and Latin." Her eyes widened. "Maybe you could teach me?"

"Teach you French?" He stretched out his legs. "Teach you how to French kiss, maybe."

Lucy almost spat out her sandwich as humiliation raced up her neck. "Was I so terrible that I need lessons?"

"Not at all," he replied softly. "You have a perfectly lovely mouth, Lucia."

She turned hot all over and tried to eat the rest of her sandwich. "This is really good."

"My mom is a good cook."

"She is. I should get her to give me some tips." Lucy's smile broadened. "And, just so we're straight on this, I'm not interested in Kieran O'Sullivan in the least. And it wasn't really a date, just two former colleagues catching up over coffee."

"Glad to hear it. The O'Sullivans think way too much of themselves."

She laughed. "He told me that his brother is going to keep trying to buy you out until you buckle under the pressure."

The pulse in his cheek throbbed. "Did he?"

She nodded. "And I told him he'd be waiting a long time."

He glanced at her. "Why did you tell him that?"

Lucy nodded. "Because I think anyone who has been a soldier on the front line for twelve years knows more about pressure and resilience than someone who sits behind a desk at a fancy hotel and barks out orders to employees all day."

He smiled and drank some soda. "I can handle Liam O'Sullivan...but thanks, it's very sweet of you to defend me."

"That's what friends do for one another."

He didn't disagree.

When he stayed silent Lucy spoke again. "Do you miss it? Being a soldier, I mean."

He nodded. "Sometimes I miss the code...the knowledge that someone always has your back. I miss the camaraderie and the friendship. Do I miss holding a weapon, using a weapon and dodging enemy fire? Not at all."

Lucy shivered. "I can't begin to imagine what you went through."

"At times it was hell on earth over there. A different world. But it was my job, so I did it the best I could while I was there."

"Why did you leave?' she asked quietly. "You were a career soldier, Brant. You're smart and could have worked in many different areas of the military... Why did you leave so suddenly and come back here and buy a burned-out tavern? It doesn't make a whole lot of sense," she said gently. "Unless something terrible happened that made you leave."

A shutter came down over his gaze. "I can't talk about it."

"You mean you *won't* talk about it," she corrected. "There's a difference, believe me, I know. I spent years refusing to talk about my mom's death and how I was plagued by guilt because I couldn't help her. But when

I did open up I stopped feeling guilty and experienced an incredible sense of freedom. It's like I'd been living in a house of glass, too afraid of what would break if I made a sound. But then I was out of this glass house and I could wave my arms around without breaking anything."

He twisted in the chair, placed the sandwich and soda into the basket and faced her. "Getting inside my head isn't helpful, Lucy. I'm only interested in living in this moment."

"This moment?" she asked. "Right now?"

"Right now," he replied.

"Is that why you're here with me…to be in the moment?"

"I'm here because…" His words trailed as he reached out and touched her chin. "Because the idea of *not* seeing you tonight was unthinkable."

Lucy's lip trembled. "And are you going to kiss me?"

"Yes," he said and took the sandwich from her hands and dropped it in the basket. "If that's okay?"

Her heart pounded behind her ribs. "It's more than okay."

His mouth touched hers gently, coaxing a response, and Lucy gave herself up to his kiss without hesitation. She waited for his advance and then invited him closer, loving how he now felt so familiar, so warm and strong, and how his mouth seemed to fit perfectly to hers. It was a chaste kiss compared to the one they'd shared in his apartment, and since they were in the hospital foyer and anyone could have walked by, Lucy was content to simply feel his mouth gently roam over hers. His hand stayed on her chin, steadying her, and she kissed him back softly, loving the connection, loving the moment. Loving him.

"Lucy…" He suddenly spoke her name in a kind of

agonized whisper. "When your shift is over, come back to my apartment."

"Brant, I—"

"I want to make love to you," he said, trailing his mouth down her jaw. "You're all I can think about."

His words were like music to her ears. He wanted her. She wanted him. It should have been as simple as that. But it wasn't.

"I want that, too…so much."

He clearly heard the reluctance in her voice because he pulled back. "But?"

"But not until you talk to me. Really talk."

"Talk?"

She swallowed hard. "About your past."

He released her and was on his feet in two seconds flat. "Blackmail? Really?"

"Not blackmail," she said in defense. "If I'm going to *be* with someone, I'd like to know who he is."

He frowned. "You know me already."

"I know what you allow people to see," she said. "I know there are things about you that you keep deep inside and are afraid to let anyone see. Including me."

"There's not."

Lucy didn't back down. "I may be naive, Brant, but I'm not gullible. I want to be with you. But I want to get to know you, too. What you think, what you feel." She put a hand to her heart. "In here. And that includes knowing what you went through when you were—"

"How has you and I sleeping together got anything to do with what happened when I was in the military?" he asked, cutting her off.

"It just does."

"No," he said irritably. "This is simply some kind of female manipulation."

"It's not," she implored. "I'm not like that. And there's nothing simple about this."

"How's this for simple?" he shot back. "You want to know about my past because you want to *fix* me. Well, I'm not some kind of renovation project for you, Lucy. I don't need *fixing*. Save that for your patients."

He turned around and walked away, his straight back and tight limbs making his anger abundantly clear.

Lucy watched as he disappeared through the doors and a blast of cold air rushed through the foyer. Her heart sank miserably and she packed up the basket beside her. So much for a romantic dinner for two.

Lucy grabbed the basket, let out a long, unhappy breath, and walked back to the ER.

The Parker-Ellis wedding was being held at Grady's ranch. However, Lucy had stopped by Marissa's place, which was next door to Grady's, to help Brooke and Colleen get the kids ready for the ceremony.

She braided their hair and the three little girls looked so adorable in their lavender-and-ivory dresses. Lucy was a little misty-eyed when she saw how beautiful Marissa was in her lace wedding gown. The other woman positively glowed. Even Brooke, who was as tough as the most ornery cowboy, had a tiny tear in her eye. One day Lucy hoped to be a bride herself. *One day*. When she was over her foolish infatuation with Brant Parker.

She left with Colleen and the kids and took a seat at the back of the ceremony next to her friend Ash. The huge tent had been beautifully decorated, and heaters were discreetly in place to keep the area warm and comfortable for the guests. The white-covered chairs with lavender tulle bows had been laid out in aisle format and, even from the back, she had a great view of the altar. And of Brant.

He stood beside his brother as best man, dressed in a gray suit, white shirt and bolo tie. He looked so handsome. But tense. His jaw was tight and his back straight. And she couldn't take her eyes off him. He turned when the music started and their gazes clashed. In the past two days she'd gone from loving him to hating him, back to loving him and then hating him again.

As she met his gaze head-on and realized he wasn't looking at the bride as she walked down the aisle, as everyone else was, but that he was looking at *her*, Lucy's skin burned from head to toe.

Once Marissa reached the altar, everyone turned to the front. The service was moving and heartfelt, and Lucy wiped tears from her cheeks once the celebrant pronounced them as husband and wife. Grady's daughters were jumping around excitedly as he kissed his bride and the guests erupted into applause they walked back down the aisle. Brant followed with Brooke on his arm and he flipped her a look that was so blisteringly intense as he passed that Ash jabbed her in the ribs.

"Wow," her friend whispered. "What on earth is going on between you two?"

"Nothing," she replied and watched as he escorted Brooke from the tent. It was a gloriously cool but clear day and the wedding party headed out for the photographs to be taken. "It's a long story."

"I like long stories," Ash said as they moved from the seating area toward the other side of the tent where a dozen large round tables were set up with crisp linen and white dinnerware. It was elegant and understated and exactly what a wedding should be, she thought as they wove their way through the tables to find their seats.

But Lucy didn't tell the story. She wasn't in the mood for any kind of post mortem about her aborted relationship with Brant. Because she was pretty sure it was over. Well, whatever they had was over. He'd made no contact for two days and she hadn't garnered the courage to call him, either.

By the time the wedding party returned it was time to be seated for dinner and then the speeches began. If she'd imagined Brant would be nervous giving his speech, she was mistaken. He was charming and funny, sharing anecdotes about his brother that made the audience laugh, and at the end there was a toast and applause.

Then later the bride and groom hit the dance floor and swayed to an old Garth Brooks love song that was so sentimental Lucy wanted to burst into tears. Seeing Grady and Marissa together was seeing real love, firsthand. They'd somehow managed to find one another despite the obstacles they had endured and made a lifetime commitment. She envied them. And felt a little sad for herself.

She looked around and noticed Brant dancing with Brooke. More couples were on the dance floor. Since Ash had been chatting with Kieran for the past hour Lucy was now conspicuously alone at her table. A band of tension tightened around her forehead and she grimaced. The last thing she wanted was a headache.

She needed aspirin so she got up, left the tent and headed around to the back of the house. Lucy let herself through the gate and walked in through the back door. She could still hear the music and laughter coming from the tent, but the house was deserted. She'd been to the ranch several times and knew her way around, so she made her way down the hall toward the main bathroom.

She was just about to open the top vanity cupboard when she heard Brant's voice behind her.

"Everything okay, Lucy?"

She swiveled on her heels. "Fine," she said breathlessly. "I was hoping to find some aspirin."

He frowned. "Kitchen. Pantry. Top shelf." He grabbed her hand. "Come on, I'll get it for you."

Heat coursed over her skin at his touch and she longed for the strength to pull away. But he held her firm and led her down the hall and toward the huge kitchen. When he released her she crossed her arms and waited while he opened the pantry and took out a small container of painkillers. He filled a glass with water and placed both items on the counter.

"Thanks," she said and took the medication.

"Headache?"

"Almost," she replied. "Just getting it before it gets me. So, how's your uncle?"

He shrugged lightly. "He seemed okay when I saw him this morning."

"I checked on him yesterday afternoon and he seems to be recovering quite well."

"I hope so." He rested his hip on the counter. "He was miffed that he missed this today. So, are you enjoying the wedding?"

"Sure," she said, placing the glass down. "You?"

His mouth twisted. "Sure." He met her gaze. "That's why we're both in here."

"I was looking for aspirin," she said and shrugged. "What's your excuse?"

"I was looking for you."

Her heart skipped a beat and she was suddenly absorbed by him. "Why?"

"You know why."

His deep voice resonated around the room and even though she was desperate to leave, she couldn't. "I *don't* know. You're confusing me, Brant. Nothing has changed since the other night."

She was right to say it. Right to remind him.

His gaze darkened as he looked her over. "You look so beautiful in that dress."

The long-sleeved deep red soft jersey dress molded to her breasts and waist and flared out over her hips. She'd had it in her closet for two years with rarely an occasion to wear it. Sometimes she wondered if it was going to gather dust along with her old prom dress. "Thanks. You look pretty good yourself. It still doesn't change anything."

Silence stretched between them and Lucy was so caught up, so hypnotized by his dark blue eyes, she couldn't move. Couldn't think. She could only feel. He looked lost and alone, and she remembered how he'd accused her of wanting to *fix* him. And she did. She longed to make him whole again. Because she knew he would make her whole in return.

"Okay," he said finally, as though it was one of the hardest words he'd ever spoken. "I'll tell you. I don't know why I want to tell you. I don't know what it is about you that makes me want to talk about things that I try not to think about. But for the past two days all I've been able to think about is you when I should be doing a hundred other things."

Lucy's breath caught in her throat. She waited. The silence was agonizing. The hollow, haunted look in his eyes made her ache inside and when he spoke again her heart just about broke into pieces.

"Three men in my unit died," he said quietly, his voice little more than a husky whisper. "And they died because of me."

Chapter Ten

Brant knew there was no taking back the words once they were out. He'd kept them inside for over a year, never daring to say them out loud. It should have felt good. Cathartic. Instead, every morsel of guilt and regret he'd felt since that day came rushing back and almost knocked him over.

Three men—whose names would be forever etched into his blood and bones and his very soul—had died to save him.

"Tell me what happened."

Lucy's voice, soft and concerned. A voice that haunted his dreams and consumed his waking hours. When good sense told him to stay away, he was inexplicably drawn even more toward her. When everyone else made him clam up, Lucy Monero did the opposite. Talking to her was, somehow, salvation.

"They were protecting me," he said flatly.

Her gaze narrowed. "I don't understand."

"I can't tell you anything in detail. This is classified information, or mostly, anyway. I can tell you that I was part of a small team who infiltrated deeply and secretly. We were on a mission and deep in enemy territory. Intelligence is often gathered via listening devices, some high-tech, other times just basic radio-frequency stuff. We'd been listening for several hours and I had information," he explained and tapped a finger to his temple. "In here. I was a translator and because of the situation we were in there was no time to document all the intelligence."

She nodded. "And?"

"Radio contact was made. A pickup point was decided. And then the mission turned bad and we were suddenly surrounded by insurgents. There seemed no way out. We were bunkered down behind a ridge of rock and held that position for eight hours, randomly exchanging gunfire. We all knew it was highly unlikely we'd all survive. Decisions had to be made. And then three other soldiers in my unit lost their lives making sure I got back safely. For the greater good, you see," he said cynically. "Funny—but nothing felt good about any of it."

She took a step closer and grabbed his hands. "I'm so sorry."

"Yeah…me, too. Do you get it now? Do you understand why—?"

"I understand guilt," she said, cutting him off gently. "And I understand why you feel as you do. But they were doing their job, right? Just as you were? Which doesn't make it your fault."

"I know that…logically," he said and gripped her hands. "But there's this thing about logic—it has a way of camouflaging truth and grief and guilt. So it doesn't matter how often I tell myself I'm not to blame. It doesn't matter that the intelligence eventually got into the right hands. It doesn't matter that the insurgents were defeated because of that intelligence. Because all that matters is that three lives were lost…three families are mourning…three men are dead…and I'm not."

She sucked in a sharp breath. "Are you saying you wish you had been?"

Brant shook his head. "Of course not. I'm grateful that I survived. I'm glad my family isn't grieving and I'm certainly glad I'm here, in this room, with you."

She shuddered and he pulled her closer. The awareness between them amplified and Brant fought the urge he had to kiss her. He wasn't going to coerce her in any way. They had heat and attraction between them, and he knew it was powerful for them both, but if they went any further it had to be her decision.

"Brant…" Her voice trailed off and then she inhaled sharply.

"Yes, Lucia?"

"I want to be with you… I do. I want it more than anything. I want you to kiss me and make love to me. But I also want everything else that goes with that."

He knew that. He knew what she was looking for. Commitment. Security. A life. Probably marriage down the track. He'd never been one for commitment and didn't see that changing anytime soon.

"Then you decide what you want to do, Lucy," he said and released her gently. "You know who I am. I've told you what happened and even though you might not understand why, it closed off something inside of me. And because of that I won't make you promises I can't keep. But I want you…and that's all I can offer right now."

Brant turned and left the room. He wasn't going to deceive her.

He cared about her too much for that.

By the time Lucy left the Parker ranch it was past ten o'clock. She drove into town with a heavy heart.

I want you...

His words toyed around with her good sense. She should run a mile. She should forget all about him. Instead she pulled up outside the Loose Moose and stared at the big door. She looked up and saw there was a light beaming in the upstairs window. He *was* home. He'd left the wedding around the same time she had, without speaking to her. If she went inside now they would make love...no doubt about it. If she drove on, Lucy sensed she'd never hear from him again.

And that was...unbearable.

Thirty seconds later she was tapping on the door.

When he opened the door he was still dressed in his suit, minus the jacket. He looked so handsome and his dark hair gleamed in the lamplight overhead.

"Hi."

His eyes glittered brilliantly. "Hello."

"Can I come in?"

He stepped aside and she quickly walked over the threshold. The door closed and she turned. He stood excruciatingly still and Lucy's dangling courage disappeared.

"You look really beautiful tonight," he said softly.

"I think you said that already."

He shrugged. "I don't think you really know how beautiful you are...inside and out."

Heat spotted her cheeks as she stripped off her coat

and placed it on a workbench. "I'm not beautiful...not really."

"You are to me," he said and half smiled. "You're also argumentative and a little stubborn and have a bad temper. But you do look really great in that dress." He took a few steps toward her. "I should have danced with you tonight. I wanted to."

Lucy swallowed hard and then grinned. "It was like prom all over again. No date. No dancing."

Brant stared at her, his gaze unwavering. He came closer and grabbed her hand, linking their fingers in a way that felt so intimate, Lucy's entire body grew hotter with each passing second.

"Come with me," he said and led her across the room.

She thought they were going upstairs, to his bedroom, to his bed, and her nerves had her legs shaking. But he walked past the stairwell and toward the back of the tavern. It had once been a pool room but was now filled with several tables and a stage, as well as two new gaming tables. There was a dance floor and jukebox in one corner. Brant didn't release her as he headed for the jukebox and flicked a few switches before it roared into life. He took a moment to choose a song and then turned her toward the dance floor.

Lucy dropped her bag onto one of the tables and went with him into the center of the floor as the music began. Kenny Chesney's voice suddenly filled the room and Lucy curved herself into Brant's embrace. They fit together, she thought as his right arm came around her waist and his other hand cupped her nape. And then they danced. Slowly, closely, as though they'd done it a hundred times before. His hand was warm against her neck and he rubbed her skin softly with his fingertips.

Lucy gripped his shoulders, felt the muscles harden

beneath her palms and moved closer. There was nothing but clothing between them and she could feel the heat of his body connect with hers.

And then he kissed her, deeply, passionately, as if he couldn't get enough of the taste of her mouth.

Lucy kissed him back and heard him groan as his fingers tangled in her hair. She held on to his shoulders and lost herself in his kiss.

When the song ended Lucy pulled back, breathless, knees trembling.

"Take me upstairs," she said softly.

"Are you sure?"

Lucy nodded. Whatever happened, she wanted this part of him. She wanted his touch and his possession and body next to hers. In that moment, nothing else mattered.

It took about a minute to walk upstairs and into his bedroom. The big bed was covered in a functional blue quilt and, other than two narrow side tables, a small chair and a wardrobe, the room was clearly just a place to sleep. He pulled the curtains together, flicked on the bedside lamp and turned off the overhead light. Then he unclipped his watch, placing it on one of the side tables.

Lucy was so nervous she was sure he could hear her knees knocking together. But she didn't move. She only watched him, mesmerized, well aware that he'd certainly done it all before, many times and with many other women. But she didn't want to think about that.

He tugged at his tie, dropped it on the chair and then began to slowly unbutton his shirt.

She absorbed him with her gaze and her palms itched with the urge to rush forward and run her hands over his chest. He was broad and muscular and so effortlessly masculine. Once the shirt disappeared, his hands rested on his belt and she gulped. Of course she'd seen plenty of naked men in her line of work. But this was different. This was Brant. She was going to touch him. Kiss him. Make love with him. And he would do the same with her. She was suddenly filled with a mixture of fear and wonderment.

"Everything all right, Lucy?" Brant asked as he kicked off his shoes.

She swallowed hard. "Yes…everything's fine."

He pulled the belt through the loops and dropped it on the floor. "*Lucia*…come here." She walked across the room and he grasped her hand. "You're shaking. Are you nervous?"

She nodded. "A little."

"Don't be," he said as gently swiveled her around. "We'll just take it slow."

His fingers found the tab of her zipper and he slowly eased it down. His mouth brushed across her shoulder and she moaned, overwhelmed by the sheer longing she felt for his touch. The gown slipped off her shoulders and fell to her feet. She stepped out of it and inhaled as she turned to face him.

"You're so…" He raked his gaze over her, taking in the red-lace bra and matching thong she'd bought on a whim months earlier and was suddenly very glad she'd teamed with the red dress.

Normally, Lucy was self-conscious of her curves. She never dressed overtly sexy and her underwear was usually the sensible nondescript kind. But the desire in his eyes was hot and real and made her skin burn.

She flipped off her heels and stood in front of him. "I can't believe we're here."

"Believe it," he said and tugged her closer. "I've thought of little else for weeks."

His words enflamed her and Lucy abandoned her

nerves and accepted his kiss. They were on the bed seconds later and she was breathless as his hands caressed her from knee to rib cage. His kissed her throat, her shoulders and the curve of her breasts. Her entire body was on fire and her hands clamored to touch him. She felt his heart beat madly in his chest, twirled her fingers on the trail of hair on his belly and heard him suck in a sharp, agonized breath. He was as weak for her touch as she was for his and the knowledge gave her courage. She didn't feel out of her depth. Touching him felt like the most natural thing in the world.

He dispensed with her bra quickly and touched her breasts with his hands and then his mouth. It was delicious, exquisite torture, and she threw her head back as his tongue toyed with one nipple and then the other. He pushed her thong down her hips and for the next half hour he gave but didn't take.

He kissed her, caressed and stroked her skin. He touched her with his hands, his fingertips and his mouth to the point that every inch of body was übersensitive to his touch. She clung to him. She whispered words she'd never imagined she would utter to another soul and experienced such narcotic pleasure than she was quickly a quivering mass of need.

He knew, somehow, that the sensitive skin behind her knee was an erogenous zone and his touch there made her head spin. He knew that trailing his tongue along the underside of her breast would drive her wild. And, finally, when he touched her intimately, she was so aroused she almost bucked off the bed begging for him to give her the release she suddenly craved. As inexperienced as she was, Lucy somehow knew what she wanted.

"Please," she begged and met his mouth hungrily.

"Not yet," he said with a raspy breath as he caressed

her gently. "We have all the time in the world. There's no need to hurry, Lucia."

There was every need. She wanted to feel him above her, around her, inside her.

But he knew what he was doing. There was a gentle rhythm in his magical touch as he continued to stroke her. And then she was gone, caught up in a vortex of pleasure so intense she thought she might pass out. She moaned and said his name, felt her entire body shudder as she came back down to earth. It was beautiful, frightening, overwhelming…and she knew there was more.

When her hands stopped shaking, she fumbled with the button and zipper on his trousers. She heard laughter rumble in his chest at her eagerness and he quickly took over the task. In a second he was naked and above her, chest to breast, his arousal undeniable.

He reached across the bed and grabbed something from the bedside table. When she realized he had a condom in his hand, she blushed wildly.

"Oh… I didn't think about that," she said suddenly self-conscious.

He chuckled. "Now, Doctor, I don't have to tell you how babies are made, do I?"

Lucy's heart did a backflip at the very idea of having his baby. It was one of the things she wanted most in the world.

"Ah…no. Just caught up in the moment, I guess."

He smiled and kissed her. A deep, drugging kiss that had possession stamped all over it. And she didn't mind one bit. She wanted to be his. She longed for it. Right then and all night long. And forever.

He moved over her and Lucy ran her hands eagerly down his back, urging him closer. She closed her eyes and waited. She knew there would be pain, knew her inexperienced body would resist at first. But she wanted him so much, needed him so much, any fear quickly disappeared. He hovered over her, kissing her neck, her jaw, her mouth, and Lucy welcomed him.

He stilled, rested his weights on his arms and stared down into her face. "Everything all right?"

She nodded. "Of course."

"You're tense," he said and kissed her again. "Relax."

She tried and when he finally was inside her she felt a sharp, stinging pain that made her wince.

He stilled again, more pronounced this time, and his gaze sharpened. "Lucy?" There was query and uncertainty in his voice. And he still didn't move. "What…are you…have you never—?"

"Brant." She said his name urgently, cutting off his words. She held on to his shoulders when she felt him withdraw. "No…don't…please…stay with me."

He knew.

And for a moment she thought she'd lost him.

His gaze bore into hers, absorbing her, asking the question and getting the answer he clearly hadn't expected.

"Lucy…" He said her name again, as if he was torn, unsure.

She gripped him hard and pulled him closer. "Don't leave me."

He gaze wavered and it seemed to take an eternity for him to relax. But he did, finally. He stayed, and that was all she cared about. She felt complete for the first time in her life. Lucy wrapped her arms around him and urged him toward her intimately. He moved against her, kissing her mouth with a mixture of passion and disbelief. And she drew strength from his mixed emotions. She kissed him back. She touched him. She told him what she wanted.

She matched him. They continued that way, moving together, creating a rhythm that was mind-blowing. And when release came again it got them both. Lucy held on as he shuddered above her, loving him with all her heart as she got lost in a world of pleasure so gloriously intense she could only say his name on a sigh.

When it was over, he moved and rolled onto his back. Lucy stayed where she was, breathless and still mindless from the tiny aftershocks of sensation pulsing over her skin. After a few minutes, Brant got up and disappeared into the bathroom. When he returned Lucy still lay on the bed, a sheet half draped over her hips.

He sat on the end of the bed and his skin dappled golden in the lamplight. Lucy reached out to touch him and he flinched. Then he looked at her. There was no mistaking it. He was angry.

"Brant, I—"

"That was your first time?" he asked quietly.

She nodded. "Yes, but—"

"Goddamn it, Lucy! You should have told me."

"It doesn't—"

"Whatever you're going to say," he said, cutting her off as he got to his feet and pulled on a pair of jeans that were on the chair. "Just save it. Because if you think it doesn't matter, you're wrong. It matters, Lucy. It matters so damn much."

He walked out of the room and she heard his feet thump on every stair. Once he was downstairs she stretched and sighed. Her body was still humming, still remembering every touch. She'd imagined making love with Brant countless times and being with him had exceeded anything she'd imagined. She had never expected to feel such a deep, fulfilling connection to another person. If she'd ever doubted that she was in love with him, those doubts were now well and truly gone.

Lucy sat up and swung her knees over the edge of the bed. He was angry and, in typical Brant fashion, when he was mad he closed down. And since Lucy preferred to face an issue head-on, she knew they had to talk.

She got up, grabbed the shirt he'd discarded and slipped her arms into the sleeves. It felt warm against her skin and the scent of his cologne clung to the fabric. She made a bathroom stop. She was still a little tender, but he'd been so gentle with her she knew it would pass quickly. Then she took a deep breath and headed downstairs.

Brant rarely drank hard liquor anymore. But he downed a second belt of bourbon and let the heat slide down his throat.

He was wound up. He couldn't sit still. He paced the rooms downstairs and tried to work out what he was feeling. Guilt. Confusion. Disbelief.

I should have known.

The words kept chanting in his head.

There had always been something innocent about Lucy Monero. She was an intriguing mix of confidence and coyness. Her kisses were sweet and making love to her had been like nothing he'd felt before. Her touch hadn't been tentative, but exploring, inquisitive…like she was experiencing something new and exciting. Of course, now he knew why.

A virgin.

He could barely believe it. Okay, so she *was* kind of wholesome. But she was also twenty-seven. And a successful doctor who'd gone to college and medical school and had lived a full life. Never in his wildest dreams would he have imagined she would be untouched.

"Brant?"

He looked up. She stood silhouetted in the doorway. She was wearing his shirt and with the light behind he could make out every curve and dip of her naked body beneath. His libido spiked instantly. Her hair was mussed and loose around her shoulders and he couldn't help but remember how he'd fisted a handful of her beautiful locks and kissed her throat and neck and breasts. He'd wanted her as he'd never wanted anyone before. Damn…he still wanted her. Everything about her was pure invitation… her skin, her lips, her curves. She was so lovely. So sweet. And sexy, too, even though he was pretty sure she didn't know it.

Brant shook off his thoughts and sat on the edge of one of the tables. He knew they needed to talk. But first he had to ensure she was all right. "Are you okay?"

"I'm fine." She stepped closer and the light behind turned the shirt translucent. "Are *you* okay?"

He shook his head. "We need to talk about this, Lucy."

She bit her bottom lip. "I know you're angry and—"

"I'm not angry," he said. "I'm a little confused. Frankly, I don't understand why you didn't tell me."

She shrugged. "Well, it's not the kind of thing that generally comes up in conversation."

"You're twenty-seven years old," he said flatly. "And up until half an hour ago, you were a virgin. I think that warrants some kind of conversation, don't you?"

She took a few more steps. "Okay… I probably should have said something."

"Probably?"

"All right," she said on a sharp breath. "I just didn't want to make a big deal out of it."

"It *is* a big deal, Lucy," he said quietly. "And if you've waited this long, you know that."

She sat on a chair by one of the pool tables. "I just wanted to be with you tonight."

Brant pushed himself off the table and dragged a chair beside her. "I wanted to be with you, too," he said as he sat. "But it was your first time, Lucy…and that should mean something."

"It did," she whispered. "At least, it did to me."

Guilt hit him squarely between the shoulder blades. "Look, of course it was…great. You're beautiful and sexy…and it's obvious I'm attracted to you."

She raised her hands. "But that's all it is, right?"

"I haven't deliberately misled you, Lucy," he said soberly. "I try not to mislead anyone."

"You're not serious?"

"What does that mean?"

"It means," she said quietly, "that for the past couple of weeks you've been courting me and haven't even realized it."

His back stiffened. "That's not true. I only—"

"Pizza and a football game?" she reminded him. "Comforting me when I had a bad day at work? An impromptu Thanksgiving dinner? Text messages? Phone calls saying how much you missed me? Really…what did you think you were doing?"

He stilled. Was she right? Was he so blind? He liked her…a lot. But the idea of it being more than that made his head ache.

"I guess… I guess I *wasn't* thinking," he admitted. He took one of her hands in his. "Did I hurt you? The first time can be—"

"You didn't hurt me," she said and pulled her hand away. "And you're working yourself up about it for some

reason of your own. I made a decision tonight, Brant…
and I made that decision because I *am* twenty-seven years
old and know exactly what I want." She got to her feet.
"Yes, I have not had a lover before tonight. And maybe
I didn't tell you that exactly, but I've told you plenty
about my life and the kind of person I am. I was a geek
in high school, *remember*?" she said with emphasis. "I
was a bookworm. I didn't have boyfriends. I didn't have
a date for the prom. And I told you I didn't date in college. What did you think that meant? That I was amusing myself with one-night stands instead?"

"Of course not," he said quickly. "I only—"

"I didn't deliberately set out to be a virgin at twenty-
seven. And even if I did, I'm sure that doesn't quite make
me a candidate for *Guinness World Records*."

"That's not what I meant to—"

"I was grieving my mom," she said hotly. "I was still
coming to terms with the accident. And the truth is, I was
so *messed up*, I didn't want to get involved with anyone.
And then when my roommate was attacked it shut something off inside me and all I wanted to do was become
a good doctor. That's all I concentrated on. That's all I
wanted. Not a date. Not a boyfriend. Not sex."

She was breathing so hard her chest rose up and down
and Brant was instantly aroused. She walked away, hands
on hips, clearly irritated. He stood and followed her
around the pool table.

"But you want that now?" he asked. "A boyfriend?
Sex?"

She stopped walking and turned, glaring at him.
"You'd make a rotten boyfriend."

He couldn't help grinning. Even when she was mad-
der than hell she was beautiful.

"You're right about that."

She looked at his chest and then her gaze rose to meet his eyes. "So, I should probably leave."

"If that's what you want."

She scowled and still looked beautiful. "You'd let me go so easily?"

"I never said it would be easy."

She seemed to sway closer. "None of this is easy, is it? Feeling. Wanting. Maybe…" she said as a hand came up and touched his chest. "Maybe it's not meant to be easy. Maybe the struggle is what makes it worthwhile."

"Maybe," he agreed and placed his hand over hers.

"So," she said softly. "What do we do now?"

Brant clasped his hands to her hips and lifted her onto the edge of the pool table. "Now," he said as he settled between her thighs and wound his arms around her, "I guess we do this."

She sighed, all resistance disappearing. "For how long?"

"For now. For as long as it lasts," he said and kissed her.

He knew that Lucy was thinking forever.

And that was something Brant didn't believe in.

Chapter Eleven

Lucy didn't want to think…or imagine…that six days into their *thing* she actually had a boyfriend. But Friday night, after they'd spent two hours in bed together and were now in her kitchen, eating enchiladas and drinking coffee, she figured she could call it a *relationship*. Of sorts.

When they were together Brant was attentive and charming and certainly seemed unable to get enough of her. They made love a lot. He arrived at her place every afternoon at five thirty and was always gone by midnight. They ate dinner, watched television, talked about mundane things and regularly had hot, uninhibited sex that turned her sensible brain to mush. But he never slept over and always called her the following morning to see how she was.

She was on day shift at the hospital and got to sleep in until eight every morning to combat the fatigue she felt, which meant a mad rush getting showered and dressed and to work on time. But she didn't care. She was wrapped in a lovely kind of bubble that had everything to do with the fact that she was crazy in love with Brant and adored every moment they spent together.

"I have the weekend off," she said and sipped her coffee.

Brant looked at her over the mug in his hands. "I know."

She half smiled. "Did you want to do something tomorrow? Or Sunday?"

"I have the kitchen going in at the tavern this weekend," he said quietly. "And the new chef is arriving tomorrow, so I'll be tied up both days. Plus, I want to try and see Uncle Joe. I'll let you know, okay?"

"Oh…sure."

He drank his coffee and then stood, collecting their plates. "There's a game on if you're interested?"

Football? She was learning to like the game and if it meant cuddling up on the couch with Brant, all the better. She nodded. "I was thinking, if you're coming over tomorrow why don't you stay the night and we could go into town Sunday morning for breakfast?"

He stilled and stared at her. "We'll see."

Code for "no chance." Right. Lucy wondered if he was worried about being seen with her. It was a small town and people talked. Although, since his truck had been parked outside her house every night for close to a week, she figured they had probably been outed already. Of course, Kayla had called every day, and Brooke and Ash, who were a little more discreet, had been texting her off and on for two days. Colleen had been noticeably absent and Lucy figured the woman was giving them space.

"If you don't want to spend the night, just say so."

His gaze sharpened. "That's not what I said."

She shrugged. "Actions speak louder than words."

She immediately saw the gleam in his eyes. "They certainly do."

Lucy smiled, caught her bottom lip between her teeth and felt a familiar surge of desire pulse through her body. "Prove it," she said and got up and raced into the living room, well aware he would be ten paces behind her.

By the time he caught up she was turned on and ready for him. He hauled her into his arms and kissed her hotly. She kissed him back and wrapped her arms around his waist. They made it to the sofa in three seconds flat and began stripping clothes off in their usual hurry. She straddled him and linked her arms around his neck.

"Contraception," he said raggedly.

Lucy dug into the pocket of her robe, extracted a foil packet and then rattled it between her fingertips. "Voilà!"

He smiled against her mouth and kissed her hotly. "Sweetheart, you never cease to amaze me."

Lucy's heart surged. It was the first endearment he'd ever called her and she liked it more than she'd imagined. They made love quickly, passionately, as if they couldn't get enough of one another. It was hot and erotic and mind-blowing. Afterward, Brant grabbed the blanket from the back of the sofa and wrapped it around her shoulders.

"It's cold in here. I've let the fire burn down too low," he said and hooked a thumb in the direction of the fireplace. "Remind me to stock up your firewood next week."

His consideration warmed her heart. He was caring and kind and she loved him. And had almost told him so a dozen times in the past week. But she always held back. He wasn't ready for any kind of declaration.

Lucy nuzzled his neck and pressed herself against his chest. "Thank you."

They watched the football game, fooled around a little on the sofa and by eleven-thirty he bailed. She gave him a lingering kiss in the doorway and watched through the front window as he drove away. As usual, once he'd gone, Lucy experienced a kind of aching loneliness. She knew it was foolish. Knew that whatever she was feeling, Brant was certainly not on the same page. He liked her. He wanted her. But that was all he was good for. She'd tried getting him to talk more about what had happened in Afghanistan, but he would shut her down every time she broached the subject. She knew he'd been to see Dr. Allenby again, but had no idea if he was making any progress or if he'd made another appointment. Despite how close they'd become, there was a restless kind of energy around him that was impossible to ignore. It had her on edge…and waiting for the inevitable fallout.

Strangely, he didn't text her Saturday morning and by ten o'clock she gave in and sent him a message. He replied about half an hour later, saying he was tied up and would speak to her later. It left her with a heavy, uneasy feeling in her heart.

Kayla and Brooke dropped in to see her at lunchtime, carrying a pizza and a six pack of pear cider.

"It's about time you came up for air," Kayla said with a grin as they all headed for the kitchen. "By the flushed expression, I take it everything is going well?"

Lucy shrugged. She wasn't sure she wanted to have a post mortem about her relationship with Brant. It felt… disloyal. That was stupid, of course, because Kayla and Brooke were her closest friends and she could always rely on their support and understanding. But she'd essentially always been a private person, and being with Brant on the most intimate level was not something she wanted to discuss or dissect.

"Yeah...fine," she said and grabbed plates from the cupboard. "How are you both?"

Brooke, certainly the most diplomatic of the pair, gave her arm a gentle squeeze when they all sat. "We're worried about you, that's all."

"I'm fine," she assured them. "I promise."

Kayla's perfectly beautiful face was marred with a frown. "We don't quite believe you. And we're here if you need to talk."

She knew that. But, strangely, the only person she wanted to confide in was Brant. She liked the way he listened. She liked the way he stroked her hair when she'd talked about her mom and the accident and how helpless she'd felt. She liked how there was no judgment, no condescending advice...only his deep voice assuring her the pain and hurt would eventually pass. The irony was, it was exactly what she wanted to say to him. They were both broken in their own way. Sure, she'd moved on and seen a therapist and didn't have bad dreams anymore, but a part of her would always grieve for the years she'd lost with her parents. And Brant understood that grief better than anyone ever had.

Sometimes when he'd dozed a little after they'd made love, she'd witnessed his restlessness. He had bad dreams, she was sure of it. She hadn't said anything to him about it, but knew he was certainly reliving the horror of what he'd seen in the war. And it broke her heart that she couldn't help him through his pain.

She looked at her friends and felt their sympathetic stares through to her bones.

"I'm fine, like I said. It's early days, that's all."

"Good," Kayla said and sighed heavily. "We just weren't sure if you knew about the woman he was with this morning."

Her back stiffened. "What woman?"

"I saw him at the coffee place next door to O'Sullivan's. They were talking. It looked serious."

He was with another woman. And it looked serious.

Lucy wondered if there had ever been a bigger fool than her. But she pasted on a smile and shrugged. "I'm sure there's a perfectly reasonable explanation."

Her friends didn't look too convinced. Heat burned the backs of her eyes and tears threatened to spill.

"I'm in love with Brant," she said honestly.

Brooke patted her arm again. "Yeah, we know that."

"I've never been in love before," she admitted, aware her friends knew it already.

Brooke offered a gentle smile. "Does he love you back?"

Lucy shook her head, suddenly hurting all over. "I don't think he believes he's capable of loving anyone."

And knowing he believed he was that hollow inside made her heart ache.

Saturday lunch at his mother's wasn't generally a chore, but Brant was in no mood to be put under the microscope by his parent or his brother. He planned to stop in for an hour before he got back to the tavern to tackle the painting. He'd had half the kitchen installed at the tavern that morning and the contractors were coming back the following day to finish the job. He'd also interviewed the new chef and discovered the thirtysomething single mom had excellent credentials and stellar references. She also had nowhere to live, since she was relocating from Montana with her young son, and Brant had assured her he would help her find suitable accommodation. His apartment above the tavern would do the job, and since he hadn't planned on making it his permanent residence, he needed to think about getting a real home of his own. A house, with a yard and a porch and a maybe a swing set out back.

As soon as he had the thought, Brant shook himself. He had no place in his life for yards and swing sets. That was the kind of life his brother had. Not him.

Only…he kept thinking about it. About yards and swing sets and Lucy Monero.

"Everything okay?"

His brother's voice jerked him into the present. Grady and Marissa had forgone a honeymoon and instead planned to head to Nevada with her father, Rex, after Christmas to meet her newly discovered extended family. Brant hadn't been home for the holidays in six years and suspected this one was going to be filled with the usual family gatherings and gift-giving.

"Fine," he said and met his brother's gaze for a moment. They were in the living room, watching a game on television. "How's married life?"

"Amazing." Grady grinned. "You should try it for yourself."

He wasn't about to admit that he'd thought about it many times over the past week. About as often as he'd thought about *ending* his relationship with Lucy. Damn… he didn't want to think of it in terms of being a *relationship*, but how could he not? She'd gifted him the most intimate part of herself and the responsibility of that gift was wreaking havoc with his integrity and moral compass. Lucy wasn't a casual kind of woman. Lucy Monero was the *marrying* kind. If he kept seeing her that's where they'd end up. He was sure of it. And he couldn't. He wouldn't. Having sex with her was addling his brain. He felt weak. Out of control.

He stared at the television and spoke. "I've done something really stupid."

Grady glanced sideways. "And what's that?"

"Lucy."

His brother chuckled softly. "Yeah, I heard. Mom's over the moon. But you know it might just turn out to be the smartest thing you've ever done."

He shook his head. "I can't give her what she wants."

"What's that?"

"Everything," he replied.

"And why do you think you can't give it to her?" Grady asked, more serious.

He exhaled heavily. "Because I'm not made that way. I don't know…maybe I was once. But…"

"The war changed you?" Grady said. "No surprise there. It would change anyone."

Brant nodded. "I've been talking to Dr. Allenby…you know, at the veterans home."

"How's it going?"

He shrugged. "He knows his stuff. He's easy to talk to and doesn't push too hard. But I've talked to army shrinks before and it hasn't made any difference. What's in here—" he put a finger to his temple "—is there forever. I can't escape it. I can't deny it. I'm just trying to camouflage it so I can lead a normal sort of life."

"And Lucy?" Grady prompted.

"She rips through that camouflage without even knowing it." He ran a frustrated hand through his hair. "Or maybe she does. I don't know. All I do know is that when I'm around her I feel… I feel so damned…"

"Vulnerable?" his brother said and sighed. "I hate to break this to you, but that's got nothing to do with you being changed somehow by what you experienced in the war."

Brant frowned. "Then what is it?"

"It's because you're in love with her," Grady said frankly.

Every part of him stilled and he quickly dismissed his brother's words. "I'm not. I just feel…responsible."

Grady's eyes widened. "For what? She's not pregnant is she?"

Brant scowled quickly, looking around to make sure his mother or sister-in-law weren't nearby and spoke quietly. "No. But she…" His words trailed off. He wasn't about to betray Lucy's confidence, as much as he felt like spilling his woes to his brother. "It's private and not up for discussion. But let's just say that she…surprised me."

His brother shook his head. "You can be cryptic if you have to, but the truth is you've always had blinders on when it came to Lucy Monero. She was the girl next door, remember? The girl who used to look at you with puppy-dog eyes and who you never noticed because you were too busy trying to score with Trudy What's-Her-Name. Now you've come to come to your senses and finally noticed her and it turns out she still has a thing for you." Grady's eyes gleamed. "Sounds like love to me."

Brant shook his head. "You can make fun all you like, but I have my reasons for feeling responsible for hurting her. You're right, she waited for me," he said, flinching inwardly, wondering what Grady would think if he knew the true meaning of the words. "She chose me and I have no idea why. All week I've been trying to work out ways to end it. But then she looks at me, or touches me, and I'm done for. I feel as though I'm in a corner and there's no way out. And the thing is," he admitted wearily, "part of me doesn't want a way out."

Grady smiled and slapped him on the shoulder. "Well, I guess there's only one thing you can do."

"What's that?"

"You should do the smart thing and marry her."

When Lucy didn't hear from Brant again on Saturday, or on Sunday morning, she began imagining a dozen different scenarios. Maybe his coffee date had turned into something else. Something more. But by midday she'd worked herself up and was so mad with him she knew if she stayed home she'd stew all day and ruin what was left of her weekend.

She drove to Kayla's in the afternoon and ended up staying for dinner. Kayla was all commiseration and support and by the time they'd consumed three cups of coffee and a packet of Oreos, Lucy had convinced herself that Brant was seeing someone else and his silence meant he was breaking things off between them. She left at eight o'clock and drove down the street, pulling over beneath a streetlight. She grabbed her cell and sent him a text.

I need to see you.

A couple of minutes later she got a reply.

I'm kinda busy right now. But I'll call you later.

Later? Right. Her rage turned to hurt and then her hurt morphed back into rage. Well, if he was seeing someone else she certainly wanted to know about it. She might be foolishly naive…but she wasn't going to be a naive fool!

I'll be there in five minutes.

She didn't wait for a response and drove back into town. Six minutes later she pulled up outside the tavern.

Lucy didn't bother with her coat, instead she grabbed her tote, got out of the car, marched up to the door and banged so hard her knuckles hurt. The big door swung back and he stood in the doorway, dressed in old jeans that rode low on his hips, a long-sleeved, pale gray Henley T-shirt and sneakers.

He was also covered in paint from head to toe.

"What are you doing?" she asked.

"Painting myself," he said, grabbing her arm and hauling her across the threshold. "More the point, what are you doing out this late and without a coat? Are you trying to catch pneumonia?"

She shivered as the cold from the air outside seeped through her thin clothing. "My coat is in the car."

"There's a fire going in the back room," he said. "Warm yourself up while I grab you a sweater."

Lucy walked to the rear of the tavern and stood by the big fireplace. She noticed a couple of ladders with a timber plank between them and a tin of paint on its side and a pool of paint on the floor. He returned a couple of minutes later with a blue zip-up sweater. She took it and placed her arms through the sleeves.

"Um, it looks like you had a little accident?" She pointed to the paint spill.

"Someone texted me," he replied pointedly. "I was on the ladder with a bucket of paint in one hand and brush in another. I went for my phone, it slipped out of my hand and almost landed in the paint. I figured a tin of spilled paint was the lesser of two evils."

Lucy bit back a grin. He still had some explaining to do. "Are you seeing someone else?"

"What?" he shot back as he grabbed a towel from the bench top and wiped at some of the paint on his face and neck.

Lucy stepped forward and took the towel from him. "Someone else," she said again as she removed a smear of paint from his jaw. "As in, the woman you had coffee with yesterday."

He sighed, clearly exasperated. "Faith O'Halloran has just moved to Cedar River from Montana with her young son," he explained. "She's the new chef. The coffee *date* was an interview."

Lucy fought the sudden embarrassment clinging to her skin. Damn Kayla and her overly suspicious mind. "Oh… I see."

He took the towel back. "So, is the interrogation over?"

She shrugged lightly. "Mostly. You've got paint in your hair." She grabbed the towel again and started on the paint smear on his throat. "And everywhere else, by the look of things. Why are you working so late anyhow?"

"I've got some of the interior fit-out next week," he said, standing perfectly still. "I told you I was working this weekend."

She avoided his gaze and kept wiping his throat. "You said you were busy."

"Yes, busy…working." He shook his head. "The kitchen went in this weekend, remember?" He took the towel and tossed it aside. "I'm going to clean up this mess, take a shower and then we're going to talk. Or—" He grabbed her around the waist, careful not to get paint on her clothes, and looked down into her upturned face. "You could take a shower with me and we could skip the talking for an hour or two."

Lucy liked the sound of that idea.

An hour later they were lying side by side on his bed, spent and breathing hard.

"Incidentally," Brant said as he entwined their fingers. "I'm trying not to take offense at the fact you thought I was seeing someone else. I'm many things, Lucia, but unfaithful is not one of them."

Lucy grimaced. "I'm sorry. Put it down to inexperience. I'm not very knowledgeable when it comes to this kind of…" She waggled the fingers on her other hand. "Thing."

"You're not alone," he said quietly. "I haven't exactly embraced commitment for the past decade."

She grinned. "Your virgin heart. My virgin body. That's quite a combination."

He laughed softly and his grip tightened. "Lucy… I'd like to know something."

"Sure. What?"

"I don't quite know how to put this without sounding incredibly egotistical…but why did you really wait so long to have a physical relationship with someone? Did it have anything to do with me? Or to some old infatuation you may have had from when we were kids?"

Lucy shrugged lightly. "Not consciously. I mean, sure… I did have a little crush on you in high school. But I was so quiet and ridiculously self-conscious in high school. And once I got to college, sex seemed like some kind of tradable commodity. The bed hopping wasn't something I wanted for myself. And then when my roommate was attacked…it just seemed like one complication I didn't need."

"But once you were working and out of college, surely there were men interested in you?"

"Not so much," she admitted. "I think that when a person puts a wall up for long enough, people stop trying to find a way over the top. And I had a wall that was ten feet high."

"What about Kieran O'Sullivan?" he asked.

"A friend," she replied. "No blip, remember?"

"So…there was no one else you were interested in being with? Ever?"

Heat crawled over her skin. How did she respond without sounding like an immature, love-struck fool? "I guess I didn't want to kiss a whole lot of frogs before I discovered princes didn't really exist."

Silence enveloped the dimly lit room for a moment. Lucy could hear him breathing and watched the steady rise and fall of his chest. After a moment he spoke again.

"Are you saying you hadn't…" His tone took on a kind of wary disbelief. "That you hadn't—"

"That I hadn't really kissed anyone before you?" she finished for him. "I guess I hadn't."

She heard his sharp intake of breath and felt the tension seep through his body. "Lucy…why me?"

Heat caught in her throat and she swallowed hard. "You know why."

He sighed heavily. "You could have any man you wanted…someone who can give you what you're looking for…marriage…family…"

When his words trailed off, Lucy's heart twisted. "And that's not you, is that what you're saying?"

He sighed again, wearily, as though he had a great burden pressing down on his chest. "A week ago you said I'd been courting you and didn't even know it…and you were right. That was unfair of me. I don't—"

"Am I being dumped?" she asked hotly, jackknifing up.

He straightened. "That's not what I meant."

"Then what?" she demanded. "Your hot-and-cold routine is tiring, Brant." Lucy shook her head and sighed. "How about we get some sleep and talk about this tomorrow?"

Brant stood, unselfconsciously naked and so gorgeous

she almost crawled across the bed and pressed herself against him. But his next words turned her inside out.

"You can't stay here."

She watched as he grabbed a pair of fresh jeans from the wardrobe and slipped them on.

Lucy scrambled her legs together. "Now you're kicking me out?"

He ran a hand through his hair. "I just think it would be best if you went home."

Lucy got to her feet and stood toe-to-toe with him. His gaze raked over her, hot and filled with an almost reluctant desire. Even when they were in the middle of a crisis, the attraction they had for one another was undeniable.

Lucy stood her ground. "No."

His gaze narrowed. "No?"

"I'm staying."

He inhaled sharply and grabbed her dress from the chair in the corner. "Get dressed."

"Forget it, soldier," she said, hands on hips. "Because if I go, I go for good."

"Then go," he said coldly and walked toward the door.

"What is it, Brant?" she demanded as she quickly got into her dress and smoothed the fabric over her hips. "What is it you're so afraid of?"

He stopped instantly and turned. "Afraid?" he echoed, his blue eyes glittering. "I'm not afraid of anything."

"I don't believe you," she snapped, going for his emotional jugular because if she didn't she knew she would lose him forever. "So, what is it? Are you scared that if I spend the night, if I sleep in your bed, that at some point I'm going to witness the *real* you? The you who paces the floorboards at night? The you who breaks out in a cold sweat at two o'clock in the morning? The you who has bad dreams and cries in his sleep?"

He paled instantly. "How…how do you know that?" he asked raggedly.

Her heart ached for him and she pressed a hand to his chest. "Because I *know* you. In here. I'm connected to you in a way I've never been connected to anyone in my life. Don't you get it, Brant? *I love you.*"

It was out.

There was nothing for either of them to hide behind.

Just her heart on the line.

Lucy stared at him, absorbing every feature, every conflicting emotion, evident in his expression. But he didn't speak. He didn't move. He simply looked at her. Into her. Through her. Time seemed to stretch like brittle elastic until, finally, he spoke.

"It's late. Get some sleep."

He turned and left the room and Lucy didn't take a breath until she couldn't hear his footsteps on the stairs. She sat on the bed and sucked in an agonizing breath. Did the man have ice water in his veins? Had she given herself and her love to someone who was impervious to deep feeling?

No…

She knew him. He was kind and compassionate and capable of much more than he realized.

Lucy lay on the bed and closed her eyes. She was so tired, weary from tension and knowing she had to go to work the following day. She inhaled, relaxed her aching shoulders and tried to rest, hopeful that at some point Brant would join her in the big bed.

But he didn't.

Lucy woke up around six and, after a quick bathroom stop, headed downstairs. Brant was awake and behind the main bar, sorting through paint swatches. He wore jeans and a dark sweater and looked so gorgeous her mouth turned dry.

"Hi," she said as cheerfully as she could muster. "Did you manage to get some sleep?"

He hooked a thumb in the direction of a narrow cot in one corner. "A little. You?"

She nodded. "I could make breakfast if you—"

"No…but thank you."

She inhaled sharply. "I guess I should go. I'll just get my things."

Lucy didn't wait for a reply and swiveled on her feet. When she came back downstairs a few minutes later he was near the front of the tavern, piling cut pieces of timber into stacks. "Will I see you later?"

He looked up and straightened. "I'll probably be tied up here all day."

Lucy nodded and walked toward the door. She grabbed the handle, lingered and then turned back to him. "You know, Brant, I've pretty much been in love with you since I was fifteen years old."

He stilled instantly, his blue-eyed gaze riveting her to the spot. The silence between them was suddenly deafening. But she kept going, too far in to back down.

"Do you remember the day you took Trudy to the prom?" she asked but didn't wait for him to respond. "I was at your ranch with my mom. Your dad and Grady were helping my mother sell our ranch and they were all in the kitchen talking and I was sitting by the counter, my head in a book, as always. I used to hang around your ranch and watch you and your brother break and train the horses. Or your mom would give me baking lessons. But that day you came into the room dressed in your suit with a corsage for Trudy and you looked so handsome and grown-up. I knew once school was over that you would be leaving for the military and for the hundredth time I wished I was older, prettier, more popular... And I wished that the corsage was for me and you were taking me to prom."

She sighed, remembering the ache in her young heart that day. "Then you left town and I finished high school and went to college and med school. Years passed and occasionally our paths would cross and you would usually ignore me, and I got used to that. When I returned to town permanently I knew I wanted to work at the hospital and settle down in Cedar River and hopefully find someone to share my life with." Her voice quivered as tears filled her eyes. "Then you came back and I tried to act like I was indifferent and over my silly infatuation. But I knew I'd been fooling myself. Because," she said, putting her hand to her chest as tears fell down her cheeks, "in here...in here I was still that insecure fifteen-year-old girl, dreaming about corsages and going to the prom with Brant Parker."

She pulled her tote close to her body and grabbed the door handle. "I know you believe you can't make a commitment, Brant...and I think I understand why. But, despite how much I love you and love being with you, I need to end this now... I need to stop kidding myself into thinking that what we have is enough for me. Because it's not."

She left the tavern and walked to her car. There was a light blanket of snow on her windshield and she flicked it off before she climbed into the car and drove home.

But the time she arrived at work an hour later, she was hurting all over.

Brant didn't call her that day. Or the next.

However, Lucy called him late Wednesday afternoon and left three messages on his cell.

Because at one o'clock on Wednesday, Joe Parker had another heart attack and was rushed into the ER by the paramedics, but tragically died forty minutes later.

Chapter Twelve

Brant ignored every message on his phone for several days. His uncle was dead and Lucy had left him. She had her reasons and it was probably the right thing. But by Friday he was so wound up he could barely stand being in his own skin.

He met Grady at the funeral home late in the afternoon and finalized the funeral arrangements for the following Monday. The service was to be held at the small cemetery on the edge of town and his uncle would be laid to rest next to their father and grandparents.

"Are you coming back to the ranch?" Grady asked once they'd left the funeral home. "The girls would love to see you."

Brant shook his head. "I've got things to do."

Grady grabbed his shoulder, looked concerned and didn't bother to disguise it. "I don't think you should be alone."

"I'm fine."

When they got to the parking lot, his brother scowled when he saw the motorbike. "Really? In this weather?"

"It was clear when I left the tavern."

Grady held out his palm and caught a few flakes of snow that were now falling. "It's not clear now. I'll drive you back and you can pick the bike up tomorrow."

They both knew he would never leave his motorbike unattended. "Stop fussing like an old woman."

Grady made an exasperated sound. "All right, just be careful riding home in this."

"I will," Brant promised.

His brother nodded and then spoke. "So, have you seen Lucy?"

"No," he replied.

Grady pulled his coat collar up around his neck. "She was there, you know, at the end, holding his hand, giving him comfort."

Brant ignored the tightness in his chest. Yeah, she was good at holding hands. Good at comfort. And good at ending things. "I gotta run. See you tomorrow."

He grabbed his helmet, straddled the bike and was about to say goodbye when his brother spoke again.

"I've always tried to avoid telling you how to live your life or give advice. But I'm going to give you some now. You need to face this, Brant."

His back tensed. "Face what?"

Grady waved a hand. "This thing with Lucy. You served three tours in the military and much of that time was spent on the front line. You're a soldier and one of the bravest men I know. So tell me, what is it about loving this woman that scares you so much?"

"I don't love her," he said coldly as he kicked the bike into life and drove off.

Twenty minutes later, after circling Lucy's block for the third time, he pulled up in her driveway and killed the engine. She wasn't home. He checked his watch. Five-fifteen. She was probably out with her friends at O'Sullivan's. Or she was working. Or on a date.

Brant climbed off the bike and headed for the small porch. He zipped up his leather jacket and sat in the love seat. And waited.

She arrived home twenty minutes later. Wrapped up in a scarlet woolen coat with fake fur trim, black boots, knitted gloves and a white beanie, she looked like she belonged on a Christmas card. Her cheeks were spotted with color and her lips looked lush and red. And imminently kissable.

She seemed neither surprised nor unsurprised to see him as she sat wordlessly beside him on the love seat. He didn't touch her. He didn't dare, despite how much he longed to.

"You didn't reply to my text messages," she said quietly.

"I haven't been doing much of anything this week."

She nodded fractionally. "I was worried about you."

He knew she would have been. "I'm sorry. I've been keeping to myself...trying to make sense of it all."

"And did you?" she asked softly.

He half shrugged. "Not so much. I miss him already."

"I know," she said, her gentle voice somehow soothing some of the pain he felt. "Are you still seeing Dr. Allenby?"

One thing he could always rely on—Lucy Monero never pulled punches or talked in riddles. She was honest and forthright and demanded the same in return.

"Yes," he replied. "I saw him Monday and I have another appointment next week."

"It's helping?"

"I think so...yes."

"I'm glad," she replied and, after a small silence, spoke again. "But what are you really doing here?"

"Grady told me that you were with my uncle when he died," he said, conscious of the heavy weight pressing down on his shoulders. "I just wanted to thank you for that and for your kindness toward him these past few weeks. It's meant a lot to us." He paused, took a breath, felt an uneasy ache in the middle of his chest. "And to me."

She nodded. "I wish I could have done more."

"If yours was the last face he saw before he passed away," Brant said quietly, "then I'm sure he would have died with peace in his heart. So, thank you."

"He was a nice man and I cared about him a great deal." She met his gaze, unwavering. "But anything I did...I did for you."

The sensation in his chest amplified and he swallowed hard. God, she undid him with just a few words. He got up and grabbed the helmet. "I know that. Goodbye, Lucy."

She was frowning. "Should you be biking in this weather?"

Brant looked at the snow still coming down. "I'll be careful."

He got to the steps and then turned. She was still sitting, still looking lost and lovely. His heart thundered in his chest. "You know, I did hear you the other night. Everything you said...you were right to say it. The thing is, I came back to Cedar River to try and forget what happened in Afghanistan. But most days, I still feel as though I'm back on that ridge, back dodging bullets and back hearing the screams of men who died so I could live.

And knowing the only reason it turned out that way is because I had an aptitude for learning another language. If I'd been good at math instead, things would have turned out very different. So, when it's two in the morning and I can't do anything other than stare at the ceiling instead of sleeping, or when my dreams are so bad I wake myself up screaming, I think about how a high school French class probably saved my life."

She stared at him. Through him. Into the very depths of his blood and bones and then further still, right into his soul. No one else had ever done that. No one ever would.

When she spoke again he could barely stand to hear the words. "Part of me wants to wish you and your guilt a long and happy life together. But I can't...because that would simply be my broken heart talking." She got to her feet. "I'll see you at the service on Monday."

Brant looked at her and every conflicting emotion he had banged around in his head. Part of him longed to take her in his arms, part of him ached for her touch. "Thanks again...for everything."

She nodded. "Sure. Goodbye."

Brant watched as she turned, walked into the house and closed the door. Lights flicked on and her silhouette passed by the window, and he was suddenly overwhelmed by an inexplicable urge to knock on her door to beg her to let him stay the night. But then she'd witness his truth—the insomnia, the pacing at two o'clock in the morning, the dampness on his face when he jackknifed out of bed in the middle of a nightmare. He'd tried medication and all it did was dull his senses. Alcohol left him hung over and weary for days. The only solution was to ride through it in private. No one needed to witness his anxiety. She already thought he needed a shrink. If she saw him at two in the morning, drenched in sweat, shaking from fear, she'd run a mile. Or worse, she'd stay. Out of pity and concern. And *that* was worse than not being with her.

It was better this way. For them both.

Brant got through the weekend by working at the tavern and on Monday ran on autopilot during his uncle's funeral. About eighty people turned up for the service, half of them Joe Parker's former army buddies. The minister gave a short reading, as did Grady and then Brant, and while most of the military crew went to Rusty's afterward to celebrate their fallen colleague with a round of beer and shared tales from the war, Brant returned to the ranch with his mother and brother and about twenty close friends, including Lucy.

By the afternoon there were just half a dozen people left, most bailing before the snow came down heavier. Brant sat on the wide veranda, an untouched coffee in his hand. Grady and Brooke were in the kitchen and Marissa was in the playroom with the kids. He spotted Lucy walking across the yard toward the stables. She had on her red coat and it was a stark contrast against the white backdrop of snow. He watched her as she walked, like a vision in red, like a beacon for his weary soul.

A surge of feeling suddenly rose up and hit him squarely in the solar plexus and he couldn't quite get enough air into his lungs. He didn't know what to make of it. Or what to think. Only Lucy could do that. No one had ever had such a profound effect on his peace of mind. His body. His heart.

They'd barely spoken all day. Strangely, it was as though they didn't need to. But during the service he'd felt her behind him and then her small hand had rested on his back. It was all he'd needed to get through the moment. And she'd known that, wordlessly. Because she knew him better than anyone.

He watched her as she walked around alone, moving in circles, almost as though she was so deep in thought she didn't care where she ended up.

"Do you remember what I said to you a few weeks back?"

His mother's voice made him turn his head for a moment. Sometimes his mom had the stealth of a jungle cat. "What?"

"That she would be a good match for you," Colleen reminded him, inclining her head toward Lucy. "I still believe it."

"Not today Mom, okay?"

"Did you know that your dad was terrified of enclosed spaces and had night terrors?"

Brant snapped his gaze around. "What do you mean?"

"He fell down a mine shaft when he was eight years old. He was trapped there for two days. He used to wake up screaming some nights. Knowing he had fears, flaws…it didn't make me love him any less."

Brant's stomach dropped. "Mom, don't."

"The fact that he could admit it," she said pointedly. "That's what made him strong. And a better man for it. And it made me love him even more."

Brant watched Lucy wander by the stables as his mother spoke. He resisted the urge to join her, to hold her steady as she trudged over the thin blanket of snow, to keep her safe.

I've pretty much been in love with you since I was fifteen years old…

Lucy's words echoed in his head and then lodged in his chest. No one had ever uttered those words to him before…and certainly not with such heartbreaking honesty. But Lucy was always honest.

Right from the start she'd told him the truth. Right from the start she'd had a way of making him think and feel when he'd believed himself too numb to feel anything. The way she'd opened up about her own past had switched something on inside him. She had demons… regrets…but she'd forged ahead, carving out a successful career and becoming a kind, compassionate and considerate person. The best person he'd ever known. And she'd shared a part of herself with him so earnestly…so honestly. It wasn't just sex. Being with Lucy was like nothing he'd experienced before. Making love to her, feeling her touch, watching her come apart in his arms, was both spiritual and physical. The perfect moment. The perfect feeling. She was perfect.

"I know you were incredibly close to your uncle," his mother said quietly. "But don't go down the same lonely road that he did. When Joe came back from the war without one of his legs he thought he was somehow defined by that…so he never allowed himself to have a serious relationship with anyone. He never fell in love. He never had a family of his own. And I don't want the same thing to happen to you."

"It won't, Mom," he assured her. "I'm not an amputee for one—"

"Some wounds are on the outside, some are on the inside," she said with emphasis.

"She's right."

Grady's voice snapped his head around. His brother came up behind them and stood to Brant's left. Flanked by his mother and brother, he felt like he was suddenly in the center of an intervention. And in that moment all he wanted to do was to head down the stairs and find solace with Lucy. Looking at her walking through the snow alone made his insides ache. And the only thing that would appease that ache would be to be by her side... by sitting on the couch holding hands or watching football over cold pizza and beer. By kissing her beautiful mouth. By making love with her and feeling the tenderness of her touch. She was the tonic he needed. She was *all* he needed.

Brant stilled and every muscle in his body tightened. *He really needed her.*

When he'd convinced himself he didn't need anything or anyone. Only solitude and time to dilute the pain and guilt that some days seemed etched into his very soul. And yet, Lucy knew that. She knew that and still wanted him. *Still loved him.* Because she was strong and courageous. She'd traveled her own road, recovering from the grief of losing her mother so tragically, and still found the strength and fortitude to allow someone into her heart. To allow *him* into her heart...even though he'd pushed her away again and again.

And he knew why.

Because he was scared. Terrified that he wouldn't measure up, that she'd think him weak, unworthy. That she would see him at his worst and still stay...out of loyalty. And pity. And that would be unbearable. He didn't want her sympathy. He didn't want her thinking she needed to fix him. He wanted to meet her head-on. Without fear.

Because...

Because he was in love with her. Wholly and completely.

Lucy Monero held every part of his heart and body and soul.

He watched her, a breathtaking vision in her red coat,

her head bent and her beautiful hair spilling out from beneath her hat. No one could ever come close. No one ever would.

Brant looked at his mother and then at Grady, and finally let out a long breath before speaking the words that were in his heart. "I'm in love with Lucy."

Grady laughed softly and his mother squeezed his arm. "Yes, we know," she said.

"The thing is," his brother said, still smiling, "what are you going to do about it?"

Brant looked toward the stables, watched her as she walked, his heart and mind filling with a kind of peace he'd never know before. "I'm going to ask her if she'll have me."

And he knew just how to do that.

Lucy was glad to be back at work. It was two days after Joe Parker's funeral and she was trying to get her life back into some kind of bearable rhythm. The hospital was busier than usual for a Wednesday, and since Christmas was only a couple of weeks away, there seemed to be an increase in the number of tourists coming into the ER with everything from stomach bugs to blisters. Lucy put on her best smile and spent the first few hours of her shift in Triage.

And she tried to *not* think about her broken heart.

It wasn't easy. Everything reminded her of Brant. Every time she walked into the ER she remembered him the afternoon his uncle had been brought in so many weeks ago, and how she'd quickly found herself in his relieved embrace. She couldn't walk through the front foyer without remembering how he'd brought her dinner on Thanksgiving. And at home the memories were even more intense. Sitting on the couch drinking beer and eating pizza, watching a silly football game together, making love as though there were no other people on earth. *Everything* reminded her of Brant. And her dreams offered no respite. He filled them, consumed them, and each morning she woke lethargic and with a heavy heart.

Kayla stopped by with lattes at lunchtime on Wednesday and Brooke called her after lunch to ensure she was okay. Ash came in around two o'clock to question a young man who'd been in a minor vehicular accident and had whiplash. She stayed to chat for a few minutes and Lucy tried to appear to be her usual happy self. She knew what her friends were doing and loved them for it…but mostly, she just wanted to be left alone.

There was nothing anyone could say or do to ease the ache in her heart and she didn't want to burden her friends with her unhappy mood. She'd get over it in her own time. Once she stopped thinking about Brant. And dreaming about him. Only then would she stop loving him.

She'd considered calling him several times in the past couple of days, but every time she grabbed her cell phone she simply stared at the screen. They had nothing to say to one another and no words were necessary. She knew how he felt. He couldn't give her what she wanted and she couldn't settle for anything less.

I just need some time to get over him.

But as she thought the words she didn't really believe them.

By three o'clock the flow of patients into the ER had eased. Lucy was about to make a final walk around the ward before she prepared to go home when she was paged. She answered the call and was asked to go down to the main reception area as there was someone waiting to see her. Thinking it was one of her friends again,

Lucy grabbed her white coat and slipped it on before she headed out through Triage and toward the front of the building. When she stepped out of the elevator she took a left turn and stopped in her tracks, suddenly poleaxed.

There were several people walking through the foyer, but she only saw one.

Brant...

He stood by the small bench seat where they had shared dinner from a basket and drank sodas. But this time he was dressed immaculately in a tuxedo and shiny black shoes and he carried a small, clear box with a flower inside.

Lucy stared at him, mesmerized. He looked so good. So handsome. His blue eyes glittered and his dark hair shone beneath the bright overhead lights. He didn't move and Lucy somehow found the strength to take a few steps toward him. Suddenly she didn't see anyone else or hear anyone else in the room. Only him.

Finally, he held out the small box and spoke.

"I just want you to know," he said, his deep voice like silk, "that you will always have a date for the prom."

Lucy's breath caught and tears instantly heated her eyes.

It was the single most beautiful, romantic moment of her life.

She wanted to race into his arms. But she held back. That had a lot to talk about. A lot to think about.

"Is...is that for me?" she asked.

He nodded. "Everything is for you, Lucia."

Lucy experienced an acute sense of joy and stepped a little closer. He was in front of her, dressed in a suit and holding a corsage, with his heart on his sleeve and no walls between them. And in that moment she had never loved him more.

"Brant…" Her words trailed off as emotion clogged her throat.

"Lucy," he said softly and held out his hand. "Is there somewhere we can talk in private?"

She nodded, took his hand and walked away from reception and up the corridor. There were several empty offices and she tapped on one of the doors and entered. If anyone walked by she didn't notice. She saw only him. She didn't care if anyone wondered why the most gorgeous man on the planet was doing with a harried-looking doctor wearing scrubs and a white coat.

The room was a small and perfunctory—typical of any administration office, with a desk, filing cabinet and two chairs. She closed the door and turned to face him. He held out the box again. She took it with trembling hands and looked at the perfect orchid corsage. "It's beautiful."

He held her hand tightly and nodded. "Shall we sit down?"

Lucy sat in one of the chairs and waited while he pulled the other one close. As soon as he sat he grabbed her free hand and spoke. "I know I've repeatedly screwed things up from the start. I know I've behaved badly. I know I've pushed you away time and time again. And I know I have no right to ask this of you…but I'm asking without any agenda, without any notion that I deserve it…but would you give me another chance?"

Her heart contracted and she smiled, seeing the love in his expression. He'd reached out in the most amazing way and she felt confident enough to meet him halfway, so she nodded. "Of course."

He looked instantly relieved. "Thank you. For believing in me. For understanding me. For having the patience to wait for me while I came to my senses."

Lucy smiled. "Have you? Come to your senses, I mean?"

He nodded. "Absolutely. I can't bear the thought of my life without you in it."

Lucy had never heard anything more heartfelt in her life. "I love you, too."

He kissed her then, a soft, slow kiss that kindled her longing for him. When he pulled back, his blue eyes were so vibrant she could almost see her reflection.

He held her hand lovingly. "What time do you finish today?"

Lucy checked her watch. It was two minutes to three. "Just about now."

"So," he said, curling a hand around her nape. "How about we get out of here and you go home and put on your prettiest dress and I'll take you out somewhere and we'll do this properly."

"Do what properly?" she teased.

"You know very well," he said and lovingly tucked a lock of stray hair behind her ear. "I'm not going to ask you to marry me while we're sitting in a hospital office room."

Lucy's heart almost exploded in her chest. "Oh… you're going to ask me to marry you?"

He smiled. "I most certainly am. But not here."

"Well," she said and leaned closer. "How about we go home and I won't put on my prettiest dress. Instead," she whispered, going closer still, "you can get out of that ridiculously sexy tuxedo and we can kiss and make up for a while and then you can ask me. Because I miss you. I miss *us*."

Brant kissed her softly and took the corsage box from her hand. He extracted the flower and carefully pinned it to her white coat. "I miss us, too."

She looked at the flower then met his gaze. "Brant what happened...what made you—?"

"What made me see sense?" he asked, cutting her off gently. He grabbed her hands and held them close. "What made me realize that I couldn't live without you? A few things. The other day my brother asked me what I was afraid of and I couldn't answer him. And then after the funeral, my mom told me not to end up like my uncle... because I had somehow come to think that my past is what defines me...and not my present. But I think..." he said, his words trailing for a moment as he softly touched her cheek. "I think that it was you. I *know* it was you. I was watching you walk alone in the snow the other day at the ranch, wearing your red coat... You looked so beautiful it took my breath away. But you looked alone, too. And that was unbearable for me. In that moment I knew... I just knew."

Lucy's eyes burned and she managed a quivering smile. "You knew what?"

He took a long breath. "I knew that I was in love with you."

They were the sweetest words she had ever heard. She reached up and cupped his smooth jaw. "I will always love you, Brant. And I'll always be there for you... through fire and rain...through bad dreams and sleepless nights."

His eyes glittered. "I wish I could tell you that I was through the worst of it, Lucy. But I can't."

She kept her hand against him. "You were in a war. And you experienced something life altering. You have to get through this at your own pace, Brant...but you also have to forgive yourself enough to let that happen. And that will take time. And patience. And probably therapy.

But there are no judges, no one here to devalue your feelings. There's just you…and me."

He groaned softly and captured her mouth in a kiss. "I love you, Lucia," he said against her lips. "I love your strength and your goodness. I love how you make the most of every moment. And I'm humbled that you want to love me back. There's no one in the world like you," he said and smiled, love in his eyes. "And I will love you and protect you and honor you always."

Lucy's throat burned with emotion. He was such a passionate, strong yet gentle man. And knowing she had his love filled her heart with overwhelming happiness. She knew they had some hurdles ahead, but Lucy was confident they would get through it together.

"So, about this tuxedo," she said and toyed with the bow tie. "Although it looks great on you, I still like the idea about going home and getting out of these clothes. And you did promise me a proposal, remember?"

He laughed softly and pulled her onto his lap. "I certainly did. Speaking of homes, in a few weeks I'm going to be homeless. The new chef is taking over the apartment above the tavern," he explained. "So unless you want to see me out on the street, I might have to bunk at your place for a while."

Lucy smiled and pressed kissed to his jaw. "Oh, I think we could come to some arrangement." Her eyes sparkled. "But that means sleepovers, you know. Cold sweats and bad dreams and all."

"I know what it means," he said as his arms tightened around her. "And although I'm probably going to struggle at first with you seeing me like that, I know I need to let go of the fear that you'll think I'm…needy…and weak."

"You don't have a weak bone in your body, Brant Parker," she said, her heart aching for him. "But I understand. And we'll simply take it one day, and one night, at a time."

He nodded slowly. "Dr. Allenby was telling me about the group therapy sessions they hold at the veterans home, you know, for the veterans and their families." He squeezed her hand. "I was wondering if you'd come with me sometime."

"Of course," she said quickly. "Of course I'll come with you. From this moment I don't ever want to be apart from you."

"Me, either."

She pressed against him. "And I love the idea of us living together."

"Me, too." He held her close. "Let's get out of here, Lucy. Let's go home so I can get down on my knee and ask you to marry me."

Lucy smiled cheekily. "Do you have a ring?"

His eyes darkened. "Of course."

"Then I accept!"

He laughed and the lovely sound reverberated through her entire body. "I haven't technically asked you yet."

"That's true," she said quickly and jumped to her feet. "Then let's go. I don't want you changing your mind about this."

Brant stood and hauled her into his arms. "Just so you know, Lucia, I will never change my mind. You're stuck with me for the rest of your life."

And that, Lucy thought as she offered her lips for his kiss, was the best news she'd ever heard.

Epilogue

"You know, you can protest all you like, but I *am* going to carry you over this threshold."

Lucy stared up at him, all green eyes and red lips. "But it's bad luck if we're not married."

Brant shook his head. "We're getting married in nine weeks. A date that *you* set, if you remember," he reminded her. "*I* would have happily eloped over Christmas."

"If we eloped, your mother would never forgive us," she said and crossed her arms. "Nor your brother or Kayla or Ash or Brooke."

She was right, of course. Eloping had never been an option. And she was right to suggest a six-month engagement. They needed time to get to know one another better, for Brant to continue with his sessions with Dr. Allenby, to arrange a wedding and to buy a house. Which is why they were now standing on the porch of their new home and she was being typically stubborn about his insistence he carry her over the threshold.

"Well, I have these," he said and dangled the keys from his fingertips. "So, I either carry you or we stay out here."

She glared at him. "You can been a real pain sometimes."

He shrugged. "I thought you found me charming?"

Her glare quickly turned into a smile. "Yeah… I do."

Brant laughed. "Well, climb the steps and come here."

She trudged up the five steps onto the porch. "This is really silly. What if someone sees us?"

"Some like who?"

She shrugged. "Our new neighbors perhaps."

He looked left and then right. "Old Mrs. Bailey plays bridge on Thursdays and is out, and the other side is Joss Culhane's house. Which you know. So, stop making excuses and get over here."

She chuckled and the sound hit him directly in the heart. Everything about her made him smile. Lucy was an amazing woman—kind, considerate, supportive and a tower of strength. Much more than he deserved, he was sure. But she loved him and he loved her in return, more than he'd ever imagined he could love anyone.

The past three months had been something of a whirlwind. With planning a wedding, opening the tavern, taking a part-time job teaching French at the high school and buying a home, there never seemed enough hours in the day. But Lucy was always at his side and unfailing in her support. She always made time to accompany him to the group meetings at the veterans home and had been with him in several of his sessions with Dr. Allenby. She'd been right about that, too. Time was a healer. Truth was a healer. He'd discovered both those things with her love and support. He'd even begun sleeping through the night.

The nightmares still came, but he was better prepared to handle them. And he'd forgiven himself, finally, for surviving the war when so many people around him hadn't.

"Where do you want me?" she asked, standing beside him.

Brant opened the security screen and then the front door. The house was big, low set and had been freshly renovated by the previous owners. Exactly what they wanted. Three bedrooms, two bathrooms, a huge kitchen and dining area, a large living room and a yard that needed a little work. But he didn't mind. Seeing Lucy's delighted expression the first time they'd viewed the house was enough to ensure he'd made an offer to the Realtor on the spot.

"I want you right here," he said and held out his arms. He scooped her up and jiggled her playfully. "Hmm... you're heavier than I thought."

She scowled and tapped him on the shoulder. "That's not very—"

"I'm kidding," he said and crossed the threshold. "You're as light as a feather."

She smiled and he carried her down the hall toward the kitchen. Since there was no furniture in the house, he propped her on the Canadian maple countertop and she smoothed her skirt down over her thighs. He kissed her cheek and then waved an arm to the middle of the dining area.

"We need to buy a new table," he said.

"My furniture arrives tomorrow," she reminded him. "Let's get it in the house and then see what we need."

He grinned. "My logical love."

She nodded and met his gaze. "While we're on that subject... I was thinking it would be logical to move the wedding up a bit. Say, to April."

Brant frowned slightly. "April? That's next month. Why would you want to do that when everything's booked for June?"

He looked at her and realized she seemed on edge. Even nervous. It occurred to him that she'd been a little distracted for days. Now he was really concerned. He said her name and she sighed heavily.

"I just want to make sure," she said softly.

"Make sure of what?"

"That I still fit into my wedding dress."

Brant stilled instantly. Her dress? He met her gaze and saw her expression change. Now she was smiling, a kind of delighted, secret smile that reached him way down. And she deliberately lay a palm on her belly.

Her belly...

A strange sensation tightened his throat as his gaze flicked from her eyes to where her hand lay. And in an instant he knew. "Are you pregnant?"

She nodded. "Sure am."

Emotion rose and hit him square in the middle of the chest. Pregnant. A baby. A dad.

And Brant didn't know whether he wanted to laugh, cry or pass out.

Lucy couldn't help smiling at the look on his face. She'd kept the secret for two days, wanting to break the news in their new home...for a new beginning...a new chapter in their life together.

"Are you okay, Brant?" she asked, taking in his sudden pallor.

"I...think so. Are you sure?"

She nodded. "Positive."

He took two steps across the room and settled between her thighs, hugging her tightly. "How far along?"

"About six weeks."

She could see him doing the math calculation in his head. "The night of the opening?"

"Yes," she replied, remembering how the night of the Loose Moose reopening they'd celebrated a little too hard and forgotten contraception. They'd joked about it at the time. Now, Lucy couldn't be more delighted that they'd neglected to use protection that night. She was over the moon, happier than she'd ever been in her life. Having Brant's baby was a dream come true. "Are you in shock?"

"A little," he admitted. "You?"

"I've had two days to get used to the idea," she said and smiled. "But I wanted to tell you here…in this house. *Our house.*"

He kissed her, long and passionately and filled with love.

"I'm gonna be a dad? Really?"

"Really," she replied.

He kissed her softly. "I can't believe how lucky I am. I can't believe I have all this. That I have you. And now…" He looked down at her belly. "And now we're having a baby together…it's as though suddenly I have this perfect life."

Lucy grabbed his hand and laid it against her stomach. "We do," she assured him and saw his eyes glittering with emotion. Lucy touched his face. "And you're going to be great. *We're* going to be great. Everything *is* going to be perfect, Brant."

When their beautiful son, Joel, was born a little more than seven months later, everything was perfect, just as she'd known it would be.

* * * * *

COMING SOON!

We really hope you enjoyed reading this book.
If you're looking for more romance
be sure to head to the shops when
new books are available on

Thursday 27th February

To see which titles are coming soon, please visit
millsandboon.co.uk/nextmonth

MILLS & BOON

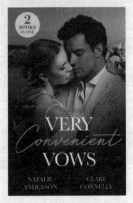

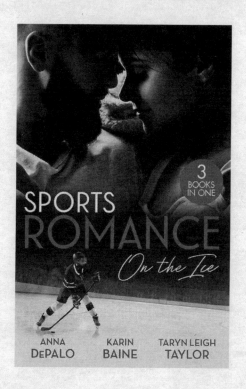

OUT NOW!

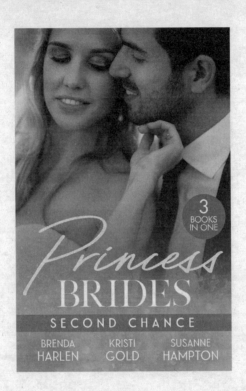

3 BOOKS IN ONE

Princess
BRIDES
SECOND CHANCE

BRENDA HARLEN   KRISTI GOLD   SUSANNE HAMPTON

Available at
millsandboon.co.uk

LET'S TALK

Romance

For exclusive extracts, competitions and special offers, find us online:

f MillsandBoon

X @MillsandBoon

○ @MillsandBoonUK

♪ @MillsandBoonUK

Get in touch on 01413 063 232

afterglow BOOKS

Afterglow Books is a trend-led, trope-filled list of books with diverse, authentic and relatable characters, a wide array of voices and representations, plus real world trials and tribulations. Featuring all the tropes you could possibly want (think small-town settings, fake relationships, grumpy vs sunshine, enemies to lovers) and all with a generous dose of spice in every story.

♪ @millsandboonuk
⊙ @millsandboonuk
afterglowbooks.co.uk

#AfterglowBooks

For all the latest book news, exclusive content and giveaways scan the QR code below to sign up to the Afterglow newsletter:

SCAN ME

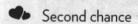
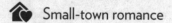

MILLS & BOON

THE HEART OF ROMANCE

A ROMANCE FOR EVERY READER

MODERN
Prepare to be swept off your feet by sophisticated, sexy and seductive heroes, in some of the world's most glamourous and romantic locations, where power and passion collide.

HISTORICAL
Escape with historical heroes from time gone by. Whether your passion is for wicked Regency Rakes, muscled Vikings or rugged Highlanders, awaken the romance of the past.

MEDICAL
Set your pulse racing with dedicated, delectable doctors in the high-pressure world of medicine, where emotions run high and passion, comfort and love are the best medicine.

True Love
Celebrate true love with tender stories of heartfelt romance, from the rush of falling in love to the joy a new baby can bring, and a focus on the emotional heart of a relationship.

HEROES
The excitement of a gripping thriller, with intense romance at its heart. Resourceful, true-to-life women and strong, fearless men face danger and desire - a killer combination!

From showing up to glowing up, these characters are on the path to leading their best lives and finding romance along the way – with plenty of sizzling spice!

To see which titles are coming soon, please visit

millsandboon.co.uk/nextmonth

GET YOUR ROMANCE FIX!

Get the latest romance news, exclusive author interviews, story extracts and much more!

blog.millsandboon.co.uk